Published by St. Frances Press
Copyright © 2016 by Gerri LeClerc

All rights reserved. No part of this book
may be reproduced in any form without written
permission from the publisher.

ISBN 978-0-9972631-1-4

Cover and book design by David M. Seager
www.gudburd1123@gmail.com

Cover illustration by Renée Easton

This book has been typeset in
Minion Pro Condensed
with heads in Emily.

GERRI LeCLERC

ST. FRANCES PRESS

"*This is a superb story, so filled with hope, joy and sorrow, grief, loss, and the pain addiction causes, especially to the littlest victims, the children involved. It is the shining story of love and loss and, finally, restoration beyond explanation. Ms. LeClerc is incredibly gifted in her writing abilities. I will never forget this story.*"

—Kathleen Marusak, *Editor*

Acknowlegements

*"WE ARE ALL APPRENTICES IN A CRAFT WHERE
NO ONE EVER BECOMES A MASTER."*

—ERNEST HEMINGWAY

I am grateful to everyone who helps this apprentice! My family all, parents, sisters, children, continue to be my uber-support. Listening tirelessly as I recite lengthy plot details and character sketches, then listening or reading again when I change them. They cheer me on, always finding everything I do to be wonderful. I go back to the keyboard uplifted and pound away. I couldn't be a writer without you. My love and thanks to you!

My friends who don't hesitate to read for me whenever I ask: Maria DeFrancisci, Joan Earnhart, Mary Ann Miller, Marian James, Louise Brady, and Susan Ferrara. I'm so lucky to have friends like you. Heartfelt thanks!

Special thanks to friends, Barbara Ulbrandt, who shared her experience of owning an online store. And Elaine Crowley, Adult Psychiatric-Mental Health Clinical Nurse Specialist, who reviewed my fictional addiction counseling. Any mistakes are mine.

The tougher scrutiny and critique, which made my book shine, was again provided by Suzanne Fox, my coach, author, teacher, and friend. Thank you for your generous support and for sharing your amazing knowledge.

Sandra Fontana, my critique partner, author, playwright, entrepreneur. You never hesitate to help, giving me your honest critique. Thank you for your gracious wish for my success, which I give back to you!

My editor, Kathleen Marusak, whose words of praise for Silent Grace lift me to the moon. Or as my husband says, makes my head swell too big to go through a normal doorway! Thank you, Kat!

To Patsy Bouzianis, who graciously explained to me what it is like to be deaf. Who can now understand words because of the cochlear implant she wears. Thank you!

Always last but never least, Ron, my husband. He's been promoted to CEO and CFO of St. Frances Press. He rides the Cape with me as I market Missing Emily, and who still has time to run our kitchen! All my love.

*This book is dedicated to
the memory of my sister, Pat Ray.*

She was an angel.

She sang like an angel.

She sings with the angels.

Chapter 1

With sleet tapping at the window of her New Bedford, Massachusetts apartment, Beth Henson sat on the floor, packing a box of books. The phone rang with her sister's unique ringtone and interrupted her off-key singing. Beth hesitated, pressing tape over the flaps of the box, and considered letting the call roll to voicemail. Instead, she wove her way through a maze of packed boxes, retrieved her phone and answered.

It was a video call from Grace.

"Mommy won't wake up," her niece said in her fragile voice, while she also signed at a frantic pace. "Scared."

"Is she breathing? Turn the phone so I can see Mommy," Beth said, while also signing, at least the principal words. Grace understood and switched the phone's camera to Patrice on the couch. Beth saw that she was breathing deeply.

"I'm coming now, sweetie. Stay on the phone with me." But the call ended. Beth must have signed incorrectly. She didn't take time to call back. She grabbed her purse from the table by the front door. "Keys. Keys!" she said, dumping the contents on the floor. She scooped up the keys and left everything except her wallet where it landed. Grace had to be alarmed to use her voice. Beth feared she knew what it was; had seen it before.

Though traffic was light, the conditions were hazardous, so it took longer than the usual five minutes to drive to Patrice's apartment. She gripped the steering wheel. Why did this have to happen now?

When she opened the apartment door, she could see into the dingy living room through to the eat-in kitchen. In the front corner of the apartment, two couches, upholstered in a worn, flower print, sat perpendicular to each other. Patrice sat dazed, but awake, on one of them. Relief mixed with ire tightened Beth's throat.

She stared at the tableau, allowing her heartbeat to drop to a slower tempo. Perhaps because she was moving, her sister and niece seemed different. Patrice, with her tousled blond hair, sat with her long legs crossed at the ankle, her fine artist's hands rubbing her eyes. Grace knelt beside Patrice, using her small body to guard her mother. Her dark-green eyes glared at Beth. Her face was pale, made paler still by the contrast of her long black hair. It pained Beth to look at her. Clearly, Grace remembered the last time this happened, and she still blamed her aunt for sending her mother away.

"What happened, Patrice?" Beth asked.

"Grace overreacted. I'm fine. Just taking a nap. I don't know why in heaven she called you."

Her slurred words and glassy eyes made Beth want to weep with disappointment. "What did you take?" She spoke with her hand near her mouth so Grace couldn't speech read.

"I'm clean; didn't take anything. I'm just tired."

Beth ignored her and started to search. Her sister rarely hid anything well. A short hall led to two bedrooms with a bath in between. She stepped into the bathroom. The sink had globs of toothpaste in it. In the corners of the vinyl floor, webs of fallen hair had accumulated. A hair dryer lay on the toilet lid, still plugged in. It was obvious by the mess, today wasn't the first day Patrice had started taking drugs again. Beth had missed the signs. Or maybe blocked them.

She pushed open the plastic shower curtain. There it was: a brown plastic prescription bottle with the remnants of a label across it. She opened it and poured the red pills into her palm. Four of them left.

She dropped them into her pocket and went back to the living room. "Grace, Mommy and I have to talk. Can you go into your room and read a book for a bit?" Beth struggled with her inept signing, but Grace seemed to understand. She looked to her mother who nodded and gave her a crooked smile.

When Grace was out of the room, Beth pulled the pills out of her pocket and showed them to Patrice. "How many did you take and what are they?"

"Just a couple of Darvocets. Nothing bad."

"They're all bad! And it was *way* bad for Grace. She was petrified when she called me."

Patrice turned her head away. "She didn't see me take them."

"Do you think for one moment she doesn't know? Do you realize what you're doing to her? What if you didn't wake up? For God's sake, Patrice, how can you do this to yourself and to Grace?"

"You think it's easy?" Patrice's voice was hoarse. "I've been clean for months. But it's so hard. You'll never know how hard it is."

"Grace might." Beth dropped onto the couch, her hands on her knees. She took some purposeful breaths. This was not the way to handle it. Anger didn't help. *Unconditional love,* she told herself.

"What made you take drugs again? Why now?"

Patrice walked on wobbly legs to the kitchen and filled a glass with water. She swallowed three-quarters of it before she looked back at Beth in the living room. "You're leaving us. That's what weakened me."

Beth raised her chin. "We agreed the move was good for both of us."

"How is it good for me?"

Beth bit her tongue. Patrice was manipulating her, and Beth had to stay on course. "I have to put myself first for my own health. Every time I rescue you, I'm enabling you and feeding into my codependence. We both need to become self-reliant. I'm going to Cape Cod to make a life, Patrice. I'll be an hour and a half away. I won't be able to run over in five minutes—" Beth clamped her mouth closed. She felt a rope pulling tight from her throat to her stomach. Though she knew it was right to leave Patrice, what about Grace? How could she leave *her* now?

Grace was a shy child, having become more so since becoming deaf. But she was strong, even feisty, especially when it came to protecting her mother. She signed well, but was only fairly accurate at speech reading, and she rarely used her voice. In fact, most of the time she was silent. When she did speak, as she had on their video call tonight, she also signed.

Patrice dropped her head and began sobbing into her hands. It was a picture of grief Beth couldn't bear. She went into the kitchen and put her arms around her sister. Patrice lifted her face. "I'm sorry. I can do it. I know I can. It's just that I'll miss you so much."

Grace peeked out at them from the hall. When Beth smiled at her, she spun both index fingers around each other in a sign for *Go*. As in *go away*.

Moving a few steps back from her sister, Beth signed to Grace, "I'll go soon. Everything is all right." She turned back to Patrice. "What do we do now?"

Grace was reading their lips. They knew to talk about addiction in code so as not to frighten her.

"I—I just needed a little help. I'm okay now. Those won't hurt me, won't start anything." She shook her head as if to clear it.

Beth turned away from Grace's view. "Call your sponsor. Get to the NA meetings. You know what you have to do." She held up both hands for emphasis. "Look. We've been over this too many times. Now it's time to think of Grace."

"I'm sorry. I want you to be happy. Don't worry, that's it. I won't slip again. I'll go back to the meetings. Really, I'm good."

"You have to be. From now on, Grace will only have you to depend on."

Grace stiffened again as Beth hugged her and said goodbye. Patrice held her so tightly, Beth could hardly breathe. But the tears in Beth's eyes weren't from her sister's tight hug; they were the cost of tough love.

Beth closed the door of her apartment and strode across the living room. She was so lost in thought she tripped over the corner of a box and went down hard. She lay still in the heap she landed in and let the tears flow. She should have expected it. Years of taking care of her sister. Years of getting her out of trouble. How many bills had she paid for therapy, for rehab? Everything was set in place at last. Patrice was clean, working. And now this. It was not the way Beth wanted to leave. *Damn!* She picked up a book and threw it across the room. Addiction was a disease, she knew, but sometimes she just resented the hell out of it.

Beth stood up, rubbing her right hip, which would surely have a bruise to remind her of this night. She looked over at the boxes. Just hours ago she was happily filling these last few containers. Now she was sick with worry. Did Beth have an obligation to take care of Patrice forever? She knew from Al-Anon meetings she didn't. But wasn't she abandoning Grace?

Tomorrow would be her greatest challenge; she had to follow through with her move. When Patrice visited next weekend, Beth would be able to tell if she was clean. She hoped with all her heart she would be.

By the time Beth finished packing the books, she could hardly keep her eyes open. She padded into her bedroom. The one thing left to do in the morning was to put the bed linens into the open box on the floor and tape it up. The coffee pot would go right into the car with her. Could she regain the joyful anticipation of her move to Cape Cod? Either way tomorrow she would leave New Bedford.

Chapter 2

On Saturday in New Bedford, the streets were clogged with residents and visitors. Patrice loved their historical hometown, and wondered how Beth could leave it. The city, the prom queen of whaling ports in the nineteenth century, was now a tired housewife, for sure, but she wwas undergoing a renewal. And the rest of the world came to see her every day.

The New Bedford Whaling National Historical Park covered 34 acres, and included the world-renowned New Bedford Whaling Museum, with its five whale skeletons and the largest whaling ship model in the world. Since the city had a population over 95,000, and the park was open year-round, the streets were usually crowded and vibrant.

Patrice took Grace to see Emily and Ruth, the Asian elephants at the Buttonwood Park Zoo. It was one of Grace's favorite places. The trip was to make-up for the scare Patrice had given her daughter.

Sitting on a nearby bench in the weak winter sun, Patrice waited while Grace communed with the elephants. In every quiet moment, she was filled with regret for taking the Darvocet pills. She was, at this moment, still struggling to resist the urge for more drugs. The NA meeting she'd attended last night helped. It was the fear of life without her sister that haunted her. Beth was her best friend, someone who could overlook all the trouble Patrice had caused her over the years and still love her and praise her accomplishments. In spite of her failures, Beth still had a dream for her: to show her art one day. Beth had bought her easels, paints, canvases, and some for Grace. Patrice had finished four paintings, which Beth knew nothing about. One day, she would surprise her. She had to keep her focus on that, on knowing that Beth wasn't too far away, and that she was close to a beach, which they all loved. With her sister's help, Patrice had her own apartment and a job that didn't require weekend work. If she could only stay clean. If she could only adjust to this huge change that she knew deep down was right for both of them.

When she was pregnant with Grace, she'd had to give up her old friends, even Frankie, the man she loved. He wasn't an addict, but many in the group were, and she'd never stay clean around them. A healthy baby had been her first priority. She'd destroyed her relationship with Frankie anyway by then, but she always believed she could earn him back.

Grace bent over and looked into her mother's eyes. She made the sign for mother and raised her eyebrows. She was still worried from Thursday night.

"No. Mommy's fine. Just thinking. How are Ruth and Emily?" she said and signed.

"Wonderful," Grace signed, moving both flat hands up and forward a couple times. Then she signed, "Bears?"

"Oh, you want a bear hug?" Patrice said. She grabbed her daughter and hugged her, swaying back and forth. She felt the bubbles of laughter rise in Grace's chest.

"No, Mommy," she signed, her hands shaking with her giggles. "See bears."

"Oh, you want to see the bears. I get it. Okay, let's go, then we can get some ice cream."

Grace skipped before her, knowing the way well.

Patrice's heart filled with love, though a little black cloud of need shadowed her.

All the trepidation of leaving New Bedford disappeared as Beth crossed over the Bourne Bridge. She looked down at the gray waters of the Cape Cod Canal and knew, once she was on the other side, her new life would begin. The nagging worry about her sister and Grace was, if only for a few minutes, forgotten, as she drove on Route 6 toward Orleans.

Two hours later, with the proof of her ownership in a folder on the seat beside her, Beth pulled up in front of her new house. The silver-shingled cottage was postcard charming, oozing the character of 1907, when it had been built.

She gazed up at the hydrangea-blue front door surrounded by an arbor woven with quiescent rose vines. The old sign nailed to the shingles on the right side of the door said, *Knoll Cottage*. An extensive front garden flowed down the curve of the hill, waiting to blossom in the spring.

She drove her car up the driveway and parked beside the moving truck backed up to the porch on the side of the cottage. It was raining softly, but the overhang would protect her possessions from becoming wet.

Beth indicated the placement of each item and checked it off the inventory, as the two movers brought in the next box or piece of furniture.

It took much less time to empty the truck than to fill it. When the truck rattled back down the driveway, the time was close to four o'clock. Beth closed and locked the door, then turned around, hugging her arms to her chest. She drew in a deep breath. The cottage smelled like snappy fresh air. It was chilly from having the doors open. She knew in her heart that this was the happiest day of her life. So far.

For a second, she wished she could share her joy with Patrice. And then a shadow darkened her mood. She'd done everything she could to ensure that when she moved, Patrice and Grace could manage without her. But because of Patrice's relapse, even though it was driven by a need to keep Beth in New Bedford, she still felt like she'd abandoned them, which left her with an aching heart.

"I can't go there. I won't! It's all right for me to be happy," she said aloud to make it feel real. She gave herself a little shake and took a walk around the kitchen. It was outdated but charming with its sage-green cabinets and maple countertops. She loved to cook, and had been cooking in a galley kitchen for years, so this was a step up. In time, this would become a chef's dream kitchen.

In the hallway that stretched from the front to the back of the cottage, she turned right. Thea Connor, the previous owner, had left the sun porch furniture behind, saying it wouldn't fit in her new house. Beth trailed her fingers over the gently worn wicker chairs and the white-painted pieces that were now hers. She sat in the old black rocker, oddly out of place, and stared out into the backyard. Thea had assured her the gnarly shade tree in the center of the yard would become a lovely surprise in May.

She jumped up and walked back into the kitchen, piled high with boxes. Beth began to open drawers and cabinets, planning where things would go. She peered inside the oven and pictured a Thanksgiving turkey roasting. Inside the refrigerator, she found two bottles of water, a bottle of champagne, a flute painted with flowers and ribbons, a chunk of apricot Stilton, and a small box of ginger snaps. Welcome gifts from Thea.

The heck with the boxes. Beth left the champagne to share later, and took a bottle of water and the goodies to the sun porch to celebrate her new, wonderful cottage. *Hers!*

The following weekend, Patrice and Grace came to the cottage. The wind was brisk as Beth stood on the side porch, which Thea had called the "farmer's porch," and waited until they got out of the car. She studied her sister's gait and saw no telltale wobble. She let out the breath she was holding in one fast exhalation.

Patrice surprised her with a large wrapped package topped by a purple bow. "Grace wrapped it," she said, holding out her arm for Grace to come closer.

"Thank you." Beth turned to face her niece. "Grace, you did a beautiful job on the wrapping." She spoke slowly and signed.

The pretty child smiled with a rare sparkle in her large forest-green eyes.

Once inside the cottage, Beth opened the box slowly, watching Grace's smile grow wider. Inside was a cobalt-blue Depression glass vase. "It's beautiful. Thank you. How did you know there would be so many gardens here? It's just what I need."

Beth hung up their coats and began the house tour through the kitchen and her office. They stood in the arch entrance to the living room. Flames flickered brightly in the fireplace, which was surrounded by built-in shelves and wood paneling.

"This is nice," Patrice said in a flat tone.

Beth glanced at her sister's dispirited profile and continued on. "This is the only fancy feature in the house. The rest is just functional." Then she walked them through the remaining rooms, ending up on the sun porch. Grace was clearly enthralled. She sat in the high-back rocker with her feet dangling above the floor, looking around at all the empty shelves. Beth knelt before her and put a finger under her chin to direct her focus. "Would you like to bring some of your books to keep here on the shelves?" Grace shook her head. She didn't understand. Beth closed her palms together then opened them up, the sign for book. She pointed to Grace and to the shelf, saying, "Bring some of your books here."

Grace's eyes grew wide, and she smiled and nodded.

Patrice and Beth stepped back into the kitchen. Beth began to assemble their lunch, *Salade Nicoise*. "Wow," she said, "I can't believe Grace. She seems so happy, and is sharing it with *me*, too." Beth remembered the first time she'd held the newborn Grace, swaddled in pink flannel blankets, so tiny and helpless. And healthy. Since then, her meningitis and resultant deafness, and her mother's drug issues, had stolen some of that innocent joy.

"She is happy. I think having you here takes away some of the threat."

"I'm still a threat to her?" Beth asked, rolling her lips between her teeth.

"You know, she worries that you might send me to the hoosegow."

Patrice laughed.

Beth's fervent hope was that this visit would begin to restore her relationship with Grace. How much Beth loved and helped her mother didn't count in that equation, and Patrice made no effort to change Grace's feelings. The contradiction that Grace also needed Beth when things went wrong made their relationship even more complicated. "Well, anyway, I'm glad to see her happy for a change. And she seems to want to have a place here. Did you see her smile when I asked if she wanted to bring some books for the shelves? Maybe she can stay with me for a while in the summer while you're working. We can visit the beach every day and have picnics on the porch."

"Maybe we'll take small steps at first. A weekend or something."

"Right. I'm getting ahead of myself." She turned away, pulling silverware from the drawer to hide her disappointment.

"You're different, too, Beth. I've never seen you so relaxed. Being away from us must agree with you."

"Ouch! You know that's not true." But it was true. She was happy and relaxed in her new cottage. Patrice could always cause Beth guilt, and manipulate her, but Beth was determined not to let anything spoil the rest of the visit. This weekend was meant to foster a new rapport, one of caring and sharing, but not of dependence. She forced a smile. "I made a huge salad. I hope you're hungry."

They filled their plates and took them to the sun porch to eat. Beth turned on the space heater against the cold seeping in around the old windows. Her heart glowed from the happy chatter and laughter they shared. It was exactly how she wanted her family's first visit to Knoll Cottage to be.

While she washed her favorite pottery salad bowl, she watched her sister out the window. Patrice had set up two lawn chairs she'd unearthed from the pile of summer gear in the garage. She was bundled in a winter coat and wore gloves with open fingers, so she could work her sketching pencil. Even as a little girl, her talent for drawing had been amazing. A woman in their father's congregation had given her free lessons when she saw the art Patrice had created.

Grace sat right beside her with her head low over her drawing pad. They were both sketching what Beth—standing at the sink with dripping fingers—thought must be the farmer's porch. Patrice sat gracefully, one leg bent at the knee, the other extended in front of her. Her blond hair shone in the weak sunlight. Her long fingers lightly held the pencil moving rapidly around the page. Beth thought any artist would love to paint *her*. Beth had had freckles on her fair-skinned face since she was five, but Patrice had a flawless, peachy complexion.

Patrice must have sensed her sister's eyes on her. She looked up and smiled. Beth waved and smiled back. If only Patrice hadn't been such a rebel. If only she hadn't met up with the high school stoners, she mused.

Patrice and Grace brought in their finished sketches to show her. Grace's was great for her age. The porch was sagging a little, but she had captured the angles, the table and chairs, the window. But it was Patrice's sketch that intrigued Beth. Her drawing was set in the summer with the large shrubs in leaf at the front of the porch. Instead of the plastic table and chairs, she'd drawn an Adirondack chair with flowered pillows. A table beside it held an open book turned face-down and a glass of ice tea with mint leaves. But it was her rendition of Beth that held her attention. In the window, a woman appeared with her head bent down. The angle of her body, the stiffness of her arms conveyed a rigid focus on her task.

She looked up at her sister. "Is this how you see me?"

"That's how you are. Working, never playing."

"And the Adirondack would be your chair. For reading and sipping tea?"

"No, that's what *you* should be doing. I'm not there. I've gone to a party. The dishes can always wait." She gave Beth a quick hug before walking away while removing her coat.

Beth dried her hands and stepped into the bathroom to examine her face. Her expression was serious. Her sister was right; Beth had always worked. Having a father like theirs and a sister who was an addict, what choice did she have? She blinked. That thought was a reality check. She *had* a choice, to let people handle their own lives. She wasn't responsible for the world. Beth smiled at her reflection. If she didn't stop trying to carry others' burdens, she would never have laugh lines. And she truly wanted laugh lines.

When Aunt Beth asked if they wanted to walk up to the beach, Grace could hardly contain herself. She'd answered, "I want to go!" Both her mom and her aunt were surprised, which made Grace laugh. It wasn't often she used her voice since she'd been sick. She hated being different now. Having to have a special lady sign to her at school so she could understand the teacher. All the kids stared, and Grace felt stupid.

Months ago in the classroom, she had mustered up the courage to raise her hand. Her teacher, Miss Royce, noticed her and smiled. She called on Grace by pointing her finger. She stood up and said the words, "The Niña and the Pinta." At least she thought she had. Her mother had helped her vocalize the words in her homework the day before. But in school, the kids eyes got big and they opened their mouths, or covered them with their hands. She knew they were laughing at her. The teacher came over and put her arm around Grace's shoulders, shaking her finger at the kids.

After that, she was silent.

Grace wished she could talk like she used to. She asked God every night to teach her again. So far, He hadn't been listening. Maybe God was deaf, too.

But today she was so excited she spoke aloud before she thought better of it. And they understood her and were happy. "Let's go!" Aunt Beth said.

Facing traffic, they walked along the street without sidewalks, and only saw one car. It was cold when the wind blew and Grace folded her arms over her chest. Then she spotted the beach ahead and started running. She beat her mom and aunt to the edge of the water that went all the way out to meet the sky. She spun around delightedly and began to search for shells. Her aunt came and knelt before her and hugged her. "You love the beach."

Her signing was pretty bad, but between her lips and hands, Grace got the gist of it. She nodded. She looked up to see her mother sitting on a bench near the parking lot, but Aunt Beth began to walk along the sand with her head down. She picked up a shell and brought it to Grace. It was a long, smooth, double white shell. Aunt Beth pulled on her sleeve then spelled r-a-z-o-r c-l-a-m. Grace studied the shell. She loved its cold silky outside, rubbed her thumb up and down its surface. She brought it to her nose and sniffed. It smelled like saltwater. Then she tucked it carefully into her coat pocket and went to search for more treasures.

It didn't seem long before her mom came down and signed she was freezing. Grace shook her head back and forth until her hair swung around. It was too soon to leave. She watched her aunt, hoping she would send her mother home without them. And she tried, but her mom came and took Grace's hand. Grace refused to look at her to see what she was saying. She didn't want to leave yet, but she obeyed. She didn't want to ruin her mommy's good mood.

Later, she was watching a Disney movie with closed captioning when her mother came to sit down next to her. She patted Grace's knee with a shaking hand. *Oh no.* Grace was afraid she was sick again. Would Aunt Beth try to send her mother away, away from her?

She signed, "Mommy, are you sick?"

Her mother signed, "No," and looked to the television.

But Grace worried.

Chapter 3

For Beth, it was the kind of morning when the toast was a little limp. The healthy margarine couldn't convince it was butter.

What was wrong?

She had packed off her sister and niece after lunch the day before. The magic that was there all day Saturday—at the beach, in the cottage, during the driving tour around town—had been absent on Sunday. She couldn't figure out why, but Grace had turned surly and stayed well away from her. Patrice had seemed fine, but she kept a close eye on Grace.

What had changed?

This was part of her new existence. Not knowing every detail of her sister's moods, her troubles. Beth had to get used to it. In time, she would, but right now, it was a struggle to withdraw from the closeness they had shared.

She had plans to meet her friend, Sandy, for lunch on Tuesday. Then she would spend about four hours at the warehouse office of her online business, Linens & Lavender. Her newly promoted manager seemed to doing a good job. Her staff had been with her for years and they were dependable, hard-working employees. Beth would continue to work on site once or twice a week. After work, maybe she'd drop in on her sister and have dinner. Make sure everything was okay.

She had to get busy. She had an appointment at the real estate agency Thea had used to list the cottage, to scout some possible sites for the retail store she planned to open. The Realtor, Annie Eldridge, had emailed several listings in Eastham and Orleans to her a couple days ago.

"How do you like Knoll Cottage?" Annie asked, indicating with a wave a chair across from her desk for Beth.

"It's still a work in progress, but I love the cottage."

"Thea will be happy to hear that. I spent many hours in that cottage. She and I grew up together. Her mother, Hannah, was a favorite of all of ours, so a group of kids was always at the house. And your wonderful sun porch? Hannah called it her 'sacred space.' All the kids thought she was a witch—a good witch—because she told us the cottage had magic, especially in the sacred space." Annie laughed. "I tried, but I never saw any magic. Still, Hannah was truly spiritual. Thea rolled her eyes at the whole idea."

"I didn't know you two were old friends. Thea didn't mention it when I talked about a store location at the closing. She just said you were the best realtor in the state."

"Well, that's true!" Annie said, laughing. "You're in good hands." She rubbed her palms together. "Now, how did you like the listings I sent?"

Beth's family worries faded as she contemplated the location for the retail store she'd dreamed about operating for years. A store where her buyers could experience her luxury linens first-hand. A chance to get to know her Orleans neighbors, and to meet tourists from other places. As she sat beside Annie, surfing through listings, Beth's excitement grew.

"All of these have good storage space," Beth said. "I'll need that to keep up my stock."

"Linens & Lavender, right? I visited your online shop. I can't wait until you open your retail store. I'll be a good customer. My husband just finished his degree in landscape architecture. We bought a house with a large front yard that he can make into a showplace to display some of his design ideas. I'm decorating the interior, and beautiful linens are on my list."

A week later, Beth signed a lease and put down the deposit required by the owner, who agreed to allow her to redesign the store's layout. She'd chosen an Orleans location with a higher rent, but also, she hoped, with a higher sales potential. The rent would keep her in the red until the shop began to make money, but the business had a decent cushion in case she needed it. A couple years ago, she'd added a commercial line to Linens & Lavender, selling linens for hotels, nursing/rehab facilities, hospitals, and taking only a slim profit. Then she'd had a big break when a higher-end motel chain came on board. Now, that side of her business thrived.

After a celebratory lunch with Annie, Beth drove home happily contemplating how she would revamp the store's interior. She entered the cottage and went immediately to browse the internet. Besides her regular stock, she planned to expand to include a line of new products, maybe sleepwear or bath accessories.

She was dreaming of a fire. She could smell the smoke and hear the alarms going off in the house. Her legs caught in the twisted blankets as she struggled to get out of bed. She was breathing hard when she woke up.

The phone was ringing. Beth fumbled for the handset as she glanced at the clock. One-twenty-two a.m. Her heart was thumping at a frantic rate.

"Beth Henson?"

"Yes. Who is this?"

"Sergeant Paul Metzler of the New Bedford Police Department. Are you related to Patrice Henson?"

Oh God. "Yes. She's my sister," she said, then held her breath.

Patrice was cold. She felt as if her eyes were glued shut, and someone had installed a carpet on her tongue. She forced her eyes open. *What the hell?*

She dragged her stiff body up an inch at a time, giving her spinning brain a chance to adjust. Floor-to-ceiling bars surrounded her. A jail cell. *Oh shit.*

She rubbed her face with her palms and looked again. Still there. The bars. The ugly stainless steel toilet and sink. The thin mattress she'd been sleeping on. Two women were in the cell with her. One asleep on another mattress; one standing against the bars, muttering to herself.

What had she done?

She stood and went to the front of the cell. An officer was working at a desk. Patrice tried to think, but she couldn't get her thoughts in order, and her head hurt so badly. What had she taken?

Her hands flew to her mouth. *Oh God! Grace.*

Patrice stumbled back to the mattress, sat down hard. She forced herself to remember. Frankie had called. The gang she used to live with was throwing him a birthday bash, and he wanted her to come by. She'd said no twice then caved. She'd lied to herself. Told herself she'd just stop over for a birthday hug. She brought her hands up to cover her face. She'd left Grace alone. Jumping up, she called out to the officer. "Is my daughter all right? Can someone check on my daughter? She's deaf. Please help me."

The female officer came over. "She's all right. But it was lucky for her the police picked her up."

"What happened? Where is she?"

"All I know is she was alone on the street around midnight. DCF has her now."

Patrice had to hold tight to the bars so she wouldn't fall. The bottom had just dropped out of her pitiful life. She was so filled with regret she couldn't breathe, couldn't hold herself up against its weight.

"Are you okay? Maybe you'd better lie back down," the officer said.

"I need to go home. Grace needs me. She's deaf and helpless."

"You should have thought about that before you got high."

"What am I here for?"

"Oxycontin in your possession. You're up for bail."

Patrice groaned. How could she make bail? How could she ask Beth to make it for her? But what other choice did she have? Grace needed her at home. "Can I call my sister?"

"Give me the number. I'll make the call."

Patrice moved, as if her body was encased in ice, back to the cot and lay down. One of the other women vomited into the toilet. The smell made her gag. Patrice pulled her shirt up to cover her nose and mouth, but she could still hear the retching. She felt as if she'd died and gone to hell, just like her fire-and-brimstone father had predicted.

She'd sunk to her lowest, bottomed-out; committed a crime and was under arrest. What would happen now? To Grace? She didn't deserve her daughter. Tears seeped into the shirt pressed to her face. How could she have done this to her little girl? Her daughter was out in the dark night looking for her. Grace took better care of her mother than Patrice did of her. Something terrible could have happened.

Patrice knew that DCF could take Grace away from her because of the drugs. She had to convince them she wasn't addicted. An occasional prescription drug helped ease the pressure. The old people in the home where she worked had plenty of bottles of prescriptions that were there for the taking . . . if you were careful.

She hung her head. Yes, she *was* an addict. She'd tried to stop. More than once, but the craving was constant. It was so hard not to want to feel that good ever again. She'd never felt this bad after taking pills, though. Someone must have given her a different drug at the party.

What would Beth think of her when she heard she'd left Grace home alone?

Patrice rolled into a ball and willed herself back to sleep and oblivion.

Chapter 4

Beth drove to New Bedford with tears running down her face. Sorrow, worry, and fear collided inside her. She forced herself to focus on driving. It seemed like hours before she reached New Bedford Police headquarters.

It was nearly four a.m. when Patrice was brought out to her. She'd been released without bail by the magistrate, pending her hearing. Her face was pale. Her eyes were red-rimmed. She walked hunched over, like an old woman.

"Patrice," Beth said, crying again at the sight of her sister. "What happened? Where's Grace?"

Patrice sobbed so hard, Beth could hardly understand her. "The Department of Children and Families has her in a foster home."

"What? Why? Oh God. Tell me what happened?" Beth placed her hands on her sister's shoulders, barely noticing that the shirt under her fingers was damp and emitting an unpleasant odor.

"It's my fault. I left her alone in the apartment. She went out to search for me."

Beth felt as if she were sinking in quicksand. She couldn't utter a word. She took Patrice's elbow and guided her outside to the car. They rode in silence to Patrice's apartment. Beth's sense of doom made her head pound. This was a disaster. She never should have left. If she'd been there, this would not have happened.

They entered the apartment. "Get in the shower," Beth said. "We'll talk after." She paced the small apartment while she waited.

Ten minutes later, Patrice came into the living room wearing a pair of old pajamas. Her hair was wet, and her skin was red from hot water and hard scrubbing.

"I'm sorry, Beth. It was a birthday party. Frankie called and asked me to come. I shouldn't have gone." Patrice leaned against the living room wall and wept.

Beth's body shook from head to toe from a toxic mixture of anger and dread. "You're charged with possession. Most people bring a present to a party. You brought drugs. And you left Grace alone. Why didn't you call the sitter? Did you consider her welfare at all?" She was angry, but she was also sick with guilt. She'd have to use all the skills she'd learned at Al-Anon not to take responsibility for Patrice's bad behavior.

Patrice crossed her hands over her heart. "This is it. This is rock bottom. I'm going to quit. I promise you, Beth. They let me sign a paper asking the court to send me to a rehab facility instead of prison. To keep Grace, I *have* to get clean and *stay* that way."

Beth sat down on the couch, spent.

"I need to find out how Grace is," Patrice said. She walked to the end table and pulled a phone book from the drawer.

Beth watched Patrice flip the pages for the number. When she couldn't find it, she picked up the phone and had directory assistance connect the call. After someone answered at DCF, Patrice identified herself as Grace's mother, answered a few questions, and then hung up the phone with a shaking hand.

"A social worker is coming over. She'll be here in about fifteen minutes," Patrice said, then came to sit on the couch near Beth.

The social worker, who introduced herself as Lynette Middlebrooks, was a large woman wearing black slacks and a green cowl-neck sweater. Her brown hair was tied in a loose knot at the back of her head.

"I don't understand. What is a 51A report?" Patrice asked.

"It's a report filed with DCF by someone—in this case, the police—about a child considered at risk for abuse or neglect. A woman reported seeing a child wandering in her neighborhood late last night. She called the police. They picked Grace up and called DCF. I went to get her."

"Is she all right?" Patrice asked.

"She was very frightened. We brought in an interpreter to sign to her, and she calmed down. Because you were arrested, we've removed Grace from your custody on an emergency basis. She'll remain in a foster home until we get this sorted out."

"She's deaf. How can they take care of her? Do they sign? Please, she needs to be with me."

"She's in good hands. You've been charged with possession and possibly with child neglect. That's up to the DA." Lynette paused. "You may go to prison. In any case, whether you get your child back is up to DCF and the courts.

"I'll be filing an affidavit for a C and P case, Care and Protection, in Juvenile Court today," Lynette said. "There will be a hearing in the next day or so. Under the circumstances, I've no doubt the judge will decide to uphold the removal of Grace from your custody."

From her seat on the couch, Beth sat stunned, her heart aching. She looked at Patrice. Her head was down. Her shoulders shook as she wept. Teardrops fell on her pajama pants. Seeing Patrice cry never failed to affect her, but Beth was too upset herself to comfort her sister.

"Can I see Grace?" Patrice asked then pressed her knotted fists to her mouth.

"Not now. It's important not to put Grace through any more trauma than necessary. We'll wait until after the hearing and court case. Once we know your sentence, we'll work on a more permanent situation." She turned to Beth. "My choice always is to place children with a relative. But first I'll need a list of all family members."

Beth sat up straighter. "It's just me. No other family members."

"Are you willing to take your niece?"

"I—" She turned to Patrice, whose face showed fear at Beth's hesitation.

Lynette spoke up. "You'll have time to think this out. We have to see what the courts decide first. Meanwhile, I have some paperwork for you to fill out. If you take Grace," Lynette focused her pale blue eyes—one slightly wayward—on Beth, "the initial eligibility screening includes a background check; a home visit and an interview; a commitment to complete the full assessment and approval process; and completion of the Family Resource Application."

Beth could only nod.

Grace sat alone at a big kitchen table. The smell of bacon cooking made her sick to her stomach. The lady who lived in the house was looking at her and making her hand move back and forth to her open mouth. It wasn't real sign, but Grace knew what she meant. But she couldn't eat. She would throw up.

She was so worried about her mommy. When was she coming to get her? Last night, when the police lady came and took her from the street, a man signed to her that her mother was sick in a hospital. He said mommy would be all right, so why didn't she come to get her? Wasn't she better? The signing man didn't come to this house. Grace tried signing to ask the lady, but she didn't understand. She'd even used her voice to ask where her mommy was. But the lady just shook her head like she didn't know. Grace was afraid. What if mommy didn't come back?

The lady put a piece of toast on her plate, then pushed some butter on a dish closer to her and pointed to it. Toast was what her mommy gave her when she felt sick. She took the knife and sliced off some butter. The woman clapped her hands together a few times and smiled. Grace buttered the toast and took a bite. It didn't taste that good, but she broke off little pieces and ate them.

A dog as high as the table snatched a piece of toast from her fingers. Grace screamed. She slid off her chair and backed away from the dog. He followed her, putting his big nose on her fingers. She screamed again and swatted at the dog's head until the woman came and pulled the dog away. Grace ran upstairs to the room she'd slept in and closed the door. Standing there, she cried. She was afraid, and she wanted her mommy.

The lady pushed the door open a little and peeked in. She walked over to where Grace now sat on the floor and knelt down. Grace read her lips, she said she was sorry. She said the dog was a good dog who only wanted her toast. The lady showed her a piece of paper then she pointed to herself. The paper said MARY. Then she held up her finger and went back out.

Grace thought of Aunt Beth. Did she know Grace was in this house? Why couldn't she come get her? Or she could go to Sophie's, who could sign with her, like she did before, couldn't she? Didn't they like her anymore?

Mary came back carrying a tray. It had new toast, a bowl of cereal, and a glass of apple juice. Grace's stomach growled. Mary nodded at her and left the room, closing the door. Grace got up and made sure the door was closed tight. Then she sat on the floor and ate the food.

Beth was packing boxes again. Since Patrice had rented the apartment furnished, only clothing and personal items had to be packed. At least she'd only have to pay two months' rent; Patrice was on a month-to-month basis with sixty days notice. Something to be grateful for in this calamitous series of events.

So much had happened in a short amount of time. The juvenile judge upheld the removal of custody. Grace remained in a foster home. The preliminary hearing was held, and Patrice had been assigned to a year in a residential drug rehabilitation facility. The sisters had clung to each other in relief. No jail.

The constant issue that circled through Beth's mind without resolution was Grace. She was more and more convinced that her niece should be with her. How to handle all the baggage that came with the responsibility was not clear. Grace would have to change schools, Beth would have to arrange for her deaf therapies on the Cape, find her a doctor, a dentist. Even though she knew none of those tasks was insurmountable, a part of her still held back in making a final decision.

As Beth filled boxes with Patrice's possessions, she found prescription bottles of narcotics and tranquilizers, and sandwich bags of unidentified pills hidden in Patrice's clothing. Frowning at the cache on the bureau, she wondered what she should do with them. She tossed them into a box and decided to call Patrice's court-appointed lawyer in the morning to ask him. It frightened her that she hadn't realized the extent of her sister's addiction. How many times was she using and putting Grace at risk? When she heard in court that Patrice would be sent for detox first, Beth hadn't understood. Now she did. Patrice had covered her habit well. By the look of it, she'd been using drugs for some time.

She loaded Patrice's boxes into her Ford Explorer. Lynette would pick up Grace's boxes in the morning.

After worrying during the whole drive back to the Cape, when she pulled into her driveway, Beth felt the pleasant glow of coming home lift her spirits. For a while, she would try not to think about all the bad that had happened. She carried the boxes inside and tucked them along the wall in the living room.

In the kitchen, with every intention of cooking a meal, she sat at the table and cried instead. She was crying for Patrice, and Grace, but also for herself. She rubbed her hand back and forth over the smooth maple top of the Hitchcock table, rimmed with stenciled gold fruit. It was one of her best estate sale finds. She'd been collecting treasures for her first house for years with her friend, Peg. They called themselves the Happy Hoarders.

She'd pictured her family sitting around this table, maybe having added a husband or two, watching Grace grow up. Now, her dream was slipping away. Her tears flowed faster. Patrice would pay for her crimes with a sentence, but so would she.

How could she take Grace and still move ahead with her committed plans? Maybe her niece would be better off with the family she'd stayed with before. When Patrice went to rehab last time, Grace had refused to move in with Beth. Wouldn't she again blame her aunt for her mother's absence?

She got up and made a cup of tea. How could she not take Grace? Leave her for a year with strangers? But was it Beth's responsibility? Would Patrice ever forgive her if she refused?

Chapter 5

Every single muscle in Patrice's body ached—no, *pained*. How could something that made her feel so good, make her suffer like this when she stopped taking it? An occasional Oxy, Big Boy, a Perc. It had never been this awful before. Her big mistake was trying to stop before going to court for her possession hearing, so she was already having symptoms of withdrawal. By the time she arrived at the detox center, she thought she would die. Then she hoped she would.

She stood in front of the bathroom mirror, really a square of shiny metal, which blurred her reflection. If it were a real mirror, she might have wanted to slit her wrists with a sliver of it. Her beauty, and Grace, had been the only good things she had left. Now, both were gone. A sob escaped her, but she didn't have the energy to cry. She hated the person in the mirror. Her complexion was ashy, her hair as dry as dead grass, her cheeks sunken. The only good news was that the worst was over. So they told her. And yet, at this minute, she was overwhelmed with *craving*.

An aide who oversaw her detox, knocked on the doorjamb. "Ready to go? Car's here."

"I'll never make it. I need something. Can you give me more of that Suboxone before I go?"

"No. Can't do it. That's only to help you over the withdrawal. Now the hard work begins."

"I thought you said the worst was over."

He frowned his displeasure and went on. "The Jenna Treatment Center has a multi-therapy program. It's going to take a while for the *need* to leave you. But you have time. Make the best of it. You want your daughter back."

"I have time, all right." She picked up her suitcase that she'd barely unpacked, having spent her three-day stay in a cotton Johnny.

It was a short drive to the treatment center, which was on the same large campus as the detox center. Patrice stepped out of the car and accepted her suitcase from the aide. He walked her to the door and introduced her to the woman at the desk.

"Mary Anne, this is Patrice."

Mary Anne had her sign some papers, and then took her to a sky-blue, homey room, with two beds, two bureaus, and two desks. The furniture was small scale. The beds were covered in chenille spreads that looked clean and fresh.

"You'll be sharing this with Angie. Like at the detox facility, we only use first names here. She's in group therapy right now." She indicated one of the twin beds. "This is your bed. Why don't you put your suitcase down, and I'll take you on the tour."

The administration office area reminded her of her high school: layers of pale green paint on sturdy walls, commercial tiles that shone from wax that left a lemony scent. Patrice saw meeting rooms, a living room with a television, an exercise room, a kitchen, and dining room, some of which were homey like the bedrooms. Patrice saw other women there; some smiled at her, others lowered their eyes.

"Can we walk around by ourselves?"

"This isn't a prison, Patrice. It's your only hope to stay *out* of prison. The doors are locked, but you can go in and out with your key card. You're free to leave at any time." Mary Anne stopped and waited for Patrice to absorb the information. "If you decide to go, or if you take any drugs, you'll serve your time in prison. It's up to you." She turned and began walking again. "You'll attend programs that teach you skills you can use to find work when you complete treatment. We have a vocational rehab therapist who comes in twice a week. She'll help you chose your program. You'll undergo individual and group therapy, and you're encouraged to attend 12-Step meetings in the evening. We have a schedule already set up for you. I'll give it to you after I finish showing you around."

Mary Anne brought Patrice back to her room and left her to unpack her suitcase, while she went to get a copy of her schedule. It took only a few minutes to unpack. She sat on the bed and waited. This would be her home for a year. How could she stand it? The walls seemed to close in on her. It became difficult to take in a deep breath. She was about to jump up and run when someone came through the door.

"Well, look here. My new roomie?" A thin woman with tight brown curls, wearing a flowered, loose-fitting dress and flip-flops, came to stand before her. "What's your name?"

"Patrice."

"I'm Angie. Just get through with detox?"

Patrice nodded.

"What of?"

She felt herself bristle. It was none of this woman's business. Besides, her drugs were just painkillers. Not hard dope.

"What's the matter? Cat got your tongue?" Angie tilted her head.

"Look. I'm not comfortable having this conversation. I don't know you and vice versa."

"Ah, it's like that, is it? Everybody comes in here with an attitude. Yours might be a little uppity. But it won't be for long. Things even up around here fast. You're going to learn that pretty quick."

Her roommate still stood with her head to one side, studying Patrice, which made her nervous. She didn't want to start out with having made an enemy. "No. I'm not uppity. I just don't know how I'm going to survive a year here."

Angie nodded. "Got kids?"

"A daughter. I already miss her so much."

"I've been here a month. I miss my boys, too. Four of them. But they're probably better off without me."

Patrice didn't know how to respond, so she didn't. Angie walked over to her bed and lay down facing the wall. After a minute, Patrice followed suit and stretched out on her own bed. Resting her arm on her forehead, she wondered where Grace was at the moment, mentally cringing. One little mistake. The one time she left Grace alone, and she'd completely screwed up their lives. If only she could start over with Frankie's phone call. She'd been so happy to hear from him, she couldn't see the risks. What did Frankie think of her now? She was hauled out of the party like a piece of meat. How could she have messed up so badly?

No one would tell her about Grace. Did her sister have her? Beth would be coming to see her in a few days. She'd have to wait until then. Tears slid over her temples, into her hair. Grace was the only good thing Patrice had. Beth had everything else. Would she have Grace now, too?

She sat up. That kind of thinking got her nowhere. It was her job to kick her dependency on drugs for good. DCF's goal was to reunite her with Grace. She had to do everything she could to make that happen.

She changed into sneakers to go to the exercise room. The craving was bad. She would exhaust herself so she could sleep at night. As she crept out of the room, Angie raised her head.

"Where are you going?" she asked with her eyebrows drawn tightly together.

"To exercise. Why?"

When Angie dropped her head back down on her pillow, Patrice left.

During the six days and nearly sleepless nights since Patrice was arrested, Beth had come to a decision. It wouldn't be easy, but she would have Grace move in with her. She'd notified Lynette Middlebrooks and filled out the paperwork. Lynette submitted her name for a background check that, by regulation, had to be completed before she could foster Grace.

Once the details of her decision and planning were roughed out, she breathed a sigh of relief, though she didn't know how she would mind her online store, settle into the new house, get the retail store up and running, and still give Grace the attention and love she needed. What she did know was it was the right decision for all three of them. Beth felt content in making it, despite a lingering sadness at recognizing her independent life was delayed. She didn't dare think beyond that.

Before Grace arrived on the Cape, Beth planned to meet with the contractor and settle on the revamping of the store space. Nick Marini had agreed to be present at the site this morning at nine-thirty.

She pulled into the parking lot in front of a strip of white clapboard shops on Route 6A. Though the shops were attached, the roof lines differed, giving the strip a cozy village feel. Each unit had a red door and a black flowerbox under the front window.

Inside, it still smelled faintly like pizza from the restaurant that occupied the space before her. She'd arrived an hour early to go over her drawings to be sure they still made practical sense before showing them to the contractor.

He was right on time. Not at all what she'd expected. He wore a red polo shirt with khaki pants and loafers. He was maybe five-eight and close to her own age, she guessed. If it weren't for the calluses she felt when she shook his hand, she would think she'd called the wrong number.

"Anything wrong?" He ran a hand over his longish dark hair.

"Oh, no. I'm Beth Henson. You're Nick?" Just to be sure.

"Here, does this help?" He flashed a smile and pulled a serious-sized measuring tape from a holder on his belt, then a notebook from his pocket. He slid a small pencil out of the notebook and tucked it behind his ear.

"Yes, that's more like it." She smiled.

He stood uncomfortably close to her at the old laminate counter, studying her drawings. "I'm thinking I'd like to have three distinct areas where I'll set up some display furniture," she said. "Across the back and along the walls, I'd like shelves deep enough to hold folded sheets and towels. I measured them out for you." She took a few steps away from him. "On either side of the front door—that's this drawing here—I'll set up bath products and smaller items."

"Nothing in the alcove?" He cupped her elbow and walked her toward a small arch, opening into a six-by-eight-foot room. "This could be a real showcase."

Though Nick was engaging, she didn't like his close presence, and once again put space between them. "That's one of the features that sold me on this store. I carry a line of lavender products. I plan to use this area for them. I was hoping to come up with a special arrangement, but I haven't yet."

"Glass. Glass with small lights under the shelves. I can also put spotlights above that you can direct to highlight any area you want."

"Yes. That would work."

Nick strolled around the area, occasionally pressing down with his foot on a floorboard. She watched as he studied the ceiling.

"Were you going to keep this?" he asked.

"I think, with my budget"—she gave him a number—"I may have to for now." She looked at the old off-white acoustic tiles, some with stains. "Maybe I could just paint it."

"Well, let's see what we can come up with. I'll be back to take more measurements. I want to see what the wiring looks like behind the ceiling panels, and I think I'd rather do that with my *uniform* on." He gave her another charming smile. "I'm big on lighting. It creates an atmosphere that can enhance your sales. Especially in this case, since you'll be selling bedding."

"I agree. I'd like to hang chandeliers over two of the display furniture areas. Sound okay?"

"Absolutely."

"Okay, thanks." She looked through the sketches she was holding and pulled out the one for her workspace, handing it to him. "Is this doable?"

"Yes. You want it near the door, so you can see what's going out." He widened his hazel eyes at her. "Since the door is off-center, how about we place the work station along the right wall?" He walked over to the space and extended his arms on each side. "You're close to the door, and people in line will be passing the alcove, which will be so irresistible, they'll pick up something on the way out."

She grinned. "Sounds good. How long have you been doing this work?"

"Two years." He raised his hand. "Don't worry. I've worked with my dad since I was a kid. He's a fantastic cabinetmaker. He taught me everything I know. Now he's retired and making wood carvings for his grandchildren. He often drops by and gives me a hand on a project, too."

"Your kids?"

"Nope. No kids, not married. Anyway, I started out with a business degree, but I just couldn't sit at a desk all day. Now I'm doing what I love."

"Me, too," Beth said with heart, imagining the store when it was completed.

"I'll give you a call when I have some numbers for you. We can work them up or down. We can also do the work in stages. Did you have an opening date in mind?"

"I'd like to open Memorial Day weekend. Does that work for you? I know you have commitments, too."

"We'll get it done."

They shook hands, Nick holding hers a little too long. Maybe he was just a warm, touchy-feely guy, but the fact that he seemed flirty made her uncomfortable. Was it because she couldn't remember her last date? Still, Nick's enthusiasm for her project was a plus. And Annie had recommended his work. She would just have to make it clear to him this was business only. Picking up her drawings and purse, she headed for the door. She'd withhold final judgment until she saw what he came up with.

The next day, she was repainting the white shelves that lined the sun porch. The lavender paint on the walls looked fresh, so she chose to keep it. Even though she felt peaceful working in the sunny room, nothing about it felt like a 'sacred space' to her. But then, she wasn't a believer in much sacred.

Finished, she sat and rocked in the perfectly balanced old rocker and took inventory of the sun porch. The cushions on the wicker chairs needed replacement. She would have to find a seamstress. Then her eyes fell on the child's chair. An image of Grace sitting there flashed into her mind at the same moment the doorbell rang.

At first, she wondered who could be at the door, but then her hands flew to her face. She'd totally forgotten.

She opened the door to a smiling woman, who handed her a business card. "I'm Sue Willis from DCF," she said, shaking Beth's paint-stained hand.

"I—I'm sorry I look like this. I was just painting, and the time slipped away from me." How could she have forgotten something so important? Beth led her into the living room, feeling a tight pressure forming between her shoulder blades.

Sue Willis sat on the couch and lifted her briefcase onto the coffee table. She was a small, pretty woman with short sandy hair and bright blue eyes, fanned with wrinkles. When Beth was seated in the wooden chair she'd pulled over, Sue folded her hands on her lap. "I'm from the Hyannis office of the Department of Children and Families. We received a referral from our office in New Bedford. Lynette Middlebrooks said she'd met with you."

Beth nodded. Her decision was about to become official, and she discovered she still held some resistance, which she quashed.

"I believe Lynette called to let you know the department supported the case, and that the judge upheld the emergency removal of Grace from her mother. As Lynette told you, DCF's first preference is to have a family member assume the care of a child. Your background check should be completed soon. I'd like to conduct the interview and home inspection today—" She frowned at what Beth knew was seeing her cringe. "Am I wrong here?" Sue asked. "Were you not planning to have your niece move in with you?"

Beth hesitated, realizing that up until that moment, she'd still held a foolish hope that the whole ordeal would go away. That maybe Grace would love the family she was placed with, or maybe her school friend's parents wanted to foster her.

"Listen. I need you to be honest with me. My concern is with Grace's welfare. You seem . . . a little reluctant. Don't get me wrong, I understand this is a big responsibility to take on."

Beth smiled at Sue then took a breath. "I will be honest with you. It's been a lifelong struggle with my sister. I love her, but I will admit I'm weary of her troubles. I just moved into my house here, and I'm opening a retail shop in the near future. It was a big step for me toward independence." She winced. "Wow. Do I sound selfish, or what? Compared to what my sister and Grace are going through, I have no problems at all."

"Everybody has problems, Ms. Henson. I know this isn't an easy decision. Grace has a disability that is difficult to handle. It's a sacrifice for you to make room in your life to take this on, but you have to be certain in your commitment."

"You can call me Beth. Will you be Grace's social worker?"

"Yes. So you may as well call me Sue." She smiled. "Your sister has given you Caregiver Authorization. That's written permission for you to make educational and medical decisions for Grace. I also have her medical records in the file." She sat back, clearly allowing Beth time to think.

"Can I offer you something? Coffee or tea?" Beth asked.

"I'd love a glass of water, with ice if you have it. Thanks."

"First thing I did was have an ice-maker installed. I'm an ice freak. Be right back."

In the kitchen, she remembered how defensive Grace had become with her. She filled the two glasses with ice and took them to the sink for water. She focused on the day Grace visited when they'd talked about keeping her books on the shelves in the sun porch. How loving and happy she'd been then; how much she had loved the beach.

Beth carried the glasses back to the living room. Her moment of rebellion was past.

"I am going to take my niece. But I want you to know, as her case worker, she is not fond of me right now. She realizes I'm the one responsible for her mother leaving her twice before when she went to rehab. My signing skills are stuck at basic, so I couldn't make Grace understand why her mother had to go. They don't teach the word *addiction* in the night class for signing. I doubt she would have a clue as to what it means anyway. I'm only telling you this because I want you to understand our relationship as it stands now. I'm sure she also blames me for this time her mother's left her."

"I'm going to put your mind at ease. It's never an easy transition, even for a hearing child, to go into foster care. I read Lynette's notes. She explained to Grace that her mother was ill and had to go to a special hospital for a while. An interpreter signed, and she felt Grace fully understood. Your niece made it clear she wanted to come here. She wanted to live with her aunt."

Beth rolled her lips between her teeth. She loved Grace, and she was happy her niece wanted to live with her. It wasn't what she'd planned, but life rarely followed a plan. Beth had to consider it an opportunity to return to her loving relationship with Grace. And to give her sister every chance to get clean for good. She returned her attention to Sue and nodded. "How soon will Grace be coming?"

"As soon as we receive your completed background check. And if you have time to answer some questions and show me the house today that would speed the process up."

After the interview and house tour, Sue spent a few minutes explaining how DCF worked and what would be expected of Beth.

"Don't try to take it all in at once. I'll guide you through the regulations." She checked her watch. "I'd better get going."

"What about her school?"

"I'll make an appointment for us to meet with the superintendent of Nauset schools Special Education Department. These few missed weeks won't hurt her. It's more important to get her settled. She'll catch up."

"I like the way you make us sound like a team. It doesn't seem so overwhelming."

Sue stood up. "We *are* a team. I'll call and let you know when Grace will be coming. If you have any questions, don't hesitate to call me."

As they walked to the kitchen door, Sue pulled a thick manila envelope from her briefcase. "These are Grace's medical records. When I bring her, we can talk about them." She tapped the envelope. To Beth, it seemed like another shoe was about to drop.

Two hours later, she heard the train whistle that was the ringtone of her cell. It was Sue calling to say that the background check was complete and she would be bringing Grace 'home' tomorrow. When Beth hung up the phone, she checked the time. Nick was due to arrive at five-thirty to finalize the plans for the store. It was three o'clock; she had two hours. First, she'd run to the grocery store. Afterwards, she would switch the upstairs bedrooms, making a place for Grace.

On her first night in the cottage, when Beth had gone to bed and turned off the lamp, she'd noticed how much darker it was on the Cape than outside her apartment in New Bedford. So, when the whole ceiling lit up with glowing butterflies, she'd been delighted. She'd realized it must have been Emily's room, Thea's adorable daughter, whom Beth had met at the closing. She'd trade bedrooms so Grace could have the butterflies. So much to do in so little time.

Chapter 6

Beth had everything ready when Sue Willis brought Grace to the cottage. But she wasn't prepared for the change in her niece. It took all the strength Beth had to keep the smile on her face. Grace had dark circles under her eyes and her face was pale as milk. Staying with strangers, coupled with all the worry and upset about her mother, had taken a toll on her. Beth's eyes burned with tears she held back. Thank God she'd made the right decision.

Beth signed, "I'm happy you are here." She stooped in front of her niece and pulled her into a hug. Grace didn't resist—or reciprocate.

"We'll go sit in Grace's favorite room," Beth said to Sue, then took Grace's hand and led them down the hall to the sun porch.

"I think Grace is pretty tired," Sue said, nodding at Beth. "She told me she didn't sleep well at the foster home. She was afraid of the dog, and she had nightmares."

"Do you sign?" Beth asked.

"No. I took an interpreter with me when I picked her up, but we managed well enough when he left." She smiled at Grace. "She seems to read lips pretty well. With your ability to sign some words, Beth, I know you'll both get along fine. I'm sure she'll be much more relaxed now that she's here."

Sue was giving her a chance to get over her shock at Grace's condition. She looked at her niece, who sat in the child's chair, staring straight ahead, not even trying to lip read. She was wearing summer-weight pants and a sweater. Her black hair was in a loose pony tail that was tangled enough to tell Beth she'd slept with it a couple nights.

"Did you get a chance to go over her medical file?" Sue asked as she opened her briefcase and pulled out papers.

"Oh shoot. I forgot all about it. Great way to start. It's just that I had an appointment last night, and today, I've been getting ready for Grace. I fixed up her bedroom. I also stocked the kitchen with food she likes."

"I'm not judging you, Beth. The thing is, when Patrice took Grace for her initial health care screen, her regular doctor filled out her Medical Passport. He noted her deafness and that a cochlear implant had been recommended by a specialist earlier. He had obtained Grace's medical files from the specialist. Those are the records I gave you, and they did recommend an immediate placement of an implant to help Grace hear."

Beth shook her head. "Patrice never mentioned anything about it."

"At some point, once you're both settled in, you might want to have Grace re-evaluated."

They chatted further for a few minutes, then Sue handed her the papers she was holding, which were Grace's Medical Passport, her Mass Health ID card, a guide for foster care providers, a schedule of family visits, and a few forms and lists. "The medical passport contains all her health information. It's confidential and must be taken to every medical or dental visit for the provider to review. Also, the provider should fill out this—" Sue pulled a form out of the group Beth was holding—"which you'll give to me on my monthly visit."

Beth was overwhelmed and must have looked it. Sue went on, "There's a great deal of information in this booklet that you can use for reference. It has everything I told you spelled out, so don't worry if it doesn't all make sense now. Ask me about anything at all, even if it seems silly. I'm here to help."

Before Beth was anywhere near ready to take over alone, Sue stood up to leave. "Don't hesitate to call me if you need me. I'll check in with you tomorrow." She bent down and told Grace goodbye, giving her shoulders a little hug.

Beth walked her to the door, and then went back to the sun porch. Grace hadn't moved.

"Come see your room," Beth signed, and then held out her hand. Grace took it, and they climbed the stairs. She showed a flash of interest in the bedroom switch Beth had made since her last visit. The twin beds were now in the front bedroom. She walked around the beds, dragging her fingers along the comforter Beth had chosen for her—white pique with embroidered yellow daises—and touched a leaf-shaped green toss pillow.

"Let's unpack your things." Beth indicated Grace should follow her. Back downstairs, she gave Grace a small box to carry upstairs and took two herself. They made two trips. A pine bureau stood along the inside wall, and a bedside table rested between the twin beds. Beth had moved in an extra chair from her own bedroom temporarily. Grace would need a comfy chair and a desk set up. Beth had an idea they could do the consignment shops together, to look for the chandeliers and some furniture at the same time.

Grace sat on the chair, staring out the window.

Beth tapped her on the shoulder. She signed, "You want to clean—no. Want to move your clothes into the bureau?" By Grace's expression of disdain, Beth knew she'd signed wrong. "Shall we put your clothes in the bureau?" she said instead.

Grace's hands flew around.

"Ah, jeez. This is going to be tough." Beth rotated her index fingers alternately toward her body, then slid her right flat-hand fingers over her left flat hand, from the fingertips to the wrist. "Sign slowly."

When Grace slowed down, Beth got the gist of what she was telling her: She wanted to go home with her mother. She wasn't going to stay with Beth for long. She didn't want to unpack her clothes.

Beth decided Grace had suffered enough trauma in the last several days; it wouldn't hurt to let her live out of boxes and her suitcase for now. One step at a time. She nodded her acceptance to Grace.

One thing was clear; Beth needed a sign dictionary handy to help them communicate. Grace obviously was unaware of the length of time she would have to stay with her aunt. Beth would have to explain that, to be able to sign words that must be delivered gently. She stood up and motioned for Grace to follow. She led her down to the kitchen and pulled out a chair for her.

"I'll make you some lunch. How about—?" She went to the pantry and pulled out a jar of peanut butter and held it up.

Grace waved her hands, signing quickly again. Beth didn't understand.

"Use your voice, sweetie."

After a slight hesitation, she said, "See mommy." Her words were childlike, her tone high-pitched. She was growing more agitated. Should Beth tell her the truth? Lynette had given her a little explanation. Obviously, Grace needed more now.

Beth began to sign the best she could as she spoke. "The lady told you, your mommy is sick. We can't go see her yet. She must get better first."

Grace shook her right index finger from side to side. "Where?"

Beth finger-spelled the words: Fall River.

"See mommy!"

Beth had to wait for Patrice to tell them when they could make their first visit, but she had to ease Grace's fear now; it was clear she was on the verge of tears. She signed, "Three or four days."

Grace worked her hands, "Want to see her now." She stood.

"Not now. In three or four days." She turned and opened the refrigerator, pulling out a jar of strawberry jam. Grace came and tugged on

Beth's shirt. When she got her attention, she began to sign, "Now. Now. Now!"

Beth knelt down and gently shook her head no. She raised three then four of Grace's fingers. Grace bowed her head. Beth gave her a quick hug then guided her back around to her chair. She made a sandwich and poured a glass of milk.

While Grace nibbled the edges of the sandwich, Beth tried again. With her limited ability, she told Grace that her mother would be all right, that nice people were taking care of her. It seemed to help. As Grace ate, Beth began to recognize the magnitude of taking care of a deaf child for longer than a weekend. She thought back to how easily Patrice had always handled it. It made Beth wonder why she'd apparently ignored the recommendation of a cochlear implant. Beth had no idea what was involved with the technology, but if it would help, shouldn't Grace have it? She'd have to ask Patrice when she saw her.

Since her online business had taken off, keeping her working long hours, Beth had given up her American Sign Language class. In the short periods she and Grace were alone together, they had managed well enough with Beth's knowledge of the alphabet and basic signing. The rest of their time together, Patrice was there to help. Though Grace had spoken early, she rarely used her verbal skills now. Beth remembered the doctor saying it was lucky she was speaking before her illness, as it would help her to continue. Shouldn't she be speaking more? Beth began to wonder how often Grace had missed her speech therapist appointments.

It was a cold day, but the sun was out. She improvised with signals and sign that they could walk to the beach. Grace shook her head, pointed to the phone and signed. "Mommy call me."

What was the sign for *today*? She couldn't remember. "Not today," Beth said, shaking her head. Grace's body slumped in her chair.

Beth tapped her shoulder. "Library?" One thing she knew about her niece, she loved to read. Grace nodded.

"First, let's get you cleaned up."

While Grace bathed, Beth ordered a sign dictionary and a couple of other books about deafness online.

Once they received their new library cards, they went to the children's section.

A woman who was putting away books turned and smiled at them. "Can I help you find something?" she asked Grace.

Grace looked up at Beth.

"Grace is deaf," she told the woman, "but she can read lips fairly well if you face her and speak normally, but not too fast."

"Okay, that's good to know." She bent down and spoke to Grace. "I'm Lauren. Can I help you find some books?"

"No," Grace said then bit her bottom lip. She began to sign to Lauren.

"I'm sorry. I don't understand," Lauren said to Beth.

"She said she'd like to choose the books herself." Beth indicated to Grace that she should go ahead. She said to Lauren, "Grace is my niece. She's come to stay with me for a while."

The woman appeared to be around Beth's age. She was short, with bob-length hair, brown with lighter highlights. Her expression was open and friendly. "Oh, that's nice. You're new here, aren't you?"

"Yes. I recently moved in."

"Where?"

"On Bay Road. Do you know it?"

Lauren's eyes widened. "Not the cute shingled cottage with the roses?"

"Yes, that's it. The roses haven't blossomed yet, but I've seen a picture."

"I am so happy to meet you. I absolutely love that house. I see it on the way to Skaket Beach, where I take my boys in the summer. Oh my God, the gardens you have! You're going to love it here. What brought you to Orleans?"

"I'm planning to open a store, so I considered towns with commercial centers. It seemed like Orleans had the most to offer. I just signed a lease."

"Good for you. What kind of store is it?"

For a librarian, this nice woman was not quiet. Beth was slightly uncomfortable, but she couldn't help but like her. And she could use a friend. "It's called Linens & Lavender. I'll carry organic linens and an array of lavender products."

"It sounds charming. Speaking of linens, do you quilt by any chance?"

Beth blinked at her. "Quilt?"

"You know, sew quilts?"

"No. Do you?"

"Yes, and if you ever want to learn, you could join our group. Since we're such a great group of women, it would be a way for you to meet people, though I guess you'll be pretty busy when your shop opens."

"Thanks for the offer. You're right, I'm going to be busy for a while, but I'd love to see the quilts you make sometime." She looked over to one of the small tables where Grace was bent over a book, sniffing the pages. Beth had seen her do that many times before. It always made her smile. "I guess we'd better get going."

"Hold on," Lauren said and reached for a piece of paper. When she finished writing, she handed it to Beth. "That's my phone number and email address. Feel free to get in touch if you have any questions about the town. I'm a native, and I know all the good things we don't tell the tourists." She chuckled.

Beth felt her spirits lift as they left the library because she sensed the beginning of a new friendship. It assured her she'd made the right choice for her new home. It was obvious by the way Grace hugged her books to her chest that she felt better, too.

Back at the cottage, Grace walked right to the sun porch and placed her pile of books on the shelf. A smile tugged at Beth's lips as she watched her. The day was definitely calmer.

Grace was exhausted by the time they finished dinner. Beth helped her into a nightgown she pulled from her suitcase. When she tucked her into bed, Beth turned off the lamp. She waited until she heard Grace's intake of breath, signaling she saw the glowing butterflies, and then Beth turned the lamp back on. "For you," she signed and smiled. She kissed her niece's forehead.

Beth flipped on the night light, turned the lamp off, and closed the door most of the way. She sighed. One day done, and she was feeling good about it. Grace had to be her first priority. Her job was to take care of Grace and help her through this terrible situation. Beth was upset enough herself. Her sister could have a record. Worst of all, it was obvious she had not been able to stay clean.

In her downstairs office, Beth turned on her computer. She had to catch up on two lost days of work. She also wanted her employees to know what was going on with her family, while skipping some parts, and that her scheduled times in the office would be erratic. When she signed into the administrative site for Linens & Lavender, a host of details popped up that vied for her attention. It was daunting. She thought about all she had to do between the online business, setting up the cottage, and opening her retail shop. And Grace was a full-time job, besides. It would be easier once the doctor visit was over and Grace started school.

She switched to answering her email and began writing notes to her New Bedford friends, whom she missed so much. Their responses would dispel some of her loneliness. Everybody she loved was far away, except Grace.

Chapter 7

On the Wednesday following Grace's arrival, Beth took her to see an ENT, Doctor Scott Adams.

Grace looked so small in the large leather chair in the doctor's office. Her hair was in pigtails and she was dressed in a purple tunic over white tights. She had slept and eaten better once Beth told her they could visit her mother on Sunday. But right now, her eyes were wide with apprehension.

When the doctor walked in, Beth saw he was holding the manila envelope of Grace's records, which he dropped on his desk. He shook both their hands then sat down, with a slight frown. He had yet to say a word.

Bedside manner wouldn't be his forte, Beth realized, but his credentials were impressive. He had curly, dark brown hair with a few strands of gray, though his face was unlined. It was difficult to guess his age. He wore rimless glasses. The lenses were distracting, appearing to float over his brown eyes.

As he laced his fingers on top of the desk, Beth noticed his fingernails were closely clipped. He gazed at her like a college professor who was disappointed with his student, then turned to her niece. Beth already knew she didn't like him.

"Grace, can you understand what I'm saying?"

Grace reached for Beth's hand. She shrugged her shoulders then nodded at the doctor.

"At least that's something. Though it may work against her speech progress. Ms. Henson, her medical workup after her meningitis-caused deafness was excellent. When a child becomes deaf post-lingually, meaning after she's learned to speak, the goal is always toward oralism. Grace was initially given a hearing aid, though her audiological studies implied that there would be little gain. It wasn't the first choice of the audiologist or the doctor. I'm sure you've heard all this before."

He seemed to be waiting for Beth to explain. She was indignant. His attitude was confrontational—evoking memories of her father. She was ready to leave. She needed a doctor who would be supportive, not patronizing. "Doctor Adams, I am Grace's aunt, not her mother. I was not privy to every decision my sister made about her daughter's care. I *do* know her mother loves her very much, and she would have done the best she could."

The doctor bent his head down. When he looked up, he said, "I owe you an apology. And your sister is. . . ."

"Away." Thinking she may seek out a different doctor, she decided not to be more specific.

"Okay, we'll leave it at that for now. Let me explain. The problem is Grace has lost some valuable time. She should have had a cochlear implant as soon as possible after she became deaf. Instead, she learned to rely on sign and speech reading, which makes the switch to oralism more difficult. How is her academic progress?"

"I don't know. Her school records have been transferred to Orleans Elementary. I've only had a preliminary meeting with the superintendant of special education. They'll be working with us to mainstream Grace, with the aid of an interpreter and a speech therapist."

"I sense a void here. Maybe you could explain the family circumstances. Are you Grace's legal guardian?"

Beth angled herself away from Grace, even though she didn't seem to be paying attention. "My sister—" she bit her lip, before starting again. "My sister is in a substance abuse rehabilitation facility by court order for twelve months. Grace is under DCF custody, and she's been placed with me." She raised her hands, palms up. "I'm still a bit confused about my responsibilities. There's a lot of paperwork involved. Even though my sister has given me caregiver authorization, I would want to consult with her on any medical decisions."

"How's Grace taking all this?"

"She's only been with me a few days. She's not happy, but I wouldn't expect her to be. Communication is difficult. I don't sign well, and she's too quick for me to understand."

"ASL—American Sign Language, or English?"

"She studied both. The teacher added English sign, because even at five and a half, she could already read some."

He nodded. "Go on."

"As far as I know, Patrice, Grace's mother, was doing what she was told to do by her doctors. Our relationship has been difficult, at times." Beth furrowed her brows at that.

"It always is with addicts. Okay, I've got a better picture. I'm going to examine Grace first then we'll talk again." He leaned forward to get Grace's attention. When she looked up, he began to sign and speak. "Grace, I'm

Doctor Adams. I'm going to look you over, and then we're going to talk about your deafness. Right now, we're going to move to a different room. Are you ready?"

Grace was holding Beth's hand in a tight grip, but as the doctor talked to her, she became more relaxed. She let go of Beth's hand and signed to the doctor.

A smile broke out on his face, producing a deep dimple in his right cheek. The dimple seemed to draw away the stern impression of his expression. "No. No shots. And yes, you can keep your clothes on. I'm mostly going to be peeking down the rabbit holes in your ears."

Grace smiled. She signed again.

Doctor Adams smiled back and nodded. "I guess she can come with us if you want."

Grace took Beth's hand again.

He gave Grace a thorough examination, all the while explaining what he was doing. Beth could tell he was gauging her speech reading and signing skills as he went along.

Back in his office, he handed Grace a book to read, called *What's it Like? Deafness.*

"Grace needs to have the implant, probably two of them. When a child has sudden sensorineural hearing loss, which means there is damage to the hair cells in the cochlea, hearing aids aren't much use. Based on her records, she's profoundly deaf. I see how little she uses her language now. Teaching a child to sign and speech read makes her depend on those skills. It's easier for her since she can't hear her voice. It's also isolating. Her social growth becomes retarded. I'd be willing to bet she's had some issues in school.

"The goal for her, as I said, is oralism. Speaking. She's had the advantage of having reached a proficient stage of language before she lost her hearing. It's best to do the implants as soon as possible after deafness occurs, while the brain still remembers how to interpret sounds as speech. Since she still vocalizes a little, I have faith she'll learn to speak again, though it will be harder now.

"Know that cochlear implants won't *cure* her deafness, but they will allow her to hear sounds. Have you read anything about them?"

"No," Beth said. "But I just ordered a book online about deafness that includes information on implants."

"Before we go any further, I need to know who can legally make medical and financial decisions for Grace. This is a long process. First, she'll have the surgery to place the implant. Then the mapping—I'll explain all this later—then an extensive rehabilitation where Grace's brain learns to connect the sounds she hears to words. It's a program that requires consistency and emotional support for both Grace and her caregiver."

His words seemed like a preamble to something huge. Something Beth wasn't equipped to handle without Patrice. "I don't know all the answers to your questions yet. My sister never mentioned an implant to me. I don't know if she decided against one or was advised not to do it. I'll be seeing her Sunday, and I'll discuss all this with her. As far as DCF is concerned, it was Grace's social worker that requested she be re-evaluated, so I doubt there would be any problem there."

"Good. I think we should assemble a team together, an audiologist, Special Ed, DCF. So you'll have Grace for a year?"

"Yes, but Patrice is also accused of child neglect. I don't know where I stand on that. It depends on whether or not the DA brings charges. And . . . I'm not sure how she'll do in rehab."

"As soon as you sort it out, let me know," he said, standing. "This shouldn't wait. I'll bet when you read her academic records, you'll find she's fallen behind. And if we don't do everything we can to guide her toward independence, she will fall further. This needs to be a group effort to give Grace every chance of speech."

Before they left, Beth took out her iPhone. "May I take your picture? I'm putting together a book of places. I read that if I could show her a picture of where we're going, she would have less anxiety."

Dr. Adams grinned. "Have at it." After Beth took the photo, he nodded and said, "You'll do just fine." She heard the patronizing tone in his voice and felt her muscles tense. She did not like the man, but she had to admit, he'd won Grace over and calmed her fears. Even made her smile. That was what mattered.

Beth was overwhelmed with information. Somehow she couldn't face going home. She drove to a soft-serve ice cream shop she'd noticed in town, The Local Scoop, where Grace could pile on her own toppings. When they walked in the door, they were greeted with a potpourri of sweet fragrances from every kind of goody. The colorful bins of toppings made Grace's eyes pop. While they waited in line to choose their cones or cups, Grace tugged on Beth's purse. She signed, "Phone." But Beth didn't hear it ringing. Grace insisted, so she took it out and looked at it.

Grace signed, "Photo."

When Beth stopped laughing, she took the picture for Grace's places book.

Chapter 8

It would happen all over again, Grace knew it. She was holding a library book on her lap, but she was gazing out the sunroom window. The kids in her new third grade class would first stare at her because she was new. Then they would stare at her because she was different from them. Because she couldn't talk right, or hear, and had to have help.

A few days ago, she went to see the new school that looked like her old school, pretty much. She met the lady, Ms. Jenny, who would sign to her what the teacher was saying. Ms. Jenny was nice, and Grace loved the way she signed. She looked like a ballerina dancing. Grace stood up, setting her book on the wicker chair, and signed words with her hands making graceful arcs and her body swaying in time. Then she giggled, knowing how funny she must look. She sat back down in her chair.

She'd been hoping her mommy would be home by now, so she could go to her own school. She didn't like that one either, but the kids didn't pay much attention to her any longer, because she wouldn't use her voice again in front of them. Why couldn't she keep doing homework with Aunt Beth at the cottage? Her teacher, Mr. Hamilton, sent her an assignment to do at home every school day. She could read mostly by herself and didn't need too much help from her aunt to do the lessons. But Aunt Beth said no, it was good for her to go to school to make new friends.

She didn't want to go. She couldn't make friends anyway, since she couldn't talk to them.

She picked up her book, and then looked at the rocker. Grace could never see the lady, only hear her, but she smiled anyway. She knew the lady could see her because she always read the words in the book with her. Sometimes she rocked her chair.

Grace began to read and the lady spoke: *Becky could no longer see her mother. Where had she gone? Everybody around her looked so big, like she was standing in a forest of people. "Mom!" Becky yelled—"*

"Want to go to the beach, Grace?" Aunt Beth poked her head into the room and asked, signing *beach*.

"No."

"Why don't you want to walk to the beach? You're in here all the time. You need some exercise and sunshine. So do I."

"I like it here," she signed, then picked her book back up so Aunt Beth would get the message and go away.

"But honey, you've read each of those books many times. And you love the beach."

Grace tilted her head and stared, pursed-lipped, at her aunt. Then she sighed and put the book down again. "I can hear the words," she signed.

"What?" Aunt Beth said, frowning.

"I can hear the words."

"In your head? Can't you usually?"

"No. I hear her voice *saying* the words."

Aunt Beth stared at her. "Who?"

Grace shrugged her shoulders.

"Can you always hear her voice like that when you read?"

"I hear her voice in here," she signed then pointed at the floor of the sun porch. "I can hear her words when I read the book. I like it." She pulled the book back up to her face, to effectively end the conversation.

"Grace!" Patrice called out as she rushed into the visiting room. It seemed like a year since she'd seen her daughter. She grabbed her and swung her around. "Mommy's so happy you came." She set Grace's feet back on the floor and knelt before her. "Tell mommy what you've been doing. I've missed you so much." Patrice smiled at Beth and patted her heart. "Thank you for bringing her. And you."

Grace had seemed subdued when Patrice first entered the room. Now she was excited, signing a straight line of thoughts without breaks. "Slow down, sweetie. What butterflies?"

"They're on my bedroom ceiling and they come out just at night."

Beth laughed. "I changed rooms after the time you visited, because my room had a ceiling full of butterflies that glowed when I turned off the light. I thought Grace would like them."

Patrice smiled. She asked Grace, "Do you like your new school?"

Grace looked at her feet. "I have to go tomorrow."

"Are you scared? I bet you are. It's tough to go to a new place when you don't know anyone. I was scared to come here, too."

Grace raised her eyebrows. "You were?"

"Just like you. But you know what happened? I met some very nice people that are helping me get better." She hugged Grace, looking over her head at Beth.

"I am getting help. It's been hard, though."

"I can imagine," Beth said, shaking her head. "How are you feeling?"

"Physically, I feel much better, but . . . it's difficult. And I miss Grace so much."

"I know. I'm proud of you. And you look great. Rested and well."

Patrice slid Grace onto her lap and signed, "How's your shell collection coming?"

"I don't go to the beach. It's too cold."

"It was freezing the day we all went and you—" she tapped Grace's nose, "You didn't want to go back to Aunt Beth's cottage. I want you to have a big bunch of shells for me to see when I come home."

They signed back and forth until Patrice noticed she was neglecting Beth. "I'm going to talk to Aunt Beth a little now." She reached out her hand and took Beth's, who was sitting beside her on the opposite side of Grace. "I don't know how to tell you how much I appreciate your taking Grace. The thought of her in a foster home made me panic. Thank you so much."

"You don't have to thank me. I'm loving it. Remember how I said she could stay with me all summer and go to the beach? Well, now we can."

"But she said she isn't going to the beach. Yes, it's March, but she loved it even in February."

"For whatever reason, she's taken to the sacred space. All she wants to do is read there."

"What's the sacred space?"

Beth chuckled. "It's the sun porch. Word is, a good witch used to live there and that's what she called it, 'her sacred space.' It seems to work for Grace. It calms her."

"She must miss me."

"She does. She's been very sad, but I know she'll be better now that she's seen you."

Patrice felt relief. And then joy. Her daughter was missing her. She wasn't having such a good time at her aunt's that she didn't miss her mother. Her imagination had been torturing her at night, picturing Grace running at the beach, having fun with Beth. "Beth, she starts school tomorrow. She's afraid. She's had some hard times with kids at school."

"I know. But her teacher is so nice and she's already met her deaf interpreter. I've been to a couple meetings with them and other school officials, and they are all working together to get her settled and happy."

"That makes me feel better. I just wish I could see her more."

Grace was yanking Patrice's shirt. "Wait one more minute, honey." She turned back to Beth. "Listen, you have no reason to believe in me. But I promise with all my heart, I'm going to make it this time. You won't have to help me again. If I had something sharp, I'd make us blood sisters like we used to do when we were kids. I love you so much, but I never realized how much I *took* from you until I started this therapy. You never asked for anything in return for all those times you saved my butt. When I get out of here, I'm going to make it up to you."

She watched through her own misty eyes as Beth stabbed at a tear that was about to spill down her cheek. "You don't have to. You just did."

On the way home, Beth saw an estate sale sign on a street corner in Sandwich. She'd seen the company's advert in the paper. Today was the second day when the sale managers often discounted the price of the unsold items by half. Maybe if they looked for some pieces for her room, it would make Grace feel better. Between leaving her mom and having to start school, it might give her something else to think about. She pulled into the sale parking area.

"Grace, this is a way people sell things they no longer want or need. Would you like to go into the house with me and see what's there?"

Grace shook her head no. But Beth encouraged her. "Maybe we'll find a chair for your room." The spark of interest was enough. Grace opened her door. Beth draped an arm over her shoulder and they walked to the house.

The sale was in a large residence. Most of the items were already gone, giving voices in the empty rooms a hollow ring. They stopped at a card table displaying odds and ends. Grace stood beside her like a store mannequin, making it plain she wasn't interested. But when Beth held up a box of water colors, slightly used, Grace's eyes grew large. "Want these?" Grace moved her fist up and down. "Yes."

Beth handed her the paints. "Let's see what's left in the bedrooms."

They climbed circular stairs to the second floor. The first two bedrooms were empty except for the beds, which held sold signs on their frames. In the third bedroom was a small desk and chair. Beth walked over to look for a sold sticker but she only saw the price. If it was fifty percent off, it was well within her budget.

"What do you think? Do you want to try sitting in the chair?" she signed to Grace.

It was a good fit with room for growth so Grace could take it home with her when she left. "Would you like it? You can do your homework, or you can sketch and paint while sitting at your own desk."

"Yes."

Hearing the verbal word, unsolicited, set off a quick little flutter in Beth's heart. "Okay. You sit right here so no one else can buy it while I go get someone to help us," she said and partly signed.

Grace pulled the chair in and stretched her arms across the top of the desk. She needed no words to convey her meaning.

Two men loaded the desk and chair in the back of the SUV. Grace wanted to ride in the back with her desk, but Beth insisted she sit in the back seat with her belt on. Still, she kept one arm stretched over the back of the seat, while she kept an eye on her desk, with the paints rattling in the drawer.

Beth stopped at the drugstore in Orleans and bought the journal her sister had suggested during their visit, along with pencils, a stapler, Scotch tape, and note pads. Grace actually skipped back to the car while holding Beth's hand.

It felt like the sky was full of rainbows.

"You pick. In your room or in my office?"

The desk and chair were sitting in the hall. The plastic bag from the drug store was on the floor beside the chair. Grace stood undecided, her finger working her thumb cuticle again. She had been giving Beth lessons in sign for about a half hour a day. They were able to communicate better, but Beth still depended on Grace's expressions, which sometimes were clearer than sign language.

"If you keep it in my office downstairs, it will be much easier to bring back to your house when you leave."

Grace held her bottom lip squeezed between her index finger and thumb while she nodded her head.

Beth crooked her finger and walked into the office. She indicated the space on the opposite wall from her own desk. This way she could keep Grace near her instead of isolated in her room. She was hoping Grace would make the decision herself, as she did.

"How about right here?"

"Yes."

"Oh boy, you're doing well in speaking. I'm proud of you."

This time Grace tucked her lips between her teeth to hide a smile.

They moved the desk in place. Beth filled a bucket with Murphy's Oil Soap and warm water, threw in a cleaning cloth, and set it beside the desk. She wrung out the cloth, breathing in the clean scent, and handed it to Grace. "Oh, wait."

Beth went to the kitchen and took out an old apron of her mother's. She tied it on Grace. "Now, you're ready."

On Monday, April Fool's Day, winds tossed the trees and shoved the clouds briskly across the sky. This was a day when she hated the deafness that kept Grace's feelings locked inside of her. Beth knew she was afraid, any child would be nervous the first day of attending a new school. Beth knew from the school meeting that Grace had been struggling in her old school. The children had ignored her after her celebrity status of deafness had worn off.

Mr. Hamilton had asked them to come in a little early. He was at the classroom door waiting for them. "Good morning. Are you ready to learn a whole bunch of neat things?"

Grace did her don't-understand headshake. Ms. Jenny, her schoolroom interpreter, came up to join them from the back of the room. She tapped Grace's arm, then signed to her. Still, Grace didn't answer.

"She's a little nervous," Beth said to Mr. Hamilton.

"We'll take good care of her. Don't worry. Why don't you tell her goodbye and take off? It'll be easier if we can peel her hand from yours." He smiled.

Beth bent down in front of Grace. "Remember all the good things that happen today so you can write about them for mommy. I'll be right outside the door when class is over." She gave her the lunch they had packed together. Then she stood and waved. And left.

Oh God, that was hard. She sat in the car, her hands gripping the steering wheel. If it was this difficult for an aunt, what had Patrice gone through? It was hard enough for a child to start school, but for a deaf child? Beth held her hands tightly over her ears. She could hear her breathing, and the amplified sound of her hands pressing on her sensitive ears. Much more sound than Grace heard, and yet, it was lonely. She took her hands down. She could hear the hoarse drag of a school bus engine, birds chirping in the trees, children's running footsteps and loud voices. A dog was barking; a sharp sound against the droning of tires some distance away on Route 6. Grace would hear none of these sounds everyone else took for granted, were even annoyed at for disturbing their peace.

She thought of Doctor Adams. His suggestion of the cochlear implant was more about teaching her to speak. But being able to distinguish sounds instead of a vacuum? If the implant could do that, Beth wanted her to have one. A team meeting was scheduled on Wednesday evening to go over all the retesting they had done on Grace. When Beth had all the information, she would discuss it with Patrice the following Sunday. The first visit was all about being together again. This week they could sneak in a little talk about the implants. She knew her sister would be excited, too.

Grace didn't hold her hand on the way to the car after school, a good sign to Beth that her first day went well. Standing next to the SUV, Grace signed to her, "I taught the kids to sign words." She held up three fingers.

"Three of them? Which words?"

She made a salute for hello. She moved both flat hands forward then down from her lips until they were palms up—thanks, or you're welcome. She pointed to her right ear, then moved her flat hands, palms down and apart, back together. Literally, ear closed, meaning deaf.

"Wow. You're a good teacher. You teach me sign. But I didn't know you could teach school."

Grace shook her head with a serious expression. "No. Some sign only," her hands said. When Beth reached past her to open the car door, Grace caught her sleeve. She signed again. Her eyebrows were raised as she made the sign for a ball then kicked out with one foot. When she saw Beth understood, she signed again, "I want to play."

Beth thought the word *conundrum* made the perfect sound to match its meaning. Could Grace play soccer when she couldn't hear? She was watching Beth's expression, holding her breath. Beth hadn't seen her so excited in years. How could she burst this bubble?

The only idea that came to her was something her mother used to say when she didn't want to answer: "We'll see." She wished she could say yes, but she would have to check first to learn if sports would be safe. It was clear Grace's heart was set on it. She seemed almost happy at times now, and Beth didn't want to dampen that.

That night, Grace unpacked her clothes and put them away in her room.

Chapter 9

On the following Sunday, Grace sat with her journal on her lap, waiting for her mother. When Patrice came in, she jumped up and ran into her arms. Again, they talked and hugged and read the journal together before Patrice acknowledged Beth.

Finally, she turned to face her sister. "How are you managing all this? Do you have any time to yourself? I know how important that is to you."

"Sure, I do. Grace is going to school every day, so I have plenty of time."

"Don't worry. It may not be as long as we thought. I understand the assignment can be changed to outpatient if I'm doing well for an extended period. Since I'm a star pupil here, I'm making that my goal. And Beth," she took Beth's hands in hers and shook them a little, "the DA decided not to bring charges of child neglect, because I was in rehab and also because he couldn't find evidence of any other incidences of neglect." She ran her fingers through Grace's ponytail. "Maybe, once I'm an outpatient, DCF will let me see Grace more than once a week."

"Such good news! I'm so happy. Just keep doing what you're doing. Don't get ahead of yourself or put undue pressure on yourself. Grace and I are fine." Beth watched her sister's expression change.

"I think it's a good goal," Patrice said, "For your sake, but especially for Grace's. The more she sees me, especially since I'm so much better, I would think the happier she will be. We have to do what's best for Grace. Right?"

Beth knew she'd crossed one of her sister's lines. She *was* doing what was best for Grace. She brushed off her annoyance. Patrice needed all her support, because what she was doing was far harder than taking care of Grace. "It's a great goal. I know you can do it. I just don't want you to worry about me when you already have so much on your plate."

Patrice ignored her for a while as she signed with Grace. Then she scowled and turned to Beth. "What doctor says she needs an operation?"

This was not going well. "DCF asked me to take Grace to see an Ear, Nose, and Throat specialist—"

"Wait. Stop. Why? Is she sick?"

"No, Patrice. It's because of her deafness, and because a doctor you took her to before recommended a cochlear implant. It was in her medical records. DCF wanted her to be re-evaluated. The ENT was asking why she never had the implant. I told him you must have had a good reason."

"Of course, I did. I researched it and decided I didn't want to put her into that dangerous situation when it might not even work. I also read all about deafness. Do you realize the deaf community thinks of themselves as a minority? There's a lot of controversy about making a deaf child talk. So, I made the decision not to have the implant."

"I've been reading about deafness, too. But I thought the argument to stay deaf, which would mean she would be in a deaf community, was only for people who were born that way. Grace was already talking when she became deaf. You were sending her to speech therapy, weren't you?"

"Oh, suddenly you're an expert on deafness." She folded her arms across her chest.

This was going downhill faster than a sled on ice. "No, Patrice. I thought it would be good to understand about cochlear implants myself before we talked about it. I'm not trying to take away your choices. DCF insisted I take her to an ENT and have her re-evaluated, based on Grace's medical records. So I did."

"Who do they think they are? She's my daughter."

Beth was worried about Patrice's reaction. She was under enough pressure trying to recover. She smiled at Grace who had looked up from the string puzzle she was playing with. Beth sat on the edge of her seat and leaned closer to her sister. "Patrice, it's nothing to get upset over. I would never tell you what to do. DCF wouldn't do that either. It's your decision. Maybe they've had some new developments since you read about the implants. One of these times I'll bring along the book I have for you to read."

"Shit. What's wrong with me? I'm sorry. My nerves are on edge." She turned to Grace and signed. "What do you think? Do you want to have an antenna on your head?" Then she laughed at her joke. Grace laughed, too, but it was clear she was confused.

Beth smiled, but she was frustrated. She didn't understand why her sister was so adamant about her daughter not having the implant.

Patrice patted Beth's hand. "I'm sorry. It's just that I miss Grace so much." She wrapped an arm around Grace's shoulders. "The truth? I'm a little paranoid about your having her. You were always such a good 'mom' to me." Patrice took a deep breath, and then looked at Beth with a sad expression. "I need Grace to love me best. She's all I have."

"She does love you best. She always will. No matter what I do, I'll only be her aunt. You're her mother."

On Tuesday, the sun shone after an early morning shower, making the sky seem bluer, and the juniper tree in the backyard a brighter green. As Beth walked out of the house, she noticed the buds had swelled on the branches of the tall bush on the side of the farmer's porch. Cape Cod had no respect for the vernal equinox, which had already passed. Winter held onto the Cape, sliding slowly off the tip of Provincetown, as if reluctant to end its rule.

Even though the full bloom of spring was still only a wish in the minds of the residents, the signs of the new birth of flora were uplifting. A reflection of Beth's own rebirth. To add to her light heart, she was on her way to see the progress of her store. She walked in and looked around, her eyes wide at how fast the changes were taking place.

"I can't believe how much you've done already. It looks great!"

Nick came down from the ladder and joined her. "We like compliments. Right, Dad?" He called to his father, who was putting up shelves in the alcove. "Come meet the nice lady we're working for." He winked at Beth. "This is my Dad. Paul, meet Beth."

A wizened man with a thick white mustache came bowl-legged toward her. The man had a map of life carved into his face. When they shook hands, Beth tried not to wince at the pain. Nick laughed. "He doesn't know his own strength." He reached over for her hand and gave it a little shake.

"Watch out for him, Beth. He's a flirt," Paul said, chuckling.

"What do you think of the new ceiling?" Nick asked.

"It looks great. Now it fades into the background. No longer an eyesore. You found it for me, didn't you, Paul?"

"Yeah. Been at this a long time. You get a sense. Nick told me all about you. That helps."

Her cheeks felt warm, so she moved around the room, trailing her fingers over the wooden shelves sanded smooth as a baby's palm. "Everything looks perfect. It's so exciting to see the progress you've made. I'm going to take measurements in the alcove, so I can figure how much stock the shelves can handle." She went to the counter and grabbed the measuring tape.

Nick climbed back up the ladder to insert more ceiling panels. "Any luck on the chandeliers? We've got the best electrician in town, but he's a busy guy, and it won't be easy to get him back in to finish the lighting. Might take a few tries."

"I've been so consumed with getting my niece settled I haven't been able to shop. I'll make a real effort this week."

"Give me a call when you find them. Don't drag them over to the store. I'll come by to make sure they don't have to be rewired or need any other adjustments before we call our guy."

New Englanders knew how to handle weather. The earliest pilgrims who settled Cape Cod, when it was a wilderness strip of land stretching seventy miles out into the ocean, not only survived and thrived, they created ingenious ways to deal with hardship. Those pilgrim genes were still walking around in New England's solid stock.

So, it didn't matter that winter continued to stake its claim with a snow storm in April. The members of Grace's team, with one exception, all made it to Beth's house for the planning meeting.

Beth and Grace had moved chairs from the sacred space and kitchen into the living room. They also baked cupcakes and two kinds of cookies. As people arrived, Grace hung up their coats and Beth took coffee orders.

Doctor Adams arrived last. When Beth opened the door, he reached back and guided a young girl, ten or eleven, to enter in front of him. "Ms. Henson, this is my daughter, Kristi. I thought she might help us out tonight. She's terrific at sign."

Beth wondered if she was deaf, too. "Nice to meet you, Kristi."

"We'll be discussing Grace's medical issues so I need your permission for Kristi to sign for Grace. If not, I thought she could keep Grace company away from the group."

"It's a great idea to have Kristi help out. Either way."

"Good. We'll start with having Grace and Kristi join us, then there's a time when it might be better to have them leave. I think it will be nice for Grace to be able to communicate with someone younger."

Grace sat snuggled close to Beth on the couch. Everyone was settled in with coffee and baked goods, so Doctor Adams began.

He spoke and signed, looking at Grace. "Grace, tonight we're going to talk about helping you to speak again. We're going to be telling you a lot of stuff you won't understand right away, but I want you to get to know the words because you're going to hear them a lot as we go along."

She didn't think her niece could get any closer, but Grace pressed harder against her side. Beth put a hand out and patted her knee.

Since Doctor Adams signed, the school interpreter hadn't come to the meeting. The doctor went on. "We want to hear from each of you who have done a separate evaluation in your particular field. My daughter Kristi signs. She'll be our interpreter for Grace tonight. She's pretty familiar with my work, and her interest has been a great help to me." He smiled down at his daughter.

Oh, Beth thought, that was why she signed. Watching her, Beth could see Kristi was hearing what was said. She had wavy brown hair and dark eyes like her father. Her features were delicate, with an upturned nose, a sweetheart mouth. What made her stand out was her poise as she stood looking into the eyes of the people in the room. She stopped at Grace and smiled at her.

"Ready, honey?" her father asked.

Kristi moved closer to Grace and stood with her arms at her side. When her father began to speak, her hands went into swift action. Beth watched Grace read the signs, but every so often, look up with awe at the older child. Beth, too, was impressed with the girl. Her father may be arrogant and short with adults, but he must be good with kids. It made Beth comfortable with her decision to choose him.

When there was a break in the discussion, Grace signed to Kristi, asking if she was deaf, too.

"No, I'm not deaf."

"Why do you sign?"

"I think it's the coolest way to talk. My dad and I can tell each other secrets that most people can't understand. I know it's harder for you because you're deaf, but you sign well."

The audiologist spoke of frequency, intensity, threshold air and bone conduction. "My apologies to you, Ms. Henson. You'll pick up the jargon as we move along. Mostly, my report shows little change from the last exam done in New Bedford." He turned to Doctor Adams. "To summarize, I agree she is a candidate for bilateral implants."

Doctor Adams further explained, "One implant compared to two is like the difference between a mono speaker and stereo. We're using two more often now. They not only balance the hearing, the wearer can more easily tell where the sound is coming from. It also helps when there's a lot of background noise. And the sound quality is better in general." He directed his words to Beth.

Before Mr. Hamilton began his evaluation report, Doctor Adams asked Kristi to take Grace out and tell her all about her new school. "Kristi goes to your school, too," he told Grace. Kristi took Grace's arm and gave it a little tug. She signed something to her that Beth didn't catch. Grace walked beside her out of the living room.

"We're going to hear from Tom now. He's already discussed his evaluation with Doctor Spencer, the head of Special Education, who couldn't join us tonight. I thought it would be better for Grace not to hear this part."

"Why, Doctor, is something wrong?" Beth asked.

"Nothing I didn't expect. And nothing we can't fix. By the way, we're all in this together. Call me Scott."

Tom Hamilton was brief. Grace worked at a first grade level in math. Her writing was a year behind. She read at a fifth grade level, which didn't surprise Beth. Plans were set for an Emerson College student, who was deaf herself, to tutor Grace in math two days a week after school. The good news was Grace's intelligence scores were high. Harder to overcome was her social delay.

"She freezes up when one of the kids tries to talk to her. Of course, you can imagine what happens. The children forget she can't hear, because they don't *see* anything wrong with her. When they talk to her and she can't understand, they might laugh in their own embarrassment. Grace sees it as laughing at her. I had her teach the kids some signs. It gives her stature in their eyes. I think it would also help if she was good at a sport. Has she played sports, Beth?"

"Not that I know of. Unless it was in school P.E. She came home last week and was all excited, hoping to play soccer. I didn't see how she could play," Beth said.

"Sure she can. Half the battle is in wanting to," Scott said.

"Soccer practice starts soon. She'll need a sports physical and some papers signed. I'll talk to the coach. Maybe we can teach her some signs she could use to direct Grace on the field. Hey, might work with all the kids that way. The more we can incorporate her peers, the better she'll be at learning to interact with them."

Beth thought how lucky Grace was to have Tom as her enthusiastic teacher.

The speech pathologist's report was limited because Grace had been uncooperative.

Sue Willis indicated she would have to confirm that DCF medical coverage would pick up the costs associated with the cochlear implants. They would also look into any benefits available from Federal or State Government funds.

Grace and Kristi were called back into the room. Grace entered first with her head held high and her shiny black hair in a new French braid.

Scott addressed her. "Well, Grace, looks like we figured out what to do. Your aunt will bring you back to my office another day. We're going to talk about how you can hear some sounds and learn the words they mean with the help of a little gadget called a cochlear implant." He finger-spelled the words. "When you and your aunt come, I'll show you what it looks like."

When everyone left, all Grace could talk about was Kristi. Her hands flew, listing all of Kristi's wonderful accomplishments and attributes, of which Beth understood about three.

"What about the implant?"

Grace made a silly expression and shrugged her shoulders.

"Enough for tonight. Go get ready for bed. I'll be up shortly."

The same dusky veil of sadness dropped over Grace's face. Nights were the hardest. She missed her mother and often cried herself to sleep. Her sadness tugged at Beth's heart.

"I want her to read me a story," Grace signed.

"Who?" Beth said.

"In the sacred space," she signed. Beth had told her the name for the sun porch. "Honey, why don't you take a book to bed? You can read for a while then turn off your lamp. Okay?"

Grace nodded but still looked sad. Beth had hoped that having a friend who could communicate with her would put an end to the bedtime blues. But not tonight. Not yet.

Before she went to bed, Beth pulled a novel from a shelf in the living room to read herself to sleep. Turning off the lights, she padded down the hall to the stairs. Moonlight illuminated the sacred space. She looked at the book in her hand, then passed the stairs and stepped into the sacred space. It was chilly. She could see the almost-full moon out the window. Turning on a lamp, she sat in the rocker.

This is silly.

Beth opened to chapter one. She began to read.

Nothing.

She read another paragraph, slowly. But she heard only the voice in her head, which she recognized as her own.

She stood up, smiling at her fanciful imagination, and went to bed.

Chapter 10

Grace could do it. Living with her aunt wasn't as bad as she thought it would be. Except the day the kids had laughed at her in school. It made her remember the time in New Bedford, when her classmates made fun of her voice. Mr. Hamilton had told Ms. Jenny to say they weren't laughing at *her*, but at the way her hands moved when Grace taught them the sign for the word, curious. She couldn't hear the sounds they made, but she sure got the chicken thing they were doing with their heads and arms. Even if it was only three boys, it still made her want to go home, want her mother to hold her while she cried. That day she'd come home and wouldn't leave the lady's space, refusing to do homework or go anywhere. Aunt Beth had been worried, but Grace couldn't tell her what happened.

She didn't know who the lady was, but she thought she must be a ghost because Grace couldn't see her. Grace only knew the lady was nice and loved her. It made her feel safe. When the lady read a book to her, she got all warm inside. She even felt better about the bad things, like what happened in school. It *was* funny. To make the sign for *curious*, you had to pinch your neck skin between your index finger and thumb, and wiggle it back and forth. Whenever she was afraid or sad, she would spend time the space and feel better.

Mr. Hamilton still made her teach new signs to the class, but now she checked in the mirror first to make sure they wouldn't be funny.

She liked Karen who tutored her in math some days after school, even though signing numbers was harder for Grace than words. But being with someone like Karen who was deaf, too, encouraged Grace. Each evening, she did her homework on her special desk, which she loved, while Aunt Beth worked on the computer at her own desk. Mostly, Aunt Beth was nice like she used to be before she sent her mother away. But Grace still missed her mommy so much.

Kristi came to her classroom to walk her from school to Aunt Beth's car, as she did every day now. They wore their backpacks instead of wheeling them so they could sign to each other. It was like having a real friend. Or a big sister. Grace used to pretend she had a sister. They would play dolls together and color in their books at the kitchen table. Now she had a real friend. And she had the lady.

She waved goodbye to Kristi, then climbed in the backseat and fastened her seatbelt.

"How was school?" her aunt signed and spoke.

"Okay," she said aloud. She only used her voice for her aunt because it made her smile. Then she signed, "Library?"

"Did you remember to put your library books in your backpack?"

Grace nodded.

"Library. Yes."

Ms. Lauren was there in the children's section. Grace was allowed to take all the time she wanted to pick new books because her aunt liked to talk and talk with Ms. Lauren. She chose her books carefully for the funny voices the lady would use when she read them in the space. Grace especially liked mysteries, though, so she also looked for ones she hadn't yet read. When she had five books, she came back to stand beside her aunt.

"I hoped I'd see you today," Ms. Lauren said to her aunt. Grace wished she was better at speech reading. Ms. Lauren said they were hanging something she wanted her aunt to see. Grace tugged on Aunt Beth's hand and signed "What hanging?"

Her aunt raised her eyes to the ceiling like she did when she tried to think of a sign, then finger-spelled q-u-i-l-t-s instead.

Boring. They continued to talk with each other.

"I'd love to see them," Aunt Beth said.

"Why don't you bring Grace to my house on Saturday? We'll have lunch with the . . . then I'll give you a . . . tour of the quilt. . . ." She couldn't catch all the words. Who would they have lunch with? And, ugh, who wanted to see a quilt?

They checked out her books and went to the car. She read the first one on the way to the doctor's office. When Aunt Beth had pointed to Doctor Adam's picture in her places book that morning, she'd shaken her head as hard as she could. But when her aunt turned to the ice cream photo, she'd agreed to go to the doctor. He was Kristi's father, and he was funny, but she didn't want that thing put in her head.

A cool girl brought them back to the room where Doctor Adams had looked in her ears the last time. The girl had black hair like her own, but it had purple streaks in it. Her uniform top had ponies all over it. She smiled and waved at Grace before she closed the door behind her.

She looked around the little room, full of cabinets with words on each door. The counter looked like a kitchen. It had jars of cotton balls and big Popsicle sticks they put down your throat, and other doctor things. It was bright white in the room from all the lights, and it was cold.

Then she saw the stuff on the tray. Doctor Adams told her he would show her an implant. Her aunt took out her phone and snapped a picture of the tray. It scared her because she knew the picture was for her places book.

The doctor came in and signed "hi" to her and Aunt Beth, who sat on the chair.

"Kristi tells me you're doing well in school. Make some new friends?" he signed and said.

Grace wouldn't talk about good stuff. She pointed to the tray. He had to understand she didn't want that.

"Okay. You want to get right down to business, I see. Good." He pulled the tray to the end of the exam table where Grace sat, and said, "Beth, come over while I explain." Grace liked that he signed everything he said so she could understand. He was good at sign; she wished her aunt could be, but she was learning.

When they were all huddled over the tray, Doctor Adams touched the first piece. "This little guy is called the receiver. We hide one of these under your skin behind each of your ears, about here." He touched a spot on her head.

She jerked her head away from his touch. "No!" Frightened enough to use her voice, she then tried to sign that she wouldn't allow it.

"Hold on. I'm not going to do anything today. I'm going to show you what cochlear implants are. Remember, we talked about them? How they can help you hear some sounds again?"

Grace held her hand over the spot the doctor had touched, but she felt a little better because he promised not to put them on her head today.

He pointed to another piece similar to a hearing aid she'd worn behind her ear once. That one wasn't bad. She would be willing to wear that again if it made her hear this time.

"This is called a processor," the doctor said. "It's smart. With its little computer, it processes the sounds you can't hear and sends them through the wire to this disk, called the transmitter. That guy sends them inside to the receiver hiding under your skin. Both the receiver and the transmitter have a magnet." He turned them both over and pointed to the magnets, and then stuck the two pieces together. "See?"

He had signed slowly, spelling the names of the things, but she couldn't understand the stuff he was saying. It didn't matter. She would never let him put that thing in her head. Never.

Aunt Beth asked him a question she didn't get, but she was pointing to all the wires.

"Call me Scott," he said to her aunt. "And you," he told Grace, "can call me Doctor Scott. Now, those are called electrodes." Even though he finger-spelled the word, Grace didn't understand. "I'll insert them into Grace's inner ears, and it's their job to send the sounds to her brain."

"No! Go home!" Grace demanded, and tried to shove the tray away. She was so scared she had to fight to hold her tears back.

"Honey, what's wrong? Don't be afraid." Aunt Beth came over and put her arm around her.

"Grace, what scared you?" Doctor Scott signed.

She touched her chin with the thumb of her spread-fingered hand.

Aunt Beth seemed to understand. "I mentioned to you that we talked to her mom about the implant last Sunday, and she isn't convinced it would be good for Grace. She made a joke to Grace, asking her if she thought an antenna on her head was a good idea."

At first he looked annoyed, and then he laughed. "What a picture. No wonder you don't want one. Hold on." He went out of the room.

When he came back, he had a big book, like a phone book. He opened it to a page and turned it around so Grace could see it. Her aunt held the book for the doctor.

Grace looked at the picture on the page, which was the back of a girl's head. The girl had pretty blond hair. She wore two of the round things, but they were different than the ones on the tray. They were cute, like pretty round barrettes.

"This is what the transmitters look like in your hair. Nothing weird at all. No antenna." He turned the page. "Here's the ear piece. It comes with different-colored covers. Does that help?" He took the book from Aunt Beth and set it on the tray, then stood in front of Grace with his hands on his hips.

Grace shrugged her shoulders. She was still afraid, and she didn't want to have something inside her head.

"Not so bad, right?"

She couldn't answer.

"You love your mother," the doctor said.

She nodded. She wouldn't cry. She wanted her mother to tell them no.

She wanted her mother.

Doctor Scott wouldn't stop. "When she talks to you, you can't hear her voice. You read her lips, watch her sign. Right, Grace? But if you had an implant, there's a good chance you could learn to hear her words."

She couldn't hold it in. Once the first tears started, she didn't try anymore. It hurt her throat to keep it all in and it felt good to let it out.

Aunt Beth moved closer to her and wrapped her arms around her.

"Grace, I would never do anything you or your mommy wouldn't want me to. I promise you," Doctor Scott signed.

And Grace believed him. Then he made her smile again before he called in the cool girl to take her out. He signed he needed to talk to Aunt Beth for a few minutes. The girl brought her back to the waiting room and gave her a kid's magazine to read. All of a sudden, she remembered the promise of ice cream.

When Beth woke up on Saturday morning, she could see the sun peeking around the window shades. It was six-ten. She felt full of energy as she went across the hall to wake Grace. Her bed was not only empty, it was made. Beth chuckled at the job Grace had done with both humor and amazement. Grace was never taught to make a bed. Not once when Beth visited her sister's apartment did she see either of the beds made. Grace had an excuse, but Patrice had made her bed every morning when she lived under their parents' roof.

She headed downstairs. She saw Grace in the sacred space, sitting in the child's chair. Her right hand rocked the rocker back and forth. Her face was serene as she stared ahead.

Beth approached down the hall. "No story today?" she signed.

Grace nodded.

Beth looked around the space but there were no open books. She must have been up for a while. "What do you think? After breakfast, let's walk up to the beach. Wait. Better yet, let's pack a picnic and have breakfast *at* the beach."

Beth went overboard as usual. She baked biscuits, cut up fruit, and mixed a sweet yogurt sauce for dipping. She hard-boiled two eggs for protein and wrapped them with cool packs. She made coffee; hot and black for her, a warm latte for Grace, who had developed a love of coffee. Another new change Patrice might be unhappy about.

An hour later, they were ready to go. "I have sand sitters we can carry on our backs. They're in the garage. We'll get them on the way out," Beth signed and said.

With the food, two woolen throws in case their winter jackets weren't enough insulation for the cold air by the water, and a book for each of them, they were loaded down. They hung the sand sitters on their backs and hiked to the beach like a couple of mules.

They spent nearly two perfect hours, eating, collecting shells. They played a game of keeping their bare feet in the frigid water until they couldn't stand it anymore. Grace bubbled with laughter, running in and out of the water until her pants were soaked. Beth grabbed her in a bear hug and carried her back to their chairs. "Time to go. You need a hot bath and warm clothes."

Grace laughed out loud, pointing to Beth's jeans, which were also soaked-through. As they packed up for the trip home, Beth saw Grace still had a smile on her face. Then she realized she was smiling, too, and knew this was a real breakthrough for both of them.

They shed their chairs beside the garage, carried the rest to the farmer's porch, and dropped it. Beth pulled the food bag toward her to take the key off. But it wasn't where she'd clipped it. She checked the smaller bag, but no key was attached. She unzipped both bags and checked inside.

"Oh no. I lost the key." She walked back to the garage and searched the area around the chairs. Grace appeared concerned when she came back, so she smiled at her. She signed what was wrong to Grace, and told her to sit tight while she checked for an unlocked window. Fat chance. Beth was religious about making sure that all doors and windows were secure before she went up to bed. And they still were.

She walked back and stepped up to the porch. Grace stood by the door, shivering. Beth took one of the blankets and wrapped it around Grace's shoulders. "I'm sorry, sweetie. The windows are all locked," she signed, with added hand movements to help convey the signs she didn't know. "I'll have to call a locksmith."

What Beth *wanted* to do was stamp her feet and release a decent string of curses. How could she ruin their lovely morning? She picked up her phone, ready to Google locksmiths in the area.

Grace touched her arm and shook her head. Beth watched as her niece reached out to grasp the doorknob. She turned it and pushed. The door opened!

Beth stood with her mouth agape. "How did you do that?" she gasped, not expecting an answer. "I remember locking it. I had to put everything down and pick it all up again."

Grace stood inside, taking off her jacket, nonplussed. Beth raised her hands to her cheeks. This was downright eerie. *Was* there magic in the cottage? Maybe she'd turned the key the wrong way. But she distinctly remembered jiggling the locked handle.

Grace came back to the door, looking out at Beth with drawn black brows.

"Nothing's wrong," Beth signed. Then she picked up the rest of the picnic things and went inside. The kitchen was cozy and warm with a spicy fragrance that reminded her of lilacs.

Beth wasn't sure Grace would like to go to Lauren's for lunch, but she surprised Beth and agreed. They drove to Barley Neck Road. Lauren's house was a Cape with a high-pitched roof. Beth whistled through her teeth at the perfect lawn, picturing her own yard full of wild violets and other weeds.

The day had grown cooler once the ocean breeze kicked in. Lauren came to the door wearing jeans and an Irish woolen sweater over a pink turtleneck. A small boy peeked around Lauren's leg and pointed his finger at them.

"Hi guys. We're all so happy you came," Lauren said, her hand on the little boy's head.

A large living room opened to their right as they entered. Pieces of a wooden puzzle were strewn across a colorful canvas floorcover. A sippy cup lay on its side atop the coffee table. A big, soft recliner was positioned in front of a large flat-screened TV. The homey room made Beth smile. A happy family lived here.

They followed Lauren and her little boy into the kitchen. Grace tapped Beth's hand and pointed to a second boy, who looked exactly like his brother. Grace held up two fingers to Beth with a question on her face.

Lauren smiled and nodded. "They're identical twins," she said, speaking slowly to Grace. "Three years old." The boys were dressed in denim overalls, one wearing a red shirt, the other blue. They had short, auburn hair with the exact same cowlick. "Jake and Benjie," Lauren told Beth, who finger-spelled their names for Grace.

Grace walked over and stood in front of one of the twins. She bent over and waved at him. The child smiled shyly and handed her the Nerf ball he held in his hand. Grace moved back and tossed the ball to him. The other twin came to join them. "Wow," Lauren said. "Look at that."

"I'm shocked. Grace is so reserved I worried about how she would handle our visit."

"You know, the boys are too small to know what deaf means. And they're pretty slow in their own language skills. Maybe Grace senses there's no pressure for her with them."

"Very possible. The boys are adorable, and I doubt Grace has ever seen identical twins before."

Beth sat at the table while Lauren prepared their lunch at the counter. "It's a reminder of what her lonely inside life must be." Beth slid the salt shaker back and forth between her cupped hands. "I hope my sister agrees to the cochlear implants. What a miracle it would be if she could hear and speak again."

"What doctor would be doing the surgery?"

"Scott Adams. Know him?"

"I met him once. The boys were born about two months premature. Their pediatrician referred them to Doctor Adams' office for testing and exams. I like him. I think he's hunky."

Beth's eyes widened. "Really?"

A big teddy bear of a man came into the kitchen. He smelled like soap and spicy after-shave. He had a full head of damp, thick auburn hair and bright-blue smiling eyes. "You must be talking about me, right?"

"Yes, we were, honey. You bet." Lauren made a funny face. "Troy, this is my new friend, Beth Henson, and that's Grace playing with the boys." She turned to Beth. "I told him she was deaf so he wouldn't embarrass her by talking a blue streak—which he will every chance he gets."

"Believe me, Beth. She hardly lets me get a word in," Troy quipped.

Grace sat at the table between the two boys in booster seats. She signed to Beth, "They look the same." She had an expression of awe on her face. She helped the boys eat and entertained them while the three grown-ups also ate and chatted. Beth liked Troy, with his good humor and obvious intelligence. And she could see Lauren adored him.

She was struck watching their interaction, at how different her relationship had been with Joe. When he'd asked her to marry him, she was so wrapped up with her sister and Grace, she had put him off. And she was so deeply involved with the minutia of her sister's life, she'd lost herself in the process—and her fiancé. Now watching the love and fun Lauren and Troy shared, and after having cared for Grace, and worked hard to maintain her boundaries with her sister, she longed again for a family of her own.

After lunch, Lauren and Beth sipped tea and talked. Troy took the three children to the basement to show them his model train set up. Every time the whistle blew, Beth started, thinking it was her cell.

"Beth, may I vent?"

Beth saw a serious expression had tightened her friend's face. "Sure. What is it?"

She swallowed. "Troy has to have some tests done. A bronchoscopy and a PET scan. He has some enlarged lymph nodes in his chest." Her eyes brightened with tears. "My good friend who's a nurse told me not to worry, but I can't help it."

"Did the doctor give him any indication of what caused them?"

"He was pretty upbeat, listed some possibilities, but he said we'd talk when we know a little more. They found the nodes on a chest X-ray he had in the ER after he fell off a ladder at work. He's an electrician."

"Well, finding it is a good thing, right? And the doctor didn't seem too worried?"

"What do you think of when you hear the words 'lymph nodes'?"

Beth nodded. "It's frightening. I'm glad the doctor told you there could be other causes."

Lauren inhaled a deep breath and said in a low voice, "I don't know how I could live without him. He's my love, my best friend, and he's such a wonderful daddy."

Beth leaned forward. "I know you have a lot of friends, but I can be here anytime you want to talk, and I can hold your hand if you need me to."

"I knew you were that sort of person the minute I laid eyes on you. I feel better, just having you to worry with me."

"I'm glad I could help. Let me know if there's anything I can do."

When Troy offered to watch Grace and the boys so Beth and Lauren could go to the quilt exhibition alone, Beth wasn't sure she could leave her. Lauren convinced her by writing both of their cell numbers on the boys' blackboard and making Troy promise to call for any reason. When they were at the door, Beth turned to wave to Grace. She was on the floor in the living room, helping Benjie or Jake—Beth couldn't tell them apart—do the wooden puzzle. Grace looked up, smiled and waved. Beth had the distinct impression her niece was thrilled to miss the quilts.

Chapter 11

Tomorrow her daughter and sister would be back. All week, Patrice had been obsessing about last Sunday's visit. The second she'd laid eyes on Grace's face, she'd seen the stress was gone from it. Her reaction then had been joy. It occurred to her later, Grace's usual pinched face and pale color had been a result of the worrisome life she'd lived with her mother—and then without her.

Grace had been clearly happy to see her. And it broke her heart when she cried at having to leave. She'd shared with her mother everything she'd done in the past week. And all through her signing, she didn't once frown. She was a happy child in every way but missing her mommy.

As the days passed, through her therapy sessions, NA meetings, and general interaction with the others, an underlying irritability with her sister had simmered. Today, she saw the whole picture clearly: She didn't want Grace to be happy with Beth. That was it. She was angry at Beth for making Grace happy.

But Doctor Harper wanted to dig deeper into Patrice's addiction. "We can help you get clean and sober, but if we don't find out the underlying cause, you won't stay that way."

"How would I know?" Patrice shrugged her shoulders. "Genetics? I started young, and it was all about having fun."

"Was it? Or was it self-medicating?"

Sudden tears stung Patrice's eyes. She'd heard this before, but she didn't want to talk about it. What good would it do now? But Doctor Harper sat and waited. *Get it over with.* "My mother. She was hardly a part of my life."

"Why was that?"

"Because my father wouldn't let her be?" Patrice hesitated. Something was percolating up in her mind. "Maybe she never wanted to be?"

"How does that make you feel?"

"Sick! Angry!"

"Hurt?"

"Hurt." One of her most haunting memories came immediately to mind. The way she had behaved at her mother's funeral.

As usual, Beth had handled everything. Their father was too involved with who the mourners at the church would be to take time to grieve himself. Patrice was angry, furious. Her mother had never had time for her own kids, but she'd made time to do every single task her husband gave her. If only her mother had tried to help *her*. If only Patrice had tried harder to make her mother proud.

She hadn't attended the funeral. It was the bravest, stupidest thing Patrice had ever done. She'd gone to a friend's house and drank instead. She was so drunk by the time she went home, she raged at her father. In front of his congregants, the most hellish sin she could commit. Worse than being drunk.

"You son of a bitch! You killed her! She was like your pathetic minion, a work horse who obeyed your every command. You took her away from her own children. She wore herself out trying to please you."

Beth had taken her arm, trying to pull her away. "She doesn't mean it. She's upset. She's grieving."

Patrice cried hard at the memory, but she could still see the stunned look on the pious faces gathered in the room. The staring women, holding flat, empty purses in the crooks of their arms; the men, shooting her nasty looks. She shook off Beth's grip and wiped her eyes. "You *all* took advantage of her. You all used her. You killed her, too." Beth had then grabbed her arm in a vise grip and yanked her toward the bedrooms.

Her stunned father finally came to life. Patrice heard him roar, "Get out of this house. Never come back through that door. My God cannot save you. You will burn in hell. Get out!"

When she'd gone out the door, she could hear Beth weeping inside. The only one who had loved her in that sad little family.

Patrice bent over in her chair, holding her stomach. "Oh God. Why *didn't* my mother love me? What was wrong with me?" She let her tears flow. That poor little girl. Poor little Patrice. All she wanted was for her mommy to love her. And then, something deeper reared its ugly head. She was a mistake. They had never wanted her from the very beginning.

For no reason obvious to Beth, Grace was inconsolable Saturday night. When she and Lauren had returned from the library, Grace sat beside Troy, turning the pages of the book he was reading to the twins, who were tucked into the crooks of his ample arms. The boys jumped up from his lap and ran to hug their mom. Grace looked up with a serene smile on her face that broke Beth's heart. It occurred to her that Grace's life with her was much busier and more social than her home life, and again, how lonely she must be inside her silence.

Beth made them tuna melts and a green salad for dinner. Grace only picked at her food. They were eating cookies for dessert when Grace began to sob. Beth went around the table, stooped beside Grace's chair, and put an arm over her shoulders. "What's wrong, honey?" she asked, but Grace couldn't see her or hear her. She'd dropped her head on her folded arms and wept with a sharp grief, which cut right through Beth's heart. She pulled up the chair next to her and sat, rubbing Grace's back and waiting for the tears to subside. When they didn't, Beth picked her up and carried her to the rocker in the sacred space. Grace curled up on her lap and continued to weep, but softer. Beth tried several times to sign to her, without success. Instead, she held her and rocked her until the tears stopped. Dry sobs continued to shake her body for several minutes afterwards, and then she was so still Beth thought she might have fallen asleep. But Grace raised her right hand and made the sign for mother.

Beth leaned down so Grace could see her face and said, "Tomorrow." She smiled at Grace, who must have forgotten visiting day. Instead of the reaction Beth expected, Grace signed she wanted to go to bed.

Sunday morning always started with a feeling of ingrained guilt for Beth.

The Sabbath had been the center of her parents' universe. The girls had bathed the night before, washed their hair, and laid out their clothes. They were awakened early so they could make their breakfast while their parents showered and dressed. When the four of them were ready, they walked to the church up the hill from their house. They were there an hour before services began so their father could practice his sermon, and their mother could arrange the organ music and Bible readings. The girls were supposed to pray away the time. Patrice usually slept. Beth entertained herself with dreams of her future: She would go to college and never come back home. She would own a business. If she married, she and her husband would have happy children whom they would take to the circus. The kids would be allowed—no, encouraged—to dance and play games. And they would have friends come to their house to play. No one would yell about sin and hell.

This Sunday, April seventeenth, Beth still had to remind herself that she was confident no God like the one her father believed in existed. Maybe there was no God, period. She'd never seen any proof of one. Her mother slaved for her father's mission, and died young. Did *she* not do enough for God? Her father ended up with Alzheimer's. Was that *his* reward for a lifetime of service?

Beth stepped into the shower, her baptism, her ritual cleansing of Sunday's heresy.

Grace looked wan and tired when she came to eat breakfast, still in her pajamas.

"Do you feel better?" Beth signed.

Her hand said yes, her face said no.

"You'll be happy when you see your mother. You'll feel much better. I know how much you miss her."

Grace sat up straight, her eyes wide, and pointed out the window. Beth turned to see the brilliant orange and black bird sitting on a branch of the tree off the porch. He tilted his head back and sang a few notes before he flew away.

Beth looked at Grace. "What a good find! I never saw a bird like that before. Do you know what it was?"

Grace shook her head and raised her hands, palms up. Beth tried again, this time Grace seemed to understand. "No," she said, with a smile. The bird had cheered her up, but the dark circles under her eyes would still be there when her mother saw her.

"How about some coffee?" Beth held up the pot with her eyebrows raised.

Grace nodded with an expression saying, it's too good to be true. Beth poured half a glass of milk, added some coffee, then sugar. She stirred it and placed it before Grace.

Grace took a sip. "Ummm."

"Don't tell mommy," Beth signed and winked.

Even though Patrice emitted the same noises of joy at seeing her daughter, Beth sensed something else: Patrice was faking it. Beth felt her insides tighten as she considered the possibility that Patrice's subterfuge was caused by drugs. But she didn't see any obvious signs.

When the two had gone over the journal, Beth handed Patrice the book she'd purchased and an informational pamphlet Scott had provided for her. Grace's eyes grew big when she watched Beth show her mother the picture of the cochlear implant on her phone. "Grace and I received a long and intense lesson on this amazing piece of electronics." Beth laughed. "Bottom line is, when you put these pieces together, a deaf person can hear sound."

"Beth, didn't you hear me last week? She's not going to go through this."

"I don't understand why you feel that way. Is it the risk of surgery?"

Patrice glanced over at Grace, who was obviously trying to speech-read their conversation, then back at Beth. "It's because it won't cure her deafness. So why put her through it?"

Beth studied her sister. There was more she wasn't saying, something she wasn't going to tell Beth. Today, Patrice looked tired, she was jumpy and restless, and that was enough to make Beth drop the subject. "Okay. Maybe something in the information I brought will relieve your anxiety about the surgery. If you want to discuss it later on, I'll leave that up to you."

Patrice changed the subject. She stood up and demonstrated some of the Tai Chi moves she was learning. "It's strangely a real workout, but you move at a snail's pace. You learn these individual moves, and then you string them together in a slow dance. I love it, it's so relaxing."

Beth watched as Grace tried some Tai Chi moves, making mother and daughter fall into the giggles. She saw Patrice's face regain color and realized how difficult the program must be for her. "You're a wonderful mom, Patrice," she said, smiling.

"Oh yeah. That's why I'm here and you're her mother."

Beth understood from her statement, Patrice was still worrying about Grace becoming attached to her aunt. "*You* are her mother and a good one. I know how much you love her. I love you and Grace. I've learned how to take care of her from watching you. But I can never replace you."

"She's my little girl," Patrice said, running her hand down the length of Grace's hair. "But you can give her so much more than I can. All your money. New house. The beach. What child would want to give that up?"

"A child who loves her mom," Beth said, with brows knit. She turned to Grace. She was busy drawing a picture for her mother.

"She has to know how much her real mother loves her. It's important she isn't confused about who that person is."

"What are you saying, Patrice? Would she be better off in the foster home?" She took a breath. She tamped down a slow burn of resentment. This wasn't about her. The pain on Patrice's face said it all. "You know what? I love Grace, too. She's an angel. I want to do everything in the world I can for her. But I'll never take your place. Look at her. When she's here, she's the happiest I ever see her. You're her world."

"I know. It's just me. It's just me worrying."

The rest of the visit was better. Patrice seemed happier. Beth felt safe bringing up the implants again. "Take a look at the stuff the doctor sent. I promise not to bug you. I think we both want the same opportunities for Grace. We want her to know if a truck is coming at her, if the fire alarm goes off in the night, to hear the thunder and run in the house. The implants can do that."

"I'll think about it, Beth. And I'm sorry. I always seem to be saying that to you lately. You're doing so much for us, and I'm not making it easy." She gave Beth a hug.

"You are doing the hardest job," Beth said. "I know how much you miss Grace, too. You never have to say you're sorry to me. You're my hero. My strong, brave little sister. I want to do everything I can to help you."

On the drive home, Beth decided Patrice would probably not even look at the implant literature. She couldn't figure out why her sister wouldn't want to give her daughter the chance to hear and speak. What was it? She could only hope Patrice would change her mind in time.

When they arrived at the cottage, Grace signed, "Are you mad at mommy?"

"No, honey. Everything is fine." Even though Grace wasn't reading their lips, she was a master at reading facial expressions, so she must have picked up on her mom's emotion. Grace grimaced and went right into the sacred space.

Monday morning, Beth called Scott's office. She'd agreed to let him know what her sister decided on the implants. May as well get this off her plate. She input the numbers he'd given her and Scott answered, surprising her.

"I haven't started seeing patients yet. How did it go?"

"I'm afraid, for now, she is still against it. I gave her the literature and a book, but I don't think she'll go through with it. I guess she has enough to struggle with right now."

There was a silence and she began to wonder if the connection was lost.

"Of course, that's her choice. If she'd like to talk to me about it at some point, I'd be happy to call her."

"That's very generous of you. I'll make that offer to her." She paused. "I'm sorry you've gone to so much trouble—everyone has. It never occurred to me that Patrice would have an objection. I mean, I can imagine she would be frightened to have any surgery performed on her daughter, but there must be more to it. Maybe I'm wrong and she'll come around."

"Let's hope. Keep me posted," Scott said.

Chapter 12

The room was painted beige, and the under-padded chairs were black. Patrice sat with a dozen other clients in group therapy. The members of the group were all staring at her, some with faces of disapproval, and one with a smug expression.

"I didn't mean it *that* way," Patrice said. "I wouldn't give up Grace for *anything*. I meant it would just be nice to be able to do something *you* want to do and not having to worry every minute about your child."

"You said you were charged with child neglect, right?" Janet said. Patrice looked at the woman's bandaged right arm. Word of her cutting habit had leaked out.

"I love my daughter. I didn't have to have her, be a single mom, but I've never regretted it. Ever. Even after she became deaf, which was so heartbreaking. That one night was the *only* time I ever left her alone, and the DA did not bring charges."

"Go on, Patrice, what were you trying to say?" the counselor urged.

"Only that it's hard to achieve your own dreams when you have a disabled child, and you don't have much money. You've got to always put your child first," Patrice said, looking around the group. "But I've wanted to be an artist ever since I can remember. I had lessons when I was young, and I have a few finished paintings I think are pretty good, but I don't have much time for that now that my sister's moved away."

"I've seen some of the sketches you did here. I think you're very good," Marjorie said, nodding at Patrice.

"You felt abandoned when she left, didn't you? Like I did when my husband walked out," Estelle added.

Patrice paused before she answered. "Yes, I did. But my sister deserves her own life."

"Were you clean before she told you she was going to move?" Eunice asked.

"Yes." Patrice glanced at the counselor. "No. I used drugs whenever I could get them."

"That's excellent, Patrice. Honesty helps us heal. Does your artwork make you feel good about yourself?"

Patrice wished she had never opened her mouth. "You know, it does, but I'm not sure I have what it takes to make it. I only think about it because I see my sister's success. She accomplishes everything she sets out to do. My parents depended on her. I think it made her strong. . . . I wish I could give Grace the good life my sister can." Patrice looked around the circle of abusers and addicts. Their faces displayed interest.

"But Patrice, we're talking about ways to empower ourselves to stay away from drugs. If Grace is your life, and you want to make a happy home for her, then you have to learn personal empowerment like we all do. I've seen some of your art. I think you're lucky to have a talent like that. As soon as my kids are in bed, I cook. I love to cook. It relaxes me. Then when I go to work the next day, dinner's ready and I have time to enjoy my family," Estelle said.

Angie said, "I take two Benadryl and go to sleep."

"Angie, taking pills of any kind is not up for discussion, as you know."

"Hey, gang, just trying to lighten things up. Art, cooking—yuk. I watch TV. I don't have the means to the dreams."

On a slow walk back to her room, Patrice tried to dig deep into her mind. She could see her young self, sitting in her room with a box of crayons. But none of the art she took proudly to her parents was hung on the refrigerator. Beth was the only one who supported her, except for the woman at Sunday school who thought Patrice had talent and gave her lessons. But her parents weren't impressed. She had never believed in her dream of becoming an artist after that. Then came alcohol and drugs. At first, they seemed to make her feel better about herself, but after a while, *need* took over everything.

When they were kids, Beth was always planning her future. She used to tell Patrice her grand schemes. Patrice had actually felt sorry for her. Right. Beth was living her dream now and Patrice was living a nightmare.

How was she supposed to get through life with a deaf child, no one to help her, and a minimum wage job . . . let alone have a dream? She was not Beth. She was a failure, a worthless failure.

Her hands were shaking and the craving was strong. She hoped Angie hadn't returned to their room. Patrice needed time to think alone. If she was going to make a go of this, she'd better figure out what else would make her happy. At what altar would she worship? It wouldn't be one in a church. What about the dream she used to have of marriage and a family? Sisters and brothers for Grace? She'd sabotaged that dream, too. She would figure it out. She had to.

Beth ached with loneliness. She'd always kept busy with her online store, enjoyed her small staff in the office, got together often with friends she'd known since elementary school. From the time she was three or four, she'd loved her baby sister. They had grown up as inseparable. Then Patrice had sunk deeper into drugs and alcohol, to the point when her outburst at their mother's funeral caused their separation. Grace had brought them back together again.

The decision to leave them behind was like losing an arm. Her codependency was bad for all of them. Moving was the easiest way to keep the boundaries she needed to maintain for both their sakes. She would learn to function in a new way, on her own. But what if she'd never made that decision? Never moved to the Cape? Would Patrice be where she was if Beth had stayed in New Bedford? Would Beth be happier than she was now?

She felt even lonelier because of the tension with Patrice over Grace. Patrice needed all the support Beth could give her to be successful at rehabilitation. But she was no saint. She couldn't help but resent that her new life on Cape Cod wasn't what she'd planned.

She should have asked one of her friends to meet for an early lunch. She missed them all so much. Even though everyone was busy with their jobs and families, they always managed to find time to get together. At least she had Grace, whom she was coming to love more and more.

She needed to get busy and shop for the two chandeliers. The sooner she had them, the sooner she could call Nick to drop by and inspect them. Nick was an enigma. She liked his sense of humor. Yet, he made her uncomfortable with his constant attempts at getting close. She couldn't tell if he was just that way, or if he was hitting on her. Maybe she could offer him a glass of wine.

"Really, Beth?" she said aloud. "Are you that lonely and needy?" She grabbed her list of consignment and thrift shops and went out, shaking her head.

Beth drove by marshes, their grasses turning bright green, eight-foot hedgerows with new growth, and the sparkling blue water of Pleasant Bay, all of which pushed away some of her sorrow. She found two chandeliers she loved in Chatham at the second store on her list. Not identical, but both had hanging crystals and delicate brass structures. It might have been smarter to buy fixtures that wouldn't show the dust, but she wanted something elegant to dangle above the beds which would be made up with fine, silky linens.

It took a while for the store owner to package the chandeliers for travel, so Beth went outside to call Nick.

When he didn't answer, she left him a message: "I have the chandeliers for the store. You wanted to inspect them before you called the electrician. I'll drop them by the store on my way home today."

As she walked back to the store, he called. "Perfect timing. The spots for the alcove just came in today. I can come by your house about five, five-thirty to check them out and pick them up."

Since she'd had such quick success, Beth stopped at two more consignment shops. In one, she found the sweetest chair for Grace's room. It was a low, upholstered armchair, not as small as a child's chair, but not as large as a full-sized one.

"It's a dog chair. Can you believe it?" the clerk said, pushing her oversized glasses back up her nose. "Isn't it adorable? One of our wealthy patrons received it as a gift, but her Shiatsu didn't like it. She even had a slipcover made for it. Look." She held up a cover of heavy drill cotton, white with a close pattern of violets and buttercups. Beth fingered the fabric. Could she buy Grace a dog chair? She didn't have to tell anyone; it wasn't an item most people would even know existed. And it was the perfect size for Grace. Besides, it was obvious the dog didn't use it; it didn't have one sign of damage or distress in the fabric or structure. She bought it and headed home.

Beth pulled her car up close to the farmer's porch. She'd be moving it shortly when she went to pick Grace up at school. She had until four o'clock, since Karen was tutoring her this afternoon.

She unwrapped the chandeliers on the porch and carried them into the kitchen where she placed them on a padded vinyl cloth she'd laid on the table.

She hauled the chair up one step at a time. Once it was in place, Beth smoothed on the slipcover. It was a charming addition, just what the room needed. A chair to cuddle up in, with a warm throw and a book to read, or a place just to sit and daydream.

She'd picked up Grace from school and fixed her a snack. "Did you have a good day?" Since Grace also received speech-reading training from the speech therapist, Beth spoke first, and signed only when Grace didn't understand. She was doing much better. But today, she barely lifted her fist and moved it up and down for "yes."

"How did your math lesson go? Okay?"

The nodding fist.

"Hmmm. What did Ms. Jenny have on today?"

It didn't work. Grace shrugged her shoulders, then put a slice of apple in her mouth. Beth didn't push it. Grace was convinced her aunt was angry with Patrice, but Beth knew it would be resolved at the next visit. She wouldn't bring up the implants. Despite Scott's having said, 'the sooner the better,' it would have to wait. It wasn't Beth's decision. Tomorrow, Sue would drop off the coverage confirmation for Scott's office and visit with Grace. She would tell her Patrice had said no.

In a way, it took the pressure off Beth. What if Patrice had wanted the surgery? It would become Beth's responsibility. And what if something went wrong?

Grace finished the last sip of her milk. Beth had bought another peacemaker for her today. She signed for Grace to put her jacket back on. It was clear Grace wondered why, but realized to get an answer she would have to ask her aunt more than a one-sign question.

Beth went to her office, and picked up the bag. She handed it to Grace who peeked inside. Her face lit up, the sulkiness forgotten, as she pulled the red-and-white soccer ball out of the bag.

"Stay there on the lawn outside the window where I can see you while I make dinner," Beth said and signed, because it was a long sentence.

Grace held the ball close to her chest. It was clear by her expression she was torn about how to react. Then she said aloud, "Thank you."

Beth wanted to run and hug her, but she didn't. She simply said, "You're welcome."

Grace ran out the door. Beth watched the joy on her face as she kicked the ball around. Again, the sense of loneliness filled her, this time for Grace. She should have a friend to practice with. Beth made a mental note to find out if one of the girls or boys in her class played soccer. Then she turned her mind to cooking.

A little later, she heard Nick's Jeep pull up in the driveway. Dusk was stealing the sunlight, but she could see Nick talking to Grace. He came to the door and leaned in. "Hold on a minute. I need to show her something." Beth watched as he demonstrated how to move the ball with his feet while running forward. Grace tried it, actually doing a good job as far as Beth could tell. Nick showed her again, running beside her as she moved the ball. Beth could see him lavishing praise on her, using his own form of sign language. Beth felt a grin spread across her face and reach all the way to her heart.

"It smells like heaven in here," Nick said when he and Grace came in a few minutes later. "What are you making?"

"Chicken pad Thai. Do you like it?"

"Even if I never had it, I'd know I love it from the awesome aroma."

Beth sent a cherry-cheeked Grace into the office to do her homework. It took Nick three minutes to check out the chandeliers. "They're perfect. Wiring's fine. Great. We'll get going on this."

An awkward silence filled the kitchen.

"Oh. Well. Great," Beth managed.

"Guess I should get going?" Nick said.

"Um. Here, let me give you some of this first. I always cook too much."

He moved closer, looking over her shoulder while she filled a plastic container. Beth was embarrassed. What had she been thinking? This wasn't what she wanted. She'd only thought it was a good idea to have him here because she'd been alone too much. First thing tomorrow, she'd learn how to quilt so she could join Lauren's group.

"Whoa. There's only one of me. You're giving me way too much."

Beth looked at the container. Four people could eat this much. She turned to face him.

"Would you like a glass of wine?"

Chapter 13

Beth had forgotten all about the new chair by the time Grace went up to get ready for bed. She was wiping down the kitchen counter when she heard quick footsteps on the stairs and turned to see if something was wrong. Grace came into the kitchen, walking barefoot across the room, and wrapped her in a hug.

She hugged her niece back for a minute, and then tapped her shoulder. When Grace looked up, Beth raised both hands, palms up. Grace swept away her long hair from her face. She screwed up her mouth and forced out the word: "Chair," then waited to see if Beth understood.

"Oh, I forgot. You like it! I'm so happy."

Nodding, she said, "Thank you, Aunt Beth."

The tears came so fast they blinded her. It was the first time in so long Grace had spoken her name, even though the words were not exactly clear. "You're welcome, sweetie," she answered, when she could speak. Then she raised her right hand, her thumb, index finger, and little finger extended from her fist: "I love you."

Grace raised her small hand with the same sign, then spun around and raced out of the kitchen, leaving her aunt to cry in private happiness.

The next afternoon, Grace brought home a paper about joining the soccer team. She was excited to show it to Beth.

No longer worried whether Grace could handle the sport, she said, "Do you want to play?" Grace nodded her head and her hand. "Are you sure?" Beth said, frowning.

"Yes!"

"Then you're going to play soccer!"

Instead of jumping around or clapping her hands, she also frowned and signed, "Mommy."

Grace relied on all her other senses. She picked up signals from people and was smart enough to apply them to other things. Beth got it. She was asking if her mother had to give permission, fearing she might say no. Beth was to make the call on this one. In any case, the doctor had said it was fine.

The answer was too long to make Grace speech read. Beth signed also. "I have a great idea. Let's give mommy a surprise. When you have your first soccer practice, I'll take a picture of you playing. We'll paste it in your journal. You can bring it to mommy and surprise her."

Now she danced and clapped. When Beth had her attention again, she said, "Ms. Willis is coming later. Do your homework now, okay?"

She grinned, watching Grace skip from the kitchen. Beth was sure, if her niece could, she'd be singing.

The first thing Grace did when Sue arrived was show her the soccer ball. They all sat in the sacred space with the heater on and the last rays of the sun helping to warm the room. Beth was watching Grace's face to make sure she understood Sue's words—ready to sign if necessary—when she saw her niece do something strange. Her eyes left Sue and stared at the corner of the room where the rocker was situated. Then she smiled. Beth turned to look, but she saw nothing except the rocker, though it swayed gently. Was that what caught her attention? By the time Beth turned back Sue was repeating her question to Grace.

"What do you think about having the implants?" Sue pointed to her ear. Grace shrugged.

Beth waved a hand out of Grace's sightline, and Sue got it. She changed the subject. "I see you can understand my words better," she said to Grace.

They chatted a few more minutes, and Sue indicated the interview was over. Grace asked to go outside to practice soccer. "Turn on the outside lights and stay on the part of the lawn where I can see you from the porch windows." Grace skipped away.

"Beth, I think you're doing a good job with Grace. She seems happy and relaxed. Such an improvement from how she acted when I dropped her off five weeks ago."

"Don't give me too much credit. It's been full of ups and downs. What you see right now is her absolute glee at the prospect of playing soccer at school."

"Whatever it takes. If you have the form, I'll sign it for you. Until you're official, DCF has to give permission for school activities, like sports or field trips. I'm all in for this one. Now, what's going on with Patrice? I got your message to drop the implants discussion."

"That's one of the downs," Beth said, lifting her arm to rest it on the table between them and tapping her nails on its surface. "My sister doesn't want her to have the surgery or the implants. I mean, I understand that she's afraid. I gave her a book on implants and a pamphlet the doctor gave me, and I'm hoping she'll change her mind. It just seems hard for her."

"Sure. It's probably difficult to take on anything but her rehab treatment right now."

"I think there's more than ordinary fear, but she's not ready to talk about it. Unfortunately, Doctor Adams thinks Grace should have the implants as soon as possible to give her a better chance to speak well. We'll just have to wait and see what happens."

"What about Grace?"

Beth laughed. "I'm pretty sure she's relieved. She's even more frightened than her mother. Doctor Adams seems to have won her trust, but she senses her mother's tension over the subject, I'm sure."

Sue studied her for a minute. "What do you think about the implants?"

"It's a big responsibility I'd have if we do it, but if it's possible she could hear again. . . . She's so smart. I think she'll definitely be able to get the full benefit out of them and her life would be better." Beth raised her hands, palms-up. "I mean, even a little bit would be an improvement. She's doing so well right now with speaking. But I can hear the mutation of some of the words she used to say clearly before she was deaf. You can still make them out. The thing is she's trying now. She seems to *want* to talk."

"Well, give it time. Patrice may surprise you."

"Doctor Adams is on hold, too. He's anxious to do anything he can to help. If Patrice is in the right place, I'm going to tell her he offered to call and answer any questions she has. I just don't want to upset her right now."

Sue nodded. "You appear to like him. A good choice?"

"We both like him. Yes, I think he's the right choice."

"All right. I have pre-authorization for Grace's implants from Mass Health." She handed Beth a sheet of paper. "Hang on to it for now."

Before she left, Sue signed Grace's soccer form.

It was an unusually balmy, fifty-degree evening for April's fickle spring. Grace insisted on washing her soccer ball before she took her own bath. She was out on the farmer's porch with Murphy's Oil Soap and water on one wad of paper towels, and plain water soaking another. As Beth sat at the kitchen table waiting for her, she was reminded of last night.

Nick had seemed happy to stay for a glass of wine, while she was still stunned that she'd asked him. Maybe it was watching him interact so sweetly with Grace that did it. They'd moved the chandeliers from the table and sat across from each other, drinking their wine. After fifteen minutes, everything seemed funny. Well, with Nick's sense of humor, it was. He told her about growing up on the Cape and about playing soccer on a travel team. He offered to work more on Grace's skills.

"I can come by a couple days after work and teach her some of my amazing soccer tricks."

"Oh, that's nice of you," she said, squeezing her crossed legs tighter under the table. She avoided an answer by redirecting the conversation. "How did you know she was deaf? I don't remember telling you."

"You didn't. She did."

"Do you sign?"

"No. She just said it."

"Oh. Good," Beth said, smiling.

With the second glass of wine, she told Nick about her sister and why Grace lived with her. Surprising both of them, she broke down and cried. Nick got up and came to sit in the chair next to her. He put an arm around her shoulders. "Listen, I know how it hurts. My brother nearly killed himself drinking and driving. He's been on the wagon for twelve years now."

Beth dried her eyes on her sleeve. "I don't know what came over me. I'm sorry."

He didn't move away. "Don't worry about it. I'm happy you felt comfortable enough with me to share it."

She didn't ask Nick to stay and eat with them. She was confused by his constant nearness and by her mixed reactions to him. Besides, Grace had enough adjustments to make. When they finished their wine and a bowl of pistachios, he stood and thanked her for the good company and the good wine. He repacked the chandeliers and put them in his Jeep. She followed him outside, carrying his container of chicken pad Thai.

Every cliché she'd ever heard about the stars ran through her mind as she gazed up at the incredibly clear heavens. It looked as if someone had punctured a gazillion pinholes in a blue-black, shimmery fabric, then stretched it out in the sky with a brilliant light behind it. As she'd continued to watch, she saw a falling star and gasped. Nick's voice startled her; she hadn't realized he was standing so close to her.

"Hard to believe there's a nor'easter hurtling toward us this minute," he'd said, staring up at the sky with her.

"Is there? I haven't listened to the weather."

"Should be here by tomorrow afternoon. Better batten down the hatches."

Chapter 14

It was Saturday morning, filled with sunshine, and the thermometer registered fifty-five degrees in the sun. Spring brought long-missed fragrances from budding trees and early flowers. Daffodils and tulips were sprouting in the garden, along with lily of the valley.

"Let's go look at the garden and see what's coming up."

Grace signed, "We're in our pajamas."

"It's early. No one will see us. It's more fun this way."

Grace frowned but followed her outside. Her long loose hair was fluffed by the light breeze, the silky strands sparkling in the sunrays. Beth lifted her face to the warm sun and her spirits lifted, too. It had been too gray for too long.

She pulled Grace down beside her to kneel in the dirt. Bending over and pointing, she finger-spelled the flowers she could name. She saw she'd caught Grace's interest. There were flowering hot pink and red azaleas and bright yellow forsythia, already waning.

"Grace, this is going to be a lot of work. I've never taken care of a garden before. Do you think you would like to help me?"

Grace agreed with a nod.

They walked under a flowering crabapple tree, whose gnarled branches gave away its age.

"Take a deep breath through your nose," Beth signed and demonstrated. Her niece's eyes grew big as she discerned the flowers' perfume. "Ummm," she said.

Around the side of the house, irises were raising their purple buds. Grace went over to cup one in her hand. "I love purple," she signed.

In the back yard, buds were forming on the big shade tree. "If I didn't know better, I'd think this was a lilac bush, but it's a large tree. We'll have to wait and see."

Grace signed, "Can I climb the tree?"

Beth moved her fist up and down for yes, then cupped her hands to give Grace a boost up. Grace wrapped her arms around the trunk, put her foot in Beth's hands, and hoisted herself to the first big horizontal branch. Beth stood back to watch her ascend, wondering if she should have said no. Grace went up with ease. At the top, as she turned to look down at Beth, her eyes went wide. She couldn't let go to sign but she had something to say. "Get down," then shook her head.

"Oh no. Grace, read my lips. Move your right foot down. There's a big branch right under it." Beth used pantomime to clarify what she said.

Holding on tightly, Grace stretched her foot below and made contact with the branch. Beth stood under her with arms outstretched, ready to catch her if she fell.

Grace tilted her head down to look at her feet. Her tongue wrapped over her upper lip. Then she let herself down to the next branch. She flashed a big smile to Beth. She got down to the last branch and sat on it. Beth raised her arms higher, and Grace slid off into them. They both hit the ground together in fits of laughter. Beth gave her niece a big hug.

As they stood and brushed off their pajamas, Beth could see something at her feet. She leaned down and cleared it with her hand. It was a piece of fieldstone with a rabbit carved into it. Below the rabbit were the words: Lizzie's Lilacs.

She looked back at the tree. So it *was* lilacs. She'd never before seen a lilac *tree*.

Grace tugged on her sleeve. "Who is that?" she signed and pointed to the fieldstone.

"I don't know. I'll have to see if Thea knows who Lizzie is. Ready for breakfast?"

They walked back around the other side of the house to go in the door on the farmer's porch. Beth heard the UPS truck before Grace saw it. It turned into their driveway. Beth grabbed Grace's hand and they both sprinted for the door. Grace's belly laugh joined Beth's as they tried to get in through the door before the driver caught them in their pajamas.

By late afternoon, the wind made itself heard. The tall trees in the back bowed and the grass flattened with the gusts. Beth turned on the weather station.

Living in New Bedford all her life, she was no stranger to storms, familiar even with nor'easters and hurricanes. This storm was different. It was her first Cape storm. It pounded a thin arm of land out in the ocean, including her town, which was nestled inside its elbow. She felt vulnerable, a little nervous. Her charming cottage had weathered many such storms in the past; she only hoped it would again.

As the afternoon turned to evening, the storm increased in intensity with wind gusts as high as seventy miles an hour. Beth heard an occasional sharp crack, which she identified as a snapped tree branch. She tried to see outside, but the black window panes only reflected her image. There were no corresponding loud bangs on the roof . . . yet.

Though Grace couldn't hear the loud noises of the storm, the occasional lightning frightened her. So when Beth had tucked her into bed earlier, she'd left the hall lights on, along with Grace's bedside lamp and nightlight. She told Grace she could read a while, hoping she would fall asleep.

Beth sat in the living room, going over the print-out of the store inventory, when a loud blast made her jump. The electricity was instantly cut off, leaving the room in total darkness. Probably a transformer had fallen victim to the storm. She stood and began to make her way to the kitchen.

Grace screamed, her voice in the full tilt of panic.

As Beth took off toward the stairs, she realized Grace would now be deaf *and* blind. And terrified. She tripped on the top step, mistaking it for the landing. She hit the floor hard with a muffled *whomp*, but she scrambled up, ignoring the pain.

Stupid! She'd rushed upstairs for Grace without a flashlight or a candle. It was so inky black she couldn't see Grace. She took cautious steps to her open door. A prolonged, fearsome flash of lightning illuminated the room. It was empty. Her instinct was to call out, but realized Grace wouldn't hear her.

An ear-splitting crack of thunder seemed to shake the house. She moved a few steps inside the bedroom. "Grace," she yelled, as if she'd get a response. She could hear her own breath coming faster. Where was she? Less familiar with the new house and this bedroom setup, she took small steps with her arms outstretched. She checked the bed, the chair, opened the closet and explored it with her hands. No Grace. She was little; she could be curled up in a hidey-hole, or under the bed. She squeezed her fists in frustration, knowing Grace wouldn't be able to hear her moving around.

But could she *feel* her?

Beth began to stomp her feet as hard as she could, which was easy with all the adrenaline pumping into her bloodstream. She kept it up. *Stomp. Stomp. Stomp.*

She heard a scuffling sound, followed by quick footsteps. Grace raced out from somewhere in the room straight into her arms, nearly knocking her over. Beth dropped down and hugged her, felt Grace's tears soaking into her t-shirt. She held her tightly until her breathing became quieter then she rose up, bringing Grace with her. They walked entwined to Beth's room where she eased Grace away from her and sat her on the bed. Beth took matches from the drawer of the bedside table and lit the votive candle.

When the little flame caught, both aunt and niece sighed aloud.

"It's just a storm. We're safe. The box that controls our electricity was damaged. That's all. You're safe," she said and signed, hoping she was right.

Grace's frightened eyes reflected the candle's flickering flame. She signed, "I'm scared."

"I'll stay right here with you." She reached past her and pulled the bedding down. "Move over a little and crawl under the covers."

Grace scooted under and pulled the covers up to her neck. She lay on her side facing Beth, her eyes big and round.

"I'm going to put on my pajamas. I'll be right back. Don't be afraid."

When she was ready for bed, Beth climbed in beside Grace and kissed her cheek. She signed, "Good night," and "I love you." Then she picked up a book, moved the candle closer, and began to read. For several minutes, she felt the pull of Grace's stare. Then she looked over to see her niece sound asleep. Beth sighed. It was scary being a new mommy.

On the following Wednesday morning, Lauren's husband, Troy, was scheduled to undergo his medical procedures. Her friends had all signed up to help, taking the boys to pre-school, or staying with them in the afternoon. Another friend would sit with Lauren while the tests were underway, so the only way Beth could think of contributing was to bring food. She wanted something she could make ahead because she planned to go to Grace's first soccer practice after school. She decided on a chicken curry casserole. Though curry was a love-or-hate spice, this recipe was mild curry, and everyone she'd served it to, liked it.

Cooking was usually relaxing for her, but today it wasn't. She stripped the meat from the cooked rotisserie chicken while the rice mix simmered, and thought about Patrice's reluctance to have the implant surgery performed. When the lights had gone out during the storm, Grace could have reached over and put on her cochlear implants. If she learned to speak again, she could call out to her mom or her aunt, at least, and she could hear them call her. Beth felt more determined to convince Patrice that the implants would be good. She knew not to push her, but when the opportunity came up, Beth would try again. Why was Patrice so frightened? Was her fear out of proportion because of her weakened state, affecting her reason? Would she worry about Grace playing soccer, too? Grace was excited about showing her mother the soccer picture they would take today, which she hoped wouldn't further upset Patrice. She chopped the celery, parsley, and onion with a speed generated by tension. When the rice was cooked, she added sour cream, curry, and white wine. While she stirred everything together, she wondered what would happen if Patrice agreed to talk to Scott. Then she wondered again about Scott.

Today, Beth brought her camera to the soccer field to take pictures. She had an idea for Grace to make a photo album of her soccer experience. She could bring it to her mother each week, along with her journal.

She met the coach, Judy, and went to sit alongside the field to watch.

Grace stood to the side of the girls who surrounded the coach. She looked adorable to Beth, standing there in her little shorts and big soccer shirt, with her knee sox and shin guards and her spikes. Her hair was pulled into a long swishy ponytail. As excited as Grace was to play the game, she looked like she was about to cry. It broke Beth's heart. As she pressed her fingers over her mouth, deciding whether or not to go over to her, the coach leaned out of the circle and pulled Grace in. She spoke to the kids with her hand on Grace's shoulder. It was clear even from a distance, she was telling them about Grace's deafness. Then the coach showed them the signs she would be using for Grace, thanks to the efforts of Tom Hamilton and Ms. Jenny. Beth could see the kids looking back and forth between her niece and the coach. She took her first picture.

Like the proudest aunt in the world, she watched Grace get right in line for the drills and perform them better than most of the other children.

After several drills of walking, running, and turning the ball with their feet, the coach had the girls line up to kick. She inserted Grace in the middle of the line. She studied each girl's moves as they kicked the ball then ran to a marker several feet away.

When it was Grace's turn, she thrust her foot out, knocking the ball a short distance, and lost her balance. The coach reset the ball. This time Grace made solid contact, and the ball skipped a distance away from her, after which she ran to join the girls on the other side. She turned with a proud smile and a wave for Beth.

The next kicker sent the ball soaring through the air, slamming smack into the right side of Grace's head. She dropped to the ground.

Beth ran.

Grace cried. The girls crowded around, staring at her with expressions of worry and sympathy. Judy knelt beside her, speaking softly.

"Shall I take her to the emergency room?" Beth said, breathing hard from her sprint. "Oh my God. Is she hurt badly?"

"I think she'll be all right," Judy said with pointed calmness. "Most of the steam was out of the ball when it hit her."

Beth stood stiffly with her fists clenched. "I don't have children of my own. Grace is my niece. I don't know what I should do." She knelt down and signed to Grace, "Are you hurt?"

She had stopped crying, but the tear tracks were still damp on her cheeks. She slowly raised her hand, her thumb and first two fingers extended from her fist and tapped each other, signaling, "No."

She began to get up. Before Beth could help her, the coach put a hand on Grace's shoulder. "Hold up here a minute—oh. She can't hear me," she said, looking at Beth.

"I think she understood. She reads lips pretty well."

They waited a few minutes then helped her to stand. Beth examined Grace's ear; it was bright red. She wondered if she should call Scott. Or Sue. Someone.

Grace signed, "Go home."

Beth was disappointed. Her first day and this had to happen. She couldn't remember ever having seen Grace so excited before this. Was it all ruined on her first day out?

As they were picking up their things, the coach walked over with the season's schedule, and handed it to Grace. She studied it. Beth waited for her to hand back the paper. Instead, she looked up at Judy and gave her a sweet smile.

Beth hummed on the way home. Not only was Grace a great soccer player, she was no wuss.

They iced her swollen and painful ear for about twenty minutes. Afterwards, Grace went upstairs to take her bath while Beth cooked dinner.

When she opened the refrigerator and saw the casserole, she gasped. She'd forgotten all about it. She checked the clock. If they rushed, they could just get the food to Lauren's in time to warm it for their dinner.

She hurried upstairs and explained her plan to Grace, who happily rushed her bath, looking forward to seeing the twins.

Chapter 15

They arrived in plenty of time. After Beth and Grace were introduced to Lauren's friend, Ingrid, they carried the casserole into the kitchen. Grace went to the family room to see the twins.

Beth sat on the couch next to Lauren, reaching for her hand. "How's Troy doing?"

"He's asleep. He was sick from the anesthesia when he first woke up, but half an hour later, he was starving." Her smile was weak. "They gave him graham crackers and apple juice. He's sure going to enjoy your dinner."

"Did the doctor tell you anything?"

"He just said everything went well," Lauren said. "It all took longer than I thought. Oh God, Beth, I feel like I've visited hell today. I don't know how I would have gotten through it without Ingrid." She turned and blew a kiss to her friend, who sat across the room, in a comfy-looking chair with her feet up on the ottoman.

"Did the doctor say when you'll have the results?"

"We see him in four days. Four long, painful, horrible days." Lauren rubbed her face with her free hand.

"We'll keep you busy," Ingrid said.

Beth turned to smile at her, letting go of Lauren's hand. Ingrid was older than Lauren and Beth, nearing fifty, she guessed. Her face was attractive but creased with wrinkles when she smiled.

"That curry already smells delicious. Will you both stay and eat with us?" Lauren said.

"Not me, darling," Ingrid said, standing up. "You need some time alone. I'm leaving, but call me if there's anything I can do…." Her voice trailed off.

After she left, Lauren explained that Ingrid was an emergency room nurse. "I've known her for years. I can't tell you how much she's helped me through this. Everyone's been wonderful. And thank *you* for bringing dinner tonight."

"I'm happy to help. And I'll echo Ingrid, call me if you need anything," she said, preparing to stand.

"Don't go yet. Can you stay and have a glass of wine with me?"

Little boy giggles came from the room where Grace entertained the twins. "Sure. It sounds like we can stay a little longer."

Lauren poured them both a glass of pinot noir and sat back down.

"I'm so scared," she whispered. "I don't know how I'll keep a happy face for Troy until we hear."

"You'll do it, Lauren. He'll make it easy, I bet."

"You're right. He had all the nurses laughing in the pre-op room." She smiled, and took a deep breath. "How's the store coming?"

"Great. It should be finished in a couple days."

"I'm anxious to see it."

They talked for a few more minutes, until Lauren relaxed, leaning back on the couch with her feet tucked up beside her, and her empty wine glass on the cocktail table.

"I'd better get going. Is there anything I can do before I leave?" Beth asked.

"You barely touched your wine," Lauren said. "Oh, you're driving."

She nodded. "No, you've been great. I think we'll eat your delicious meal and all go to sleep."

Later, with Grace fed and tucked into bed, Beth sat in the living room and listened. The house was as silent as an empty church. She'd been trying to read a book, but the day had left her nerves on edge and she couldn't concentrate. Now, the silence made her feel like some huge bubble was about to burst. She stood up. She'd go to bed and put an end to this day. Maybe set the timer on her clock radio with some soothing music to help her sleep.

She checked the window locks, turned off the lights in the living room. She moved through the dining room and office, into the kitchen. She went down the hall to check the windows in the sacred space. It was always cold in that room. Even during the sunny hours. Tonight was no exception. She sat in a wicker chair, wrapping her arms across her chest.

A vision of the airborne soccer ball, soaring toward her smiling niece flashed before her. What if something bad happened to Grace? How would she ever face her sister? The responsibility she'd taken on hit her hard. She hugged herself tighter.

She thought of Troy, facing a possible life-threatening diagnosis. How quickly fate could stamp out a life. How vulnerable humans were, and how catastrophic the loss of a loved one could be.

A whippoorwill began to sing. Beth was so grateful for the sound, she smiled. Then she noticed a fragrance. Lilacs. She breathed in the sweet perfume with her eyes closed. The backyard tree must be in bloom. She'd been so busy, she hadn't noticed. The fragrance was calming; she could feel herself slowly melting into relaxation.

Seconds later, Beth came to. She must have dozed off. She went up to bed and fell into a peaceful sleep.

At ten o'clock the next morning, she was on her way out the door when the phone rang.

"It's not cancer! It's not terminal. Praise God!" Lauren yelled into the phone.

"Great news! I'm so happy for you both. What's the diagnosis?"

"Sarcoidosis. They don't know the cause, but it's like his body is fighting an infection but the process gets stuck in inflammation and doesn't turn off. Maybe from something he breathed in on the job. Anyway, he'll have to be on steroids for a while, and the doctor doesn't want him to go back to work yet. His job is too physical. He's working at a site where he's on a ladder and crawling around attic space. But that's the least of our worries. Who cares? It's such an unbelievable relief."

Beth was on her way to the garage when she remembered to look at the lilac tree. She walked around the house and saw the buds on the tree were still tightly closed. She moved closer, sniffing, but she couldn't detect a scent. She shrugged her shoulders and headed for the garage.

Today the store was ready for her final inspection. As she drove, she wondered about Lauren's phrase, "the least of our worries," and figured she meant it would be an economic hardship for Troy to be out of work.

A small bell emitted a soft ring when she entered the store. Beth turned slowly, taking in the whole space. It sparkled under the indirect lighting. The shelving shone with gloss white paint. The crystals on the chandeliers acted as prisms where the sun hit them, casting rainbows on the white walls. The wood floor was buffed to a warm glow. And the alcove, lined with spotless glass shelves, was like a softly lit stage, waiting for the props.

She took in a deep breath, moving her head from side to side. "I can't believe it's ready. It looks terrific," she said to a grinning Nick.

He followed as she walked through the back room—whose deep storage shelves were all painted white, ready for stock—then into the newly tiled bathroom.

"It's beautiful," she said on a sigh.

"I like the soft colors you chose," Nick said.

Back in the main store, Beth scanned the length of the work counter, and imagined wrapping purchases in white tissue and placing them inside lavender shopping bags, stamped with *Linens & Lavender*.

She turned to Nick, who seemed oddly quiet. "It's great. I can't wait to get started."

"Glad you like it," he said, smiling.

The bell chimed and they both looked up. A slight man with long, dark hair masking his face hauled in a large palm plant with a big red bow on it. Nick went over to help him.

The man walked over to Beth, brushing loose dirt from his hand before extending it to her. "I'm your neighbor, Charlie Sawyer. Welcome!"

He was older than she expected from his dark hair, but handsome, with an olive complexion and brown eyes so dark, she couldn't see the pupils. "Thank you. The palm is the perfect finishing touch," she said, then paused. "You're right next door. Sawyer's Books and Music?"

He nodded. "My wife is the musician. She sells sheet music, new and old. I'm also a purveyor of antiquities—rare or gently used books. We set up a small café for folks to sit and read, or just sit and sip. Come over for coffee when you have time."

"I'll be there."

"Good. My wife, Jane, is minding the store right now, but she's anxious to meet you, too."

On his way out, Charlie turned and said, "I can't tell you how delighted we are we won't be smelling pizza all day anymore. We're thrilled to have you."

Beth had been smiling so long, her cheek muscles were tired, but she couldn't stop. She stood behind the counter, rubbing her hands over the smooth wood top, while she tried to take everything in. It all felt magical.

In a soft voice, as if not to disturb her, Nick said, "So, you open on Memorial Day weekend?"

"That's the plan."

"If there's anything I can do to help, call me. If you want me to move the furniture around, carry heavy boxes, any kind of macho stuff like that, I'm your guy."

"Thanks," she said, with another smile at his humor. "You're invited to the grand opening."

"I wouldn't miss it, of course. I'll be working the crowd for more business."

She chuckled. "Good for you. I'll see you then."

"Maybe sooner? Now that our business is completed, I was wondering if you'd like to have dinner with me one night."

She swallowed. "Thanks for asking me, Nick, but I sort of have my hands full with Grace and the store right now."

Two weeks later, Grace clutched her photo album and journal close to her chest on the way to the Jenna Treatment Center. Beth could tell she was excited because she could hear the tap of her foot kicking the back of the passenger seat. Their last two visits to the center had been good, focusing on Patrice's rehab progress and Grace's schoolwork. Beth hadn't brought up the implants and neither had Patrice.

They walked hand in hand into the foyer. When the woman at the desk saw them, she stood and came to stand before them.

"Ms. Henson. Your sister asked me to bring Grace in alone. She thinks it would be better if you waited outside today. Here's a note for you." She handed Beth an envelope.

Is my sister all right?"

"She's fine. She asked me to tell you not to worry."

Beth was still holding Grace's hand when the woman took her other hand and led her away. She remained standing, stunned, holding the blue envelope. Grace turned her head to look back at her with a worried expression. Beth forced a smile and waved her on.

She was about to sit on a bench in the foyer when she changed her mind. She didn't want to see the woman return, so she went to sit in her car.

She pushed the seat back and reclined it slightly, then opened Patrice's letter.

Beth,
Please don't be mad at me. I need to talk to Grace alone. I read the information you gave me on the implants. What I didn't tell you was how my friend's son died when he was only having his tonsils out. Grace is all I have. I couldn't go on if anything happened to her.

Her doctor came to see me. He offered to talk to me on the phone, but I knew I'd rather look into his eyes as he told me what he was going to do. You know me and people. He is so nice, and he spent a long time helping me to understand everything. Scott told me why it was better to do the implants as soon as possible. I'm still scared to death, but I'm sure now, it's the right thing for Grace.

They won't let me come to the hospital to be with her. It's a lot to ask, but you were right. I want her to hear the sirens and horns honking, and as Scott said, my words to her. Will you do this for me?

I know you're willing. You'll take good care of my little girl.

Beth wasn't mad. After all, she was the one who had made the decision to encourage Patrice to live her own life. Beth recognized her need for the same. So why did she feel left out right now? Why did it sting that Patrice didn't seem to have needed her in this decision, and in telling Grace, the way she used to need her?

And why was *she* filled with this all-encompassing loneliness that made her sister's exclusion of her worse? She raised her eyes to the front of the treatment center building. It had to be hard for her sister to watch Beth take over the care of her daughter. When this was all over, and Patrice was clean, they would end up in a healthier, loving relationship. Beth had to be more understanding and less sensitive. But, *damn*, it was hard.

Grace had become even dearer to her now. All Beth wanted was to do the best for her. She shook her head, imagining Grace speaking and hearing like the other kids—almost. She shouldn't raise her expectations too high, but at least now Grace had a chance.

She pulled a pen from her purse, turned the letter over and wrote:

I knew there was something frightening you. You don't need anything else to worry about while you're working so hard to get better. Yes. I'm willing. I will take the best care of Grace. I know you're putting your trust in me to keep her safe. I'll do everything I can. I'm glad you met Scott. He's the best. He's such a dedicated doctor who cares so much. She'll be in good hands.

I miss seeing you today, but I understand. I love you and hope you're doing well.

When Grace was brought back to her, she was sitting on the bench in the front hall with a smile on her lips.

"Mommy said I must do the implants," Grace signed.

"Is that what you want?"

"I want to talk," she said aloud, while her right index finger made a small forward circular motion in front of her mouth. The sign for *say* or *tell* or *speak*. And she did all three with passion.

Chapter 16

They were in Doctor Adams waiting room. Beth hid her smile when Grace's eyes adored the nurse with the purple hair, who talked to her like they were friends, as she led them to an exam room. Beth liked everything about Scott's practice: The professional, friendly staff; the cleanliness; the orderliness; the doctor's care for his patients. It all gave her confidence.

Scott smiled when he opened the door. "So, Grace, are we ready to go?" As always, he both spoke and signed everything.

"Yes," she said aloud, smiling back at him.

"Excellent! Today, I'm going to tell you everything we'll be doing. There's nothing to worry about. Have you ever been in the hospital?"

"Yes," she said in her small voice. She signed a few words then stopped, with a scowl.

"Meningitis?" he finger-spelled.

"Yes." She nodded.

"This is different. You're not sick, for one thing. And you'll go home the same day."

Grace smiled. Beth could see that was one worry gone. She thought how difficult it must be to not be able to speak freely. The words needed to ask certain medical questions would not be common in sign language. Still, she had a feeling that when Scott finished his explanation, all the stones would be turned over.

He talked to Grace about the hospital, the room she'd be in, what she'd be wearing, who else would be there, the needle in her arm, and the good nap she would take while he did all the work. At one point, Grace reached for Beth's hand. Scott noticed.

"Aunt Beth will be with you every minute until you fall asleep, and as soon as you wake up, she'll be with you again." He turned and smiled at Beth, a warm dimpled smile that said he knew it would also be something she'd want to know. Again, he'd anticipated her thoughts, but this time, she had to suppress a smile in return.

Grace was signing, and Scott waited until she finished to answer her. "No, you won't hear anything when you wake up."

She looked disappointed.

"You'll have a little incision—a small cut—behind each ear that has to heal first. Remember the processors you'll wear over your ears?" Grace nodded. "That's where the incisions will be." He reached over and touched an area behind one ear. "So we don't want to put anything on them until they're healed."

He explained about the pre-operative tests that needed be done before the procedure. Then he walked them to the business office where a woman would set up the surgery date. Beth asked her to delay the surgery by a week. It was set up for next Monday. Beth wanted to talk to her sister one more time before she'd feel completely comfortable. Besides, this way Grace would able to play in the first soccer game on Saturday.

The woman gave Grace a lollipop and showed them into Scott's office. After about fifteen minutes, he walked in.

"All set?"

"It seems so," Beth said. "It made all the difference when you went to explain everything to Patrice. Thanks for doing that."

"My pleasure. How about you? Any questions?"

"I think you've made everything clear. I'll see Patrice this Sunday and we'll put our heads together and let you know if we come up with anything you haven't covered."

Beth gave Grace a kiss on the cheek, and watched her run off toward her coach and team. She set up her lawn chair as close to the edge of the field as she could. She had her phone and her camera. It couldn't be a more glorious May day.

She stayed on the edge of her chair, leaning forward, and cheering the girls on. When Grace kicked in her first goal, Beth jumped up, clapping and yelling. Grace had her arms extended as she also jumped up and down. Her celebration was ended quickly by the coach. But as Grace ran past her on the field, she stuck out her fist to give Beth a thumbs-up.

Officially, no score was kept for this age group, but everyone kept one in their heads. You could tell when the home team went ahead of the visitors by the roar that went up from the local crowd.

It was like watching the Red Sox down by one at the bottom of the ninth with two outs and one on. But the pressure Beth felt watching the tied soccer game was even greater.

The soccer ball was in play. A bunch of little girls were somehow advancing the ball up the field toward the goal. Beth was on her feet, giving them her full-throated support. Grace pulled away from the pack. She moved in front and to the side of the goal. The goalie moved over closer to her. The ball rolled toward Grace. She lifted her right foot, smacked the ball sideways. It flew into the net right before the whistle blew.

If that last Red Sox player at bat had hit a home run, Beth could not be more excited.

Patrice watched Beth and Grace enter the visiting room. Her daughter ran into her arms. She hugged her and held on until Grace squirmed.

"Mommy," she said, her face animated as she held up the books she carried. "See pictures."

Patrice, smiling, held up an index finger to her, and turned to hug Beth. "I'm sorry about last week. It was important to have Grace focused on me alone, so I could discern if she really wanted the implants. I already know what you think is important for her."

"I would never talk her into something you didn't want. I'm glad you explained your fear to me. I couldn't understand why you seemed so hesitant. But I didn't push Grace at all. I wouldn't do that."

"I just needed to see that for myself. And she is scared, Beth."

"Of course, she is. But I think our visit with Scott took some of that away. It seemed to do the same for you. Do you like him?"

"You picked a winner. I like him a lot," she said, then turned to Grace.

Patrice signed her excitement about Grace's soccer game, the pictures, and read the journal entries her daughter had written. She felt much more relaxed and her mood seemed stable. In fact, she had a sense of confidence she hadn't felt in a long time. It didn't even bother her that Beth made the soccer decision without asking her. Maybe this time, rehab was really helping her.

When Grace closed her books, Patrice turned to ask Beth the question that had been on her mind since the doctor came to see her. "Is Grace's doctor married?"

"Doctor Adams? I don't know. Why?"

"He spent a lot of time with me. I thought maybe he was attracted to me. I've been thinking about my future. I want to have a husband and another child. They tell you no new relationships for six months to a year after you finish rehab, but I think it would be easier to stay clean if you were with someone you love." She rubbed her cheeks to hide the blush she could feel on her face. "They talk here about putting trust in a higher power, but that doesn't work for me. I've had enough higher power growing up." She looked away for a moment. "I need to find what's right for me. And I think my dream of a little family helps keep me on course."

"I don't see any harm in having that dream," Beth said.

"Yes, but you know me. It's hard to be patient." She smiled at Beth, before changing the subject. "I wish I could be there for the surgery."

"You're sure you're feeling good about this? I want to know you're fully behind me."

"I'm sure. Call me as soon as it's over. They'll find me wherever I am. Even better, have Scott call me."

"I'll ask him. I think he does all his surgeries in one day—"

Patrice put her hands on her hips. "Is it too much to ask for him to tell Grace's mother that everything went well?"

Grace tugged on her mother's arm and signed, "What's wrong?"

"Nothing's wrong, sweetie." She turned to Beth. "Don't get her upset before her surgery."

She watched Beth's expression change. She didn't mean to hurt her, but she couldn't seem to control her resentment. It was in part due to her anxiety about Grace's surgery, and she knew it was her own fault that she couldn't be there. She had to stop sniping at Beth.

Grace was frowning at Beth, as if she had made her mother cry, and God help her, that made Patrice happy.

Beth sat in the surgical waiting room with her hands wrapped around a paper cup of coffee. It was two hours into the surgery, and her mind kept replaying the morning.

A teary-eyed Grace had been surrounded by nurses and doctors in the pre-operative area. Beth had held her hand while they started her IV and took her vital signs. Scott made her smile when he introduced the anesthesiologist, with his white beard, as Santa Claus.

And then Beth stood with her fingers pressed over her mouth as she watched them roll Grace down the hall.

She wished she'd taken her friends' offers to come with her today, but it was too long a drive from New Bedford, and they all worked. Lauren had spent the first hour with her before she had to leave, and Beth was grateful for the company.

She tossed her empty coffee cup into the trash and went out to pace the hall, keeping watch through the waiting room window.

Scott surprised her by coming down the hall instead of through the waiting room.

"Grace did fine. She's almost fully awake and ready to leave recovery. I'll show you where they'll bring her."

"It's over?"

He grinned at her. "It seems to last forever when you're pacing out here, doesn't it?"

She took quick strides to keep up with him as they moved through the corridors. He stopped at a door. "The nurse will give you an instruction sheet and some prescriptions before you leave. Call the office and make an appointment for Thursday. But call me if there's anything at all you need to talk to me about. Don't hesitate." As he walked away, Grace's bed was being rolled toward her.

It was over.

And it all went well.

She walked up to meet the gurney and took Grace's hand.

Chapter 19

Patrice sat on the bench in the front hall of the Jenna Treatment Center. She'd already run on the treadmill, worked the weight machines, ordered the flowers, and paced the hall. She stared at the hands of the clock over the reception desk. It was going on three hours since Grace's surgery had begun. Beth had called and left her a message when Grace went to the OR.

Patrice jumped up when the phone rang, but dropped back down when the receptionist shook her head. She was so tired, having spent hours during the night staring at the ceiling.

It was ten minutes more before Beth called.

"How is she? Is it finished? Did it go well?"

"She is fine, and yes, it went great. Scott said to tell you he'd call later, after his other surgeries. I didn't want you to wait another second, though. Patrice, you should have seen her. She was so brave. I told her you would be very proud of her."

Patrice couldn't speak. Tears were streaming from her eyes and her throat felt closed. But it was all from happiness and relief.

"Patrice? Are you still there?"

"I'm here."

"You're crying. Honey, she's fine. Really great."

"She wasn't afraid?"

"She cried a little when the nurse started her IV, but she was the best little patient."

"I'm so glad it's over. Thank you, Beth. I just wish I could hug her and kiss her. I feel so alone here right now. I wish I could be there."

"I wish you could, too. So much. The nurse said she'll be sleepy most of the day, but when she's awake and ready, we'll video-call you to talk, okay? Right now, I have to get her home."

"Home? I wish. To your house, you mean. I guess it's the only home she has until her mommy is back out in the world."

Patrice walked slowly back to her room. The surgery was over. Everything went fine. She'd worried herself sick. Beth sounded happy and relieved, too. Patrice had half a mind to run right out of this place and go to her daughter. She stopped walking, stared ahead. *Goddammit.* Why couldn't they have given her leave to be with Grace? Really. If she missed a few sessions of the same old thing, would it have mattered? She still had cravings. Other people took pills to keep them calm when the going got rough. Why was she the one sentenced to a year of rehab for doing the same?

These were dangerous thoughts. She walked faster to her room and lay on the bed. If she didn't make it through rehab this time, she would never do it. If she didn't want to miss the next big events in Grace's life, she had to learn to live without the drug crutch. It all sounded doable in this place, but when she went back to her old life, could she stay clean? She flipped over and stared at the table beside her bed. She noticed a letter there and sat up. It was addressed to her, but it was opened. She took out the note and her heart sped up when she read the signature: *Frankie*.

Aunt Beth heated up some soup for Grace when they got home, and made her peanut butter crackers. They sat at the table in the sacred space. The lady wasn't there. Grace was tired and her head hurt, but she was so proud of herself. Aunt Beth said she was brave, because even though she was scared, she still went through the surgery. She said her mommy was so proud of her, too.

She raised her arm to look at the bandage where the needle went in. She didn't remember too much after Doctor Scott said Santa Claus was going to make her take a nap. Then she woke up like a minute later. Aunt Beth said it was hours, but it sure seemed like only a minute. Doctor Scott told her how good she was. She was proud.

She raised a cracker to her mouth when she felt a tap on her knee. She giggled because it seemed like she was dreaming.

Aunt Beth had a surprised look on her face as she pointed outside. Grace looked. Lizzie's lilac tree was like a bride with her veil made of white flowers. "Pretty," she signed.

The doorbell light flashed, and Aunt Beth went to answer it. Grace felt dreamy again.

She came back carrying a white vase with two pink roses in it. "Look, Grace. Somebody sent you beautiful roses." She took the card in a little white envelope and handed it to Grace.

She pulled out the card and smiled. She signed, "Mommy," and handed the card to Beth.

For my little angel. One pink rose for each cochlear implant. I love you, Mommy.

A few minutes later, Aunt Beth gave her a pill to swallow. "It will take any pain away. Now, let's get you upstairs for a nap. Those eyelids are getting heavy, aren't they?"

They went upstairs, and Aunt Beth brought her roses along. For once, Grace didn't mind going to bed. Her aunt left a bell on her bedside table next to the vase, and told Grace to ring it when she woke up. She said she shouldn't get out of bed until Aunt Beth came back. Grace turned her nose into her pillow. It smelled so sweet and clean. Then she gently turned her head until she felt the bandage behind her ear. It didn't hurt. She stared at the roses until she had to let her eyes close.

"Mommy," Grace said, running into Patrice's arms.

"Hi, Beth," she said over Grace's head as she hugged her daughter. "I'm so happy to see you both. I want to hear all about the surgery."

They sat huddled together. "Scott said he called you and gave you the technical details, but we'll fill you in on all the rest. Grace was unbelievable. Show her your pictures, Grace."

Grace signed as she flipped through the few pictures on Beth's phone. Then she showed her mother her healing incisions.

"Do they hurt, honey?"

"Only if I forget and scratch," Grace signed, "and I got sick."

Beth told Patrice about the dizziness and vomiting Grace experienced after her surgery. "We healed it with ice cream and ginger ale."

"Ummm," Grace said.

Grace sat on Patrice's lap while her mother brushed and braided her hair. "Beth, I'm doing so well here. I would be back home by now if I had gone to the short rehab program again. What a difference. I like the therapist who does my individual therapy, and the counselors who do group are all great. I've made friends, and we help each other work on issues that could cause a relapse. I'm sure this time, as hard as it is on you and Grace, and me, I'll be able to stay clean."

"I'm so glad it's going well. I can see it on your face. You're more relaxed and happy. I believe in you."

"My vocational work here is cooking. I love it. I'm learning all kinds of things. Must be in our genes." She wrapped a band around one of the braids. "Each week a vocational therapist comes in. She's part of my treatment plan and she'll be helping me find work as a cook when I'm released. She has employers willing to hire recovering addicts. They get tax breaks, and I get a chance."

"That's terrific. Now you can help cook our holiday dinners," Beth said, bumping shoulders with Patrice.

Patrice patted Grace's head. She slid off Patrice's lap, feeling her long braids with both hands.

Patrice went on. "Maybe someday I'll open a little bakery or a coffee shop. You can help me with the business part. I'm dreaming happy dreams."

"I'm there!" Beth replied, beaming. "I'm learning a lot about retail, so I'll be ready to help you."

"Are you still on track to open on Memorial Day weekend?"

"Yep. I have two women hired who have experience in retail. I'm going to start training them on my POS, point of sales, system this week."

"Something I need to know?"

"You'll learn. It's easy. It does everything for you, inventory, reports, order management, tax calculations. It's all synchronized to the online business, too. Want to see it? I have an app on my tablet." Beth reached for her bag.

Patrice laughed. "I'm sorry I asked. Not yet. I'm still learning to cook!"

It wasn't until after they left that Patrice remembered she wanted to tell Beth about her letter from Frankie. She allowed a private smile. It was another of her happy dreams. She could tell from his note, Frankie still cared for her. He wrote to say how sorry he was about what happened to her at his party. Patrice hadn't discussed the letter with Doctor Harper yet. She wanted to hold Frankie's words in her heart a little longer before she shared them.

Lauren had invited Grace and her for dinner, so they left the treatment center and went directly to Lauren's house. Benjie and Jake were waiting for Grace. She'd brought her soccer ball, and they all went out to play in the fenced backyard.

"You ready for a drink?" Troy asked, handing her a glass of wine, and then gave one to Lauren.

"I'm ready, thanks. You're looking pretty darn healthy, Troy."

"I wish," Troy said, as he settled carefully onto the couch with a full stein of non-alcohol beer in his hand. "I'm getting restless. I don't know how some women stay home every day with nothing to do."

Lauren made a harrumph sound. "Huh? Nothing to do, he says.

What about the dishes, the meals, the kids, the wash, the housecleaning, watering the plants, working in the—"

"Uncle!" Troy said. "I'm just saying, I wish I could be busy at work."

They ate meatloaf and mashed potatoes, with cherry crisp for dessert. After dinner, while they were doing the dishes, Lauren asked Beth to drop by the quilting group to meet her friends the next day.

"I wish I could. I'd like to meet your friends, but my store inventory is being delivered tomorrow. It'll take me days to unpack it. After that, I'll be arranging all the displays. With two stores now, I'll be hopping back and forth."

"You're going to be busy, all right. Is there something I can do?" When Beth hesitated, Lauren said, "Jeez. I could help you get the store ready. The quilting circle can get along without me. I suspended my volunteer work at the library when Troy was diagnosed. I won't start up again until he's able to go back to work. Meanwhile, he's my live-in babysitter." She laughed. "And, trust me; I don't need to make one more quilt." Lauren dried her hands on a dish towel. "Follow me."

She led Beth down the hall and opened a good-sized linen closet. On every shelf colorful, neatly folded quilts were piled high. "Really, Beth, as you can see, I can afford to take some time to help you set up. Besides, I worked in retail before I married Troy. It'll be fun."

It occurred to her on the drive home that she could offer to sell Lauren's quilts in her shop. It would be good to add local talent to her store, and bring in extra money for Lauren's family until Troy could return to work.

Chapter 18

Patrice told them she was sick. She lay on her bed, curled up, facing the wall. She was sick. Sick at heart. It happened every Monday after she'd seen Beth and Grace. She wanted her baby back. And she wanted something to make her feel better. Something to keep her on a steady track. Yesterday, she felt so good, and today she was miserable. Always riding the elevator of emotions.

She'd been clean for more than two months. What good did it do? It only made her pain more real, her situation less tenable. Ever since she was twelve, she'd needed some form of help to exist in her world.

When she became pregnant, she fought to get clean and have a healthy baby. With Beth's help, she'd done it. Her new life was going to be dedicated to loving her baby, and making sure Grace always knew how much she was treasured.

She had Beth as her example, in how she shared her life; how she loved her sister, no matter what. Beth's love and care had been the only thing that kept Patrice from the streets. But right now, all she felt for Beth was resentment, and she couldn't fight it.

Patrice knew she was being unfair. With every cell in her body, she'd wanted to be there for Grace's surgery. She knew the reason was at least partly about trying to reclaim her daughter. Now, Beth would end up the superhero. Making the blind see, the deaf hear.

Why hadn't she followed up years ago when the doctor recommended a cochlear implant for Grace? Maybe because she'd needed to keep her daughter dependent on her. She still did.

Now, the two people she loved the most were happy and together. She was alone. She was sure Grace loved Beth more than her. Would she hate to have to come home? The pain made her curl her body tighter.

"Are you awake?" Doctor Harper said in a soft voice.

Patrice ignored her.

"We need to talk."

"Not now," Patrice said, knowing she wouldn't go away.

"The worst thing you can do in here is bottle up your feelings. I know you're hurting. This is an opportunity to solve your problems without drugs. If you learn how to do that where you're protected and supported, you'll be strong enough when you leave to resist the temptation to use."

Patrice didn't move. The doctor was right. But all she wanted was something to ease the pain. And she didn't care about working it out.

"What's wrong?"

Before she could stop it, a sob escaped her.

"Sit up. Let's talk it out."

When she was upright, the doctor made her get out of bed and sit in a desk chair. Doctor Harper closed the door and pulled up the other chair. "What's going on?"

Tears kept rolling down her cheeks, in spite of her deep breathing and swallowing. "She's taken my child. The only good thing I've ever done in my life."

"That's not true. Don't belittle yourself. Be honest. She may be the best thing in your life, but I'm telling you, there's so much more to you that's good. You've been here long enough for us to get to know you. You've made friends. You've helped others."

"Why can't I help myself?"

"You have. Setbacks happen. It's why we have the tools to deal with them without taking drugs. Not only have you made good relationships, you've made great progress in a short time. Your desire to be free of your addiction is something you can be proud of. It shows how much you love your daughter, and how hard you're working to get her back. That's all good stuff."

Patrice forced her words through her throat, thick with emotion. "Grace will never want me. My sister is too *fucking* good. She can part the oceans, she can make rainbows appear, she can make Grace *hear*. Why would she ever want me back? Come home to a crummy apartment, with no money. Some job I'll hate that will make me tired and angry. Doctor Harper, tell me, who you would pick?"

The doctor was silent. Patrice knew the drill. She was supposed to vomit up all the rest of her shit. *Oh God, I need something.*

"I'm angry at her for making me see who I am, for showing Grace the alternative."

"You know, Patrice, in my practice, I treat quite a few children. One truth that never changes, no matter what, is children want their parents' love. It's instinctual. Even in cases of abuse. Your daughter will love you forever. Your life is just beginning here. You can do this. Before you finish your assignment, we'll help you connect with job training, housing, and employment. We're not going to send you out cold. You have the desire, more than almost any other woman here—and don't you dare repeat that. You're made of the same genes as your sister. You have amazing talent in art. And you have a loving heart." She paused and watched Patrice dry her tears with a tissue. "It's not easy to climb this mountain, but you have the best equipment possible to make it to the top."

The doctor sounded like she meant it. As if she cared. Understood. "Thanks, Doctor Harper."

"You're welcome. Now come to group with me. They're waiting for you."

Beth woke up thinking of quilts. She'd called Lauren when she got home last night, and had taken her up on her offer to help with the delivery today. She was anxious to talk to her today about selling her quilts. And if she found a way, offer her some hours at the store. Cindy, one of her two new hires, couldn't work on Friday afternoons. If Lauren could fill in, Beth would have some time to get her computer work done at home where she wouldn't be interrupted.

"How could you get here so early?" Beth said, waiting for the Keurig to brew Lauren's hot chocolate. They were standing at a narrow counter in the back room of the store. It was seven-thirty.

"I set up a car pool with a couple mothers whose kids go to pre-school with Jake and Benjie. I should have done it sooner. I realized that when Troy went in for tests. I can stay all day and help. Troy will watch the kids this afternoon." She laughed. "Secretly, I'm loving that he is so impressed about what a mommy/housewife does all day."

"I could see that last night. Is he feeling better?" Beth handed Lauren her hot chocolate, and popped her coffee choice in the holder.

"Not too great. He's still tired and he's a little irritable, which I know is because he's worried." She turned away and looked around. "Seems like you got a head start." She indicated with a wave a nearby fully packed shelf.

The aroma of brewed coffee blending with that of Lauren's cocoa made the back room smell like mocha. "I brought some items from my online store when I moved here. I didn't know what I might want to use in the cottage, and I had a bunch of smaller items and lavender products delivered earlier."

"Have a seat. We still have some time to chat." Beth unfolded a snack tray and set it between the two director's chairs she'd picked up at a thrift store. They had new burnt-orange, canvas covers.

"Lauren, I wonder if you're interested in consigning some of your quilts? It would be great for the store and . . . you do seem to have a bunch of them." Beth raised her eyebrows.

"I would love that. I know Troy would get down on his knees if I could reduce my inventory." She chuckled. "In fact, my group talked about selling quilts on Craig's list or eBay, but it seemed too complicated. I think we could keep you in quilts for quite a while."

Beth took in a breath. "Great! We'll get that going. Another thing—" Beth stopped, rolling her lips between her teeth. "I was wondering if you'd like to work in the store a few hours a week? You won't offend me if you say no."

Lauren slid a little lower in her chair. She took a sip of her chocolate, swallowed, and then smiled at Beth. "I would love that, too."

"I'm glad. One of my employees can't work on Friday afternoons this school year. I thought you could fill in that day, and maybe others, if someone needs time off?"

"As long as Troy is home, I can fill in anytime. After that, maybe I can switch off play dates with a friend so I can continue Friday afternoons. You'd better bring me up to snuff on modern retail. It's been years since I worked in a store."

With a little more discussion, the plans were set. Beth asked if Lauren and Troy could take color pictures of the open quilts for sale, and put them in a binder. Once Lauren had her inventory and price list completed, Beth would be her first customer. She wanted to buy one of the quilts for a raffle on the day of the grand opening.

When those matters were settled, Beth stood up and said, "Let's begin your refresher course by having you log into our digital time clock. You're starting work right now."

Lauren, her cheeks hot pink, began to stick out her hand to shake Beth's, but changed mid-way to give her a hug.

Lauren was tearing up the empty cardboard boxes in the back room. Beth was flattening the air out of all the plastic bags to be recycled, and shoving them into one big bag, when the bell jingled.

Nick walked in, looking as grubby as Beth felt. She stood up and shoved her hair out of her face. "Now you come. When the work is all done."

"I've been told my timing is impeccable." He rubbed his palms together. "Having said that, who's going to put all this stuff you unpacked on the shelves?"

"You can come do that tomorrow."

"Ah gee," he said, grimacing, "I'd love to, but I have to build a deck."

"Too bad. I guess I'll just have to manage without you." Beth kicked the pile of plastic away from the middle of the room.

"I can take that out for you. I'm stopping at the Transfer Station on the way home." He grabbed a corner of the bag and began dragging it toward her. "I stopped in to ask you to dinner Saturday night," he said, looking into her eyes.

She should have expected this, but she'd had no time to think it over. She kicked herself for that glass of wine invite. Nick came on strong, but she couldn't deny he was fun. What would it hurt to go out? But she couldn't. "I'm sorry, but I can't leave Grace alone."

"Could we arrange for someone to stay with her?"

"I haven't found a sitter for her yet. It's so tough with her being deaf. Besides, she's been through so much I've been keeping her close."

Lauren walked out from the back room. "Excuse me," she said, looking Nick over. "Beth, could I see you for a minute back here? Got a little problem."

"Be right back," Beth said, then followed Lauren to the back room.

"Do you really want to pass up a date with this guy? Because if you want to go, you know we'd take care of Grace. We love her, and when she's visiting, the boys are so happy."

Beth laughed. "You heard?"

"It wasn't easy, but I got most of it."

"Thanks, but that's not the problem. I'm only using Grace as an excuse because I'm not sure if I want to go out with him."

"Well, if you decide to go out with that hottie, don't worry about Grace. We'll watch her, and you can watch the boys another time for me."

"Hmmm. Maybe a night out would do me good."

She went back out front to tell Nick. His face lit up. "I'll pick you up around seven?" Then he scooped up the plastic bags and left.

Chapter 19

Grace's incisions were healing well. Every so often, Beth saw her reach up to explore them with her finger. Otherwise, her life was back to normal: school, soccer, therapy, and tutoring. On the way to see Patrice last Sunday, they had stopped at some estate sales where Beth had found an easel and more art supplies, which they would keep in the back room of the store. Grace could sketch and paint when she was there after school. Beth had taken an old stool from the garage and cleaned it up for her to sit on at the counter to do her homework.

Her three employees were up to speed and enthusiastic. Everything was falling into place. The Grand Opening was scheduled for Saturday, May twenty-sixth, Memorial Day Weekend, just a little over a week away. The ads were ready to be published in the local papers and an online blast was already out. She'd created posters to hang in shop windows, and any other places around town that would allow her. She'd joined the Chamber of Commerce. She was making an effort to meet all the owners of the other stores in the strip, including Jane Sawyer, with whom she enjoyed a delicious cup of coffee in her café. In their discussions, Jane offered to run over if Beth needed an extra hand for the opening. "There're two of us here most of the time. We just like being together. Keeping the shop doesn't require two people. So, I'm free if you need me."

She'd accomplished all the necessary preparations for the opening without one frayed nerve. Yet, here she sat on Saturday night, fumbling with her make-up, still in her underwear, because she couldn't decide what to wear.

Grace, who at first balked about going alone to Lauren's, was already there, happy after choosing the flavor of ice cream they would bring to Lauren's house for dessert. The house was quiet, and Beth's ears were burning from listening for the doorbell.

She took a Q-tip and cleaned off a clump of mascara below her eyelid, then reapplied. When she looked as good as she thought she could, she went to stand in front of her open closet door. She couldn't remember the last time she'd shopped. She moved closer and, for the fourth time, slid the hangers down the rod one at a time. Finally, she picked a pair of navy blue slacks and grabbed her navy flats. She pulled a soft-weave white sweater from the shelf above.

In the third week of May, the Cape was still chilly, but the sun was shining, the hydrangea blooms were formed, the peonies were covered with the ants that would eventually open their tight buds. And that morning in the sacred space, through the one open window, Beth had smelled the fragrance of wild roses mixed with the salty scent of the ocean. There, she'd been reduced to the texture of bread dough, so relaxed, and as always in the sacred space, she was full of peace.

But now she was full of angst. Her wavy black hair curled every which way, a small pimple blossomed on the side of her nose, and she hated the boring clothes she'd chosen. She pulled off the sweater and pulled on a red cable-knit with a V-neck. She added a gold chain and locket. Red always improved everything. She went downstairs to wait.

Nick was dressed in black pants and a button-down white shirt under a gold herringbone-pattern sweater. His hair was slicked back and his cheeks were ruddy. Seeing how nice he looked when she opened the door made her nervous. He was looking at her like she was sexy, which she knew she wasn't. Pretty maybe, but not sexy. Not like Patrice.

"What happened to your freckles?" he asked, touching her nose with a warm fingertip.

She laughed, relaxing a little. "I took them off. I don't wear them everywhere, you know."

He took her to the Orleans Waterfront Inn, a Victorian inn and restaurant, which had a bar and casual restaurant downstairs, and a dining room upstairs. The inn was built on the banks of Town Cove, and both dining areas faced the water.

"I asked to sit up here with the seniors, because it's quiet," Nick stated in a stage whisper.

Beth looked out at the water, where a few colorful boats were moored. "It's lovely. Serene."

He chose a bottle of red wine, and they ordered an appetizer to share.

Nick lifted his glass. "To a perfect night."

She tapped her glass to his, and took a sip to cover her growing anxiety. The sip was more like a gulp, and she hoped he didn't notice, but he didn't take his eyes off her. She turned to look at the view again. She had no reason to be nervous. This was just dinner.

Nick seemed to sense her discomfort, and began to talk easily about the house he was planning to build for himself someday, on an acre of land he already owned. Beth was impressed with the floor plan he discussed, and his ambition. As they chatted, she realized they had much in common.

By the time she was halfway through her second glass of wine, she was feeling better. A flash of her sister's alcoholism and drug addiction came into her mind, as it never failed to do when she enjoyed a drink. She pushed it away and smiled at Nick.

"I'm having a good time. It's been a while since I've enjoyed dinner out. I work too much. And now with Grace...."

"I'm glad. Someone could have snatched you up before I had a chance to meet you." He leaned over the narrow table and kissed her. "I want you all to myself."

She was relieved that before she had to answer, their food came. She'd ordered scallops au gratin; he'd chosen the fisherman's platter.

After dinner, drinking Irish coffee and sharing a dish of bread pudding, they talked about their childhood. "I had the greatest parents," Nick said. "My mom died two years ago and my dad still cries when he talks about her. I have a sister in Pittsfield. She's married and they have two girls, ten and eight. I told you about my brother. And I know about your sister. How was your childhood?"

"It's a boring story. My father was a tough pastor of a small rural church. He and my mother lived for the congregation."

"Admirable," Nick said.

"Patrice and I didn't think so. Our life was all about the church. My dad had a string of mottos: 'Always be on your best behavior.' 'Be a role model for the other children.' 'Do good works of mercy.' Of course, as you know, my sister rebelled. I was the good girl. At least I tried to be. If my father ever knew the lies I told him to save Patrice's butt, he would have disowned me sooner than he did."

"Did he?"

"I insisted on college. By then, my mother had died. He wanted me to stay home and fulfill her mission. He came to my graduation. He patted me on the back and told me now that college was out of my system, I could come home and stand beside him to serve God."

"But you didn't."

"No. I didn't. And he never spoke to me again. Never took my calls, returned my letters."

"Is he still alive?"

"Yes, but he has Alzheimer's. He's in the later stages. I'm in touch with the nursing home where he is, but he probably wouldn't know me anymore. Jeez. How did you get me on this topic? Let's talk about something happy."

He leaned forward, beckoning for her to do the same. "I'd like to take you to bed this minute."

She knew her face was glowing red, so she just laughed. "Nick, you sure know how to change a subject."

"It hasn't changed for me since I picked you up."

"Really?" She swallowed hard.

He looked at his watch. "Want to . . . see my *blueprints* before we go pick up Grace?"

She laughed again, more of an embarrassing twitter. "Maybe another time. I tend to move a little slower. Besides, I hate to be practical, but it's the first time I've left Grace with someone this long. I think I should pick her up soon."

They moved on to easier subjects for the rest of their coffees. For some reason, when Nick said he was thirty-eight, she blurted out, "How come you never married?"

His face turned immediately red, and he pressed his lips into a tight line.

"What, Nick?"

"Well, I told you I wasn't married, because I'm separated. We were married for eleven years. No kids. It just sort of fell apart."

Beth didn't know what to say. She fiddled with the handle of her coffee cup. This was not a relationship she wanted to pursue. She knew there was something wrong there. Why hadn't she followed her instincts? Was she that lonely?

"Say something."

"I think separated is too complicated for me. Anyway, I should be getting back soon."

It was drizzling and cool outside, which was a perfect fit for her mood.

Chapter 20

The week was full of last-minute details for the opening. Grace was home from school for two days with a low temperature and a cold. Two days lost in a crunch of a schedule.

Luckily, she was too busy to think about what had happened with Nick. In spite of a few mishaps, everything was arranged to her specifications, and the store was now ready. Flower bouquets of roses, peonies, irises, and daisies, cut from her own garden, were set around the various areas to add color. The computer was ready for the first sale, and she and Grace had baked dozens of cookies. Beth was sure she'd remembered everything.

Grace walked into the kitchen and smiled at her. She was dressed in her soccer gear and carrying her clean soccer ball under her arm. She placed the ball by the door, and then pulled a chair over to the cabinet to reach a cereal bowl.

A sudden sharp pang stabbed Beth in the gut. "On no." She had forgotten to check the soccer game schedule. Grace didn't hear her. She was blissfully preparing her sport star's breakfast. She reached out and tapped her niece's arm. Grace turned around.

"Sweetie, today is the grand opening of the store. I forgot you had a soccer game."

The look of panic that crossed Grace's face told Beth she'd understood. She began to sign quickly, "I go to game."

"I can't let you go without me. I'm sorry, honey. You'll have to miss the game today."

"It's my last game. No," she signed, purposely turned her head away and filled the bowl with cereal, then hefted the gallon of milk from the refrigerator shelf. She sat down, without looking at Beth, and poured milk over her cereal.

How could she have made such a mistake? She glanced at the soccer schedule, taped to the side of the fridge. But Grace couldn't go without her. No one signed well enough to understand her if anything went wrong. Darn it, it had to be the *last* game.

Besides, she wanted Grace to be with her today. She was her only family, since Patrice could not attend. And Grace had been excited about the opening and loved baking the cookies.

Grace was sneaking peeks at her. Beth hated to disappoint her. They had settled into a great rapport. Even telling her she would make it up to her wouldn't do. Grace loved soccer more than anything she'd ever done.

Nothing to do but be firm. "Finish your breakfast and then go change, please. I know how disappointed you are, but I'll have to call your coach and tell her you can't come."

Grace put down her spoon and pushed out her chair. She came around to stand before Beth, making counterclockwise circles over her heart with her right flat hand. "Please. Please. Please."

Beth made the same sign, but with a closed fist, "I'm sorry."

After Grace stomped upstairs, Beth called Judy, who offered at least ten variations of ways to make it possible for Grace to play. With more apologies to make, Beth was steadfast. It was too much responsibility to have a stranger care for Grace. And she wouldn't be able to pull off her grand opening, into which so many of her reserves had gone, if she was worrying about Grace's safety. No. Her decision was the right one. But she felt like a rat.

A sulking, red-eyed Grace pouted all the way to the store. Beth remembered when she was a child, her parents didn't allow crying. Not for long, anyway. She'd always promised herself when she had her own children, she would allow them to cry until they were finished. Now she understood her parents' philosophy. After the first few minutes of guilt and self-flagellation, Grace's crying set Beth's nerves on edge. Even the reminder of Kristi joining them at the store couldn't end the tears. By the time they had settled in the car, every muscle in Beth's back was strung as tight as a high-wire.

As if she wasn't already a bundle of nerves, she wasn't sure her knee-length blue skirt and muted print blouse were appropriate. She'd never paid much attention to what store owners wore. And her mind was full of all that could go wrong today. People wouldn't come. Or they would come but not buy a thing. Or someone would be allergic to the cookies she'd baked, and the rescue truck would have to be summoned. Or someone would spill lemonade all over the pricey duvet on the high-poster bed.

While Beth filled the trays with cookies, Grace sat at her easel, using mainly black and red to paint an angry picture. At least painting didn't make noise.

Lauren arrived in hot pink-and-green, tropical-patterned capris with a lighter pink top. "Good morning, Beth and Grace. I bear gifts." She set down three coffees and a dozen donuts. "I'll never lose weight," Lauren said, choosing a sour cream donut for herself. That did it. Grace put down her brush and came for her coffee, smiling at Lauren and signing her thanks.

"She's not speaking today," Beth said, opening the pop-up on her coffee cup.

"Oh? Something wrong?"

"I forgot her last soccer game was today. I don't know how I could have done that. There's nothing she loves more."

Lauren laughed. "I think you had a few things on your mind. I don't know how you do what you do. It makes me dizzy to even think about it."

"God, Lauren, I'm so glad you're here."

Scott dropped Kristi off at nine-fifteen, on his way to the office for his morning appointments. He held the door open, ushered in his daughter. He called out to Beth, "Break a leg!"

The doors opened at ten. Several people were already waiting to come in. Beth breathed a thank you prayer to anyone who would listen.

It was Grace's job to pass out raffle tickets to everyone who entered. As shy as she was, Beth was surprised she wanted to do something so social. Beth had set up a stand with pens and pencils for people to fill out the tickets and drop them into her prized salad bowl. The drawing was scheduled for four p.m.

It was a cool but sunny day, crisp and clear. Perfect for shopping but not for the beach. By eleven-thirty, a decent number of shoppers were ambling through the store. Lauren was working the check-out, while Beth moved around greeting the guests and answering questions. One woman wanted to know about organic cotton. A motel owner asked if she carried cot-sized sheets. She did. To another young woman, she explained the different cottons, and how the thread count impacted the comfort of bed linens. She was amazed at how many people expressed pleasure that she only sold products made in the USA.

The lavender items were a big hit; the alcove had a waiting line. Kristi worked the crowds with drinks, cookies, and chit-chat. Grace was handing each new person a raffle ticket and indicating the stand. No one seemed to notice her silence. As a consolation prize, Beth had let her wear her new denim shorts and white eyelet blouse. She also had on her new tie-dyed Vans, and an ankle bracelet she'd made of beads. Cute, and now smiling. Crisis over.

Kristi came up to the counter while Beth was helping Cindy void a sale. "Ms. Henson, everyone loves your cookies, but we're almost out."

"No, I have plenty more in the back. I made extra in case we needed them. I'm glad we did, that means we're seeing a lot of customers."

"I know where they are, I saw them. Ha! I sampled them," Nan, her other new employee, said, chuckling.

Later, Beth set the girls up in the back room with the lunch she'd packed for them that morning. Grace looked a little tired. She was better, but still coughing. "You two are off-duty for a while now. Take a break and enjoy your lunch." Beth shot a longing look to the back room on her way out, wishing *she* could sit and rest a while.

Around twelve-thirty, Troy arrived with the twins. "Hey, how's it going?" He scanned the store. "The place is a knock-out. Great job, Beth." He rubbed his palms together. "What can I do?"

Three of her friends from New Bedford made a surprise visit. After hugs all around, they showed her they'd all bought something. It made Beth realize how much she missed them.

The Tuesday Morning Quilters came in together a little before two o'clock. After Lauren introduced her friends to Beth, she showed the group around the store.

Beth was wondering how many of the eighty-six-thousand, four-hundred seconds in a day were already used up. Her feet were hurting, and her body felt about twenty pounds heavier, harder to drag around. Her smile muscles were shaky, and her stomach was growling. She was thinking about grabbing the stool from the back room, when the bell jingled. She glanced over to see Nick walk in.

He looked great. His hair was wet, as if he had just gotten out of the shower. He was dressed in a pair of khaki shorts, a red t-shirt, and loafers, no socks. Her hand moved, as if it had a mind of its own, to smooth her unruly hair. But inside, she was still angry that he'd misled her, though she knew relief was mixed in. He'd called a few times since their date, but she'd told him she couldn't accept any new problems.

He walked right over to her. "How did it go? Looks like you still have a few people." He checked his watch. "Almost four. Isn't that when you close?"

"It's been a great success. I'm ready for bed." As soon as the words left her lips, she began a slow death of embarrassment.

He smiled. "Really? I see a bed right over there for you." He pointed to the display bed in the front corner.

He must know why her face was red, but she was grateful he didn't make the obvious joke.

"Listen, Beth. Can we get together to talk? I want to explain my situation. I should have told you right away. You just knocked my socks off from the first minute I saw you."

"Nick. Not here. Not today. I'm exhausted and—"

Scott's deep voice interrupted her. She hadn't heard the bell or seen him approach. "I can see what a good day you had, Beth. You look dead on your feet." He turned, extending his hand to Nick. "I'm Scott Adams. You're the contractor, aren't you? Nice work."

If Nick looked surprised, Beth's eyebrows were practically up to her hairline. Scott seemed to know all about Nick, but she couldn't understand how.

"I provided the manpower, Beth drew up the design," Nick said.

They talked together a few minutes, ignoring Beth, which gave her a chance to compare the two men. Nick was nice-looking in a boyish way, with a great sense of humor. Scott was solid and kind. Handsome in his own way. He hadn't addressed himself as *Doctor* Scott Adams, and Beth gave him points for that. Yet she detected an edge of superiority in him as he watched Nick speak. On Nick's part, he stole glances at her, looking as confused as Beth was in his ongoing discussion with Scott.

Kristi tapped her arm and she jumped. "Ms. Henson, it's four o'clock. Aren't you going to pick the raffle winner?"

Beth looked around. It seemed the store had filled up again. Her idea for the raffle had obviously been a winner. "Yes, I will. Right now. Is Grace in back?"

"No, she's over near the bowl."

"Okay, let's go."

Nick and Scott were still conversing. As she and Kristi passed them, Scott put his hand out and touched his daughter's head. A love pat.

The disadvantage of Grace's inability to speak became obvious when one of the Tuesday Morning Quilters won the raffle drawing.

"No, please! I have too many quilts already. Draw again," the woman said, laughing.

On the second drawing, a young boy, nine or ten, came to claim his prize. Beth thought he was cute, and judging by the expression on Grace's face, she thought so, too. Beth smiled. Already? At only eight years old?

As the people filed out, Beth warmly thanked each of them for coming. When she closed the doors the sudden quiet was palpable. She turned around to find Nick standing right in front of her. Over his shoulder, she saw Scott leaning against the counter, his eyes on them.

"Do you have something going on with that guy?" Nick said. "I mean, I'd like to take you out for a drink to celebrate, but I'm not sure where I stand."

"Nick. I told you, I'm not going to go out with you. Even if I was, I wouldn't tonight. I'm dead, and I still have work to do." She noticed Scott heading toward the back of the store.

"Promise you'll give me a chance to explain—and apologize—sometime soon."

Beth nodded her head. "We'll talk." She walked Nick to the door, locking it after he went out. Scott was coming toward her from the back room with Kristi. Beth wondered how much he'd seen or understood of her conversation with Nick.

She joined them, gave Kristi a hug. "Thank you so much, Kristi. You were terrific. What would I have done without help from you and Grace?"

"It was fun, Ms. Henson. Everybody liked your cookies and your store."

"Did you save me some?" Scott asked her.

She looked at Beth and grinned. "Oops."

Beth thanked her two new employees as they left. Next she hugged Lauren. "What a great day. I'm anxious to see the sales report, but I'm too tired to run it tonight. Go home. And Lauren, thank you from the bottom of my heart."

An hour later, the bell jingled one last time as Beth closed and locked the door. Grace fell asleep in the back seat on the half-mile trip home.

The night was warmer than the day had been. A soft scent of ocean saltwater wafted on a gentle breeze. In the stillness, Beth sat on the farmer's porch, sipping Chamomile tea. She felt as if a small engine was still revving inside her, and she hoped the tea would help her sleep. She stared up at the canopy of blinking stars as she thought about the day. Why did she feel like crying? She was exhausted. She was also overwhelmed with the success of the opening. It was a dream she'd had since she was young, and now it had become a reality.

What next? For years and years, she'd had goals, and the last one was now fulfilled. How would she fill the void it left? It should be fun to plan the future, but she had no time right now. She'd be flat-out busy until Grace went home.

Ouch. The thought cut. Beth was playing mommy and loving it. She loved Grace. With all her heart. How would she bear it when she left?

Chapter 21

A sharp ray of morning sun slanted over the sketch pad on Patrice's lap. Sundays were bittersweet. She had childhood memories of spending long, boring hours in church, while her father ranted on about sin. Now, Sundays brought her beloved daughter to her. But they also took her away.

Tomorrow was going to be an exciting day, and she was going to miss it. Beth would take Grace to the audiologist to begin creating the hearing map, which Patrice understood as tuning up the electrodes already implanted in Grace's ears. Then they would turn on her processor, and Grace would hear sounds for the first time since she'd had meningitis. Patrice ached to be there to watch.

Her pencil moved over the scene she was sketching of her daughter, surrounded by the things she would learn to hear again: birds, television, buzzing bees, music, the voices of her mother and aunt. The picture made her feel good. She was happy Grace would hear again. At least she'd *better* hear after all the emotion Patrice had wasted over the implants surgery. She stopped sketching and shook her head. She was her own worst enemy.

Every day she was thankful for the enormous favor Beth had undertaken for her. She'd so looked forward to being on her own, and the delay must have frustrated her. But it didn't keep her from taking on this implant business. Patrice had finally read all the medical literature. It was a long process. What a sister.

Patrice was now stronger. Her cravings were more manageable. And hearing from Frankie had given her another reason to stay clean.

An hour later, she sat in the visiting room. She watched her sister and Grace enter. She noticed how much more Grace looked like Beth than her. Both with shiny black hair, fair skin, and dark eyes—Beth's caramel brown; Grace's deep, forest green. At the thought, her hands tightened into fists. Then Grace spotted her and all doubts flew from Patrice's mind. Grace's face lit up with a big smile as she let go of Beth's hand and ran to her mother.

They sat together, looking at pictures and reading Grace's journal. At one point, Grace told her how much she loved drinking coffee, after which her face went white.

"Beth, Grace tells me she's drinking coffee now."

Beth, seeing Grace's fright, smiled and patted her on the shoulder. "She has a tiny bit to flavor her milk. It won't hurt her."

"I'm proud of you, Beth. You're not the goody-two-shoes you used to be. You'd never have done that without asking me before."

"I wasn't a goody-two-shoes. I just obeyed our parents. For all the good that did me."

"Come on, you were their right-hand man, or girl. But you thought they never appreciated that. You think they never *saw* you. In fact, they relied on you." Patrice smoothed her hand over Grace's hair. "You haven't talked to our father since college, but you're still trying to please our parents."

"Wow. You have me all figured out."

Patrice ignored her remark. "When I think back to those days, you were always working, helping out."

"There's nothing wrong with helping out, Patrice."

Patrice watched as Beth crossed her legs and set the top one swinging. "Do you make Grace do chores?" Patrice asked, smiling.

"No."

"That says it all. I'm proud of you."

Beth changed the subject and Patrice let her. They discussed the first mapping session. She could see Beth was nervous about it, too. What if it didn't work? They would all know tomorrow. Beth had permission to call and tell her how it went. If she believed in God, Patrice would have prayed that Grace would be able to speak again.

Beth was rubbing mineral oil into the kitchen's maple countertops. As soon as the oil sunk in, she began vigorously polishing the surfaces. Every so often, she let her right arm drop by her side to rest it. Then she'd be at it again. She couldn't rub out her thoughts, though. Tomorrow was hours away. After school, Grace had the appointment with the audiologist. Beth had to remind herself why she'd taken on the cochlear implants: because all the doctors recommended them; because Grace was profoundly deaf, and no hearing aid would help; because Patrice and Grace both wanted her to have them. Mostly, because of all the good she'd read about them, that they were Grace's best chance to hear and speak like other kids.

But would she?

At ten o'clock, she put away the oil and rags. She'd worked off some tension, but not enough to go to sleep. She picked up the pile of the day's mail and carried it to the rocker in the sacred space. Dumping the junk mail on the floor, she opened the bills and sorted them, then placed them on the floor in a separate pile. She leaned her head on the back of the chair and began to rock. As she closed her eyes, a sense of peace washed over her. Her arms and legs felt heavy, relaxed. She was sure Grace would be able to hear something when they turned on her processor tomorrow. She didn't know why, but she was positive it would happen. Breathing in the scent of lilacs, she became drowsy. A thought drifted into her mind: Who was Lizzie, the one whose name was carved into the fieldstone? Grace was curious, too. Maybe they could find out.

The hearing room was full of people Grace knew; even Kristi was allowed to come, and the cool girl with purple hair. Her teacher, Mr. Hamilton, smiled and nodded at her, but she couldn't smile back, her cheeks wouldn't work. Ms. Jenny came, and her speech therapist. They were all talking to each other and laughing. Grace wished she could hear what they were saying. Aunt Beth sat close to her, in front, so she could take a video for mommy. She looked scared, like she felt. Why couldn't mommy be here? She wasn't sick anymore. She was always smiling now.

Why didn't she come home?

Grace shivered again and wrapped her arms tightly around herself to get warm. Aunt Beth signed, "Cold?" Grace nodded and pumped her fist. Aunt Beth stood and looked around the room, but then everybody got still. Julie also stood. She smiled at Grace. "Hold your hands like this," she signed, and then cupped her own hands together. Still smiling, she put the four parts of the implants into Grace's hands. Then she picked up one of the processors, put it over Grace's left ear, and wiggled it around. Next, she took one of the transmitters, with the pretty purple cover Grace had chosen, and leaned behind her. The weird feeling when it attached to her head made her jump.

Julie signed, "That's just the magnets."

Grace squeezed her hands together. What if it didn't work? What if she couldn't hear?

While Julie worked on her right ear, Doctor Scott stooped in front of her and put his warm hand on her cold ones. "Are you ready?" he asked.

"Yes," she signed, and he moved away.

Julie tapped her on the shoulder. She raised three fingers. Grace couldn't breathe. Julie counted down, three, two, one. Then she tapped her computer keys.

She heard sounds! *Sounds*! She started to cry but it turned into a laugh. Then her mouth dropped open as she *felt* the sound, and she cried out. Then she jumped when her own voice made a sound in her head.

"Grace, can you hear me?" Doctor Scott said.

She covered her mouth with her hands to hold in a big burst of laughter. She breathed in and signed, "I can hear you!" Then she let out the peals of joy. Everyone was clapping and laughing with her. She heard the noise of them but not the words.

She reached up and touched the transmitters on her head with the tips of her fingers. Then she signed, "Doctor Scott, you sound like Mickey Mouse." Then she laughed harder.

Aunt Beth came to hug her. She was crying, so Grace put her hands on her aunt's cheeks. "Thank you, Aunt Beth," she said, hearing the noise of her voice. Aunt Beth hugged her again.

Grace stood and walked over to Kristi. "Speak," she signed.

"Pretty soon you'll be talking like me," Kristi said and signed, shaking with giggles.

"I didn't understand the words, but I can hear you!" Grace signed, and clapped her hands.

She put her fingers gently over the transmitters again and giggled as she turned and looked at the people in the room. She felt like she was going to burst. All she wanted to do was run and skip and laugh.

Everyone crowded around her, signing congratulations and good job and patting her shoulder or giving her a hug before they left the hearing room.

Aunt Beth came and held out her arm. It was time to go home. She was so happy she wanted to cry again. And then she was so sad, she wanted to cry. She wanted her mommy so bad. Aunt Beth understood and signed, "I know." Then she held up her phone. "Let's go home and send mommy the video."

Doctor Scott came and stooped before her. Before she knew what she was going to do, Grace hugged him as tight as she could. She felt him laughing and heard the rumble of it.

When she let him go, he rose up. "I have to go back to work, but I won't miss the celebration later." He smiled again then gave Aunt Beth those funny eyes he always had when he looked at her. It made Grace giggle again.

Kristi held her hand as they walked out to their car. She was coming home with Grace now, and her daddy would come at dinnertime.

It happened again. She wanted to cry. Why couldn't her mommy come, too?

Dinner was in the oven. The two fat taco pies Beth had assembled early that morning were filling the kitchen with the aroma of chili powder, onions, and melting cheese. She was chopping tomatoes, lettuce, and onions to go on top when the pies were finished baking. The girls were upstairs in Grace's room. They were quiet. Beth wondered what they were doing.

Scott sat at the kitchen table, a glass of scotch over ice in front of him. Beth felt a little nervous. This was a switch from their professional relationship, now having become something homey. She didn't want to say the wrong thing, but she couldn't think of the right thing.

"Am I making you nervous?"

"No, of course not. Why?"

"You've had your lips squeezed between your teeth for the last ten minutes. I'm thinking I may have to operate before I leave here tonight."

Beth laughed. "I didn't realize. Yes! You do make me nervous."

"After all this time?" he said. "Why?"

She took her glass of wine and sat at the table with him. "I don't know. You're the *doctor*."

"I'd like to be more than that to you." He watched her, and then said, "You're biting your lips again."

Beth smiled and bowed her head for a minute. When she looked back at him, he was waiting. Not a man to waste words. Inside, she felt the same warmth she had every time he looked at her lately.

"What are you thinking?" He took a swallow of scotch.

"I'm trying to make the switch. To think of you without your stethoscope, so to speak."

Scott nodded. "I think I've diagnosed the problem: You don't know anything else about me. Do you want to?"

"I do."

"I was born in Boston. My parents were teachers. I have one brother and two sisters. Everyone lives either in the Boston area or Connecticut. I went to medical school in Virginia, did my internship and residency at Mass Eye and Ear. I was married in my second year of internship. It lasted six years. She's married to a banker now, I think. It isn't easy being married to a doctor in training. Or maybe at all." He paused, giving her a direct stare for a few beats. "Anyway, we had Kristi, and I'm eternally grateful for that."

"You have custody?" she said, trying not to bite her lips again.

"Kendra takes her a couple weeks in the summer and here and there. She lives in Seattle. I was awarded custody with visiting rights for Kendra. She wanted it that way; she had to go find herself."

Beth could hear the pain in his voice. She picked up her glass and drank. The fragrance of the pies was stronger now. The girls were playing loud music, and someone was stomping around. *Joy.* She focused on Scott. "I was never married. I went with someone for quite a while. He got tired of waiting for me. I was always too busy with my family. He wanted his own family, and I was too wrapped up in my crazy life."

"Your sister and Grace."

"Yes. You know about my sister." She chuckled. "Things haven't changed much in that respect. I guess I'm still mired in her issues. There wasn't a choice, but you know, having Grace turned out to be the most wonderful thing for me."

The oven timer went off, and Beth rose. "I made a Jell-o mold for the girls, in case they don't like the pie. I need to unmold it."

"How about I set the table?"

They fell into kitchen work together. After Scott set the table, he poured everyone a glass of ice water. When it was time, he went to call the girls, while Beth took the pies out of the oven.

The girls clattered down the stairs and entered the kitchen. Beth looked at their red and sweaty faces. "What have you been doing? You both look like you were working out."

"I was teaching her how to dance," Kristi said, glancing over at a grinning Grace.

Beth laughed. "Really?" Then, "Wait. Could she hear the music?"

"Not much yet. She had to hold onto the box so she could feel the beat. I was getting her ready."

Beth sliced the first pie and slid a piece onto each plate. Ten minutes later, she served seconds to Scott and Kristi. Scott ate half of the Jell-o mold by himself. They laughed and talked in-between bites. Beth watched Grace straining to interpret their words. At one point, Scott noticed her, too. "Don't work so hard, Grace, it will be easier after Julie turns on the next level."

Everyone had stopped to hear what Scott was telling her. When Grace signed, "Okay, Doctor Mickey," they all laughed again.

When dinner was over, the girls went to the living room to watch one of Grace's DVDs. Scott was loading the dishwasher. Beth smiled at how precise his method was compared to her own willy-nilly placement.

They carried the coffee Beth had made into the sacred space. Once they were seated, Scott faced her and said, "I am truly amazed at Grace. She's already hearing and seems to understand some of what is said. She's been deaf for over two years. I don't know how she's doing it."

"I'm surprised, too. Deliriously happy, but surprised. And you should have heard my sister. She called after she saw the video I took and was almost hysterical with joy." Beth tilted her head at him. "You kind of prepared us for the worst-case scenario."

He was sitting in one of the wicker chairs, with his legs stretched out in front of him and crossed at the ankles. "I had a feeling Grace would get more benefit. She's smart. I could tell by her level of speech-reading and signing. And her desire to communicate is strong. But I expected it would be slow going with that much time being deaf." He shook his head. "I'm glad we were able to do the implants. I can see she'll be talking in record time."

"Scott, this is something a little strange. Grace tells me she can hear the words in her books when—and only when—she reads them in this room."

His smile was warm and dimpled. "She's quite the kid."

"But don't you think that's strange?"

"She reads a lot?" Beth nodded, and he went on. "That may be why she can already make out some words from the sounds she hears through the implants. She's accustomed to hearing her own inner voice."

"Maybe, but she calls the voice she hears reading her books, 'the lady.'"

Grace begged for Kristi to stay longer. While Beth was signing to her that it was a school night and Kristi had to leave, she was aware of having the same feeling as her niece. She didn't want the evening to end. She didn't want to go back to Scott the doc. She liked Scott the man.

Chapter 22

It was Saturday, after dinner. Grace's ice cream cone was melting faster than she could lick the drips. She giggled in-between slurps. They sat on the benches outside her favorite ice cream shop, The Local Scoop. Beth marveled at how happy they were together. Not the way Grace was with her mother, but as a team, making it through a tough time with mutual respect. And love. The thought made her ache a little around her heart. How could she go back to her life without Grace? Beth pushed the worry away. It would work out. She would adjust. They both would.

"When you're finished, let's go over to the bird store. See it, over there?"

A fat drop of ice cream plopped on Grace's sneaker. She laughed again, and then shoved the last part of the ice cream cone into her mouth.

After Grace washed her hands and face in the shop bathroom, they left the car there, and walked to the Bird Watcher's General Store.

"I've never seen so many different feeders for birds. Look at them all," Beth signed. Besides the plethora of feeders hanging from the ceiling and walls, there were also squirrel baffles, poles, all kinds of seed, and bird books. Even dishes and clothing, all with a bird motif. They stood and laughed at a video of a squirrel being spun off a feeder. "Should we get that one?" Beth asked. "Or that one?" She pointed to another.

Grace chose the model in the video.

When they left, they carried a feeder, enough seed to get started, a book on the birds of North America, and a pamphlet on Cape Cod birds, all back to the car.

Now it was June and the days were growing longer, fooling Beth into thinking she had more time. It had been two weeks since the store opening and life had changed. Cindy and Nan were up to speed and Lauren's Friday afternoon help gave her time to share with Grace. The rest of the time, her life *was* the store, and a thought occasionally surfaced: Maybe the store was more work than she meant to undertake. She considered the possibility that this fear was only because she was not yet adjusted to two stores. When Grace was back with her mother, being a shopkeeper would be easier.

The store was open ten until five, six days a week. On weekday mornings, they were up early, eating breakfast and packing lunches. Beth dropped Grace off at school and went right to the store. She did her accounts, refilled shelves, and neatened anything out of place. Sales were still good. She knew the novelty of the new store hadn't worn off yet, and she expected sales to drop off some, but she was happy to make up some of her initial investment while it lasted.

In the afternoons, Cindy or Nan took over, so Beth could pick up Grace from school and run a few errands. She would come back to the store with Grace in time for closing. Sundays, they drove to Fall River to visit Patrice. It was a crazy schedule and Beth was up late most nights. But she was having fun, and Grace didn't seem to mind spending time in the store with her. She was even helping Beth replenish the stock.

When they finally arrived home and emptied the car of their birding collection, Beth felt the weight of fatigue. Dusk was fading to darkness, but Grace was excited to hang the feeder. With a loop of wire from the garage, Beth stood on a ladder and secured the filled feeder to a strong branch on the Butternut tree outside the kitchen window.

"Will the pretty bird come back now?" Grace signed.

Beth usually encouraged her to speak now that two more mapping sessions had advanced her ability to hear. Tonight, she didn't mind the relapse. "I don't know. We'll have to watch," she signed back.

Grace sat on the grass under the tree, obviously prepared to wait for the first bird to arrive at the feeder.

Beth knelt beside her. "Grace, try hard. Can you hear any birds singing?" she asked, holding her index finger in the air, as if she was testing the wind direction.

Grace's eyes dropped to the grass, not moving a muscle. After a few minutes, she signed, "I don't. Do you?"

"No," Beth said. "I think it's past their bedtime. How about we go in and watch TV. Tomorrow we'll listen again."

On Sunday morning, Beth woke up after eight. She jumped out of bed; she rarely slept so late. She padded downstairs in her nightgown and searched for Grace, who had already made her bed. She wasn't in the sacred space or the kitchen. Beth walked faster to the living room, dining room, and office. She ran back upstairs to check the bathroom. It was empty.

Almost panicked now, she flew back downstairs and screamed, "Grace!"

She heard something and ran to the kitchen. Grace had her nose pressed on the screen, her hands cupping her eyes to see inside.

"Did you hear me?" Beth asked, opening the screen door and stepping out on the porch.

"Yes, did you hear me?" Grace signed with a serious expression.

"I heard something. What did you say?"

"I said, 'outside.'"

Beth grabbed her and hugged her. "I can't believe how amazing you are!"

Grace smiled, took Beth's hand and led her to a chair. She put her finger to her lips. "The birds were here. They'll come back," she signed.

Patrice was waiting in the visiting room. "You're late. I was worried."

"Sorry, I overslept."

"You know, Beth, I get a couple hours a week with my daughter. That's all."

Beth bit back a retort that came to mind, she knew, only because she was tired. Patrice was right. This should be a happy time for all of them. She smiled at her sister. "I know," she said, with compassion clear in her voice.

After mother and daughter talked for a while, Grace looked to Beth with an expectant smile.

It was her signal to make an announcement. Beth cleared her throat to get her sister's attention. "Patrice, Grace has something to say to you." She nodded at her niece.

"I love you, mommy."

Beth's breath caught. It was pitch perfect.

Patrice had tears in her eyes as she hugged Grace. "I love you, too," she said into her daughter's shoulder.

"I heard you, mommy," Grace said.

Patrice laughed as Grace told her all about the progress she was making with her implants. And how Kristi was teaching her to dance.

When Beth could get a word in, she told Patrice about the store, and then Grace went on about the bird feeder. When there was another break in the conversation, Patrice said to Beth, "You remember meeting Frankie, don't you?"

"I do. Years ago. Why?"

"He was the one whose party I went to. . . ." Patrice swept her hair behind her ear.

"Yes. I know." Beth didn't want to have this conversation. Patrice had a dreamy smile on her face that worried her.

"He wrote me a note to apologize. Beth, he's still in love with me." She patted her chest over her heart.

Beth felt a sinking sensation in her stomach. "Didn't you tell me you aren't supposed to be in a relationship for a year?"

"Six months to a year. But this isn't a new relationship. Frankie is like my significant other. We've been in love forever."

"Patrice. You haven't seen him in years. And then when you did, he had a houseful of addicts. What are you thinking?"

Patrice knitted her eyebrows together. "It wasn't his house. It was a friend who threw the party. Frankie doesn't do drugs. He is not an addict."

That made Beth feel only a smidgeon better. "So, he said in the note he was still in love with you?"

"He didn't say it that way. But I could read between the lines. He said how sorry he was about my being in rehab because of him and how much he wished he'd never asked me to come. He said it was a rare event when he got together with the old group because he's so busy with work and all. And he said he hoped we could still be friends."

"He does sound like a nice guy," Beth said with some relief. "I hope that you'll wait until you're back on your feet with Grace home before you attempt to get together again."

"Why? It's not like he's a new boyfriend. Remember my dream? Even when I told you I would like to marry and have kids, I was thinking about Frankie. I knew I still loved him when he kissed me that night." She knotted her fists. "If only I hadn't taken anything. I could just kick myself."

Grace tapped her mother's shoulder, looking from her to Beth with a question in her expression. Patrice smiled at her. "It's nothing, honey."

"Mommy," Grace said, then went on in sign. "Why won't you come home? You aren't sick anymore. Don't you want to come home?"

Patrice hugged her. "I want to come home but not until I'm completely better. The doctor has to say when I'm all the way better. Just like your doctor does."

"But when will he tell you? I wish you could come to live at Aunt Beth's now. She could take care of you."

Beth sucked in a breath and held it.

"Honey, when I'm well, we're going to have a brand-new place to live. You and me."

Grace glanced at Beth, and nodded at her mother.

On the way home, Beth experienced a sense of uneasiness. This could not be good. Frankie was at a party where people used drugs. Patrice should not associate with that group again. Then a new worry formed: Could Frankie be Grace's father? Patrice would never talk about Grace's father. A chill ran over her as she pictured a home with Frankie and Patrice and Grace. And drugs.

Chapter 23

Lauren arrived at Linens & Lavender at two p.m. "I have news," she sang out as she sailed through the door.

"It must be good, you're smiling," Beth said.

"Troy's going back to work. His doctor gave him permission two days before a great job came up. He'll be the master electrician. That guy is one happy man. No way he'll ever want to be Mr. Mom again." She leaned in front of Beth, standing at the checkout island, and tossed her purse underneath.

The first thought that went through Beth's mind was: She would miss her Friday afternoons off. But she said, "That is wonderful news. Troy must be so relieved. You went through a bad time, but you never complained. You and Troy qualify as my ideal couple."

"Ah, thanks. I came in early today to talk about summer when the boys are out of school. Troy starts his new job next week, right when school lets out. So, he won't be able to watch them when I come to work in the afternoon."

"Don't even worry about it. I'll work things out with Cindy and Nan."

"Hey, lady. Are you firing me?" Lauren asked, with her hands raised in front of her.

"What?"

Lauren laughed her great, deep chuckle. "I still want to work for you if you'll have me. I love being here. I love chatting to the customers and making sales. It's adult stuff that's manna to me after being with Jake and Benjie for hours on end."

"I'll take you anytime you can be here. I'm sure Cindy and Nan would love you to fill in so they can have a little beach time this summer. Who will watch the boys when you're here?"

"I've got it all worked out. Troy's niece is home from college for the summer until the end of August. She cleans rooms at a motel four hours every morning, and I hired her to babysit the boys on the afternoons I work. She's agreed, so we're all set."

Beth drove Grace to the speech therapist later that afternoon. It was a lovely warm day, one of the first beach days of official summer. It lifted her spirits. She was thinking how well it all was working out and what a waste it is to worry when Grace tapped her shoulder.

"I know Lizzie."

It took Beth a few seconds to interpret what Grace had said. "Lizzie?"

When they pulled into the parking lot, Beth shut off the engine and turned around to face Grace. "What about Lizzie?"

"She died. She was five," Grace signed.

"You mean Lizzie's Lilacs? How do you know?"

"The lady told me a story," Grace signed, then watched her aunt closely.

"Oh, a story. From one of your books?"

"No. True story. I asked her." She spoke the word 'no' and signed the rest.

Didn't she just tell herself how great this was all working out? Did she now have to worry that her niece was hallucinating? "Let's talk more about this when we have dinner. I want to hear the whole story, but, right now, Mrs. Murphy is waiting for you."

"She got sick and died," Grace said, each word distinct, as if she'd practiced.

Beth wasn't sure what to say. Grace had been through so much trauma, she might be upset about the garden plaque and need to settle what it meant in her mind. It seemed harmless, and Grace was telling her the story in a calm manner.

"That's too bad," Beth could only say.

"She had shoes with a button strap on them. And she only wore dresses," she signed.

"The lady told you that?"

"And the rocking chair was her mommy's. She rocked Lizzie until she died."

"Take a bite of your dinner." This was more than a simple explanation. It was an interesting story. Maybe she would make Lizzie's story a summer project for Grace.

As soon as she swallowed, Grace put down her fork. "Aunt Beth," she said. Then she signed, "Where do you go when you die?" The last word, die, was a graceful sign: flat hands held out in front, one palm up, the other palm down. Both moved in an arc to the left, reversing the up/down positions on the way.

She decided to be as honest as she could without showing the scars of her own upbringing. "I don't think anyone knows for sure. Some people believe you go to heaven and live forever happy. Others believe you come back to live again."

Grace's green eyes stared out the window for a moment. "The lady came back."

Beth couldn't answer. She had to remember to ask Patrice to have this discussion with Grace. It was clear she needed to know more.

"Grace, let's go to the Historic Society and see if we can find out about Lizzie. You could write her story. What do you think?"

She nodded with her fist. Beth was pleased.

As Grace cleared and Beth put the dishes in the dishwasher, Nick came to the open door.

"Anybody home?"

Grace ran to let him in. She gave him a salute, which he returned.

He looked across the kitchen at Beth. "I thought I'd stop by and see if you had a few minutes to talk."

Beth tapped an adoring Grace on the arm and waited until her eyes were on her. "Nick and I are going to talk a while. You go do homework. I'll call you to say goodbye to Nick later."

"Okay," she said, clearly understanding Beth's words. Grace worked hard to hear everything she could. She got excited at each new type of sound enabled by the regular tweaking of her implants. Beth never tired of watching her growing mastery.

"Cup of coffee?" Beth asked Nick after Grace disappeared.

"Love one."

"I'll make a pot. You talk."

Nick laughed softly. "I'd rather wait until we're sitting face to face. I want to look at you while I explain, see your expression, because I need to know how you feel."

Beth took her time, trying not to anticipate what was coming. She knew there could be no relationship while Nick was still legally married, and she was pretty sure it wouldn't make any difference if he was free. But he was a nice guy, and she didn't want them to be enemies. Besides, he was a great contractor, and she wanted him to update her kitchen at some point.

"Go ahead, Nick," she said, once she served their coffee and was sitting across from him.

"Thanks for agreeing to hear me out. I'm not trying to make excuses. I should have told you right away. I didn't realize how fast I would be attracted to you, and by then, it was too late. I just hit you with it. I don't blame you for being mad."

"It wasn't anger. You caught me off guard. The way you told me you weren't married made me think you were *never* married."

"I didn't mean to deceive you, but I did want to give you that impression. It was easier than explaining, and I didn't think you'd go out with me if I told you the truth." He took a sip of coffee. "Mmm, good."

"You've been separated for two years, you said?"

"Yep. And you're wondering why I'm not divorced."

Beth nodded.

"We were married young. I was twenty-two. Seven years into the marriage, my wife was injured. She was in a car accident and her knee was smashed. She had surgery, but her saphenous nerve was crushed. From then on, she's been disabled and still suffers bouts of pain.

"The truth is, our marriage was floundering before the accident, but I'd never mustered up the nerve to suggest divorce. We were just two different people and were growing apart. Once she was injured, it seemed cruel to bring up divorce, but a year later, I moved out with her blessing."

"Is she better?"

"She's limited. There are still times when the pain knocks her down. It's hard for her to work a steady job."

Beth smiled. "You're taking care of her."

"Yep. It wasn't a problem before. But after our dinner, I went to talk to her about a divorce. She was pretty upset. She asked for time to find a way to support herself. Maybe disability. I gave her six months. I'm going to do everything I can to help her. She's covered right now on my insurance plan."

Beth dropped her head into her hands. "So, you *are* the good guy I thought you were." She looked up.

"Don't overdo the credit. I've been pretty lazy about it all. You gave me a reason to rethink that."

She didn't know what to say. Here was this nice man sitting across the table, who was basically telling her he would work to be free for her, and she wasn't having the reaction he seemed to hope she would.

"You're not answering." He raised a hand. "You don't have to. I wanted you to understand. I was living in the status quo, and now I'm going to fix that. Can we be friends until I'm free to ask you for more?"

"Thank you for telling me. Yes. We're friends." Should she tell him now that's all they could ever be? No. She had to take the time to think it out.

Grace came to say goodbye. Nick patted her on the head, and then shook Beth's hand. When the door closed behind him, and she could hear the fading sound of his Jeep's engine, she felt a little sad.

The Orleans Historic Society was open Thursday through Saturdays during the summer. On one of their free afternoons it was pouring rain, so Beth and Grace went there to research Lizzie. It looked like a simple clapboard building from the outside, so when they entered, Beth was surprised. A plaque told her the building had served from 1834 to 1971 as the Meeting House of the First Universalist Society of Orleans. The ground floor had alcoves along both side walls, filled with historical exhibitions. An upper gallery ran along the sides and back of the building.

"Can I assist you with something?" a small, bent-over woman with silver hair asked in a high, soft voice.

Grace frowned at Beth and pointed to her cochlear implant. She could not hear the woman's words.

"I'll tell you after," Beth signed, then turned to the woman. "We have a cottage on Bay Road. I think a child named Lizzie lived there years ago. If you point us in the right direction, we'd like to do some detective work on her."

"My name is Dianne. I'm happy to help you. It's been a quiet summer so far." She turned to Grace. "So, you want to know about another little girl who once lived in your house?"

"I'm sorry," Beth said. "I'm Beth and this is Grace." She put her hand on her niece's shoulder. "She's deaf. She's learning to hear and speak again with her cochlear implants. It will be a while before she can hear different pitches of sound and learn to understand them as words."

"Oh, poor dear. She is sweet. So pretty." She raised a crooked hand to her white hair. "My hair was the same color as you and your daughter's when I was young." She turned and gestured upward. "You should start with the census records. Do you know the year the child lived there?"

"We only have a hint. The child wore only dresses and the straps on her dress shoes attached with a button."

"You have a picture?" she asked, leading them upstairs to the gallery.

"Not exactly. I think we should start looking a couple years after the turn of the century."

They searched through census records and town directories for two hours. Dianne kept bringing them more to research. It was in a 1913 directory where they first found her: Elizabeth Porter. Daughter of John and Abigail Porter, residing in Knoll Cottage.

Beth sat back in her chair, savoring the historical connection. A family, years ago, had lived in her house. What had it looked like then? Was there indoor plumbing? How did they cook their meals? Wash their clothes?

Grace was busy writing the information in her notebook. Meanwhile, Dianne brought the next ten years of directories. They were quaint. Some entries had personal information, such as: so-and-so's daughter is attending teaching college. Or their businesses: barber, shopkeeper, fisherman.

Little additional information was written on the Porters until 1919; then the directory listed only John and Abigail. Beth felt a chill rush through her. The child would have been six years old, but she was not listed. She decided not to mention it to Grace. She leaned forward to look at Grace's notes.

"What a great job. Are you ready to go?"

"We need more," Grace signed, then pursed her lips.

"Ten more minutes. It's getting late and I'm getting hungry."

As she cooked dinner, Beth turned the story of Lizzie she'd heard from Grace over and over in her head. She tried to figure out how she would have known the child was five years old when she died.

Chapter 24

"I was hoping you would want to discuss this with me, Patrice," Doctor Harper said. "Of course, I read the note."

"I know. I wasn't keeping anything from you. I needed time to figure out what to do. Frankie and I were in love years ago. I did something stupid and ruined the relationship. Drugs." She stared at the doctor.

"He took drugs with you?"

"Oh no. Frankie didn't use. I took the drugs and went off with this other man I thought I was mad for. Long story, but Frankie moved on. My friends told me he finished college and went to work. They didn't see him much. Then I got pregnant with Grace, and I knew I wouldn't ever have another chance with him."

"This is the first time you've heard from him since then?"

"Yes. When he called and asked me to the party, I was so excited to hear from him. I knew I shouldn't go, but I still loved him, and I couldn't believe he might still be interested in me. Now I know how I should have handled it. If he wanted me at the party, I should have invited him to do something another time instead. Meet for coffee or something else safe."

"You have better tools to stay clean. That's very good, Patrice. So you should realize you need to use those tools now. Right?"

"I've been thinking about what to do. I'd like to communicate with him. Explain to him that I need to work on my rehab right now, and get my daughter back as soon as I can." She swiped at her nose with the palm of her hand. "But I'm so afraid I'll lose him again." Patrice spoke in a whisper.

Doctor Harper pushed back in her chair, making it squeak.

"What if you helped me write a note to him? Explain it?" Patrice raised both hands in supplication.

"I don't think it's a good idea. You're not ready to get reacquainted. And think of Grace. She needs to be home with you without suddenly having a stranger to deal with."

"I wouldn't do that. I couldn't. I can't wait to have Grace back. I only want him to know I need time, but that I still love him."

Doctor Harper remained quiet.

"You know I'm not religious," Patrice filled the silence. "I wish I were, but my father took care of that. I envy these women who find strength in some god. I made my own higher power someone to love and have a family with. That's my goal. For me and for Grace. She needs a father, a brother or sister. I've never loved anyone else the way I love Frankie. Doesn't that count for something?"

Later, Patrice walked the grounds. The smell of fresh mown grass and the warmth of the sun made anything seem possible. She had to make a decision. Only a note, maybe, asking him to wait for her?

Grace was afraid to go on the boat, so Beth had turned down the invitation the first time Scott invited them.

"Grace, why are you afraid of the boat?" Scott asked on her next check-up appointment. "Kristi loves it, and she wants to teach you how to fish."

"I could drown," she said.

"Your pronunciation is terrific. You're my star patient." He tweaked her cheek. "But I would never let you drown."

"I'm afraid."

"I bet you don't know how to swim."

Beth was captivated. She was sure Scott was assessing her speech and hearing. He was keeping Grace distracted, so she wouldn't think about being tested.

Grace shook her head.

He looked at Beth. "We should fix that," he said, smiling, as if they were coconspirators. He turned back to Grace. "We have jackets on the boat that won't let you go under the water. Everybody has to wear one on my boat. Even if you can't swim, the jacket will make you float. Did you understand that?"

Grace nodded her fist.

"What? What did you say?" Scott said, one hand cupping his ear.

Grace giggled. "Yes."

"Would you like me to teach you to swim?"

Her eyes grew big and she reached for Beth's hand. "No."

Scott rubbed his chin. "Did you ever see a seal?"

"Yes," she said, running her fingers down her long braid.

"How close?"

She shrugged her shoulders.

"If you come onto the boat, you will wear your jacket, and I'll bring the boat close to a special place where there are a number of seal families."

She took the bait. The following Sunday afternoon, weather permitting, they were going for a boat ride. Beth, almost as excited as Grace, volunteered to pack a picnic for them.

The visit with Patrice on Sunday morning was pleasant. Beth tried to remember the last time her sister had seemed so carefree. They sat outside in a private garden. It was a beautiful late June day. She hoped the weather would stay that way for their boat ride later. By unspoken agreement, neither Beth nor Grace mentioned their afternoon plans.

Beth was surprised at the sight of Scott's house. It wasn't showy or overly large, but rather homey and inviting.

Kristi came to greet them. "Come on. We're all ready to go," she said, relieving Beth of one of her tote bags, and then led them around the side of the house. The back of the property jutted out into the channel. A long staircase led down to the water, where a long dock extended out into the water. Scott was already on the boat, and when he saw them, he jumped off and strode down the dock to greet them.

He smelled like a combination of soap and coconut as he reached over to take Beth's insulated food bag. His feet were bare. He was wearing navy blue swim trunks with a white t-shirt, which gave her pause for a few beats until she readjusted to Scott the man. Since the dinner they'd shared when Grace had her implants activated, she'd only seen Scott in the office. Summer was his busier time as more elective surgeries were scheduled. But he'd called in between appointments to chat with her about Grace's progress.

Grace seemed to be changing her mind. "Don't be afraid, Grace. It's fun!" Kristi encouraged.

Scott brought her a bright-yellow life jacket. Without a word, he helped her into it and zipped it up, then clasped the belt. "Now you are drown-proof."

Beth knew how frightened Grace was. Life with her addicted mother had left her full of fears, but she'd worked hard to overcome them. Beth wanted to run over and hug her.

Kristi walked in front of them along the dock to the boat. Scott waited until she climbed aboard then lifted Grace over the side. When the boat wobbled, she let out a small cry. Kristi led her to a seat and sat beside her, keeping up a running conversation.

Scott took Beth's hand and held on as she stepped over the side and settled her sea legs. Then he joined them. "Kristi's my first mate, so why don't you sit with Grace as we get underway?" He turned to his daughter. "Kristi, see that everyone has a life jacket on, then report to the Captain."

When Kristi's mate chores were completed, she went over to her dad. "All set, Captain."

Beth, sitting in the mate's chair, put on a visor to help keep her hair from blowing about as they sped across the water. She looked back at Grace. She'd turned her baseball cap backwards, like Kristi's, and her right hand was nearly white from gripping the side of the boat. But she was laughing at the sprays of water splashing on her face.

Scott looked back at the girls then smiled at Beth. "I think Grace likes it."

"I think she *loves* it."

"Want to drive?" he asked with a grin and raised eyebrows.

"Sure." She moved over to the wheel. Scott explained the different dials and apparatus to her. "Ready?"

He stayed close by her side while she drove. Not the first boat she'd driven, growing up in New Bedford, but the biggest. A Bayliner 340 cruiser, he'd told her, thirty-three feet long. When she turned to smile her delight, Scott was looking at her with a pensive expression that made her catch her breath.

After three slow passes around a gray seals' family compound, during which Grace took multiple pictures with Beth's phone, they dropped anchor in a nearby cove. The circle of blue water was surrounded by high, wooded lots with gray-shingled houses nestled in the greenery.

Scott set up a table where they sat and ate their lunch. He raved about Beth's lobster rolls, macaroni salad, crisp veggies and dip, and dark fudgy brownies. He went on long enough to make her glow.

When what remained of the food was cleared away, the girls went below deck to the galley to make drinks with a soda machine.

"I'm so happy," Beth said. "Grace is having a ball. She's forgotten all about being afraid. I've watched the way you handle her. You expect she will do a particular thing, so she does it. You've done a great job with Kristi, too. She's wonderful." Her lips parted a little as it occurred to her that it wasn't control, it was support Scott gave, and encouragement.

"Thanks. Kristi's special. So is Grace, brave and intelligent. She's opened up so much since she's been with you."

"I'm sure it's the implants. She's learning quickly. I can't believe the progress she's made."

"Don't underestimate your influence on her. She loves you and she watches for your approval. How's her mother doing?"

"Really well. She's like her old self."

"All good news. What about you?"

"What about me?"

"You know, all you do for Grace, busy with your store. How's that working out?"

"If the timing weren't so bad, I'd say perfect. It's hard on Grace. She's stuck there with me for long days, but she's doing fine."

"More than fine, I think." He stood. "I hope you have your bathing suit in that bag. We're going swimming."

"You're kidding, right? The water must be 60 degrees."

"Suit yourself. That's a pun." He grinned. "It's invigorating once you get used to it. The water's warmer in the cove, too. Trust me." He removed his glasses and slid them into a cubby on the side of the boat.

"I think I'll just watch you instead."

Kristi was in her swimsuit and had talked Grace out of her life jacket long enough to put on her own suit. She climbed up from the cabin with big, dark eyes, walked right over to Beth and sat close beside her. Beth noticed she'd removed her cochlear implants, and wondered what it must be like to not hear again. Not the boat engine, the voices around her, or the lapping water. Only silence.

Scott came and stood before them and signed, "Aha! Look at this! Grace isn't being a party pooper. She's going in." He pointed. "You and Aunt Beth, come stand in the back. Kristi and I will go into the water first. Your aunt will help you over the ladder, and I'll be right there to help you down."

He didn't give her a chance to say no. He went to the back of the boat and jumped into the water. When his head popped back up, he let out a howl. Laughing, Kristi jumped into her father's arms. They both swam back to the ladder.

"Okay, Grace. Come on in," he signed, while kicking to stay afloat in the deep water.

To Beth's utter surprise, Grace pulled her by the hand to the ladder. Grace then crab-crawled over the side, and Scott helped her put a foot on the second rung. She looked up with pleading eyes to Beth, but only for a second. She scrunched her eyebrows, pressed her lips together, and started down.

When she hit the cold water, she stopped. Scott came to her side and signed. "Go for it, little daredevil."

Grace reached one arm out to Scott, but still held onto the ladder. Kristi swam up behind her dad and waved her encouragement at Grace. Grace looked up at Beth again, then let go of the ladder. Beth saw the panic on her face, and was just reaching out to pull her back up, when Grace began to scream. She thrashed, kicked, and struck out so much that Scott lost his hold for a moment—long enough for Grace to gulp seawater in her sheer panic.

Without a thought, Beth jumped into the water. By then, Scott, his expression pained, had a good grip on Grace, who was gagging and coughing. Beth wrapped her arms around both Grace and Scott.

When Grace saw her, she grabbed Beth's neck with one arm, but held onto Scott with the other. The three worked their way to the ladder, while Kristi climbed on board. It was like a silent movie, in which everyone did their part but no one spoke a word. Grace was the one who needed verbal consolation, but they were all aware she couldn't hear them.

Kristi put her arms around Grace and held her until Beth was on deck and hugging her niece, and then Kristi ran below to retrieve some towels. Grace was sobbing and shaking and her lips were blue.

Scott knelt in front of her and signed, "I'm so sorry, honey. I would never let anything happen to you." When he signed 'you' by pointing a finger at Grace, she reached out a hand and wrapped her fingers around his. Beth felt her heart melt. For Grace. For Scott.

The weeks were rushing by. Grace and Beth were enjoying their easy summer schedule. Grace was bringing a new sketch or painting each week for her mother to critique. She had pictures of the beach, seals, shells, lifeguards, sand castles, and sundaes from The Local Scoop. The Fourth of July parade pictures made up a whole new album. She was excited to show her accomplishments to her mother each week, but Beth worried that it might seem as if Grace were no longer missing Patrice. That she was having a terrific vacation without her. But Patrice was nothing but happy for her daughter every Sunday. And every Sunday, Beth breathed a sigh of relief. Patrice seemed at peace and so strong.

Before Grace walked all the way into the visiting room, she began to sign, "Mommy, I can swim by myself. Watch." She air-demonstrated her freestyle stroke.

Beth smiled. Scott had been so upset about Grace's water trauma, for which he'd felt responsible, he was teaching her to swim on Sunday evenings, when most of the crowds were gone. They met at Skaket beach, a short distance from Beth's cottage. Most weeks, Lauren and her family joined them, and Troy and the twins joined in the swim lessons.

The water was shallow enough at the bay beach for Grace to stand. Scott had her wear the life jacket at first, so she didn't associate it only with the boat. He told Beth he planned more outings, and he didn't want Grace to be afraid to go back on the boat. Beth liked Scott the man more and more, though it was confusing to her where she stood in their relationship. It seemed to be all about Grace. He couldn't treat all his patients with this loving attention. He hadn't made another move toward Beth since he said he'd like to be more than a doctor to her. Except for a few special looks that made her heart thump a little harder. Patrice's answer to Grace interrupted her reverie.

"Pretty soon, mommy can come and see you swim. Keep practicing," Patrice said, and then turned her smile on Beth.

She blinked. "What are you talking about?"

"I could be an outpatient soon. I'd be moved into the halfway housing, but I'd still go daily for therapy and group. I would have to be in job training or working, but the vocational rehab therapist will help set that up. If I continue to do well, the rehab center could petition the court for my early release."

"Really? Patrice, I'm so proud of you." She patted her sister's hand.

"Thanks. That means a lot to me."

Beth wanted to jump up and down. Patrice was making such great progress. And the fact that she could move to a halfway house instead to transition into her new life on the outside was awesome. Beth hoped they didn't release her entirely before she'd spent some time there. She complimented her sister again, and then she began to talk about the great sales at the store and the new sleepwear products she carried. In spite of her excitement for Patrice, she had a hollow feeling in the pit of her stomach. The reality of life without Grace was creeping up on her. How would she adjust? How much harder was it for Patrice to have been without her daughter all these months? Beth resolved to get to work on a plan. Another reason to get something going was the strange fact that Patrice hadn't mentioned Frankie again.

Chapter 25

Angie was leaving rehab. Though Patrice couldn't say they were friends, she had to admit they were comfortable with each other. Angie was a known factor, and now she'd have another roommate to get used to. Patrice hoped it wouldn't be for long before she was packing her own suitcase. She sat on her bed and watched Angie pack her duffle bag.

"Where'd all this shit come from?" Angie asked. She shoved the items deeper so she could close the zipper.

"How long have you been here?" Patrice said.

"Six months, two days and some long minutes more. I can't wait to go out that damn door."

"Will you be all right?"

"Of course, I will." She lowered her voice. "Once I get some stuff in me."

Patrice stood. "Angie, what are you saying? You worked so hard to get clean. Don't fall back into drugs."

Angie gave her a slow smile. "Never been off for long."

Patrice stared at her. "What do you mean? You had drugs in here?"

"Shut up. I never said that." She looked worried.

Patrice sat back down, staring at the floor. "Take care, Angie," she said, without looking up. She waited until the door softly closed. Her shoulders drooped as she cradled her head in her hands. Angie had somehow smuggled in drugs? It was clear she couldn't wait to be free to take more. Would Patrice be strong when her time to leave came? Could she deal with the temptations out in the world? She thought she could. She had to.

It was her free time. No exercise today. She went to sit at her desk to write to Frankie. She'd written several letters to him, but only one of them she'd sent. Now she wrote to him because it made her feel as if they were connected. Today instead of words she made him a sketch. She drew herself walking with her suitcase toward him, holding Grace's hand. He held his arms open. He was grinning at them. When the picture was completed to her high standards, she tore it up and took the pieces with her to the bathroom.

※

It was a slow day at the store because it was a gorgeous day for going to the beach. Kristi's Aunt Lisa came in with Kristi, who ran to the back room to get Grace.

"Grace is so excited to find out how much she can hear at the movie. It's so nice of you to take the girls."

"I wish it had worked out that you could join us," Lisa said.

Lisa had come to the beach with Scott and Kristi a few times, and Beth liked and trusted her. Still, she was nervous letting her niece go without her. "Not as much as I do. But I'm sure you'll give me a blow by blow." Beth grinned. "So will Grace."

The girls came out signing to each other. Grace was wearing jeans on this hot day. She told Beth she didn't like her skin to touch the seat at McDonald's, where they were going to eat lunch before the movie.

After they left, Beth finished every bit of busywork she could stir up in the store. She'd flipped through online catalogs for what seemed like an hour but was only twenty minutes. Now she was leaning on the checkout counter daydreaming.

She was thinking about Patrice. Beth was thrilled that if the court agreed to Patrice's outpatient status, she wouldn't have to continue her treatment in Fall River, as long as they could satisfactorily place her on the Cape. Beth would continue with custody of Grace until DCF approved her return to Patrice. When Patrice left the halfway house and was able to live on her own, Beth thought she could stay at Knoll Cottage until she found a home. She grimaced. It could only be for a short while. There could be no return to Patrice's dependence on her, or her own codependence. Though she would support Patrice any way she could, her sister would have to live her own life. She knew the treatment center would help find employment for Patrice, and that would decide where she would live. Beth hoped it would be on the Cape. Once her sister was settled, after a delayed start, Beth would focus on her new life. Without Grace.

She was more than impressed with Patrice's accomplishment. Beth realized, deep down, she'd never thought her sister could be successful at rehab. Now, she was full of confidence. Especially with the controlled steps Patrice would take from inpatient rehab, to outpatient in a halfway house, to work, to independence, to having Grace back with her. She liked the plan to invite Patrice to stay with them for a short while. It would fun. Beth couldn't wait to tell her.

Lauren came in and broke the doldrums for Beth. She cleared her throat, then said, "I've noticed at the beach, Scott's pretty attracted to you."

Beth wrinkled her nose. "Do you think so? It seems to be all about Grace."

"Ha! No, it doesn't." Lauren pulled a bag of Dove dark chocolates from her purse and dumped them into the candy dish on the counter. "You think that?"

"This conversation feels like high school." She looked down at her feet then back at Lauren. "But I'm glad you brought it up. I just can't tell whether he's interested in me or not."

"Do you want him to be?"

Beth searched the ceiling for an answer. "I do," she said, unwrapping a piece of chocolate.

"It's a good thing, then, because he is. It's written all over his face when he looks at you. I can't believe he hasn't said anything. You know, like: Let's do dinner." She bobbled her head.

A slow grin crept over Beth's face. "How *does* he look at me?"

"Like he wants to jump your bones. Wow, this guy sure has shown restraint. What's that about?"

She crossed her arms over her chest. "I wish I knew, I'm not even sure you're right, Lauren. If he's interested, why doesn't he say something?"

Lauren reached for a chocolate. "I'll start my diet tomorrow. No, on Monday. It's always good to start at the beginning of the week. Don't you think?" She slapped her hand on her forehead. "Why am I asking *you*?" She chuckled, then slid the candy into her mouth and closed her eyes. "Anyway, you have one man with too much restraint and another with none. Speaking of the devil, how's Nick?" she said, around the chocolate.

"I don't have time for a romance, let alone figuring out men. Nick's getting a divorce in about six months. For me, he says. I don't want him to do it for me. He's a nice, successful guy, who's taking care of his wife instead of divorcing her. Wouldn't you think I'd be ecstatic this guy wants me to wait for him?" She threw up her hands. "But I'm not."

"You probably don't love him. Simple. He should get a divorce anyway. A guy that cool shouldn't be allowed to prey on women. He needs another wife to nail him down."

Beth laughed. "I thought I wanted to marry another guy a couple years ago. It didn't work out. How did you know Troy was the one?"

Lauren tilted her head and smiled. "It was the kiss. When he landed the first kiss on these lips," she pointed to her mouth, "we locked onto each other. I knew right away. So did Troy. We never went out with anyone else again." She focused on Beth. "Nick's kissed you, right?"

Beth nodded. "I didn't feel the lock."

"Has Scott kissed you?"

"No. I told you, he never shows any inclination of wanting a relationship with me."

"*You* kiss him."

"What?"

"You do it. Kiss him."

Beth was still snickering when a customer came into the store.

Chapter 26

"Beth, may Grace stay at my house for a sleepover? My dad says it's okay if you agree. Grace says she wants to. May she?" Kristi's excited words were strung close together.

"Oh, honey, I don't know. She's never stayed anywhere overnight without me."

She heard some background discussion, before Scott came on the phone.

"The girls put me up to this. They're having a great time. The house smells like popcorn and cupcakes. I don't want to unduly influence you, but remember; independence is our goal for Grace."

"I know the hesitation is only on my part. She adores Kristi. I'm sure she'll be all right. You'll be there, for heaven's sake."

"Not the whole time, I hope. But while I'm gone, Lisa will stay with the girls. She really took to Grace when they went to the movies."

"Oh. I'm sure it's okay. I'm just a little nervous. She hasn't been away overnight before. Will you be gone long?"

"Depends, Beth. Will you go out to dinner with me?"

They sat on the deck of the Pearl Restaurant overlooking Wellfleet Harbor and Marina. A slight breeze cooled the still-warm day. The open umbrella over their heads added a sense of privacy. Scott wore a black polo shirt and khaki slacks. His face and arms were tan from the boat and beach. He smiled at her and she watched the dimple form. She'd grown quite enamored of that dimple.

"I didn't think you'd come, Beth," he said, clinking his martini glass to hers.

"Why not?"

"I wasn't sure you were free."

Beth laughed. "My social life is extremely demanding. *Not*. It's such an unusual pleasure to be out to dinner." The words echoed in her memory. She hoped this dinner would turn out better than what came to mind.

"I'm glad you're enjoying it, but that's not what I meant by being free. I thought you might be involved with Nick—to be blunt." He sipped his drink while keeping his eyes on her.

"No, but I understand where you got that idea. The day of the store opening. I did have dinner with Nick once, but we're only friends." She cringed at what sounded like disloyalty. Saying it out loud made her face the truth, and she realized she had to let Nick know how she felt.

Scott grinned. "That was the hard part. I was sure you were going to say something else."

Beth smiled back at him. "I was sure you were never going to ask."

Scott ordered a bottle of Chardonnay to go with their fried scallop platters. Beth didn't worry about the glow she was feeling from the drinks. She was having the best time she'd had in years. Scott was entertaining and funny. She'd seen hints of his humor before, but tonight he made her laugh out loud. They shared a piece of decadent chocolate cake surrounded by whipped cream and strawberries. Spooning a dessert while looking into Scott's warm brown eyes seemed more intimate than it should have. When their knuckles touched, her skin tingled.

After dinner, they strolled around the town pier then sat for a while on one of the benches. The sun was low and the evening breeze soft, seaweed scented.

Scott let out a long sigh. "I'm so glad we did this. Let's do it again. Often." He kept his eyes on the horizon as he spoke.

"I'd love to," Beth said, hearing Lauren's words inside her head, *you kiss him.*

When they arrived at her cottage, Scott came around to open her car door. He draped his arm around her shoulder and walked her to the porch. He leaned against the doorjamb, watching while she pulled out her key and unlocked the door. Her hands shook a little. She couldn't stop thinking about Lauren's advice, and she felt like a nervous schoolgirl.

"Thank you," she said. "It's been a wonderful evening."

He reached for her wrist and gently pulled her to him. He lifted an unruly curl of her hair and let it spring back. Then he bent over and whispered in her ear, "If I don't kiss you, I'm going to die."

"Please don't do that," she whispered back. Then she slid her arms around his neck and kissed him. He wrapped his arms around her, pressing them closer, and deepened their kiss. She felt like she was floating, melting, hot. She never wanted the kiss to end. Before it did, though, she felt the lock.

Her own feeling of total joy, and the sensation of levitation as she walked around the next few days, was what made Beth realize that Patrice was in love, too.

On the next Sunday, she watched the loving interaction between Patrice and Grace. Her sister raved over the pictures of Kristi's room and the twin bed Grace had slept in. Grace read three sentences out loud to her mother from her journal. Patrice kissed her and hugged her. They talked together for a while.

"You have a cell phone?"

Grace nodded and pointed to Beth.

"You did that for her? Bought her a cell phone? That is so sweet of you, Beth. Isn't she a little young, though?"

"It's for her safety. She has limited use of the phone part, but I wanted her to be able to get in touch with me at any time. When she stayed overnight at Kristi's, I was pretty nervous. I knew I'd have felt better if she'd had a phone to check in with me.

"She's a great photographer, as you can see. So I don't limit the number of pictures she's allowed to take." As soon as the words reverberated in her mind, she waited for her sister to react in the negative. But she didn't. She was smiling. There were no sharp words about who should make decisions for Grace. Patrice didn't challenge a thing they talked about regarding Grace.

Patrice was too happy. The same kind of happiness Beth had been enjoying since her dinner with Scott. And a couple follow-up phone calls. Could Patrice be this happy from only her *dream* of life with Frankie?

"I'm dying to talk to you about moving to the halfway house," Beth said when Patrice and Grace finished catching up. "I'll bet you can't wait. Have they talked anymore about placing you? I was hoping they could place you somewhere on the Cape. That would be wonderful for Grace; me, too. I've researched 12-Step programs and there are plenty around. I'm sure DCF will want you to visit Grace more often. Then, once you finish your assignment and leave the halfway house, you can stay at the cottage for a couple of weeks. I'll help you find your own place—"

"Mommy! Mommy! You can sleep in my room with me like before." Grace had been listening with interest to the conversation. She'd frowned at her lack of understanding about the words *halfway* and *assignment*, but her smile grew as she heard the invitation to stay at the cottage. Grace understood that she couldn't live alone with her mom for a while yet. She clapped her hands together and did a little pirouette between the sisters.

Beth was laughing at her when she glanced at Patrice. For the first time in a long time, she seemed angry. "What's the matter, Patrice?"

"Beth, you can make a decision to buy your niece a phone without asking me, but you have no right to make any decisions about my life."

Beth gasped. What had just happened? "It wasn't a decision. It was an offer to help."

"You can't control me. I'm not going to the Cape. That's your place. My home, and Grace's home, is in New Bedford."

"Why would you stay there? Do you have job prospects?"

"I've given a lot of thought to our future, Grace's and mine. I have a plan, too."

"Good," Beth said, trying to smile, but shaking inside. "What is it? Or don't you want to say?"

"My plan is to get a job as a cook. And to live back home."

Beth stared, dumbfounded. It was clear to her that she was falling into her old habits. She was trying to control Patrice's life. She was arranging it for herself so Grace would still be close to her.

"You are the one who left us. Remember?" Patrice whispered, facing away from Grace.

What could she say? Patrice was right. It seemed like years ago, and that they were different people. Now she desperately wanted to be close to Grace. Couldn't imagine life without her. Grace was so happy and she loved her school, her teachers, her soccer friends, Kristi. Beth pushed her hair off her forehead. She'd made a complete circle. For months, she hadn't given a thought to her need for independence. Only about how hard it would be when Grace went home.

"There's more." Patrice broke into her thoughts. "I plan to marry Frankie. I love him."

"How could you make plans to marry him? You haven't seen him since that party."

"Don't worry. I'm not rushing into anything. The center's going to help me find an apartment when I finish my assignment. I'll work day hours so I can be home when Grace is out of school." She turned to her daughter. "Sweetie, won't you be happy to see your old school friends? Won't it be wonderful to be home together again?"

Beth heard the vulnerability in Patrice's voice. She turned to see Grace's reaction. She shrugged her shoulders and pointed to her cochlear implant. But her face had turned white, and her eyes were glistening with tears.

Patrice leaned over and hugged her. "It's going to be wonderful. It won't be for a while, though. Mommy has to finish getting better, but maybe in another place. But it's not going to be much longer."

Grace turned into her mother's arms and buried her face in her shoulder. Patrice smiled down and kissed the top of her head. "I can't wait," she said to Beth. "Right now, I don't even think about drugs. Haven't for ages. They make sure we understand we'll go through periods of weakness, but they teach us to recognize trigger points and how to overcome them." She reached over and squeezed Beth's knee. "I'm so happy, Beth. I've never been this happy *and* drug-free." She laughed.

Maybe she was wrong about Frankie. Maybe he was just the anchor Patrice needed. Maybe he really loved her. He had a job, a career. Patrice insisted he didn't take drugs. The thought of a life with him surely made Patrice happy. She took in a deep breath. She worried about Patrice too much and had to stop. "I'm sorry, Patrice. You're right. I only want the best for you."

"I know. It's just that you have to trust that *I* know what best is for me." She put her hand on Beth's. "We'll still come visit you and you'll come to our home to see us. I want you to see how strong and grounded I am. I love cooking and I'm looking forward to working at something I enjoy. I'll even have time to make some art. I'll be fine. I promise, big sister."

Beth told herself she still could have as much as six months to get ready, during which she'd remember how much she'd wanted to be independent. Loved building up her retail business. And wasn't she happy? Didn't she have a whole new wonderful relationship with Scott? She was overjoyed about that. How could she not want the same joy for her sister?

The shoe was on the other foot. Was this how Patrice felt when Beth moved away?

"You deserve to be happy," Beth said. "We'll see each other often." She raised her index finger. "We'll cook together. I'll share the recipes that you love."

"Thanks, Beth. I'm sorry about your idea. And I'm grateful for the offer, but I have to be independent, too."

The ride from Fall River to Orleans was quiet. Beth was looking into her future. She wondered what Grace was thinking. They both would work it out in time.

Chapter 27

It was nearing the end of August. Beth was shopping with Grace for back-to-school clothes. She'd grown a couple inches taller since she came to live with Beth. DCF was delighted with her progress in speaking and growth, as were her teachers, her audiologist, and her speech therapist, and especially Scott. Beth was now officially her foster parent. DCF's goal remained the same: to reunite Grace with her mother. Beth felt she was emotionally prepared for that. She would adjust to seeing Grace on visits, and she fully expected Grace to pull away from her and be closer to her mother. As it should be.

Everything in her life was good. She was madly in love with Scott. He loved her back. They both loved Grace and Kristi.

The store sales had dipped over the summer, both online and in Orleans. It wasn't unexpected, but she hoped it wouldn't last. Lauren was planning to work more hours when the twins went back to school. Beth was busy lining up promotions to stimulate gift buying for the upcoming holidays. Life was good. She could manage the changes coming.

She was holding up a pair of jeans to check the length against Grace's legs when her cell phone rang. She'd changed the ringtone to rock music so Grace could hear it. It thrilled her every time Grace looked over when she heard it ring. It was Patrice.

"Really? September? When in September?"

"The Thursday after Labor Day."

"Oh my gosh! That's soon. Grace will be so excited. Me, too. We can't wait." Grace was tugging at her arm. "I'll call DCF and let them know."

"There's even more exciting news. My halfway house is on the Cape! I'll be able to visit your cute cottage again. Hey, can I do some of the cooking?" She laughed.

"Really? What happened to going home? Never mind, don't answer that. I'm thrilled. And not only can you do some of the cooking; you *must* do some of the cooking!"

When she ended the call, Beth stooped down in front of Grace. "Mommy is moving to the house I told you about. It's going to be near us, too."

Grace clapped her hands and danced around, and quickly came back to Beth. "Then she will live in our house after?" she asked with big eyes.

Beth gritted her teeth. She had to set things straight right away, and begin the process of separation. "Mommy will visit the cottage for a few weeks. Then Mommy will get her own place ready for you to move in with her a little later."

"Why can't we stay together?" Out of habit, her fists, in the A-position, joined to make a forward circle: *together*.

"Oh, we'll be together for a long time yet. Don't worry."

It was enough. They went back to shopping, Grace often skipping beside her instead of walking.

Dianne from the Historical Society called to say she'd gathered some interesting information on Lizzie Porter. Grace was eager to go. Their summer had been so busy they hadn't been back to do more research. This morning would be their last chance before school started.

"You did an amazing job on this," Beth told Dianne, looking at the stack of papers, postcards, and photos.

"I enjoyed it. I wanted you to see it all before we end our summer hours. And besides, I had plenty of time."

Beth put a hand gently on Dianne's shoulder. "Do you want to tell us about what you found?" She watched the woman smile at sharing her discoveries.

They sat around the table. Beth signed as Dianne spoke, though she thought Grace could understand a good deal of it.

"When Abigail and John Porter died," Dianne began, "Abigail's niece came to empty the house to get it ready to sell. She found a large box in the attic filled with all these papers and pictures. She read through everything, including letters Abigail's sister had written to her, and thought they might have some historical value. She donated all of it to the town. When the Historical Society was opened, the town passed on the information."

"Why did the niece think it would have historical value?"

"Because Lizzie died in one of the deadliest pandemics in 1918, the Spanish Flu."

It took over an hour for the full story to be told. Grace was enthralled, and it was clear to Beth she was empathetic at hearing about the life of another little girl who had once lived in the cottage.

"You see, Abigail and John never thought they would have a child. They were so happy when Lizzie came along. The letters from her sister and notes in the baby book show her delight. "When the first case of flu was found on the Cape, they took Lizzie to Abigail's sister in New Hampshire to keep her safe. Unfortunately, despite this flu having been less common in children, Lizzie became ill with the flu anyway, and her parents brought her back to nurse her at home.

"According to a letter John Porter had written, Abigail sat in a rocker and held Lizzie as she died. Her grief was so deep she couldn't accept that Lizzie was gone. John had to have help to take the dead child from her mother."

Beth looked at Grace. Her eyes were bright, but she turned and rifled through the box. She held up a picture and showed it to Beth. A little girl with short hair posed for the camera in a white dress with a dropped waistline and a pair of white shoes with a strap that buttoned.

"Yes," Dianne said, "exactly how you described her."

Beth stared at Grace, who was holding the picture close to her chest. The hair on Beth's arms was standing up. "Grace, is this the same picture you saw? Do you have it at home?"

She bit her lower lip and shook her head.

"How did you know about her shoes?"

She shrugged her shoulders.

Dianne was looking from one to the other. "I wanted to tell you one more thing. The Porters were buried in the old town cemetery. I made you a map," she said, giving the paper to Beth.

No matter how she tried, Beth could not get excited. She was nervous about picking up her sister and taking her to the halfway house in Hyannis. Oddly, after days of breathless anticipation, Grace was also subdued on the way to Fall River. When she ran ahead to greet her mother, her gait seemed stiff to Beth. Exactly how she felt herself.

Mother and daughter walked toward her, holding hands. The three had a swaying group hug then climbed into the car. Patrice got into the back with Grace. Beth told herself she understood. Patrice was making an approved visit to the cottage for dinner before she checked into the halfway house.

Beth had so much extra food from her Labor Day cookout she had plenty to serve for their first dinner together. They fixed their plates in the kitchen, and ate al fresco at the table on the farmer's porch.

Grace talked more than she ate. She kept up the conversation by signing while she chewed. "Mommy, will you come to school with us tomorrow?"

Beth cringed, but Patrice smiled and said, "I'd love to see your school.

What's your teacher's name again?"

"Ms. Simpkin," Grace said, working hard on her pronunciation.

Patrice looked at Beth. "Who?"

"Ms. Simpkin. Some consonants are hard for Grace to hear in the new words she's learning."

"Simpkin," Grace said again, clearer. Then nodded.

Beth leaned over and hugged her, and watched Patrice do the same. As if they were tugging a rope back and forth. It would take a while for them to settle in. The visits would be twice a week now. One after school on Wednesdays and one still on Sundays. Patrice was enrolled in a training class for cooking, and the vocational rehab counselor was researching employment for her.

When Grace went off to take her bath, since they were taking Patrice home soon and would be back late, Beth and Patrice were alone. Mosquitoes were biting on the porch, so they moved into the sacred space.

"Can you tell me why you changed your mind and came to the Cape?" Beth asked, rocking in the black rocker.

"I had time to think about it. It was something I hadn't considered until you brought it up. Being close to you—not too close," she smiled, "sounded better and better."

Patrice was lying. Beth had too much experience with her sister's lies not to see it. She could pick it right out. "What happened to your dream of Frankie?"

"Nothing, Beth." Her voice was petulant. "I told you I wasn't going to rush into anything. It's not fair to Grace. And besides, I was thinking of you. I know how close you are to Grace right now, and I thought it would be mean to move so far away."

"I'm very grateful you changed your mind. I love you both. We'll work on our skills to keep our relationship healthy."

"Right. And if Frankie wants me, he can come to the Cape," she said, a small smile tugging upward on one side of her lips.

Grace had dried her shampooed hair and pulled it into a high pony tail, which partially hid her purple transmitters. They got back into the car and drove to Hyannis. When they pulled up to the halfway house, Beth was surprised.

"It looks so homey and welcoming."

"Wait till you see inside. When I came before, I met my new roommates, three of them. We've already vowed to help each other through this last step before we're back on our own."

The house was an old white farmhouse, well-maintained and freshly painted. There was a front porch surrounded by high blue hydrangea bushes. They climbed the stairs and went through the front door. The living room was furnished in brown faux-leather couches and chairs, covered with colorful toss pillows.

"Welcome, Patrice. Glad you're here," a fifty-something woman, who introduced herself as Greta, greeted them. "And who is this beautiful little person?"

"This is my daughter, Grace, and my sister, Beth."

They were given a tour. All the while, Greta talked about the rules of the house. "Of course, we have a no-tolerance policy for drugs or alcohol. We all clean up after ourselves. We expect you to keep up your medical appointments. You are responsible to keep your bedroom clean. This is a non-smoking house. If you smoke, you get one warning. If you smoke again, you are evicted.

"We have rehab programs that run through the day, there's group and individual counseling. In addition, you are expected to attend at least three 12-Step meetings a week, and any house meetings are mandatory. You'll be subject to random drug testing."

They were standing in what would be Patrice's bedroom. There were four beds. Posters decorated some of the walls.

"Mommy, will I come here to live, too?"

"No, sweetie, mommy will be here a little while and then I'll be all better. But you can come visit, and I can visit you and Aunt Beth once in a while."

"Make sure you inform the house manager if you'll be away overnight," Greta added.

Grace cried when she said goodbye to her mother. Beth knew it was overwhelming for her to see her in a new place that didn't include her again. Patrice had a discussion with her before they came. She told Grace that some medicines made her sick, and it was hard when she had to stop taking them, but she had. Now she was learning to cook and starting a job soon, so she could afford a house for them. During this trial period, she would keep learning about being healthy. When Grace came to live with her in their new home, her mother would teach her, too.

In spite of Grace's tears, Patrice was ecstatic. "I can't believe I'm finally here. Almost on my own again. I can't wait to get to work and earn some money. My life is so different and happy." She hugged Beth. "Thank you for helping me get through this. I can never repay you for all you've done for Grace, but I'll keep trying," she said, laughing.

Monday morning, Beth was in the store working on the computer. There was a predator online writing nasty things about Linens & Lavender, which she deleted. She could hear Lauren telling Nan about the twins. They all looked up when Nick came in.

"Good morning, ladies. I see we have a new employee?" He waved at Nan.

When the introductions were given, Nick asked if he could speak with Beth. She could feel the eyes following them into the back room.

"How's it going?" Nick said.

Beth's palms felt damp. Though she'd had every intention of telling Nick her feelings and about her relationship with Scott, as with everything else, she hadn't found time. Secretly, since he hadn't been around, she'd hoped she'd never have to tell him. Now he was here. "What did you want to talk to me about?"

"I wanted to tell you, it seems my ex has found a way to take care of herself." Two vertical lines over his nose were deepened by his frown.

"Isn't that a good thing?" she said.

"Yes, sure." He paused and looked around. "It's a guy apparently."

"Uh-huh. So, good for her. And you."

"Who knows if it will work out?" He smiled. "I wanted to update you. You know, I'm not letting you get away." His smile was a little lopsided.

"Nick. I don't want you to do this for me." She watched his eyebrows go up. "I mean, it's something you should do for yourself. And your ex-wife, right?"

"I don't think he's good for her, at all. It sure didn't take long to replace me. Did she just glom onto some guy to pay her bills? What does she know about him?"

Beth felt herself relax. He was letting her down easy! She felt like giggling. He was upset about his wife dropping him on demand. She wasn't sure how to answer. Or even if he wanted an answer.

"Look. I just wanted you to know what's going on."

"Thank you, Nick. I hope everything works out."

He took her hand and gave it a little shake as he'd done before. "I'll let you know," he said, flashing his great grin.

Lauren and Nan were quiet while Nick walked out, then Lauren turned to Beth, who couldn't stop smiling. "You told him?"

"I didn't have to. He sort of told me he was still in love with his wife." Lauren laughed out loud. Nan looked confused.

"He was a guy I went out with once," Beth told her. "He assured me he was going to divorce his wife, but it didn't work out that way. Thank goodness for me. I didn't have to tell him about Scott." Nan had met Scott previously in the store.

"So, you're sure?" Lauren said.

"About Scott? Oh yes. He's my man. My one and only." Beth grinned.

"Good choice. I was rooting for the hunky doc." Lauren sighed. "Poor Nick, back with the ball and chain."

"I think that's just what Nick wants. I'm not sure he realizes it yet. I hope he does before her new guy scoops her up."

Chapter 28

Grace was laying out her shells on the floor of the sacred space.

"Quahog, jingle shell, deep sea scallop, moon shell, boat shell, common razor clam." She looked up at Beth and Patrice, brushing sand from her hands.

"Where did you learn all those names? In school?" Patrice asked.

Grace shook her head.

"Aunt Beth?"

"Not me. I only know two of them."

"Grace, who taught you the names of the shells?" When Grace shrugged her shoulders, Patrice said, "Is it a secret?"

"Yes." Grace stared at the old rocker Beth was sitting in.

"Was it the lady?" Beth asked in a low voice. She had seen the same unfocused look on Grace's face before when she looked at the rocker.

"Who is the lady?" Patrice said.

"She's a friend of Grace's who reads stories to her." Beth nodded at Grace. "Right?"

"Yes." She picked up the shells, then ran off down the hall.

Patrice looked at Beth. "Someone at school?"

"No. At the library." A white lie. It bothered Beth that Grace was still seeing her lady. She seemed to be so well-adjusted otherwise. Patrice had come for a supervised Sunday visit. Beth decided not to worry her with it. When they moved away, the lady business would surely be over. A pang shot through her, but she ignored it.

Patrice wasn't at the halfway house at the usual time after her therapy. Beth and Patrice spoke daily since her sister had her own cell phone. The call rolled to voice mail, and Beth left a message.

When Patrice still hadn't answered her phone by two o'clock, Beth began to worry. It was foolish, she knew. It could be any number of things, as simple as being caught up in some chore. Beth mentally kicked herself and went back to work.

Later, as she waited by her car for Grace after school, she tried Patrice again, but didn't leave another message. She watched Grace running to the car. Her expression was gleeful; she was excited to play soccer.

"Did you have a good day?"

Grace nodded and jumped in the car.

"How did you do on your math quiz?" Beth tried again.

"I got all the problems right."

"OMG, Grace!"

It always made her niece laugh when Beth used the kids' jargon.

When they pulled in to park at the field lot, Beth put her off her worry and watched Grace practice.

"What happened?" Beth asked, when Patrice finally called.

"They changed my appointment. I forgot to tell you. Sorry. Now I have another afternoon group I have to attend. It's mandatory."

"Your phone was turned off," Beth said.

"I know, I know. I'm sorry. I forgot to put it back on after my therapy session." Her voice turned sad. "It was such a difficult session."

She's lying again. Beth felt a cold knowing chill seep into her bones.

❦

Frankie's small silver cottage had two bedrooms; one had bunk beds, the other a queen. The living room and eat-in kitchen, and a tiny screened porch, looked out onto a small pond. The cottage was probably no more than 800-square-feet, but to Patrice, it was a dream house.

She'd decided to actually mail one more letter to Frankie. She'd poured her heart into it and knew it was too good to rip up and flush. Just one letter, so she could stop fearing that he would meet someone else before she could see him again.

They had continued to correspond, hiding it from the center, and Beth. He loved her. He loved her so much he told her he began the process of finding a job on the Cape. Patrice had everything she wanted now: sobriety; the love of a good man; a hearing, speaking daughter; and a loving sister nearby, who would want to babysit. Everybody would be happy. Patrice couldn't believe how lucky she was. In time, she would tell Beth, but not yet. She would use these private visits to get reacquainted with Frankie.

They met every day after her lunchtime NA meeting near her cooking class. Patrice told herself as soon as she'd completed her assignment, she would start the discussion with Sue at DCF about her relationship with Frankie. Before she told Beth, whom she knew would be negative about it. If she could only understand how happy Patrice was. How wonderful Frankie was. What a great father he'd be for Grace. Patrice was going at this slowly, carefully. Today was the first day she'd come to his cottage.

Frankie led her to his bedroom and pulled her close. His hands slid up her shirt and caressed her back. When was the last time someone had touched her like that? She felt him unhook her bra while he kissed her, his tongue exploring her mouth, his breathing hard and fast. When his hand sipped under her bra and held her breast, she was helpless. He'd carried her to his bed and they made love. She'd heard her phone ringing, but hadn't come down from the cloud of their love making. Before they'd made love a second time, Frankie had reached over and turned off her phone.

By the following week, traffic on the Cape had lightened. The children were back in school, and summer vacations were over. The days were growing shorter, but the September weather was perfect, cool, dry, and sunny.

Sue Willis came to meet with Beth and Patrice. They were sitting at the table on the farmer's porch. Beth served afternoon tea, iced, and lemon-lavender cookies.

"These are delicious," Sue said, taking another small bite. "The flavor is so delicate. Did you make them, Beth?"

"*We* did. All three of us. Grace won't eat them. She says they taste like flowers."

Sue got down to business. "Patrice, how are you doing?"

"Great. No problems. I'm happy and healthy."

"Are you having any difficulties in your relationship with Grace?" Sue asked. She leaned her elbow on the table and rested her chin on her fist.

"We had a little bump in the road when she saw the halfway house. I gave her an explanation why I couldn't be home with her yet, and she seemed comfortable with that. Now that I'm given more freedom, Beth and I have started taking her for ice cream and once we went out for dinner. The halfway house has strict rules but it's nothing as confining as the treatment center."

"Great," Sue said. "What are your work plans?"

Patrice leaned over and smiled. "I have an interview tomorrow at a lovely Victorian Inn. If I get the job, I'll start when the current cook leaves in a couple of weeks."

Beth widened her eyes. This was news to her.

Sue smiled. "Good luck on the interview. Where is the Inn?"

"Falmouth. I'll find a place to live there when I'm released."

"Oh. That's a commute to Orleans. It would be best to keep Grace in her school, if possible. Since Grace will be changing her home situation, it would be better if she could keep her school situation the same."

"I hadn't thought about that. I don't think there's an employer closer to this area that would hire a recovering addict." She turned to give Beth an inquiring look.

"This is something you'll have to handle with Sue." Beth wanted to say more, but she couldn't fault her sister for where the job was. Besides, Patrice seemed to be thrilled with the idea. She should be.

Patrice nodded. "If I have to start Grace in a new school, I think she'll adjust to our situation, especially since she'll be able to communicate more with the kids. And she'll be back with her mommy." She turned to Beth. "We won't be so far away we can't see each other whenever we want."

Sue went over some further points with Patrice. "As soon as you're released, you'll move into your home first and get settled. Then, we'll begin supervised visits with your daughter with either Beth or me present. We'll work out a schedule."

"But why do I need that?" Patrice's cheeks were pink. "Aren't I doing that now with Beth? You've already seen us together, too."

"Right now, you have great support around you in the halfway house. You have a place to stay, food on the table, and a sister who is taking care of Grace. Being on your own after months of help from others isn't going to be easy. Things will come up that stress you. Grace is doing well with her cochlear implants, but she still requires therapy. She should continue with her sports. And you'll need to be working—"

Beth interrupted. "I can still help with Grace. We can work that out."

Patrice's smile was tight. "I can do it, Beth. Sure, if there's something that comes up, you can, but you need your independence. That's important to me. You've done more than your share in helping us. You have a life here, and it's time you enjoy it without worrying about us."

Beth clasped her hands together on the table. She stared at them as if they had moved there on their own. Did Patrice not understand that all the help she had given was out of love for her and Grace?

"And I'm sure she will, eventually," Sue said. "I know Beth enjoyed every moment caring for her niece." She made some notes on her tablet then went on. "It won't be easy to juggle all this, Patrice. I don't want you to go into it with rose-colored glasses. You have a drug problem. You'll need regular testing, and you'll be required to attend NA meetings.

"Until the court releases you from rehabilitation, your daughter can't be returned to your custody. In fact, DCF will retain custody of Grace until you've met the provisions in the Service Plan we'll develop for you. Since the court upheld the removal of custody in this case, they will also have to approve the return of your daughter. It will take time. I just wanted to talk to you both so you could become adjusted to all these new developments. The court could cut your assignment at any time if your therapist recommends it." She looked from Patrice to Beth. "Do you have any questions?"

Beth was sitting in the car with Grace when the question she should have asked came to her: Why did Patrice seem so happy to move so far from Orleans? About as far as you could go before you had to cross a bridge. Was it really the only job opportunity, or did she think it would be easier for Grace to adjust living farther from her aunt? That she would be more focused on living with her real mom again at a distance, and that she would settle in faster? Was it also because she wanted to remove any competition with Beth? It would take time and work to prove to Patrice that she was content to be just Aunt Beth again.

They were sitting at a red light on Main Street. Beth was still lost in thought when Grace spoke.

"Aunt Beth, look. Nick."

His car was stopped beside them in the left-turn lane. Nick was looking at Beth with a sheepish expression. Beside him sat a woman who was speaking with animation. She turned her head to see what Nick was looking at. She was pretty.

Someone honked, and Nick's car jerked forward. He gave a backward wave and was gone.

"Who's that lady?" Grace asked.

"I don't know. A friend of Nick's, I guess." She smiled to herself, wondering if the woman was Nick's wife, or a new conquest. He was obviously embarrassed that she and Grace had seen them together. Beth let her head fall back and breathed out a long sigh. The light turned green. She was free to go, possibly in more than one way.

Chapter 29

Bundles of dried lavender had arrived at the store in a large wooden crate. Beth and Nan were wrapping them as individual bouquets with aqua tissue and orange ribbons.

"These smell so gorgeous, I could take them home and put them in every room in the house," Nan said, then inhaled a deep breath.

"Take home as many as you like. I will, too."

A little while later, when Nan was gone and there were no customers in the shop, Beth picked up the phone and dialed the number on the card she was holding.

"Uh, yes," Beth began. "Could you please confirm some appointment time changes for me?"

The voice on the other end sounded young. She said, 'sure,' and asked for the name. Beth gave Patrice Henson. "The appointments are weekly, on Tuesdays and Thursdays at two-thirty now, right?" Beth's hands on the phone were damp. She hated what she was doing.

"Nope. I see appointments at eleven a.m. on those days. Do you want me to change the times? Uh-oh, sorry, that time is taken."

"No, thank you. Just leave them as they are. It's not a problem."

Oh, but it was a problem. Beth knew it. Her sister had lied. Dammit. She didn't think Patrice was taking drugs, but something was going on she didn't want Beth to know about. She had to think before she took action. If Patrice flunked one drug test, her stay of possession charges would end. She would go to prison. What would that do to Grace?

A week had passed since Beth had called about the therapy appointment change. Nothing else had changed. When Patrice broke the news that her therapist announced she would petition the court to end her treatment, Beth thought everything was all right. Maybe Patrice had needed some personal time. Beth would give her that.

Scott and Beth made a plan so they could have a Saturday evening alone. Lisa was coming to the cottage. She would bring dinner from Wendy's for herself, Kristi, and Grace, and had a bunch of DVDs for them to watch after dinner. The girls were having a sleepover. Lisa would take the living room couch so they could have the bedroom.

Everybody was excited, but no one more than Beth. Scott was going to pick her up and take her to his house. He was going to grill swordfish, using his special marinade recipe. Kristi had made them butterscotch pudding for dessert.

For Beth, it was her own celebration of thanksgiving. She'd moved to the Cape in February to make a new life. In her wildest dreams she could never have imagined it turning out as it had, becoming so wonderful. Her sister was healthy and happy and responsible. Grace loved Beth as much as Beth loved her. No amount of distance could change that. And she'd made a loyal new friend, Lauren. Opened a solid business. And then there was Scott. She was so in love with him she could hardly breathe sometimes. The problem was, whenever they were together, a crowd was around them, too. Kristi and Grace would giggle when Scott came up behind Beth and wrapped her in a bear hug, then spun her around and kissed her.

Even though Scott had not said a word about a future together, she was sure they would take a step closer tonight. She donned her most dainty underwear and covered it with jeans and a soft, white cotton blouse with buttons down the front. She even wore slides, so she could slip out of her shoes in a hurry. Her heart pounded just thinking about it. She put on small gold hoop earrings while she checked in the mirror to ensure that her makeup was perfect.

When she opened the door for Scott a few minutes later, he never took his eyes off her. She began to breathe faster. The small crowd of people behind them yelled their goodbyes, and Scott took her hand and led her to his car. He didn't say a word until she was settled in with him beside her. Then he leaned over to kiss her. His lips were warm and soft. She raised her fingers to his cheek, prepared to stay as they were forever.

He started the car then said his first words. "You look beautiful."

They were quiet on the drive. When he helped her out of the car, he placed an arm around her waist and they walked in step to the side door of the house where he stopped and faced her.

"Kristi and I have a surprise." He pushed open the door and a dog began to bark. Beth could see the animal in a crate. It looked like a black lab mix with a fluffy black coat and one floppy ear.

"You got a Hearing Dog! Oh how cute! Is it male or female?" she asked.

"Her name is Clara Barton," Scott said, smiling, while he opened the crate and attached a short leash to her. "Come meet her."

When Grace removed her implants, she was completely deaf. Beth had installed lights for the doorbell, lights for the phone, lights for the smoke alarms. Months ago, she'd read about service dogs for the deaf and had asked Scott about it. He told her they were hard to get, and could be prohibitively expensive. He'd explained it could cost upwards of 25,000 dollars to train a service dog, and take as long as two years. But, he told her, he'd worked before with a trainer who owned Wonder Dogs. They bred and trained Hearing Dogs and Service Dogs. They would not refuse a service dog to any disabled person because they couldn't pay. Scott had promised to look into it.

"Don't worry," Scott was saying. "There is nothing permanent in your agreement yet. No obligation. I know you'll want to talk to your sister. We won't show Grace unless her mom says yes. Meanwhile, Kristi's seeing what it's like taking care of a service dog in training. It's something she's wanted to do for a long time. A service dog spends its first two years with a foster/volunteer. It's a lot of work, so, I put her off until high school. This gives her an idea of what it entails so she can be sure before she commits. I wanted you to meet Clara first and learn what you think."

Beth knelt down before her, extending her hand to let the dog sniff it. She knew right away Grace would love this dog. And it would help keep her safe. She petted the dog, who licked her face in return.

Scott knelt beside Beth. "Like her?"

"She's a love. I hope Patrice decides to take her. Grace will be so happy. How were you able to get Clara Barton so quickly?"

"She'd been committed to another person, but it didn't work out. Mark called me about her. If Patrice agrees, the trainers first need to see the dog interact with Grace, and then set up training sessions at their site before they'll give the final okay. Clara's smart," Scott said, ruffling her fur. "She's able to let her person know if the fire alarm goes off, someone knocks at the door, an oven timer buzzes, or the telephone is ringing where she can't see its lights. For Grace, the other great thing is that Clara will help her make friends because kids love dogs."

Scott pulled Beth upright with him. She put her arms around his neck and hugged him. "Thanks."

He kissed her eyes, her nose, her mouth. "Are you hungry?" he asked. His voice was deep, hoarse. "Because, if not, I have some other entertainment planned."

"Not hungry," she murmured while she kissed him. "For food, I mean."
He laughed. "Follow me. I have another surprise for you."

In between making love, they talked and talked. At one point, Scott got them drinks; his scotch, hers wine. Then they made love again.

They ate peanut butter and jelly sandwiches and potato chips at midnight. Then Scott drove her home. They kissed on the porch like teenagers, neither wanting to part.

"Do you think our clan would mind if we did this again tomorrow?" Scott said when Beth was finally unlocking the door.

She laughed softly. "I had a *really* good time," she said, then clasped a hand over her mouth to hold in her giggling. "I'd sure like to do it again tomorrow."

"Okay, and every night from now on, except when I have surgery in the mornings and need my wits about me."

"That might be a little difficult."

"Not if we were married," he said. His merry expression changed to intense seriousness.

She studied his face. "What did you say?"

"I said, will you marry me?"

"Yes. I would love to marry you," she whispered.

"Are you busy this weekend?"

They kissed again then Beth went inside without answering his question. She watched him drive away and took a deep breath. "I love him, love him, love him," she whispered to the kitchen. Then she tiptoed up the stairs. In the bathroom, she nearly laughed out loud when she saw her face. It was red and chafed all over from Scott's beard. And that wasn't the only chafed place on her body. She couldn't stop smiling. She hoped with all her heart that he would understand why they couldn't be married 'next weekend.' Why she would want to wait until Patrice and Grace were settled in together. A memory of Joe walking out the door gave her a start. But Joe wasn't Scott. He would wait.

Chapter 30

Beth asked the question over the phone. Patrice wasn't as excited as Beth had hoped. She told her sister she'd have to look into it herself. A few days later, they met for lunch.

They were eating Five Guys hamburgers and French fries in the Hyannis restaurant.

"So? What do you think about the dog?"

"Well, I was shocked at how expensive they are."

"But not in this case. Wonder Dogs depends completely on donations and fund raising, so they can give dogs to people who can't afford them."

Patrice took a bite of her burger. "So you said," she returned, with her mouth full. "I found out rental places had to allow service animals, even if they're not pet friendly. And, she can take the dog to school, anywhere."

"Right. So?"

"Eat something. I'm thinking yes, but I have to meet this puppy and make sure. I also have to consider the cost of having a dog, like for food, vet, and all the other stuff. Remember, Beth, I have to make my own decision."

"I think you're beginning to believe I'll be fine when Grace goes home," Beth said. "And how good I feel seeing you so strong and determined. I promise I won't be telling you what to do. I won't interfere or drop in unless I'm invited. So, please, please, let me do this one thing."

Patrice dipped a potato into Ketchup and popped it into her mouth, chewing with her eyes closed. "Damn, this is good. I'll say yes to anything if you take me here every week." She swallowed and grinned at Beth. "Let's hear it."

"Let me be responsible for Clara's expenses. Make it a Christmas present or a birthday present, if it makes you feel better about it, but let me. It won't mean you're dependent on me. It's a gift for now. What do you say? You let me buy things for Grace before."

"Oh, stop. I can't take anymore. Yes, yes, okay. You pay. But I reserve final judgment until I see this dog. She has to love me as much as Grace."

Beth leaned over the table and hugged Patrice. "Clara will love you both. I promise. Can we all go on Sunday to meet her?"

※

The next day, Patrice skipped her meeting and Frankie took her home. His new job was starting in a day, hers soon after, so they were going to treasure their free time together now.

They were barely in the door before they began to undress each other. They fell onto the bed, kissing and caressing.

Frankie chuckled when Patrice slid off him. "That was our best performance so far."

"So, you've been rating us?"

"I have, and I ordered a mirror for the ceiling so I can get a better perspective." He turned on his side to face her. "I love you, baby." He kissed her.

"I love you, too. Where are you going?" she asked when he jumped out of bed.

"You'll see. He walked naked over to the bureau and opened a drawer. He came back to the bed with a box. Patrice sat up and accepted it. He sat beside her. She opened the box and gasped when she saw the diamond ring. It was a nice size in a plain setting, just as she would have picked out for herself. "I love it," she said, turning to him.

Frankie smiled. "Does that mean yes?"

"That means absolutely yes. Oh yes, yes, yes!"

"I think it's time we told everyone, don't you?" he said, sliding the ring on her finger.

"I don't know. I'm not sure what'll happen. I don't think anyone at the halfway house should know. I'm waiting for the court decision before I'm free to be me. Still, I don't know how DCF will react. I can't lose the possibility of getting Grace back as soon as possible." She turned her hand so the light caught the diamond's facets.

"It's time we found out. Talk to that woman. Tell your sister. We've waited long enough. If it takes a while longer to get Gracie back, we can handle that."

"No. I cannot handle that."

Frankie nudged her shoulder. "So, get going. Talk to the lady. Let's get Gracie home."

"You already have a nickname for her." She smiled. "You'll love her, Frankie, and I know she'll love you, too."

Something bothered her but she couldn't place it. She'd have to think about it later. They made love again, to celebrate, and then it was time for her to get back. While they drove back to her drop-off place, she asked him about the dog.

"It's a Hearing Dog. Beth says she's a medium-sized lab mix and very cute. I'm thinking it would make Grace really happy, and with the pond and all—"

"I don't know, Patrice. A child is one thing, but do I have to be taking care of a dog, too? Dogs are an expensive upkeep."

Then she knew what was bothering her.

On Sunday morning, it was pouring rain when Beth and Grace went to pick up Patrice, but it didn't dampen Beth's mood. It did seem to affect Patrice, though. She was in a mood Beth hadn't seen in a while. "Have you changed your mind about the dog?" Beth whispered.

"No. I didn't get much sleep last night. I'm nervous about starting the job."

An hour later, the rain had stopped, but heavy clouds clung to the sky. Beth looked over at Grace, eating an apple at the kitchen table. "When you finish, how about we use our map and take your mom to find Lizzie's grave?" Beth winked at Patrice. "Is that all right with you?"

Grace's eyes lit up. "Yes."

They stopped at Friend's Market and bought a yellow chrysanthemum plant in a pretty pot. At the cemetery, Grace held the map and Patrice helped her locate the Porter family site. Beth followed along behind them. The Porter gravestones were gray granite, mottled with lichen. Lizzie's stone was tiny. All it said was *Lizzie, age five*. John and Abigail were buried on either side of their only daughter.

Grace set the flowers down. "Is she in there?"

Beth bit her bottom lip and looked at Patrice.

"You know what I think? I think when you die the angels come and take your soul to heaven. But they leave your body where you're buried," Patrice said.

Grace shook her head. "The lady says you take your body. God makes it all well again. The lady got a new heart."

"No, honey. That's not what she meant. You can get a new heart while you're living. And nobody really knows what happens after we die, but that's what my father told me. All good people go to heaven."

Grace shook her head at her mother again. "The lady knows because she died." Patrice frowned at Beth. "What else did she tell you?" she asked Grace.

"Lots of things. She tells me God loves me and everybody. She said He doesn't live only in church because He wants to be with everybody."

"Beth, who is this woman putting ideas into her head? You know how I feel about religion. How could you let someone talk to her like this?"

"Can we discuss this later? I'll explain." Beth signaled the best she could to her sister that they drop the subject. But Patrice wouldn't. "Look at me,

Grace. Tell me more about this lady."

Grace smiled. "She's pretty, Mommy. She has long hair like me, but hers is red. Her face and hands shine white. And she wears pretty skirts."

Beth swallowed a lump of fear. She should have prepared Patrice for this. Explained to her about this imaginary woman Grace had conjured up when she was missing her mommy.

"How does she know who Lizzie is?" Patrice asked.

"She knows her and Emily, too. She loves little children."

A creeping chill was travelling up Beth's back, making her cold all over. She ignored Patrice's angry look and asked Grace, "Do you know what Emily looks like?"

"She's my age but she has red hair like the lady."

Beth stared with her mouth open. Grace had described the daughter of Thea Connor, who sold her the cottage. She'd met Emily at the closing.

"Does the lady show you pictures of these people?" Beth asked, softly.

"Yes."

Ah. Grace had obviously found a scrapbook or picture album Thea had left behind. Beth was beginning to relax when Grace went on.

"She shows me in my head," she said, staring at Lizzie's headstone.

Patrice was looking at her daughter with awe on her face. "Grace, will you ask the lady if I can meet her?"

"Yes," Grace said, then reached out to put her hand on the stone. "It's cold. Is she cold, too?"

"No, honey. She's warm and cozy in her mommy's arms."

"Does she have a new rocking chair in heaven?"

"You can have anything you want in heaven," Patrice said. "You can play, ride a horse, watch movies, even make art. Anything you want."

What? Was this her sister going on about heaven? Beth stared, wide-eyed.

Grace walked back to the car in front of the sisters. "You have a lot of explaining to do," Patrice said. Beth was surprised that her sister didn't sound angry.

Kristi and Scott were sitting on the steps to the kitchen door when they arrived. Scott came over and kissed Beth. His kisses were never a thoughtless gesture, but an intense moment of pleasure. He gave her a quick squeeze then put his hand on Grace's shoulder.

"Kristi, why don't you take Grace to show her your secret hiding spot in the yard?"

"It's far enough out that they'll be a few minutes. Kristi is going to keep Grace busy so you can meet Clara Barton," he said to Patrice. "Come on in."

Scott took Clara out of her crate and introduced her to Patrice. A smile broke out on her face when the dog's tail wagged hard enough to convince Patrice to offer her face for doggie kisses. "Oh, you are a sweet dog. You must be a smart dog, too. Are you a smart dog?" Patrice asked while she accepted the love. Clara barked once, and everyone laughed.

"What do you think, Patrice?" Beth asked.

Her expression changed from joy to worry. "I don't know. I'm not sure." Beth noticed her lack of eye contact. "Why? What's bothering you?"

"It's a big undertaking with all we're going through, you know, Beth."

"Yes, but you seemed to think a Hearing Dog to protect Grace was worth it. What's making you doubt?" Beth tried to ask the questions without making her sister defensive. Something had changed in her attitude.

Scott was looking from one to the other, but he didn't interfere.

"What if someone I meet doesn't like dogs, or is allergic to them?"

Beth stared at her. Then Patrice's expression became more relaxed.

She laughed. "I'm really looking ahead, aren't I? Maybe if Grace and the dog get along with each other, I'll just ask anyone I meet if they like dogs first."

Beth let out a breath. "Oh, good. Yes, let's show Grace her surprise!"

Scott turned and let out a loud whistle. Soon the two girls were running back to them.

"Kristi has a big surprise for you, Grace." He glanced over at Patrice and winked.

"What?" Grace asked with big eyes.

"Kristi, go get Grace's surprise."

Kristi giggled and disappeared through the side door. A few minutes later, everyone watched as she brought Clara Barton down the steps and stopped in front of Grace and Patrice.

Patrice bent down to pet the dog. "Grace, her name is Clara Barton and she wants to meet you." Clara's eyes were alert and her ears perked up as if she understood Grace was her new charge.

Grace looked at the faces around her, as if she were in a dream.

"Go ahead, Grace, you can pet her," Patrice said. "She's very friendly."

Grace moved close, dropped to her knees, and wrapped her arms around the dog's neck, laughing. Clara pulled away and licked her face, making Grace's laughter bubble over.

Beth looked at Scott, smiling. His eyes were bright when he returned her smile.

"Grace, Kristie will tell you about how special Clara is," Scott said, standing beside Patrice. "Listen to this," he said.

Kristie stood back up, spoke and signed. "Clara Barton is a Hearing Dog for the deaf. She's specially trained to help you, Grace. If you don't have your implants attached, you can't hear anything. She knows how to tell you if someone's at the door, or if your alarm goes off to wake you for school. Watch." Kristie took out a kitchen timer and showed it to Clara, then set it beside her. Kristie moved over to sit on the steps. When the timer went off, Clara ran and put her paws on Kristie's knees. She gave the dog a treat and petted her. "Good girl, Clara."

"Why don't the adults go inside and let Kristie work a little with Grace and Clara. The trainer will be here soon." He turned to Patrice. "He wants to make sure the dog and Grace are compatible. It doesn't look like that'll pose a problem."

Scott showed them into the living room. "Let's make ourselves comfortable. What can I get you to drink? Patrice? I have iced tea, all kinds of soda—God, do I have soda."

Beth laughed, remembering the fun the girls had with the soda machine on the boat.

"I'll have iced tea, thanks," Patrice said, taking in the large room with a view of the water. The right side held the dining area; the rest of the room offered comfortable seating around a fireplace, a desk area with a computer setup, and a large-screen TV mounted on the side wall.

Scott nodded. "I know what you want, Beth. I'll be right back."

Patrice looked at her sister. "He seems like a great guy. He sure does love you."

"I know how lucky I am. He's wonderful," she was saying when Scott walked in and handed her a glass. The deep crimson of the wine seemed to glow before her like it was radioactive. How could Scott forget Patrice was an addict and an alcohol abuser? She glared at him, trying to get his attention, but he ignored her.

"Here's your tea, Patrice."

Scott held his glass of scotch up to make a toast. "To Patrice and Grace and Clara. May they live together in safety and joy."

Beth took a dainty sip of wine and put the glass down. She hadn't had a drink in front of Patrice for years. She didn't know what to do. How could Scott have made this mistake?

He sat in the chair across from Patrice. "I've connected some other of my deaf patients with Mark, the man who owns and trains these dogs. I know how difficult it is to get one. The waiting list is lengthy. It takes a long time and lots of hard work to train the dogs. Mark gave me a call and told me about Clara. He offered me first dibs. I grabbed her, since I might not have another chance for a while, but I can always give her back, if you say no."

"What if we take her and it doesn't work out?"

"By the time Mark's finished working with Grace and Clara, there'll be no doubt if they're good for each other. But, sure, if something happens that you can't anticipate, Mark will take her back. It happens. That's how Clara became available."

Beth stood watching the girls out the side window, tense with the hope Patrice would allow Grace to have her dog. She turned to Patrice. "While Grace is still with me, you'll have time to watch how it goes and take your time making the final decision."

Patrice laughed. "Oh yeah, good try, Beth. I'm sure Grace will gladly give her up if I change my mind."

"I wasn't thinking of that. You're right. I guess I already love the dog, too. Your decision, but like Scott said, you aren't tied to it."

Beth turned and let her eyes go back to the happy scene outside the window.

A prolonged silence filled the room. Beth said, "Kristi is so unbelievable. She is so happy for Grace. What a beautiful spirit she has. It's obvious how much she loves that dog herself." Beth walked over and sat down. She took a sip of wine.

Scott smiled. "After she worked with Clara for over two weeks, she asked me if she could have a dog of her own instead of training them. When I explained how hard it would be with our schedule, she wanted to cry. It was all I could do not to tell her Mark is bringing *her* a dog. As a matter of fact, he'll be here in a few minutes. She's always wanted a golden lab. Today, she'll have one. A female, she's a year old. I can't wait to see Kristi's face. Mark is going to honk when he gets here, so we'll have time to get out there and watch."

Scott kept the conversation going and away from Clara Barton. He was kind to Patrice but didn't try to force her decision.

When the horn sounded, they all got up and went outside.

Scott shook Mark's hand and patted him on the shoulder. He introduced Beth and Patrice. Mark looked across the lawn and saw Grace running with Clara. "That sure answers my first question. Looks like a good match. I'll work with them a little before I go."

"We can't thank you enough for this, Mark," Beth said.

"Yes," Patrice said. "Scott was so kind to arrange this for my daughter." Beth looked at her, waiting for more, but Patrice just smiled.

"My pleasure," Mark said. He raised his eyebrows to Scott. "When do you want me to bring out the new dog?"

Scott called the girls, signaling them to come. They were both breathless when they arrived, as was Clara. "Sit," Grace said to Clara, with her hand palm up. Clara sat.

"Wow!" Mark laughed. "You already know that? I'll bet Miss Kristi taught you, am I right?" Mark, used to deaf people, spoke and signed.

"I can hear you," Grace said with a serious expression. "Yes, Kristi is my best friend." Her words were full of adoration.

"Kristi," Scott said. "I know how hard it's going to be for you to give up Clara." He turned to Patrice. "You're going to take her? Try her out?"

When Patrice hesitated, Beth watched Kristi's face light up with hope. Beth looked from one to the other, holding her breath. She clamped her teeth tightly to keep herself from saying anything.

Patrice smiled at Kristi and Beth wanted to scream. *She's going to say Kristi can have Clara!*

"I can see how much you love her, Kristi," Patrice said, "But I think Grace needs her to keep her safe."

Beth pressed her hand against her smiling mouth and Scott hugged her. "See?" he whispered in her ear. Then he left her and went over to Kristi. Grace was standing beside her with a worried expression. Beth knew she was upset for her friend, but it wouldn't last long.

"Kristi, you are the best daughter any dad could ever have. But sometimes when I come home late, or get called in during the night, I worry about you. I think you need a dog, too."

It took a moment for the words to sink in, but then Kristi's mouth opened wide. She watched Mark come out of his truck with a fluffy golden retriever on a leash. She turned to her father, her face radiant. "For me?"

He nodded. She gave him a quick hard hug and ran to meet her new dog. Grace's grin extended almost to her ears. Beth had tears in her eyes, and Patrice was still smiling.

"God, that felt good!" Scott said.

Chapter 31

She was sitting by the pond with Frankie. It was a warm October day and they were relaxing in Adirondack chairs, eating a late lunch. Patrice's phone was sitting on the wide arm of the chair so she could keep an eye on the time. It rang and she checked the number. "My lawyer," she said to Frankie, then answered the call.

By the time the call ended, she was up and pacing. She ended the call, then threw her head back and laughed. "Frankie, it's over!" She ran to hug him. "I'm free! The court allowed the suspension of my rehab and dropped the charges for possession." She put a hand over her mouth in her astonishment. Frankie pulled it away and kissed her.

"Now we can start our life together. Tell your sister, and move in with me."

"It's not that easy. I still have to deal with DCF. But I'm sure we can work this out."

"Yep. We can just get married and skip the other stuff. Then Grace would come home to a mom *and* a dad."

She hesitated. "I'm not sure. I told you I needed time for Grace to adjust before we added you to our family."

"But you'll be living with me, right?"

She shrugged her shoulders. "Oh, it doesn't matter. We'll see what happens. But Frankie, I'm free!" She twirled around on the grass with her arms extended to the sky.

She was breathless when she walked into the halfway house to make arrangements for her departure. She went first to her room and called Sue Willis to tell her the news. She didn't pick up, so Patrice left the message and asked her to call back as soon as she could.

Patrice had already told Sue about Frankie in confidence that they were engaged, and Patrice had asked what effect that would have on getting Grace back. Sue told her she would discuss the matter with her supervisor. She thought her engagement would not prevent the return of custody of Grace to her when the provisions of the service plan were met, but that her fiancé would need to be included in a new service plan and he may be subject to screening.

She wondered if Frankie would agree to whatever screening was required, worried that he might be annoyed. Patrice hadn't told him yet that she'd allowed Grace to have the dog. How could she deny Grace something that would keep her safe, make her so happy? She wouldn't.

It was time to tell Beth. She would plan to stay at the cottage a few days, before moving in with Frankie—provided Sue's answer was positive. After she broke the news to Beth and Grace, She would have Frankie come to visit. Then he would see the dog and fall in love with her like everyone else had.

For the first time in a long time, she wished for something to help calm herself. She grabbed her cell and went out for a fast walk.

When Patrice called the store, her voice made Beth's adrenaline flow. "What's wrong?"

"Not a thing! I'm so excited I can hardly talk." She took a big breath and then said, "I've finished rehab! The court let me go. No crime, no more time!"

"Patrice! I'm so happy for you! I'm happy for all of us. Congratulations, honey! When are you coming?"

"I'm going to get some exit counseling first. How about the day after tomorrow?"

"We'll be there bright and early. Oh my God, I can't believe it's over. I'll be back in the store by three o'clock with Grace so you can call and tell her. She'll be so excited." Beth felt like dancing and then she did, taking a few steps behind the counter. It seemed too good to be true.

"Aunt Beth, can we go to the library first? I need a book for school."

"Uh, how about after the store closes? I'm working on an important report and I need to send it off quickly."

Grace didn't want to go to the store and do homework. Her aunt hardly ever said no to the library. She felt grumpy. But when they stopped at the cottage to pick up Clara Barton, her mood brightened. She walked Clara to do her business and then they hopped into the car. Clara had a safety harness which Grace attached before she put on her own seat belt. Clara loved to ride in the car. Once they were belted up, Aunt Beth opened Clara's window and she stuck her nose out, keeping it there all the way to the shop.

Going through her school papers for the day was always fun. Her marks were good and so was her art. Mr. Hamilton wrote nice notes on her papers and Aunt Beth got excited every time she saw them. She was smiling at her when her cell phone rang. Aunt Beth nodded for her to answer.

"What's today, Grace?" her mommy said on the video call.

She tried to think. Was it somebody's birthday? She couldn't think of anything. "I don't know."

"It's Wednesday, silly. How about if mommy comes to see you on Friday?"

"Yea!" she said, but there was something on her mommy's face that made her wonder.

"How about if I never have to go back to the hospital?"

"Mommy! You're coming home!" She was so excited she shoved the phone at her aunt and began hopping around the room making happy sounds.

When her aunt ended the call, she came and hugged Grace, picking her up and swinging her around, making her laugh so hard she lost her breath.

"Mommy's coming home with us," she told her aunt when her feet were back on the floor. "Can she sleep in my room?"

"Of course, she can. Mommy has another surprise to tell us when she comes."

"We have a surprise, too, don't we? Clara Barton is with us now, too." The dog's ears perked up when she heard her name.

"We do. Mommy will be so impressed with how you take care of her."

Aunt Beth shook her head in a funny way and opened her eyes wide. "I think we need to celebrate. Let's go the Hot Chocolate Sparrow and get an ice cream."

Later, Grace was doing her homework when she stopped and stuck her pencil eraser in her mouth and bit it. Her mommy was not sick anymore. She'd been gone for a long time. Grace was very happy. She'd asked before if she and mommy could live with Aunt Beth. The grown-ups said no. Maybe mommy changed her mind and they could. Was that the surprise? She put a hand over her stomach where it hurt. Were they going back to New Bedford? Would she have to leave her aunt, her school friends? Her best friend, Kristi, would be sad, and so would their dogs who liked to play together. Grace was already sad because she thought her mother's surprise might be a new place to live. She put her head down on her desk and tried to hold back her tears.

Beth brought home a bakery cake on Friday that said *Congratulations*. Dinner was almost ready: meatloaf, mashed potatoes, and corn pudding. Comfort food. She was chopping veggies for the salad. Grace sat at the table, drawing a picture for her mother. Beth had suggested it to settle her. It was a long day to wait. Patrice had called yesterday to say there was a change of plans. She'd get home on her own steam by dinnertime."

"Wash up. Our celebration dinner will be ready in ten minutes, and mommy should be here soon." Grace attached her drawing to the fridge with a magnet then raced off to the bathroom. Beth was biting her bottom lip. What was all this mystery about? "Ouch!" She dropped the knife and went to the sink to rinse her cut finger.

A car came up the driveway. Clara started barking, but Grace hushed her. "Can I go out?"

"Go, girl," Beth said. She watched as a man stepped out of the car. She was about to run after Grace when she saw Patrice's blond head as she stood up outside the passenger door. Grace flew into her arms.

"Grace and Beth, I would like you to meet Frank Keenan, Frankie," Patrice said with a big smile.

He was tall with brown hair, lots of it. He had a warm smile as he reached his hand out to Grace, who was staring at him. "Hi, Grace, I've heard good things about you from your mom." He turned to shake Beth's hand. "We met a long time ago. It's nice to see you again."

"Likewise," Beth said, and then couldn't think of anything else to say. Patrice came to hug her.

Clara Barton made it her business to check out Frankie with her nose. He looked at Beth, smiling. "Your dog?"

She glanced at her sister then answered. "This is Clara Barton. She's Grace's Hearing Dog." As she watched, Frankie looked at Patrice and raised his eyebrows. It made Patrice clearly nervous. She walked off through the kitchen, babbling to Grace.

When they were seated around the table, Patrice raised her hand. "Before we begin this sumptuous feast, there's something I have to tell you both." She swiped at the tip of her nose. "It's about where we're going to live. Grace and me."

Beth felt relieved when Patrice specified Grace and her. "Oh good, I want to hear all about it." As soon as she said it, the relief left. Patrice's hands were shaking.

Patrice turned to Grace. "Sweetie," she said, reaching out for Frankie's hand. "My surprise is mommy is going to get married."

Neither Grace nor Beth said a thing. Grace pressed her fist to her chin.

"Hello? Anyone want to congratulate us?"

"Congratulations, twice!" Beth said. She stood up and walked around the table to hug Patrice, then Frankie.

"Grace, see how happy mommy is? I want you to be happy, too. Frankie has a nice house for us and it has a pond. And he's going to put in a swing set for you. It'll be a while before you come to live there, but you will *love* it, like I do."

"Hey, little girl, don't you worry. When you get to know me better, you won't feel scared about the new place, and me. We're going to have such fun together."

Beth thought Frankie said the right thing, even though Grace was still mute, and her finger was working her just-healed cuticle.

After dinner, Beth suggested Grace do her homework so that she'd have all weekend to enjoy with her mother. She went off with no argument. Patrice brought Frankie into the living room so he could watch the news while the sisters cleaned up.

"I thought you weren't going to rush things? Does DCF know? God, did you see Grace's face?"

"You know Grace is my first concern. Frankie gave me a ring and proposed. Why would I say no to the man I love. Beth, he makes me happy. It'll be good for Grace to have a dad. A dad with a job who can help support us. He's an engineer." She drew out the last syllable of engineer. "Most of all, he loves me. He's not a druggie, Beth, he never was, and I'm not either anymore. He'll help me stay out of trouble. I promise."

The words echoed in Beth's mind, over and over: *IpromiseIpromiseIpromise.*

Grace came into the kitchen and tugged at her mother's arm. When she had her mother's attention, she said, "I—I don't want him to live with us."

"I know it's hard, baby, and it's scary, but it will be wonderful. I promise." She pulled out a chair and sat, bringing Grace close to her. "How about this? You will have plenty of time to get to know Frankie before we're anywhere near ready to move you in. If you don't like him, we'll make our own plans."

Grace nodded and smiled. "I'm so sure you will love him, though, I think we'll be living on the pond." She put her finger under Grace's chin, saying, "Mommy and Frankie love each other. I love you and Frankie will, too. You'll see."

Chapter 32

On Tuesday morning, Beth walked into the store, threw her purse under the counter, and slapped down her travel mug of coffee. Drops of coffee shot out the open tab top, like little rockets.

She turned on the lights and one of the chandelier bulbs popped and died. "Great. Just great," she said aloud. She booted up the computer and headed to the back of the store. The three-day Columbus Day sale had performed above expectations, and by the time she'd locked the door yesterday afternoon, she'd been worn out.

She stood in the back room trying to shake off the pent-up anger she still felt from over the weekend. Grace seemed content to go back to school this morning, and Frankie and Patrice took off for their own place. Poor Grace. Beth kept telling herself it was none of her business. It was now between Patrice and Sue Willis. Beth was only sorry for Grace. She'd been pale and subdued all weekend. Patrice did her best to reassure her, but it had no effect. Frankie made several attempts to befriend her but was rebuffed, until they all decided to play UNO one night. He then had her laughing. It made Beth feel better. It was none of her business. He seemed like a nice man. Patrice told her Sue was already working on a new service plan that included him. It was a done deal.

The shelves all needed restocking before the store opened. She began dragging out piles of merchandise and stacking them on the floor beside their respective shelves. Then she neatened the items still on the shelves and laid out the new merchandise.

Why had she ever thought her sister would change? She was still a rule-breaker. It irked Beth to see Grace yanked away from her new friends and school, her soccer team, her speech therapist, everything she loved. A package of pillow cases slid to the floor. Beth picked it up and jammed it back in the pile. Then she stood still and covered her face with her hands. She was doing it again! What was wrong with her? She needed an attitude adjustment. Patrice had outdone herself in rehab. She was about to start a job doing what she loved. With a good marriage, her life would be solvent, comfortable. Beth resolved to be happy for the new little family. Happy!

When Lauren walked in the door, Beth started to cry.

Lauren dropped her purse on the floor and wrapped her arms around Beth. "What's wrong? What happened? Tell me."

"I'm sorry. I'm just so happy to see you."

"Yeah. That's what people do when they're happy to see me. Bawl."

Beth laughed and picked up Lauren's bag. "I'm happy to see *you*, but I'm not happy in general."

"Okay, hold on. Let me get us some coffee and then we can talk."

Beth held up her cup. "Get yourself some."

Besides her coffee, Lauren carried in the wooden stool from the back room and put it down beside the counter stool. She'd taken off her jacket and was wearing a denim skirt and a yellow boat-neck jersey. Small yellow-and-blue beach balls bobbed at her ears as she climbed onto the stool.

"Let's hear it. What's wrong? Please say it isn't Scott."

"It isn't Scott. It's Patrice. It's Grace." Beth hoisted herself up on the counter stool and turned to face Lauren. "They're going to live in Falmouth."

"No way. I thought it was all settled. They're taking Grace out of her school?"

Tears welled up again. "Yes, but it's because Patrice is getting married and her fiancé lives in Falmouth. Her job is there, too. It's all working out for her. He seems very nice, but I haven't adjusted to it all yet."

"How's Grace taking this?"

"She only knows she's moving to Falmouth. She doesn't know how far away it is or that she'll have to go to a new school. Patrice is right, she'll do fine; she's so strong." Beth lowered her head.

Lauren patted Beth's knee. "I know she will."

Beth shook her head. "It's the surprise of it all, I guess. Really, I'm happy for her. I don't know why I'm crying. I *am* happy for her. We'll be visiting back and forth." She took the tissue Lauren offered and dabbed at her eyes. "There. I feel better. Hey, maybe we'll have a double wedding." She tried to smile then said, "Oh Lauren, I'll miss Grace so much."

⁂

Patrice couldn't understand why she was so nervous. She'd looked forward to this job. She liked the owners of the inn, Meg and Tom, and they must have liked her, they hired her right away.

"I hope I don't feel this way tomorrow."

"Just a little stage fright. You'll be fine as soon as you start working," Frankie said.

They were lying in bed together; he was falling asleep. She listened to his dreamy voice with a heart full of love. But she knew she had to be careful, relax, use her skills. She closed her eyes. She was strong. She would not falter.

Patrice had made one of Beth's recipes, mocha muffins, and brought them along to her interview. It helped get her the job. Meg told her she would be on *probation* for two weeks to see how she worked out. She said it was not only for Patrice, but policy for every new hire.

This morning she pulled into the parking spot assigned to her behind the large white Victorian Inn. It was god-awful early, five a.m., but that was part of the job, and she was a morning person. Once Grace lived with them, Frankie would take her to school on his way to work, and Patrice would be home by noon.

Her job was to make daily breakfast for the guests, keep the buffet filled, then clean up. Afterwards, she would prepare cocktail snacks, leaving the covered platters in the refrigerator until the owners served them at five.

She used her key to open the back door. Everything was dark, and she switched on the lights. She hoped Meg had bought all the ingredients on the list they'd made up during Patrice's three afternoons of orientation.

First she put on a pot of coffee then she checked the cupboards and pantry. The weekly menu she had worked up with Meg was attached to the inside of the pantry door. It was Monday. The menu called for homemade granola, cranberry orange muffins, raisin bran muffins, hot oatmeal, and fresh fruit, besides the staple hard-boiled eggs and sliced meats. Patrice would cook for about forty people. The Inn had twelve guestrooms, all en suite and decorated in period. Besides the guests, the dining room was open to the public for continental breakfast.

She poured herself a cup of fragrant French Roast coffee, then filled the large thermos server for the early bird guests, and carried it to a table in the lobby. She went back for the hot water thermos, the tray of cups, sugar and cream, stirrers, teabags, and hot chocolate packets.

"My mouth is watering," Meg said, coming into the kitchen. She poured herself a cup of coffee from the new pot Patrice was brewing. "It looks like you're in total control here. Mmmm, those muffins smell fabulous. I'm so glad we were able to find you."

"Thanks. I'm glad I have a job doing what I love."

Tom held open the swinging door to the dining room. "It's almost seven, are we ready in here?"

Patrice felt a stab of panic. It was curtain time and she was sweating. Something to calm her flashed in her mind. *No! You can handle it.*

Patrice took a deep breath and called back to him, "Ready."

She could hear voices in the dining room. Mandy, a young woman who helped in the kitchen, entered. She tied an apron over her khaki pants and short-sleeved black t-shirt that didn't hide the tattoos on her arms.

"Hey, you the new cook?" she said, gesturing with a hand at Patrice.

"Yes, I'm Patrice. I'm sure glad to see you. I'm a little nervous."

"Relax, girl. We'll get this done together."

Patrice and Mandy carried the loaded trays to the buffet table in the dining room.

It disappointed Beth that Patrice rarely made soccer practice in time. She was always exhausted from her new job with 'early hours and so much stress.' Grace was used to going to practice with Beth, so she didn't seem to feel slighted by her mother's spotty attendance.

Grace ran off down the field. The full impact of the changes coming up hadn't been explained to her yet. Beth refused to do it; Patrice planned to tell her when the time was right.

Grace did love visiting the little cottage on the pond. Beth was concerned about a deaf child near a body of water, however small. Thank goodness Frankie agreed to take Clara Barton. And he'd put up the swing set as promised. Patrice was probably right to wait, since by the time Grace moved in with them, she'd be comfortable with her home situation.

At fifteen minutes before the end of practice, Patrice showed up. She looked content and well rested. It was all working out. Once Grace made the adjustments, it would be fine.

"I got my first paycheck today!" Patrice said as she slid onto the bleacher next to Beth.

"Congratulations."

"I'm taking you both to dinner."

Beth turned to look into her sister's happy face. "Thanks, but save your money."

Patrice gave Beth's knee a light slap. "Stop telling me what to do. I'm taking you to dinner. Somewhere cheap," she added, and laughed.

"Thank you. I'd love it. Jeez, I'm always telling you what to do. Old habit. I don't even realize what I'm doing," she said, tapping her head with the heel of her hand.

Patrice laughed, and hugged Beth. "The light dawns! Thank heavens. I know you only want to protect me. But you know what I want? I want you not to worry about me anymore. Marry Scott and live happily ever after. So will Frankie and I. And Grace. We'll be close. We'll visit a lot. Share holidays. You're just not used to a sister who is self-sufficient. That's what I want for us."

Patrice smiled, and Beth noticed her pupils seemed tightly constricted. A frisson of fear wriggled in her stomach, but then she realized Patrice was facing into the strong afternoon sun. She was doing it again. Concerned about Patrice. She had to stop.

A few minutes later, she watched as Patrice and Grace walked away. Sue was going to Falmouth to present her service plan—which included Frankie—while she conducted the first supervised visit that included all three of them. Afterwards, Sue would bring Grace back to Beth's house, and then go over the service plan with her. If everything went well, DCF would allow Grace to move into the Falmouth cottage after a period of more supervised visits. Sue might be able to give Beth a time frame for Grace's move. Her hands tightened into fists as she headed back to her car.

The weather for Halloween night was crisp and clear. Patrice was planning to come to take Grace Trick-or-Treating at six p.m. Beth was applying face paint to give her a black nose, a pink mouth, and long black whiskers, while they waited for Patrice to arrive. She was already late.

Beth thought Grace looked adorable in the costume she'd been wearing since four o'clock. She was a black cat. Her long hair was held back by a glittering pair of cat ears on a ribbon. She wore a one-piece velvet suit with feather ruffles at the end of the sleeves and pants. She also had on warm black socks and black shoes.

"When's mommy coming?" Grace asked, looking at herself in the mirror of Beth's vanity table.

Beth glanced at the clock; it was nearly six-thirty. She hoped Patrice wasn't going to disappoint Grace. "I'll call her and see. She's probably on her way."

"I can't get Frankie to leave this party," Patrice yelled into the phone.

"Patrice, Grace is ready to go. How far away are you?"

"We're in Hyannis. It's at his office. You know, the boss wants him here. We'll be leaving soon. Do you want to start ahead of me with her? Does she look cute?"

"Mommy's going to be late. But we can't miss all that candy. What do you think? Shall we get going?" Beth said when she ended the call.

"But what about the kids who come here? They won't get candy."

"Oh yes, they will. I have an idea." They went together to the kitchen, Clara Barton at their heels. Beth pulled out her treasured salad bowl. "Help me dump in all the candy. We'll make a sign to tell the kids to help themselves."

They set everything up on the farmer's porch. "Okay, Grace, let's hear that meow one more time."

Grace let out a perfect imitation of a cat. Beth hugged her, and Clara barked. They went off down the street, Clara in her nurse's cap, Beth in her witch's hat, and Grace prowling along in front.

Chapter 33

On Saturday evening, Beth sat beside Scott on a bench at Coast Guard Beach in Eastham. He wrapped his arm around her shoulders, pulling her close as they watched a group of migrating Eider ducks fly over the ocean. It was the golden time of day, with cool air, and a low, warm sun.

"You can handle it," Scott said.

"Handle what?" she said, wondering what she'd missed.

"Grace leaving."

"How do you always know what I'm thinking?"

He sighed. "I guess I'm going to have to tell you. It's such a burden to keep it secret."

Beth frowned. "Tell me what?"

He touched the space between her tightened brows with a finger. "It's not bad. It's just that, well . . . I'm psychic."

She grinned when she saw his dimple forming as he held back a smile. "No. Honestly, Scott. You've done it since I first brought Grace into your office." She drew her knees up on the bench and wrapped her arms around them.

"Only for you. I can't do it for anyone else." He turned his hands palm-up.

She took a hand and kissed it. "Do you know what I'm thinking now?"

He placed his fingers on his forehead and closed his eyes. Then he turned to her with wide eyes. "You want to go to your house so we can make love. Am I right?"

Beth laughed. "See! You did it again."

Kristi had gone to a sleepover to celebrate her friend's birthday, and Grace was spending the full weekend with her mother and Frankie. If all went well, Grace would move into Frankie's cottage soon after this trial getaway.

They stood up and headed for the car. "I know I can handle her leaving, Scott. I just don't want to."

"You have to set some new goals. Let's go back to your house and brainstorm."

They had the unusual luxury of time. Scott brought in the duffle bag he'd packed to spend the night. No one would bother them. Beth thought it was like a dream. They made slow, lazy love—the first time in her bed—then they both fell asleep. Later, she cooked dinner for him. They did the dishes together.

Scott built a fire in the living room fireplace, and they cuddled together on the couch, letting the flames mesmerize them. Beth couldn't remember a time when she was happier. He was right; she'd be fine once she was over Grace's leaving.

Scott's legs were stretched out over the coffee table. His head was leaning on the back of the couch. Beth was sitting sideways with her legs tucked under her. She was studying the face of the man she loved. Sensing her eyes on him, he turned his head and looked at her. "Nice fire, huh?"

"Nice nose. Great kissers," she put a finger on his lips, "and cute dimple."

"So your attraction to me is only physical?"

She leaned over and kissed him on the lips. "Mostly."

"Mine, too." He turned back to the fire with a wide smile. "Ready to brainstorm some new goals?"

"No. Not yet."

"Here," he said, shifting his position to address her. "Let me get you started. Close your eyes." Beth did. "You loved being a foster mom, right?"

She drew her brows together. "Yes."

"What about a new child?"

She opened her eyes and looked into his but didn't answer.

He cupped her cheek with his free hand. "Beth. I'm in love with you. I am *so* in love with you. I want to marry you and have children with you."

"Scott." His name flowed out softly on a sigh. "I love you, too." She leaned in and kissed him.

"Is that a yes?" he asked in a husky voice.

"A definite yes. Marry you. Children. Yes."

"Oh good, because I can't bear to be away from you any longer. I want you right by my side every day, in my bed every night. I want you to be Kristi's mother right now. She already loves you."

Beth was now crying. "I love her, too. And I want to be able to see your beautiful face day or night. To cook for you. Walk the dog with you and Kristi. Make her little brothers and sisters. I love you so much." Even as she said the words, she knew she wasn't ready to commit to a time, and she hoped Scott wouldn't press her.

He pulled her up from the couch and gave her a full-body hug. "Let's go to bed and get going on your new goals."

Every worry flew out of her mind.

"Aunt Beth, please. Can't we stay with you?" Her nose was red from crying. The afternoon sun slanted through the windows of the sacred space. Grace sat in one of the big wicker chairs, her feet dangling, in every way looking like the little girl she was.

Beth lifted the hair curtaining Grace's face and moved it over her shoulder. "Sweetie, it's going to be okay. Clara is going with you, and you'll be with your mommy. How long have you been waiting to go home with her?"

She nodded, took the tissue Beth gave her and blew her nose. "I can't play soccer anymore," she said, and began crying again.

"Sure you can. The season's over now, but in the spring, you can play at your new school."

"Can I bring my soccer ball to mommy's house?"

"Of course you can. It's yours. And your desk and art supplies. And your special chair."

"I don't want to miss you, Aunt Beth. Can you come, too? Please?"

"No, honey. But I'll visit you often. Sometimes you can spend time at the cottage, and we'll go to the beach and the Scoop." The statement was bittersweet for Beth. Patrice was beside herself with joy to have Grace home again, which made Beth so happy for her. So proud of what she'd accomplished.

"I'm afraid. I don't want to go to a new school. What if the kids laugh at me?"

Beth took Grace's hand, led her to the rocker. She sat and drew Grace into her lap. She handed her another tissue, then wrapped her arms around her. Grace put her head on Beth's shoulder, and they rocked.

"I won't see the lady anymore."

Beth stiffened. "Is the lady here now? Can you say goodbye to her?"

Grace slid off Beth's lap and stood. She looked around the room with the unfocused stare Beth had noted before. She nodded, looking toward the doorway.

Beth did the same, but the doorway was empty, as she expected. Still, if Grace could say goodbye, it might help her detach from this invisible friend. "Can you tell her goodbye for now? Maybe she'll come back to see you when you visit."

Grace stood still. Beth had a creepy sensation, as if she was in the middle of a bubble of static electricity. She could smell lilacs, stronger than ever. "Grace, does the lady have flowers?" she asked in a soft voice.

Grace nodded, as she continued to stare. Then she turned to Beth and smiled. "Everything will be all right."

"Is she gone?"

"Yes."

"Do you feel better?"

"Yes." She pushed her hair back from her face.

"What kind of flowers did the lady have?" Beth asked, goose-bumps rising on her arms.

"She always brings white lilacs, like on the tree outside."

"But there haven't been flowers on the tree for months."

Grace shrugged her shoulders. "I still want us to live here. All of us together."

Beth was shivering. She did not believe in ghosts. There must be a reasonable explanation. She just couldn't think of one right now. But Grace had enough to worry about. Beth made an effort to tamp down her fears.

"Think about all the wonderful things that are going to happen. You're going to have a new room your mommy has fixed up for you. You have a pond where you can fish or catch tadpoles with your net. Frankie bought a little rowboat so he can take you for rides on the water. It's going to be fun."

"I like Scott's boat." Her green eyes glistened with new tears. "Kristi is my best friend."

"I know, sweetie." Beth felt the press of tears behind her own eyes. She took a breath, didn't know what else to say. She frowned. Then it came to her—what to say. "Grace, if I tell you something, do you promise to keep my special secret?"

Grace straightened and focused on her. "Yes."

"Scott asked me to marry him. And I said yes. You promised not to tell, right?"

"I promise I won't tell. Does Kristi know?"

"I think her dad told her. But, listen to this. When we get married, we're going to live in Scott and Kristi's house. So, every time you visit me, you'll see your best friend, too."

She settled right down after that. Beth felt inspired. It gave her niece something to hold on to. In minutes, she was up and out in the yard to kick her soccer ball. Clara ran by her side with little yelps of joy.

Beth, still in the rocker, shook her head. God, what had happened in the sacred space? Would anyone believe her if she told them? Then she remembered she'd never given an explanation of the "lady" to her sister. Patrice had never asked.

"I guess the honeymoon's over," Frankie said, rolling over onto his side.

Patrice pulled up on one elbow. They had just made love and said goodnight. "What do you mean? It wasn't good for you?"

"Oh, it was great for me. Just thinking, though, tomorrow night we'll be parents. And we'll have to be quiet, too."

Patrice lay back down and moved closer to his back, spooning her body with his. "Being parents won't change a thing about us."

"Sure it will. Pretty soon you'll be too tired for sex. You'll be sitting up with a sick child. We'll be eating chicken tenders for dinner." He chuckled.

"Is that what happened when you lived with that woman and her two children? Because that's not what's going to happen here. And Frankie, you're scaring me. It's going to be tough for Grace to come here. She has to start in a new school and she's scared. She doesn't know you. It's a lot for her to handle."

Frankie rolled over to face her. "Sorry, Patrice. I'll adjust. Gracie will, too. It may be a rough ride, but she's a sweet kid and I like her. We'll be a family soon enough."

"Thanks, Frankie. It's going to be wonderful." She felt his hand slide over her thigh.

"How about one for the road?"

Next to Sunday, Saturday was her busiest day at work. She was running short on muffins and whipping up batter to make more. The bacon was sputtering grease all over the stove, and she ran to flip the strips and turn down the heat.

Mandy came through the door. "Need more coffee. Jeez, what's going on out there?"

"It's the holiday weekend," Patrice said, pouring batter into the muffin tins. "I'm backed up on everything, and I'm all thumbs today."

"Relax," Mandy said. "You're doing fine. Tell me how and I'll make the coffee."

"How do you stay so centered with everybody wanting service before they even ask for something?" Patrice said, once the muffins were in the oven.

Mandy smiled. "You have to keep your priorities straight."

Patrice went to make the coffee, but turned to take the bacon off the heat first. "How did you want those eggs? How did I become a short order cook? What made Tom think it was a good idea to start taking individual orders?"

"When you turned out to be such a good cook and business picked up.

Your own fault. I told you not to work so hard. Sunny side up."

"Thanks for the compliment, I think," Patrice said, smiling. She wiped the sweat off her forehead with the back of her hand then washed her hands before she picked up two eggs.

"I'd better get back out there. I'll fill the carafes when the coffee's brewed. Want me to ask Meg to come help you?"

"No, I'm handling it. No."

What would she do without Mandy? She was only twenty-two, but she had it together. She was becoming a friend. She'd even invited Patrice to join her group one night at a local restaurant. Of course, she'd said no. She had enough to do at home, and riding back and forth to Orleans so often sucked up a lot of her time. At least that would end today when they brought Grace home. She was basting the eggs when she smelled the muffins burning. She'd forgotten to set the timer. "Shit!"

Cindy's husband was having surgery and Lauren's boys had respiratory infections. Beth spent every minute of Thursday and Friday at the store. Lauren was going to work on Saturday afternoon while Troy watched the boys, so Beth could be home to see Grace off.

Beth had a miserable cold of her own. Her stress level was soaring. Last night, she and Grace had packed up her clothes. Grace took one of her green-leaf pillows for her new house, and left the other for when she came back to visit. Everything was ready downstairs in the kitchen except the furniture. Frankie told her not to lift a thing, that he could manage it by himself.

Grace was crying a little, but Beth thought it was more for fear of change than sorrow, and that made her feel better.

The red truck came up the driveway and Frankie and Patrice climbed out. Beth watched them from her window in the office and noticed neither looked happy. Were they fighting? Oh no, they had to be happy today. For Grace. It was hard enough for her to make this change without angry adults.

By the time she went around to the kitchen door and opened it, Patrice was smiling brightly. A little too brightly?

"Where's my little angel? Mommy and Frankie are here to take her home."

Grace came into the kitchen and hugged Patrice.

"Here you are, sweetie. Are you all ready to go?"

"Yes." Beth watched as Grace lifted her arm and nodded her fist, the sign for yes. She only signed now when she felt deep emotion. Like an older child sucking her thumb when she was afraid.

Patrice and Beth went down into the basement for her boxes. "Oh Lord, I'll never fit all the rest of this stuff into our little cottage. I've been barely managing with what I already took out. Do you mind if I leave these here a little longer? It's probably mostly going to Salvation Army anyway."

"No, leave them. It's a reason for you to come back."

"We'll never need a *reason* to visit you, Beth. And vice versa."

They went back upstairs into the kitchen. Patrice hugged her. "Beth, you've been the best sister in the world. You've done so much for me. I wouldn't be standing here today without you. Thank you."

Beth smiled. "You're welcome. You're worth every bit of it."

Patrice went on, quickly, as if she had to get the words out fast. "I want you to know how grateful I am. I will never forget all you've done. I love you so much."

There were tears in Patrice's eyes, but Beth pretended not to notice. She held back her own for Grace's sake. "I love you, too, little sister."

The kitchen was silent when Frankie passed through, carrying Grace's chair. "What's going on here?"

"Just sister love. We're trying not to cry," Beth said.

And then it was time to say goodbye.

Beth knelt down and reached out for Grace. "See you next weekend. Mommy wants me to come for dinner."

"Yes," Patrice said, "and you can help me cook for her."

Grace hugged Beth's neck, then quickly let go and went out the door. Patrice hugged her a little too long. So much emotion. Her sister's life would be going through a major change with Grace back home, a new job, and Frankie. She was probably nervous.

Beth walked out with them and stood on the porch, waving as they left. Grace's desk was bumping along in the back of the truck. It seemed like yesterday when Beth had carried it into the house.

She went back inside and locked the door. Then she went to rock in the sacred space and let out her pent-up tears. She prayed for the first time since she was younger than Grace. She sent prayers of gratitude wafting out to somewhere, to something she wasn't sure she believed in, but just in case. Lilac fragrance drifted by her, and she wondered again where it came from.

Could there really be a ghost? A lady who carried around white lilacs and loved children? She was beginning to seriously wonder, but she was too peaceful to dwell on it.

Chapter 34

"Sweetie, you have to go to school," Patrice said.

"You come, too."

Grace's eyes were red and swollen. It was Monday night, tomorrow would be her first day in the new school. Patrice and Sue had taken her to see the school and her classroom last week. Her teacher seemed very young to Patrice, but she kept telling her Grace would be fine. "Don't worry."

"You know I can't go with you. Mommy has to work. You have to be a big girl, be brave. Remember how brave you were when you went to the hospital to have your implants?"

"I want to take Clara Barton with me." Grace, in her pajamas, was sitting on the edge of the couch cushion. She'd been crying for fifteen minutes.

"The school said no. You don't need her there because they will take care of you, and you'll be wearing your cochlear implants. Clara is for when you have them off." She leaned down to pet the dog sitting next to Grace's feet. She seemed upset, too, whining from time to time as if she were crying with Grace.

Grace broke into another wail and Patrice flopped on the couch beside her, spent.

"What's all this racket?" Frankie asked, coming in from the bedroom.

"She's afraid to go to her new school. Poor baby."

"She's not a baby, Patrice." He knelt in front of Grace. "Gracie, everybody has to go to school. Mommy went, I went. Now, it's your turn."

Grace frowned at him. "You say my name wrong," she said, then put a finger to her transmitter. "Say, Grace."

Frankie stood up and put his hands on his hips. "Now she's telling me how to say her name? Me thinks this child is a little spoiled." He went into the kitchen for a can of soda.

Patrice followed him. "Frankie, she's trying to learn to hear and speak again. Using a nickname she's never heard before confuses her." She wrapped her arms around his waist. "At least you stopped the crying."

"I have a feeling it's only a reprieve. I think you have to put your foot down. I'm the one who has to bring her in the morning. I can't be dealing with rebellion. I have to get to work myself. New job." He raised his eyebrows at her.

"Frankie, she's not spoiled and she's not faking. You can't turn off her emotions like a faucet. She's been through hell. She did the same when Beth first took her. It was all new and frightening. More so for her because she's deaf. But she settled in pretty quick with Beth."

Frankie put a hand on her shoulder. "I know. Sorry. I guess I don't know much about kids. But I'm a little nervous about how to handle her tomorrow when you're at work. Could you beg off for one day to take her yourself?"

Patrice backed up. "I don't know who could take my place. And that's a lot to ask when I'm new there, too."

"I see you take my point."

Patrice bowed her head. "Yeah. But I can't take off. I'll just have to get her over this tonight. If she cries tomorrow, let the teacher take care of it. She's not worried at all."

She went back to the living room. "Come on, time for bed. I'll read you a story."

Grace stood up, rubbing her eyes, and followed Patrice to her room.

Two weeks later, Patrice was tucking Grace into bed. Bedtime remained an ordeal for Grace. Most nights she still sobbed a little that she didn't want to go to school, and Patrice had to reassure her it would get better. Tonight, thankfully, Grace seemed composed.

Patrice took a book from the shelf and sat on the side of Grace's bed.

"That's a little kid's book, mommy."

"You're still my baby, Grace," she said, smiling. She looked down at the book. "Hmmm, you're right. You're too grown-up for this story. How about we buy some new books tomorrow? We can go to the store after school."

That made her happy. Patrice tucked her in with a heavy heart. The joy of having her back was chipped away daily by her own mistakes. So much had changed since Grace had lived at home before. She rarely signed now. She played a sport, cooked and baked. All things Beth had done for her. The biggest feat was helping Grace hear again. She could speak quite well. Patrice was still not used to the implants. They made her nervous, but she tried not to show it. She had to learn how to clean and care for the equipment, work with Grace on new words, take her to therapy. She had a dog to manage, even though Grace was very responsible in feeding and walking Clara. Still, it was one more task she didn't need to take on. Some days she just wanted to cry herself at the realization of her own inadequacy. And she was so tired, some days she wanted to cry for no reason.

Back downstairs, she joined Frankie who was watching TV. She plopped down on the couch next to him and reached out a hand for his bottle of beer.

"You don't want this, Patrice."

"I do so. Just a sip. I need it."

"Hey. That's not a good thing. Needing. It's how you got hooked, remember?"

"I *wasn't* addicted to alcohol. Just drugs. I won't drink often, but tonight, I need to chill a little."

Frankie handed her his beer. "What's the trouble?"

"Just trying to work it out with Grace. I keep doing it all wrong." She took a long draft of beer and gave it back to Frankie.

"You're her mother, and a good one. You two will settle in. It'll take a while. Don't let it get you down." He leaned over and kissed her cheek.

"You need to help more. You haven't really tried to get to know her."

"Yeah. I know. It's weird having a deaf kid around. I can never tell what she's thinking. And you have to watch her every minute." He glanced at Patrice's expression. "I mean, it's a lot of responsibility. But you're right, I'll work on it." He took a swig of his beer then offered it back to her.

She took another swallow. She could feel the beer take the edge off, but Patrice was still obsessing about Grace. So many times she brought up Beth. How she did things, which to Grace was the only right way. She talked about her old teacher, her soccer team. Patrice kept telling herself it would all get better. But in her heart, she wasn't sure. Was the new life she offered with Frankie good enough to compare to the one Grace had lived with Beth? She didn't think so. Was loving her more than life itself enough?

Chapter 35

Since Scott and Kristi were so much a part of her and Grace's life, Beth had talked Patrice into coming to Knoll Cottage for Thanksgiving dinner. Patrice had planned on doing it at her own cottage, but it wasn't large enough for all of them. So, she was bringing some dishes to Beth's, including a pumpkin pie Grace had helped bake.

Patrice, Frankie, and Grace entered the cottage on a blast of frigid air. When all their food was stowed, they went to sit in the living room. As they began to talk, Beth was aware of tight smiles and fast words. Something was wrong. At first she thought Patrice wasn't happy about moving the celebration to Beth's place. But when Frankie didn't look once at Patrice over time, Beth knew it was something else. Grace's face was thinner and there were dusky smudges under her eyes.

"Aunt Beth, may I go into the sacred space?" Grace asked.

"It's really cold in there now, honey. If you want to go in, I'll turn on the heater, but don't stay long, okay?"

Grace nodded and followed her down the hall.

Beth went back into the living room where there was total silence. "Hey, guys, is anything wrong?"

"Nothing," Patrice said. Frankie snorted. "Frankie, shut up."

The doorbell rang, and Beth was happy for the excuse to leave the room to answer it. Dread filled her until she saw the two smiling faces at the door. After group hugs and kisses, Kristi ran off to find Grace.

"I see they're here. How is everybody?" Scott said.

Determined not to ruin the day, Beth smiled. "Everybody's good. I love that we're all together. It's going to be the best Thanksgiving we've ever had."

Scott pulled her into his arms and gazed into her eyes. She couldn't hide anything from him, but he didn't state the obvious. He kissed her. "Yes, it is."

The girls went upstairs together and the adults chatted in the living room. The fire was roaring; Frankie had piled up the wood. The conversation became more relaxed, and soon Patrice and Beth were happily working together in the kitchen.

When they were seated around the table, Beth said, "Scott, will you say some Thanksgiving words before we eat this feast?"

Scott took the hands of Beth on one side and Patrice on the other. Everyone followed suit.

"I want you all to know what I'm thankful for. I'm thankful that Grace and Beth came into our lives. That Grace has made amazing strides at hearing and speaking. And especially, I'm thankful that Beth has agreed to marry me." He raised her hand and kissed it. "Okay, your turn, Beth."

"First, I'll say ditto. I have never been so happy in my life." She smiled at Scott. "I'll add how thankful I am to have Kristi in my life. I'm so thankful for my sister's recovery and her joy in having Frankie and Grace with her."

Grace said. "Thank you, Doctor Scott, for helping me talk." Then she rolled her lips between her teeth and looked expectantly at her mother.

"I have so much to be thankful for," Patrice said. "Every person at this table." She looked around, then down at her hands, clasped together on the table.

Kristi said, "Can I say ditto to everything? But I have to add Lilly, my dog. Thanks, Dad."

Everyone turned to Frankie. After a too-long pause, he said, "Okay folks, I'll be thankful if someone would pass this food around!"

Scott and Kristi were the last to leave. At the door, hands full of leftovers, Scott said, "A little trouble in paradise?"

Beth took a deep breath and blew it out. "It seems so. I don't know what to do." She held up a hand. "Yes, I do. I will let them work it out. They can call if they need help. It's Patrice's life now."

"That's a good answer," he said, and kissed her goodbye.

In spite of her words to Scott, when she didn't hear from Patrice, she called and set up a lunch date. Patrice at first hedged, but Beth wouldn't let her off the hook. Especially since her voice was a little strange, enough to generate an acid blast in Beth's stomach.

They met at Olive Garden in Hyannis. Beth thought her sister appeared fatigued, but that was no surprise with the hours she worked.

"Beth, don't be looking for a problem."

"I'm not. Why do you say that?"

"Your eyes are like microscopes."

"Well, you do seem tired. I know you always liked to get up early, but it must be a long day."

"It's hard work, but I've learned a lot. Meg and Tom love me. They keep giving me more work, but at least they pay me by the hour. They've asked me to do an event. At night."

"Are you going to do it?"

"Frankie's not too happy about it. It's a Friday night. He likes us to go out for pizza on Fridays. The money's good, higher than my usual pay rate." For the first time, Patrice's eyes lit up, and she went on. "My friend, Mandy, who I told you about?"

"Yes?"

"She wants me to start a catering business with her. We have such a good time working together. She doesn't cook, but she said she'd learn to, and her friends would serve for us. She lives in Yarmouth." She ran a fingertip down the condensation on her iced tea glass.

"Nice. It's a good idea, but wouldn't it be evening work?"

"At first, to get established. But then I thought we could specialize in lunches, day weddings, that sort of occasion." Patrice grinned. "I'm still dreaming. I have to start with the event."

"*If* you agree to do it."

"Crap. I'd do it, but I don't want to upset the apple cart. I think it would be a good experience for me. If I can handle a large party, I could think about starting some catering on the side with Mandy."

"Wow, you have sure embraced cooking. That's awesome."

Their soup and salad arrived. Beth picked up the salad utensils and mixed the salad, then put some on both of their plates. Patrice stirred in the pile of cheese on her soup.

"Honey," Beth said, "maybe you should take it a little slower. You're making such big adjustments in your life already."

Patrice didn't answer and Beth wanted to kick herself for giving advice again. "So how's Grace doing in school?"

Tears formed in Patrice's eyes. Beth reached over and took her hand. "What is it?"

"I'm just worn out. Grace is doing much better. She misses you." Patrice looked at Beth. "She's not too fond of Frankie."

"Why not? He seems so good to her."

"I don't know. He thinks I baby her. That she'd do better with a little discipline."

"Is he doing that? Disciplining her?"

"No, I sweet-talk him out of it. I baby him, too." She smiled, but her eyes were sad.

"Can I say what I want to say?" Beth pulled her hand back and sat up straighter.

"No, I'm not taking drugs."

"May I?"

"Go ahead." Patrice put down her soup spoon and sighed.

"You may not be using, but do you want to? Are you craving? Are you going to therapy and 12-Step meetings?"

"Yes, yes, and no. But I'm *not* taking anything. I'm strong. Don't worry about me."

Beth was clamping her teeth together. Should she push it? Would it backfire and cause a fight if she did? "If you need me, anytime, I'm here for you. Make use of me. Please?"

Chapter 36

It was three weeks later, on Christmas Eve, when the pounding on the front door woke Beth. She jumped out of bed and ran to the window. It was too dark to see anything. She went to the phone on her bedside table and lifted the receiver to call 911. She was shaking and her breaths were coming in short pants.

She heard yelling. Then barking. With the phone still in her hand, she listened. Someone was calling her name. A sense of dread weakened her knees. It was Frankie, and he was frantic. *Grace!*

She flew down the stairs and fought to open the rarely used front door. Grace stood before her. Her face was soaked with tears, and she was holding onto Clara's leash.

"What? What's wrong?" She pulled Grace to her and hugged her. She turned up to Frankie's tortured expression and felt a freeze clamp around her heart.

"Frankie? What is it?"

"Patrice is in the hospital. I didn't want to leave Grace alone. I have to go right back." He stood bent over, as if Grace's booster seat in his right hand weighed a hundred pounds. "Can she stay here?"

She eased upright, still holding Grace close to her. "Frankie, calm down. Tell me what happened." Her own panic made her voice level just under a scream.

"I—I'm not sure. I was visiting my brother for Christmas Eve dinner. Patrice didn't want to go with me. She was going to have her friend Mandy visit, but when I got home, no one was around. Grace was in bed asleep. It was real quiet in the house. I went to our bedroom, but Patrice wasn't there. Then I found her passed out in the bathroom. I couldn't wake her. She looked real bad. I couldn't feel a pulse, so I called an ambulance." He paused, swallowed several times. "I did CPR the best I could." He dropped his head back and looked up at the sky.

"Go on, dammit!"

He glanced at Grace, then away. "It was déjà vu all over again, you know what I mean? Jesus Christ!" He scrubbed his face with both hands, leaving it dark red. "The EMTs worked on her—got her heart beating. They asked me how long she'd been unconscious, but I didn't know.

"I followed the ambulance to the hospital, but I had to leave her at the ER to go back and bring Grace to you. You'll keep her, won't you?"

"Yes, of course I will. Call me, Frankie, as soon as you know something. Do you understand?"

"I'll call. Listen, the hospital asked me about a living will. I don't know if she has one, do you?"

She went rigid, and Grace noticed and looked up at her with big eyes. She tried to hide the fear Frankie's words produced. "I don't know. Her papers are here. I'll check. Call me as soon as you can. Don't forget. I'll be waiting." Frankie turned to leave. "Wait, what hospital?"

"Falmouth," he said, before disappearing into the darkness.

Only a month since Grace had moved in with her mother, and now this. Beth swept her hand through her hair, grabbed a bunch of it, and squeezed. *Oh, Patrice. Patrice.*

She led Grace into the living room where they sat together. When she removed Clara's leash, the dog leaned on the couch at Grace's knee. Grace wasn't wearing her cochlear implants. Frankie must have rushed her out. She must be so afraid.

"Do you know what happened?" Beth signed.

"Mommy's sick. She had to go back to the hospital." Tears rolled down her cheeks. "Will she be gone a long time again?"

"I don't know. Frankie will call and tell us what the doctor says." Beth noticed the cuticles of both thumbs were raw and ragged.

"Can't Doctor Scott take care of her?"

She shook her head, signing, "It's better for her to be in the hospital. Would you like to go to sleep in your bed?"

"No sleep. Scared," she signed.

"How about we lie down in my bed and watch TV?"

"No, I want to be in the space." They took the couch cushions and carried them to the sacred space. Beth went upstairs for one of her bed pillows and a blanket. Grace lay down, her big green eyes staring at the wall. Beth rocked in the chair beside her.

It took an hour for Grace to fall asleep. She never mentioned Christmas. Beth wrote her a note saying she went downstairs to get some papers her mother needed. She knew if Grace woke and found herself alone, she'd be frightened. Clara Barton lay on the floor beside her. She looked up when Beth tiptoed out, then rested her head back on her paws. She was on duty.

Once in the living room, Beth let out her tears. She allowed herself to weep for a few minutes, but pulled herself together. It might not be so bad.

She shouldn't jump to the worst case scenario. Frankie hadn't called her yet; that might be a good sign.

Seven boxes that belonged to Patrice were still in the basement. Beth carried up two at a time to the living room, where the Christmas tree sat alone in the corner, making her task sadder. She opened three of them before she found the items from Patrice's desk. The contents were not organized, just a jumble of things. She dumped the contents on the floor and began to search for anything that looked like a document.

She cried again when she saw the greeting cards. They were gathered together with a pink ribbon. She untied the bundle and sorted through them. Patrice had kept all the birthday cards Beth had given her since they were teenagers. And Beth knew, when pressing the bundle of cards to her chest, how much her sister loved her.

She wiped her tears away and went back to work. She took every letter-sized sheet of paper and skimmed it one at a time, then tossed each back in the box. There were several different-sized envelopes; some used, and some new. She picked up a stack, checked each and returned it to the box. She stopped and grabbed the last envelope she'd dropped into the box. It was old, eight years old, judging by the postmark. Beth didn't recognize the name on the return address, Phil Levin. She peered inside. A letter. She took it out and read.

Dear Pats,

I know you don't want to hear from me, but this is important. First let me say, I'm sorry about what happened. I still regret it. I don't blame you for not wanting to have anything to do with me, ever again.

I'm writing because one of our mutual friends told me you were pregnant and going to keep the child. I know that child is mine. We were together night and day and we never looked at anyone else.

I want to help take care of the baby. I want to be responsible. We could even get married if you could find a way to forgive me.

I'll be out your way next week. Don't shut me out, Pats. Just let's talk about it.

Still loving you, Phil

The letter was shaking in her hands. Oh my God. Patrice *did* know who Grace's father was. Beth wondered what had happened when he'd come to see her. Patrice never mentioned anything about Phil. She'd maintained she didn't know who the father was. Whatever happened must have been bad enough for Patrice never to see him again.

She went to add the letter to the box, but instead stuck it in her pocket. When Patrice was better, Beth would bring it up. She patted her pocket and went back to the pile.

When she finished going through the rest of the contents, without finding a living will, she went to the kitchen to check the time. Two and a half hours had passed since Frankie left. Why didn't he call? Then she realized he may not know her number. He may not be able to ask Patrice. The thought threw her into action. She googled Falmouth Hospital and called.

"I believe my sister was admitted to the Emergency Room there. Can you tell me her condition, please?"

She answered the woman's questions, and then waited on hold. Finally, the woman came back. "Your sister has been moved to the ICU. She is listed in critical condition."

"Oh God." The operator wasn't able to get any further information. She called ICU and was told the same basic details. She left her phone number and asked to have Patrice's fiancé call her.

"They're doing tests," Frankie said when he called back. "They don't know if she took drugs or it's something else. I went back home and looked for a bottle or other evidence of something, but I couldn't find anything." He paused. "Beth, she's in a coma." His voice broke.

"I'm coming."

She hung up and called Scott. He answered on the second ring and sounded alert. It was four a.m., and he promised to be there in fifteen minutes. She ran upstairs and threw on her clothes.

Scott came into the cottage kitchen and held her. She could feel some of his strength flow into her.

"I'm so sorry," he said. "Remember, we don't know what the problem is. She's getting good care. You go see her. I'll take Grace and Clara home with me. Call me when you can." It was Saturday, but not Scott's weekend to see patients.

They woke Grace. Beth got together some of her clothes and her toothbrush. Downstairs she grabbed the booster seat and they went out to Scott's car. She kissed Grace and Scott, and minutes later, she was on her way to Falmouth.

During the drive, her mother and father came into her thoughts. She was almost hyperventilating with anxiety about her sister, so thinking about their parents changed her focus. Her anger trumped her fears. She wondered if her father had any memory left. Had he thought about his daughters at all over the last nine years? He had never forgiven Patrice after her drunken words at their mother's funeral. Then, once it was clear Beth would not come home after college to serve him and his beloved congregants, he'd never answered any of her calls. He was slowly deteriorating from his early onset Alzheimer's, and that's all she knew. Every time she called the nursing home, he had slipped further. He was only sixty. He had left orders that his daughters could not visit until he was dead.

Would the pearly gates of heaven open for him? Did a man who controlled his wife so completely that she'd died from exhaustion have a free pass because he was a minister? Was there no sin in his lack of forgiveness for the perceived wrongs of his daughters? Did he ever have an inkling that he might have been the one who was wrong?

She thought about Patrice. What had made her so dependent? Most of her brashness was a false facade. Inside she hurt. She must, or why would she need drugs to deaden her feelings. Had she done it this time for good?

Chapter 37

Beth pulled into the hospital visitor lot. It was still dark and the air was damp and cold. She pulled her jacket tighter around her and rushed to the door.

As she entered the ICU waiting room, Frankie stood there to greet her; his face pale and unshaven.

"How is she?" Beth asked. Now that she was there, her whole body began to tremble.

"They won't tell me. They said she took something. I told them she was clean, but I'm not really sure she was. I smelled Spice on her once."

"What! How could you let that happen? She could be drug tested at any time." She moved in front of him, her hands knotted into fists. She wanted to hit him.

"I didn't give it to her. I wouldn't know where to get it, even. I smelled something, and *she* told me it was Spice. She said it was just synthetic pot made from herbs, it wasn't a drug and it didn't show up on drug tests. That was just once, and maybe she had an occasional beer." He stepped back and dropped into the chair. "Do you think I'd let anything happen to her? I love her."

Beth had no answer. She sat in the chair next to him and dropped her head into her hands. After a while she looked up at him. "I'm sorry. I'm just upset. After all that time. She did so well in rehab. What could have made her. . . ." She dropped her chin to her chest. Three times in rehab was not the charm Beth had hoped for. Patrice had seemed so confident, happy to have Grace home, and in love with Frankie. She'd been her old self. She pressed the back of her hand against her mouth. For a while, but then there had been the strain. Beth had tried not to interfere. "Can I see her?" she asked, looking up at Frankie and taking note of his red face.

"You have to call them on the phone." He pointed to a wall phone without looking at her. "Just lift it. Someone will answer. They don't let you stay long."

With permission, Beth went through the door to the nurses' station. A bank of machines was beeping, and complicated graphs and lines were tracking her sister's progress on a stack of CRTs. A horseshoe of white counter, with three-wheeled chairs pushed under it, separated rooms on either side of the station. The ICU was a strip of glass-fronted, cubicle-like rooms, each with a computer mounted on a shelf outside the door.

"Ms. Henson?" an older nurse in a snap-front blue smock asked.

"Yes. May I see her?"

"I'll take you in. First, let me say, your sister is still unresponsive. She has a ventilator to help her breathe, and she's being monitored with machines that can look frightening. Have you been to an ICU before?"

She couldn't stop the tears from falling as she shook her head.

Nothing could have prepared her. When she saw Patrice, she lost her breath.

The nurse patted her on the shoulder. "It's all right. Takes a minute to get used to it."

The woman made no denial, like: It's worse than it looks. No words of hope. Beth moved to the bottom of Patrice's bed and held onto the footboard. She hardly recognized her sister's beautiful face. It was puffy and pale.

"Why don't you sit in the chair beside the bed? You can touch her and talk to her. Will you be all right alone for a few minutes?"

Beth couldn't speak, so she nodded. Her eyes were glued to the stranger on the bed. Clicks and whooshes from the ventilator filled the room. Her sister's heartbeats were sounding with loud, regular beeps. The tube from the ventilator hid some of her face. Multiple IV lines from her arm connected to plastic bags hanging behind the bed. The head of the bed was raised slightly.

She moved to the bedside chair. Leaning over the rail, she ran her shaking fingers down her sister's cheek. "Oh, Patrice. Don't do this. Don't leave me." She picked up the edge of the sheet and wiped the tears from her face. "Please. You're my baby sister, and I love you so much. I always have. Even when I was tough on you. I just wanted you to be happy." She took Patrice's cool fingers into her hand. Those long graceful fingers that drew such beautiful pictures were now red and rough from the scrubbing required by her job.

"Patrice, Grace needs you. You can't leave her. You can't leave me." She sobbed. "What will I do without you? Damn it. Don't do this. Open your eyes. Look at me!"

Patrice was still. Only her chest rose and fell with the ventilator's pace.

Beth tilted her face to the ceiling, causing her tears to seep sideways from her eyes into her hair. And then she wept, as silently as she could. And through it, she prayed, using words she remembered from her father's church, never letting go of her sister's hand.

She was dry-eyed when the nurse came back.

"The drug screen showed oxycontin and cocaine."

"Where would she get that? And she never took cocaine before. Her addiction was to prescription drugs. She just finished rehab a month and a half ago." Tears began to flow again. "She was doing so well. How could this happen?"

"Sometimes when an addict has been clean for a length of time, the first drugs they take can have a more profound effect. Their tolerance drops, but they may not realize it, and they overdose. Especially if it's a drug they're not used to taking."

Beth stared at her sister's face. "Is she going to die?"

"We don't know. I'm sorry. The neurologist ordered some tests to check her brain activity. We'll know more after we get those results, and the doctor will talk to you. Why don't you go have a cup of coffee, some breakfast? Nothing is going to happen while you're gone."

It was over an hour later when the doctor came to talk to her and Frankie. He was fortyish, tall and lean, with straight, salt-and-pepper hair. He was wearing green scrubs. "I'm Doctor Abernathy. I'm the consulting neurologist for Patrice. I have some information for you. I'm sorry it seems to take so long. We can speak more privately in another room. Would you come this way?"

Beth entered the small, dark room lined with wooden chairs. Two Christmas stockings hung on either side of the door. Her heart began to pound and she put her hand over it, as if to slow it. She sat beside Frankie, and the doctor pulled up a chair in front of them.

"I believe you've both been made aware of the drug screen results. A high dose of cocaine mixed with oxycontin apparently caused cardiac arrest. We don't know how long Patrice was unconscious before you found her, Mr. Keenan.

"Here's where we are right now. So far, Patrice remains unresponsive. We've done several tests, starting with a physical exam. We perform different stimulations to test the brain function. We watch her reaction, for example, when we test her pupils' response to bright light, or when we touch the cornea of her eye. We check her gag reflex. These tests gauge brainstem reflexes. We've also done an apnea test, which was inconclusive. We'll repeat that later." He paused, rubbing his palms together.

"Doctor, can my sister recover?" Beth asked, her laced fingers tightening on her lap.

"It's difficult to say with certainty at this point. When drugs are involved it complicates and delays our diagnosis. Her EEG, electroencephalogram, showed little or no reactivity, so, unfortunately, we know Patrice has suffered brain damage. Because of that fact, you must understand, even if she lives, she may not regain full function."

"Oh no. No, please. Oh God." Beth's body sagged in the chair.

"I'm sorry," the doctor murmured.

"But there's a chance, right? She could still pull through," Frankie said through his tears.

"We're going to repeat the apnea test in an hour or so. We're also going to do an MRI."

Beth tried to feel a sense of hope, but even if Patrice lived, how would she live? Would she ever recognize her daughter or her sister? Would she languish in a nursing home for years being fed by a tube? Beautiful Patrice—she would *hate* that. She looked into the doctor's compassionate face. "Will the other tests be definitive?"

"Yes. We'll know if she is brain dead. If that's the case, there is nothing we can do. Don't try to make any decisions right now. Why don't you visit her again before we take her for more tests? It will be at least two hours before we have the results."

Beth wanted to scream, to lash out at someone. She wanted to groan and weep, but she was blocked. She couldn't cry. She couldn't move. How could she go on without her sister? And Grace. How could she tell Grace her mother was gone?

"Do either of you know if Patrice has a living will?" the doctor asked.

Frankie shook his head.

"I looked through her papers, but I didn't find one," Beth said. "We never talked about it. Who thinks they're going to die at twenty-nine years old?" Her voice was growing louder; she pressed a hand to her mouth to stop the rising fear.

"I understand. Did she ever mention her wishes to either of you?"

"We talked about living," Frankie said. "We talked about getting married, having our own kids. We never talked about dying." He looked at Beth. "She was struggling a little, but we were getting it together. She wasn't taking anything. I know she wasn't. How could she just die from some goddamn cocaine or oxycontin? Where the hell did it come from?" He bowed his head and ran his fingers through his hair.

The doctor put a hand on his arm for a moment. He said to Beth, "We'll talk again when we have the test results. Are you her next of kin? Parents?" He shrugged his shoulders.

"My father is alive, but he has Alzheimer's, and I'm not sure he's cogent at all. But she has a little girl, Grace. She's eight. I don't know what to do about her."

"Let's take one step at a time. Have another visit with Patrice, and we'll get her tests underway."

After a few minutes of sitting with Patrice, bawling while she held her hand, Beth heard the nurse say it was time for the MRI. Frankie, who had been standing on the other side of Patrice's bed, turned and walked back to the waiting room. Beth followed.

"Frankie, I have to go out for a while. Are you going to stay here?"

"Yes, I'm not leaving her."

"I'm sorry, Frankie. I know you love her. I know how much she loves you, too. I'll be back as fast as I can. Give me your phone." Beth inserted her name and number into his contact list. "Call me if you need me or if anything happens at all."

She drove like she had nothing to lose. On the way, she called Scott and told him what the neurologist had said.

"I'm sure you'll be staying at the hospital until you hear more," he said.

"Is Grace all right?"

"She's doing fine. Kristi hasn't left her side for a minute."

"Scott. Is Patrice going to die?" She squeezed the steering wheel tighter. He fell quiet, but Beth could hear him breathing.

"It doesn't sound good, honey. Listen, Lisa is coming in an hour or so. She'll stay with the girls so I can drive to the hospital. I'll meet you in the ICU."

She stepped harder on the gas. She needed Scott more than anything she'd ever needed in her life. But she had to do something right now. Right now.

Chapter 37

Beth hated the place as soon as she crossed the threshold. It was dark, depressing, in spite of the fake Christmas tree decorated with red satin balls. She passed patients in wheelchairs, some staring blankly from slack faces, others talking in groups of two or three.

"I'm Beth Henson," she told the frazzled-looking woman working on the computer inside a circular counter. "I need to see my father, Thomas Henson."

"You're his daughter. The one I spoke to on the phone?" She pressed stray hairs behind her ear as she spoke.

"Yes. I need to see him."

"He made it clear you could not visit him. I'm sorry. We have to follow his wishes."

"Is he coherent? Can you ask him?"

"Once in a while he's lucid. Not much anymore."

"Go ask him please—Agnes," she said, making a point to read her name tag.

The woman sighed and spoke into a microphone. Beth could hear her distant voice asking for Jane Shepherd to come to the desk. She ignored Beth when the young woman—Jane, she assumed—arrived and spoke in tones too low for her to hear. Jane walked off, but not before Beth saw the frown on her face.

"Just have a seat." Agnes indicated a chair and went back to work on the computer.

"I'm in a terrible hurry. I'll stand." She hated the sound of her own angry voice, but she couldn't shake the emotion.

Jane came back and shook her head.

"Sorry, he wasn't able to give permission. We tried," Agnes said.

"Is his *wish* a legal statement?"

Agnes stared at her with pursed lips.

"If it's not a legal requirement for you to ban me from seeing my father—whose daughter is *dying* at this moment—then I'm going to see my father. Please show me; where is he?"

If she'd expected sympathy, she would have been disappointed. "Follow me." The woman left her at the door. "He's in the bed by the window."

Beth stood still. Now that she was here, what was she going to do? She was so full of rage, she was shaking. She took a deep breath and pushed the heavy wooden door open. A man in the bed closest to the door was lying on his back with his mouth open. He was old, and she thought he might be dead until he made a choking noise, and turned onto his side. She rushed past him and stepped beyond the pulled curtain between the two beds.

Her father seemed so small. As if his body had shrunk, as his brain had. He was almost bald, but what hair he had left streamed around his head in strands way past needing a trim. He hadn't been shaved for days, but his bedding was clean and the area neat. She stared at his face, as he was lying on his side facing the window. His head had slipped to the bottom of the pillow, causing the loose skin on his face to fold into layers and scrunch his right eye closed.

"Pastor Henson," she said, using the name he'd built his life around. He didn't respond. She shook his shoulder gently. "Pastor Henson?"

His left eye opened.

She leaned down and peered into his face. "Do you know who I am?"

"He can't understand you. He's got old timer's disease."

The voice came from the other bed, so Beth walked around the curtain. "Does he ever respond at all?"

"Once in a blue moon. Not much lately."

She went back to her father.

"Dad, it's Beth, your daughter."

He frowned. "I don't have a daughter . . . I don't think."

"You have two daughters. Beth and Patrice."

A small smile appeared at the mention of her sister's name. "Do you remember Patrice?" she asked.

He studied her with eyes that seemed cut off from his soul. Vague and blank. "Who are you? Are you my nurse?"

Beth pulled a wooden chair closer to his bed. Why had she felt such a strong compulsion to come? She was wasting time, sitting beside the wrong sick bed. As she gazed at him, she realized he was only a pathetic man, and a small crack opened in her wall of anger. "No, Dad, I'm not your nurse. I'm your oldest daughter, Beth. I came to tell you Patrice is sick, deathly ill."

"Patrice draws pictures. Where are they? Are they here in the house? Ask Mary, she knows." His hands began to pick at his blanket.

"Patrice is dying. I came to tell you. She's your daughter who draws beautiful pictures." She stood. What's the point? She felt cheated, deprived of telling him how he'd failed his daughters. How they grew up without parents and how much it wounded them. How his stubborn refusal to forgive Patrice helped make her drug problem intractable. How he took their mother away from them, first with all-consuming church responsibilities, then with her early death from trying to do it all. But she couldn't relieve the anger she'd been carrying with her for years. Her father was safe behind his destroyed mind. She'd wanted to make him suffer like she did, knowing Patrice was dying.

"Goodbye, Dad."

"Beth." It came out as a statement, not a question. His eyes held a flicker of knowledge. "Get your mother. It's time for my dinner."

Scott was waiting in the hospital lobby. As he stood she ran into his arms. He held her tightly, telling her he loved her and he would be there for her. She buried her face in his neck and listened to the soothing tones of his deep, melodic voice.

When she pulled back, he smiled at her. "You look exhausted. I know how much you're suffering and I'm so sorry."

"I can't believe how devastating this is. How could she die from an overdose? It's just not fair. She worked so hard, and she was happy."

"We never know what's in a person's mind."

Beth bent over and began to weep. She wanted to ask him the question that had been haunting her, but she couldn't stop sobbing. Scott walked her to a chair, and she collapsed into it, her tears coming as if they'd never stop. He knelt before her, and she looked into his eyes, full of love and compassion. "Scott—please tell me. . . ."

He handed her a handkerchief. "What, darling, I'll tell you whatever you want. Take a breath. I'll be right here." He cupped her cheek with his hand.

"Did she—do you think, oh God. Did she kill herself?"

Chapter 38

Beth walked into the ICU waiting room with Scott. A small group of people stood by the window, holding each other and crying. She turned away from their grief.

Frankie stood, and so did a man who was sitting beside him. Frankie introduced Phil Levin.

"Phil Levin?" Beth repeated his name.

"Did Patrice tell you about me?"

"No. I found your letter," she said, feeling the blood drain from her face.

"Look, I'm sorry about Pats. Once upon a time, I was in love with her."

Beth nodded. Scott stood beside her with his hand pressing on the small of her back. She didn't know what to do or say. She couldn't handle more than her sister's illness right now.

Frankie said, "My sister told his wife about Patrice."

"Why doesn't everyone sit down," Scott said.

When they were seated, Phil went on. "If you found my letter, then you know I'm probably—almost certainly—the father of Patrice's little girl. Is it Grace?"

Beth felt Scott stiffen beside her. She pressed her lips together and didn't answer him.

Phil put his hands on his knees and leaned forward. "Here's the thing; I discussed this with Rachel—she's my wife. She agreed we should do the right thing. I only wanted you to know, if the worst happens, I'm prepared to take my daughter." He jerked his head once, as if to finalize his prepared speech.

Beth glanced over at Frankie, who seemed somehow relieved. As if she would let him, or *anyone,* take Grace from her. She was sick to her stomach. If she had to lose Grace after losing Patrice, she thought she would die of grief.

"What? You expect to walk in here and take a child who's never even met you? No. You can't do that. If you're so sure you're her father, how come you never made an attempt to see her? My sister would have told me." Her voice was rising, and the people across the room were now looking at them.

"Listen. What do you think the letter was about? I wanted to take responsibility—I wanted my daughter, but your sister refused to acknowledge me," he said. "I could be her only real parent—"

"I'm her only parent—"

Scott caught her arm. "Do you need a little time to think about this?"

"Yes. I can't think about this now," she said. "*Please*, leave me alone. Let me take care of my sister. Oh God, don't you understand? I'm praying she'll *live!*"

In the silence that followed, two people came through the ICU door and joined the three by the window.

Phil stood. He had black hair, thin on top. His eyes were small and deeply inset, but she thought they were brown, not dark green. "I'm truly sorry to upset you more. I thought you might be happy to know, under the circumstances, that Grace would have a father. I'll be in touch." He handed a card to Scott on his way out.

A few minutes later, Beth was still stinging from Phil's words, when a nurse brought them back to the small room to meet with the doctor again. Scott introduced himself as Beth's fiancé and added that he was also a doctor.

"Good," Doctor Abernathy said to Scott. He drew a deep breath and began, "The second apnea test was positive—"

"Thank God," Beth whispered. Scott took her hand and squeezed it. She looked at him, and he shook his head.

"I'm sorry," Doctor Abernathy said, looking from Beth to Frankie, "positive results for this test support the clinical diagnosis of brain death. The MRI, unfortunately, confirms the diagnosis."

Frankie cried, and Beth put an arm around him, crying herself.

"Are there more tests? What if she gets better?" Beth said.

"There will be more tests, but these are definitive."

"Wait! What about those people who wake up from deep comas, sometimes years later? What if Patrice does that? We can't just let her die. We have to give her a chance, don't we? Please, we have to." She turned her head in the direction of Patrice's room, tears streaming down her face.

"Those are different cases," the neurologist said, "Those people were in a coma with some brain activity. Brain death is permanent and irreversible. In Patrice's case, we know there is complete cessation of all her brain function. She cannot wake up."

Scott asked him a few other medical questions. Frankie got up and told them he was going to say a last goodbye to Patrice. Before he left, Scott told him he would pick up Patrice's belongings tomorrow, Sunday, but he would stop on the way home for Grace's cochlear implants.

The doctor asked Scott and her to stay a moment longer. "There are some decisions to make. Right now, Patrice's body is being maintained by machines. Did she ever discuss being an organ donor with you?"

"Can drug addicts be organ donors?" Beth asked, frowning.

He pursed his lips for a few seconds before he spoke. "In some cases, yes. Every donor is tested and some organs may not be suitable for transplantation, but from what we know about her drug history, it's possible she could be a donor. The waiting list is long. Did she ever talk to you about it?"

Beth looked down at the vinyl square-tiled floor, blinking her eyes. "We did talk about it once. She thought it was sad that people who needed transplants died before an organ became available. But she never said she wanted to be a donor. Could we check her driver's license?"

Doctor Abernathy shook his head. "Mr. Keenan already did. She's not a registered donor. As her next of kin, you can make the decision. Why don't I have you speak with the transplant coordinator? She can answer all your questions. There's no hurry."

He stood up and extended his hand to Beth. "I'm truly sorry." He shook Scott's hand and left.

Beth sobbed through the whole meeting with the transplant coordinator. The slender woman with red curly hair seemed too young to be dealing with something as serious as organ donation, but she was compassionate and knowledgeable.

"Though your sister is legally dead, the mechanical support will keep her organs functioning, so you don't have to make the decision right this moment. I realize it's a lot to take in. Just know how much a donation of her organs could help someone who may have days to live. It's a wonderful gift."

Beth blew her nose and took a deep breath. "I need some time. It feels like the right thing to do, but . . . I have to be sure."

"I understand. Take my card and give me a call. If you decide to donate, I'll alert the surgical team."

Beth went back alone to sit beside her sister. She picked up Patrice's hand. It was warm. She could see the blue veins under the pale skin. Blood was pumping through her body, and everything but her brain was still alive. *Legally dead.*

"Oh, Patrice, how can I make this decision?" she whispered. "I want to keep you with me forever, but what good would that do? But if your good heart saved a life, I think you would be happy." She felt like her head was about to explode. She kissed her sister's hand and tucked it back under the sheet. "Be back soon."

Scott encouraged her to come home with him for a while. She had some serious decisions to make. On the ride home, after a quick stop at Frankie's cottage, Scott silently listened as she talked in circles about allowing Patrice to be a donor, of whether she should bring Grace to the hospital to see her mother, about what if Phil Levin was her father.

They stopped at Beth's cottage, where she took a quick shower. She pulled on fresh jeans and a long-sleeved t-shirt, followed by a wool sweater. She couldn't seem to warm up.

It was late afternoon when they arrived at Scott's house. Kristi met them at the door. She held a finger to her lips and whispered, "She fell asleep on the couch." Scott pulled his daughter close and hugged her. Lisa, standing in the hall behind her, gave Beth a sad smile.

Kristi's golden retriever came running to greet them, barking her joy.

"Oh no, Lily," Kristi said, trying to hush the dog.

"She can't hear, honey. She's not wearing her implants." Beth said.

A minute later, though, Grace stood in the hall. Her hair was tousled, and she had a pillow crease on her cheek. She opened her eyes wide when she focused on Beth's face. She splayed her fingers and touched her chin with her thumb. "Mommy."

Beth went to her, gave her a hug then offered her the implants and the processors. Once they were attached, she took her niece's hand and led her to a large upholstered chair in the living room. She scooted over to share the seat with Grace, whose bottom lip was already trembling.

"Your mommy is very sick," Beth said.

"Why are your eyes like that? Were you crying?" She'd turned her sneakered feet inward, the tips touching.

"Yes. I'm sad because . . . your mommy may not be able to get well again."

Grace tilted her head back and wailed, "I want mommy."

"I know, sweetie, but sometimes people have to leave us before we want them to," she said, her breath catching between her words.

"No, Aunt Beth. She can't leave. She's all better," her voice pleaded.

Beth looked up and saw Scott standing in the doorway. She knew he was there in case she needed him. His presence strengthened her. "Your mom has a kind of sickness that can go away and come back. This time it came back and was very bad. The doctors can't make her better."

"Mommy's not dead!" she yelled, and began to kick her heels into the chair.

"She's dying, honey. The doctor can't save her, she's too sick. I'm so sorry." She hugged Grace while she keened. "You cry all you want. I wish I could take this heartbreak away from you—and me—but I can't."

When she settled down a little, Beth brushed the damp strands of black hair from her face. Scott was there with a napkin. She took it and wiped Grace's face. Scott sat down quietly on the floor next to their chair.

Beth took a deep breath. "Grace. Do you want to go see your mommy and tell her goodbye?"

"No! I don't want to tell her goodbye!" Tears flooded her eyes again. "I don't want her to die."

"I know you don't. I know. You don't have to go see her, sweetie. She's sleeping, and she wouldn't be able to wake up and talk to you."

Grace sniffled and coughed. She turned her eyes, filled with despair, to Beth. How many disasters could one little girl have to face? She thought of Phil Levin and wished with all her heart he would go away.

"Would you come, too?"

"Yes, I would be right beside you."

Grace rubbed her eyes with her fists like a little child. "I'm afraid. Can Clara come with us?"

"No. Not this time. Do you want to think about it a little while?"

"I don't want her to die."

"I don't either, Grace. We are all going to miss her so much."

Grace grew quiet and still. Her tears dried on her cheeks; her mouth was slightly open. Beth sent a pleading look to Scott. He raised a hand and ran it gently over Grace's head. "It's hard, honey. I wish you and your aunt didn't have to suffer like this."

Grace slowly turned and focused on his face. "Can't you fix her like you fixed me? Please, Doctor Scott. Can you try?"

"I would give anything in the world if I could, little one. But I can't. She's too sick."

Another ten minutes went by. Beth held her, rocking her. Finally, in a scratchy, tiny voice, Grace said, "I want to see mommy."

Scott called ahead to the ICU, so they could prepare for Grace to see her mother. Although none of the machines could be removed until after they retrieved her organs, they would move her to a regular room, which would make the scene seem less frightening. On the drive back to the hospital, Scott explained the equipment she would see, and how it was helping her mommy wait to say goodbye to Grace and her aunt.

Despite of the warnings and preparation, Grace panicked when she entered the hospital room and saw her mother.

"That's not mommy. I don't want to go in. I don't want to see her." She spun around and sprinted down the hall.

Beth followed. "It's okay, Grace," she breathed, when she caught up with her. "You don't have to go in. We can say goodbye to her from right here."

Grace backed up against the wall, her thumb and index finger between her front teeth. She was crying and her nose was running.

Patrice's evening nurse approached them. Standing a short distance from Grace, she said in a soft voice, "Do you know your mom can hear you? She can't answer you, but you can talk to her, even in a whisper, and she'll hear you. You can do it from right here, or you can get closer to her door, but you don't have to go into her room."

A veil of hope slipped down over Grace's face.

"I'll go with you. I want to tell her things, too," Beth said, holding out her arm.

They walked hand-in-hand back to Patrice's room. Beth set Grace up in the doorway with the nurse by her side then went to sit beside her sister. She drew Patrice's hand out from under the sheet and held it in both of hers. Leaning close to her, she began to speak. "Grace is here to see you, Patrice. But first I have to tell you something." She put her lips together to hold back her tears. "I will miss you so much, little sister. You have always been my best friend. I never minded helping you because I loved you more than anything. I still do. I love Grace the same way. I'm sorry you couldn't stay with us longer. It won't be the same without you. I promise I'll never forget anything we ever did together." She cleared her throat, which was nearly closed with grief. "I found the greeting cards I sent that you saved. That was the best gift you could have given me." She glanced at Grace, who was staring at her mother. "I promise you I will always take care of Grace, asking myself, 'What would Patrice want me to do?' before I make any decision that affects her." She raised her sister's hand to her cheek and held it there. "I love you so much." She bowed her head and wept.

She felt a pat on her back and looked up. It was Grace. Beth put an arm around her waist and pulled her close. "Patrice, Grace is here with me." She turned to Grace, saying, "Do you want to hold your mommy's hand with me?" She gently lowered Patrice's hand back onto the bed.

Grace nodded and put her hand on top of her mother's and Beth's.

"Would you like to tell her something?"

Grace began to sob. Beth let her cry it out. When she was quieter, they sat and looked at Patrice in silence for a while; then Grace began to speak.

"I love you, mommy. I don't want you to go. The lady told me she would take care of you. She's nice. Her name is Hannah. She said you wouldn't ever be sick again. So, that's why you have to go." Grace pulled her hand away and slid past Beth, moving closer to her mother's shoulder. When she dropped her head on Patrice's chest and cried, Beth cried, too. They stayed that way for a long time.

Finally, Beth managed, "We have to say goodbye now, sweetie." She stood and eased Grace back up. "Goodbye, my beautiful little sister."

She looked at Grace.

She faced her mommy, raised her small hand, signed "goodbye," and then she signed the words, "mommy," and "I love you."

Watching her was so overwhelmingly sad, Beth broke down again. Grace wailed in her arms. They staggered together out to the waiting room where Scott rushed over and wrapped his arms around both of them.

Chapter 39

"I've decided Patrice would want to be a donor," Beth said. "I'm going to go talk to the coordinator. Will you take Grace home? I'll follow soon in my car."

Scott wrapped his arms around her and kissed her cheek. "We'll see you at home."

She watched Grace walk down the hall, holding Scott's hand. Maybe another child would benefit from Patrice's gift of life. A most wonderful Christmas gift. Someday she would tell Grace. Scott leaned over and picked up Grace. Beth could tell she was still weeping. She followed them with her eyes until they were out of sight.

She made her way to the transplant coordinator's office. Her heart was in agony, and it felt like it would be forever. But she was sure of her decision to donate Patrice's tissue and organs. After she signed the papers, the coordinator shook her hand, and Beth left the hospital.

Scott encouraged Beth to stay the night at his house. Grace was too tired to cry; she was almost stoic. He prescribed a mild sedative for her. When it began to work, Beth took her to the guest room and stayed with her until she was sound asleep.

It was near midnight. She sat with Scott in the living room.

"They said it would take four to six hours for the organ retrieval surgery. I know she's already gone, but it feels like that's when she'll be really dead."

"Yes. It's hard to see her breathing and accept that she's gone. You made the right decision, honey."

"It helps me to think part of her will live on in someone whose life she saved. I think she'd feel good about that, too." She paused. "Do you believe there's a God, Scott?"

"I've seen things as a doctor that leave me no other explanation."

"My father's God would have sent Patrice to hell to burn for eternity. I could never believe what he preached, even as a kid. If that was the kind of God who created us, why would He bother?"

"I don't think there'd be any purpose to life," he soothed.

"My sister had a good heart."

"She did."

"What am I going to do about Phil Levin?"

Scott rose and went to her. He pulled her upright and into his arms. "We'll tackle one thing at a time. It's late. Let's get some sleep."

They climbed the stairs and he kissed her then left her at the guest room door. Inside, Beth tiptoed around the room, undressing and pulling on the t-shirt Scott had given her to sleep in. A nightlight cast deep shadows over Grace, asleep in the bed. Beth was worried about her. She hadn't spoken a word since they came home from the hospital. Beth stood over her niece, loving her with her eyes. She'd promised Patrice she'd take care of her. What if she didn't get the chance? She couldn't say no to a paternity test. She spun on one foot and left the room, closing the door behind her quietly.

The door to Scott's room was ajar. She pushed it open. The room was large with two windows overlooking the water, glistening in the moonlight.

"Beth," he said.

She closed the door and padded across the room. He pulled back the blanket for her to slip in. He was lying on his back. She moved close to him, rested her head on his chest, and his arm went around her. She breathed in his scent and a sweet wave of love for him filled her. Scott was kind, funny, compassionate, and devoted; and he loved her. In time they would marry. She would have a new daughter, Kristi. Would Grace be a part of their family, too? How could she be so happy and equally so sad?

Scott kissed her temple. She trailed her fingers over his chest. He turned to her, wrapping her tighter in his arms. She was overcome with a painful need for him. She kissed him, leaving them both breathless. A fire ignited in her. She clung to him; she couldn't get close enough. She arched her body until there wasn't a slip of air between them. His passion matched hers.

"Please," she whispered. "Scott. I love you."

As if a small tornado had whipped around them, their love-making was over in minutes. Still entwined, they lay facing each other. She tried, but couldn't stop the tears running down her face. "I don't even know what of all of it I'm crying about."

"It doesn't matter. There's so much emotion, crying is good for you," Scott said, catching her tears on his fingertip.

"I don't want you to think it has anything to do with our making love. It doesn't. But I do feel a little guilty. How could I be thinking about sex when my sister died today? When, by now, her cold body is lying in the hospital morgue? God."

"Making love is nature's way of reinforcing the fact that life goes on. I read it in a book somewhere," he said, smiling at her in the moonlight.

Beth turned on her back and looked out the windows at the starry sky. "She's gone now. I can feel it in my heart." She sighed as a gentle sleep eased away her pain.

In the morning, Grace was pale and she didn't speak. Her silence concerned Beth, but she understood since her own grief weighed her down, and she knew they both needed time. Grace sat slumped on the couch, staring out over the water. Clara, breaking training, was curled up beside her with her head on Grace's lap.

Kristi had gone to her Aunt Lisa's for Christmas brunch, but Scott stayed to help Beth do all the duties that had to be done when someone died.

They sat at the table in the dining area of the great room, the fragrance of the balsam tree they'd decorated days ago scenting the air. Cheerfully wrapped presents sat untouched beneath it.

Beth decided on cremation for Patrice, and burial near their mother's grave. She called the funeral home in New Bedford and made the arrangements. The funeral director was going to call her tomorrow to discuss the particulars of a memorial service, sans liturgy, as Beth wanted it. There would be no wake. In truth, she, Frankie, and Grace already held their wake in the hospital. She would not put Grace through another viewing.

When all the preparations were made, as much as they could be, Beth prepared to leave. Though Scott wanted them to stay longer, she thought it best to take Grace home. In spite of the disaster of their lives, she also had to think about the store, buying groceries, canceling appointments, contacting people to tell them about Patrice. And she had to talk to her friends. She needed her friends.

Beth was surprised to see the cushions were still on the floor in the sacred space when they arrived home. So much had happened in two days, it seemed more like two months.

Grace set up Clara's food and water, and then went into the sacred space. Clara took a quick bite and followed her. Grace was still silent.

Beth sat with her for a while. "I think you could keep writing in your journal. I know mommy can see you. She's watching over both of us."

Grace looked up at her with hope. She was fingering the thin gold necklace Patrice had always worn. Beth put the chain on Grace when they got back to the cottage. It was in the bag of her sister's possessions the hospital gave them. She reminded herself to ask Frankie about the engagement ring that wasn't with her belongings.

"Should I take pictures, too?" she signed.

"Yes. She would love that."

Grace began to cry. It broke Beth's heart and brought back other painful memories of the loss of her own mother. She held her niece and cried with her. When they were spent, Beth said, "The sun's shining. Let's bundle up and walk to the beach. Bring your phone, and you can shoot some photos."

Though the walk had invigorated them both, it didn't give them much appetite for dinner. They watched a little TV, and finally, it was bedtime. Grace fell right to sleep. Beth stood beside her bed and watched her. *Her daughter now.* She'd grown taller, would turn nine in late January. Beth's heart was filled with love. She would do everything in her power to give Grace a happy life.

She went downstairs into the living room. Patrice's boxes were where she'd left them. She knelt in front of an open one with clothes in it. A yellow cotton sweatshirt with a rendering of an artist's palette on the front was on top. She pulled it out and put it on. Rubbing her hands over it, she breathed in the lingering smell of her sister, and mourned the loss of her life, her amazing artistic talent. She decided Grace would have art lessons to honor her mother. The thought made her think of the drawings Patrice and Grace had done of the farmer's porch.

She went into the sacred space. The sketches were still lying on the shelf. She picked them up and set them on the table. A smile crossed her face at her niece's work. Grace had talent, too. Then she picked up Patrice's drawing. Her eyes widened. What she saw, what made tears race down her cheeks, was completely different from what she'd seen before in the same sketch.

It wasn't a serious Beth at the window. It was a grieving Beth. The empty chair was Patrice's. Her glass of tea, partly drunk. A life interrupted in its summertime.

She sat and wept for a while longer, wondering at the endless source of tears. Had her sister sensed she was going to die less than a year from that day? She'd been so happy, but something had gone terribly wrong. Something wrong enough for Patrice to seek out drugs. Or was it only the weight of the world and the lure of oblivion? Was the overdose a mistake? Those questions would never be answered. In that moment, Beth promised herself not to think or speak of the possibility again. To only remember her sister's joy at being healthy and having her daughter back home, and being in love with Frankie.

She took the drawing to the sink, struck a match she took from the drawer, and set the paper on fire. Grace would never see what her aunt had seen and begin to wonder.

Lauren arrived the next morning. She brought a casserole and a variety of bakery items. She hugged Beth, and they both shed tears. "Troy wants you to know how sorry he is, too."

"God, Lauren. I still feel like I can pick up the phone and call her. My refrigerator has all the makings for the dishes I was going to bring to her house for Christmas dinner. The remnants of her whole life are here in my house. I can't believe she's gone."

"When my mother was dying of cancer," Lauren said, "the family set up shifts, so she wouldn't be alone for one minute. My Aunt Terry, her sister, was sitting with her one night. She had a terrible cold, not that anyone was worried about making my mother sicker—there was no such possibility. But the nurse told her our mom was holding her own, and she could leave early. Mom's other sister would be arriving at midnight. So, Aunt Terry went home."

Lauren patted her chest a few times and took a breath. "A floor lamp fell over in our living room at eleven-thirty. It woke Troy and me. We were standing in the living room, trying to figure out how the lamp could have possibly fallen over, when the hospital called."

"She'd died?"

"Yes, and tossed our lamp on the way out, apparently." Lauren grinned.

"Do you believe that?" Beth asked then held her breath.

"There's no doubt in my mind at all. My mom was that kind of person. She made sure none of us were around when she died, so she could leave without fanfare. But she wanted us to know she was still around somewhere. It's the greatest comfort to me." She smiled, though her eyes were glistening.

"I wish Patrice had done something for Grace. And me."

Three days later, under naked oaks and maples, and blanketed by a cloudless azure sky, Patrice was buried. Grace was inconsolable, and Scott carried her the whole time. Kristi was crying, too, so Beth held her close with her arm around her. Her other arm was extended to hold Grace's hand.

All her friends were there from New Bedford, hugging Beth and comforting her. A decent-sized group of Patrice's friends attended also, and Frankie stood in their midst. Phil Levin stood a little apart. She avoided him. The owners of the inn where Patrice had worked stood together with a young woman. As Beth looked at her, she turned her head away.

On the way back to their cars, she caught up with Frankie. "I didn't find Patrice's engagement ring in the hospital bag of her possessions. I just wanted to make sure you have it."

Frankie's face turned bright red. "Yeah. I have it."

"They gave it back to you?"

"Uh. . . ."

"What is it, Frankie?"

"Nothing. I have it, okay?"

Beth stared at his red face. "She didn't have it on, did she? Did something happen? Why didn't she have it on, Frankie?"

He turned and marched off, shaking his head.

Beth stood staring at his back. Was it a broken engagement?

After a subdued luncheon at a local restaurant, the group dispersed.

The week after the funeral, at Lauren's insistence, Scott, Kristi, Beth, and Grace joined her family for dinner. The delightful aroma of simmering beef stew made Beth think about the dinner she'd planned with Patrice, but she pushed the thought from her mind.

Grace was on her tenth day without speaking. She refused to wear her implants, so she was completely deaf again. Clara seemed to sense the change and stayed close to her charge.

"C'mon," Jake said, tugging at Grace's sleeve, "go see the trains." He was too young to understand the change in her. She just shook her head no.

"She's sitting out there by herself," Beth announced, coming into the kitchen.

"She'll come around," Lauren said, dropping dumplings on the bubbling stew. "Maybe if I ask her to help with the meal."

"I can't figure out why she's not talking. She was deaf for years and only understood parts of what people said to her. Why would she want to go back to that? I'm afraid she's somehow connecting her implants to her mother's death."

"Did you talk to her about it?"

"Not yet. I wanted her to have time to grieve. She doesn't need any more pressure. I'm taking her for bereavement therapy starting Monday." She shook her head. "That's enough about us. I don't want to put a damper on your dinner."

A little past six, they were gathered at the dining room table, covered with a rust-colored tablecloth. Flickering votive candles stood in a row in the center of the table. The only sign that Christmas had happened were the two Poinsettias by the fireplace in the living room.

Grace's chair was between the twins. She helped them with their food without speaking. Both boys were subdued, watching Grace, curiosity on their cute faces. Beth sat across from her, next to Scott. Kristi was between Troy and Lauren.

Troy said a heartwarming grace, but his last sentence made Beth happy her niece could not hear him and was not reading his lips.

"God, we ask you to hold Patrice in your loving arms and to ease the grief of those who love and miss her. We give thanks for the happy memories of Patrice that will bring her family comfort and healing."

His words sucked up all the air in the room. No one spoke, and Beth could feel many eyes on her. She looked down at her dish, holding back tears.

"Food, everybody," Lauren announced, breaking the spell. "Start passing those dishes."

The noise level rose as chatter filled the dining room. Beth looked up at Troy and smiled. "Thank you so much," she mouthed to him. His expression turned from worry to relief. "You're welcome," he mouthed back.

The letter came the following Monday.

Beth was worried sick about Grace's ongoing refusal to utter a word or wear her implants. In fact, they were missing, and she was turning her niece's room upside down, frantic to find the cochlear implants whose replacement cost would be dear.

When the doorbell rang, she was on the floor checking under the bed. She stood and shoved her hair off her face. "Shit." Even the sound of the doorbell she was so fond of made her tense.

Downstairs, she rounded the hall and went into the kitchen. Her mailman was smiling at her through the window, holding up a letter.

She opened the door. "Thanks for the door service, Henry."

"I have a registered letter you need to sign for. Seems like I'm doing more of this type of delivery every day. What's so important?" he asked while Beth signed her name. "I'm always behind on my route." He handed her the letter. "Hey, Happy New Year," he said, stepping off the porch.

Though she didn't recognize the return address, she knew by the three names that it came from lawyers. Oh no. On top of everything else? She tore the envelope open and read the first few lines. She tried to throw it across the room, but it boomeranged back to land at her feet. She collapsed heavily onto a kitchen chair, dragged her palms back and forth over her jeans-clad thighs. Grace was already so traumatized, what would this do to her? She looked up at the clock; it was four-twelve. Grace was in the sacred space doing the school lessons Mr. Hamilton provided. It was where she spent most of her time. Beth stared at the letter on the floor. She had to pull herself together. Once Grace was in bed asleep, she would figure out what to do.

The fact that Phil Levin was so sure he must be Grace's father left little hope he was wrong. But by the date on his letter to Patrice, he'd suspected for years that Grace was his child, and he'd done nothing about it. How could she give over her grieving niece to a stranger who had only now decided to become her father?

Beth was gearing herself up for a battle, but she knew the chances of winning custody of Grace over her biological father would be slim. But maybe he didn't want her. Maybe he wasn't even her father. Meanwhile, she was keeping any hint of the situation away from Grace.

Scott went with them to the designated lab for the DNA test required by the letter. They led Grace to believe the test was to help determine why she couldn't speak.

After the swabs were taken, Scott treated Beth and Grace t Grace chose Wendy's. Aunt and niece sat across from him in the booth. He leaned forward, removed his glasses, and signed to Grace, "You know how hard we all worked for you to be able to hear, honey. I think when we see what the test results are, we can fix the problem, and you'll be able to speak again."

She shook her head hard enough to whip her face with her ponytail. Then she signed," I won't hear. No."

"Why?"

She began breaking her fries into small pieces, ignoring him. Scott tapped her shoulder and repeated, "Why?"

"I don't want to." She raised her chin in defiance, but tears glimmered in her eyes.

"How will you learn at school?" he signed.

"I don't care. I'm not supposed to hear or talk."

"Who said that?" he asked.

Beth watched Grace glance away.

Scott reached over and turned her face to him again. "Who told you that? Because I'm the doctor, and I know you *are* supposed to hear and speak." His hands moved with authority as he signed. "Did Aunt Beth tell you?"

Grace gave a worried glance to Beth then shook her head.

"How are you going to play soccer this spring? How will you be able to dance to Kristi's music? What if Clara is barking and you can't hear her?"

She took her hands, slowly raised them to cover her eyes, and held them there. End of discussion.

Chapter 40

Ms. Jenny was back in the classroom, but reported to Beth that it was hard to keep Grace's attention on the schoolwork. Grace's friends helped. With Beth's permission, the students were told about her mother's death and asked to be patient and kind. Under the circumstances, the school permitted Clara to stay in the classroom. Mr. Hamilton explained to the students that Clara Barton was a service dog and had an important job to do, and they should not pet her. Still, Clara worked as a magnet, bringing the kids close to Grace. She began to speech-read some, nodding or shaking her head in response.

In the three weeks since Patrice died, Grace had not yet uttered a word. Beth wanted to rip her hair out. She'd cajoled, bribed, cried, and yelled. But her stubborn niece wouldn't speak. The bereavement therapist had determined that Grace blamed herself for her mother's death, because she was sure her mother didn't want her to have the implants.

One night, Grace was in the sacred space doing her homework. Beth came in with her decaf coffee and sat in one of the full-sized wicker chairs. Grace was sitting in the other, which was drawn up to the round table so she could study.

Beth leaned over and tapped Grace's arm. She signed, "Do you still hear the lady?"

Grace nodded her fist.

"Do you talk to her?"

A head nod.

Beth banged her open palm on the table, startling Grace. "Why her and not me?" she signed, then felt bad when Grace looked like she was about to cry.

"Please, Grace. Please talk again. Your mommy was so happy you could hear her voice. I know you can't anymore, but there are so many wonderful sounds she'd want you to hear." She wasn't sure how accurate her signing was, but she could tell she had Grace's interest. Her expression was almost hopeful. "Doesn't the lady tell you to talk again?"

Grace looked over at the rocker, which by now, Beth was sure was haunted. Then she looked at Beth and nodded.

Beth raised her shoulders and held her hands out, palms up.

But Grace looked down at her workbook and again picked up her pencil.

Silent Grace

Later, when Grace was reading in bed, Beth went into the sacred space and closed the door. She turned on the space heater then sat in the rocker. "I hope to hell I'm sitting on you, lady, Hannah, whatever your name is. I don't know what you're doing in my house, but it isn't helpful. Oh, maybe when you first read to a lonely, traumatized little girl you helped, but now she needs help and what are you doing?" She waved her hands in front of her, frustrated. "I hope you're here, and you can hear me. *Do* something! I love this child so much. I don't know what I'll do if I lose her to some goddamn stranger. You may never see her again either. I'm going to rent the house out when I get married and never live here again. There may be only days before Grace is gone."

Beth dropped her chin to her chest and sobbed softly for a moment. She wrapped her arms tightly across her chest and shivered. The room was freezing. She extended her fingers to the heater. It was warm.

"If you care about this child, you'll help her before she leaves. We've all tried everything we can imagine. I don't even believe in you, but you're my last ho—" A whiff of lilac scent stopped her. "Is that you?" She stood. "Listen to me. I'm going nuts! There's no such thing as a good ghost. I know that. But what am I going to do?" She rubbed some warmth into her shoulders, looked around at the rocker she'd vacated, shook her head, and left the room.

Chapter 41

Kristi and Beth were making chocolate chip cookies in the warm cottage kitchen. Since Grace had declined to help, her only job was to move the cooled cookies into the tins. That way she could sit at the table and watch without participating in the baking. Both dogs were sleeping at her feet under the table. Scott was joining them later for dinner.

The therapist felt Grace was making progress, and told Beth to give her niece more time. Grace was actively signing and speech reading again, but still refused to speak. Beth planned to launch an all-out happy attack over the three-day weekend for Martin Luther King, Jr. Day. Her three employees were going to cover the store while Beth would make each day special for Grace. She would make her so happy she would burst into words. She hoped. At least she had a plan, which helped her to relax and be more patient.

Scott arrived at five-forty-five and was immediately forced to eat a bunch of cookies. Beth had put a casserole of lobster mac and cheese in the oven to cook. All the samples didn't ruin Scott's appetite when they gathered around the table for dinner. After they ate, the girls cleared, and Scott put the dishes in the dishwasher, while Beth stored the leftovers.

She felt a tightness in her throat from squelching the need to cry. Tonight, they were a perfect family. A picture of how their future would be together. Beth never believed it was possible for people to love each other this much. She and Patrice had grown up in a cold environment with an intractable father whose main requirement was for them to serve him and his congregation in every way he demanded. Patrice had rebelled; Beth had complied. But she'd done it by promising herself never to be controlled by anyone else; to be the master of her own life, to make her own decisions. Now, this golden family was all she wanted. She shook her head. It was *all* she wanted.

It was too cold in the sacred space—twenty degrees outside—for the electric heater to warm it. So instead, the girls went up to Grace's room after dinner. Scott and Beth sat in the living room, side by side on the couch. Beth reached for the TV remote, but Scott put his hand out and took hers.

"What is it?" she said when she saw his expression. She felt every muscle in her body tense.

He pulled an envelope out of his pocket. "The results came from the lawyer today." They had arranged for the DNA report to go to Scott's office, so Beth wouldn't be alone when she opened it. He handed it to her then wrapped an arm around her shoulder, moving closer to her.

Beth was chewing her bottom lip. Her fingers trembled while she unsealed the envelope and pulled the folded letter out. She looked up at Scott.

"We'll deal with it," he said "Whichever way it comes out. We'll take it to court, if you want. If it's bad news, it's only the first step. Go ahead." He tightened his arm around her.

She unfolded the paper and began to read. Legal gibberish slowed her down. She skipped over it and found the words she searched for. Her hand went to her mouth and her eyes filled.

"Scott, she's not his daughter!" She threw the letter down and hugged him while she shed tears of joy for a change. "I can't even tell her and make her happy, because she had no idea in the first place."

When she pulled away and looked at Scott, he was grinning like a fool. "You sure made me happy. That little girl is going to be my second daughter. I love her, too."

It was an outcome neither expected, but Beth would not question it. She would never read another letter in Patrice's box. She would never wonder about Frankie. Ignorance was bliss. Grace was now their daughter.

"Don't you think since we already have two kids we should get married pretty fast?" Scott said, laughing.

"Yes! Who needs a big wedding and a white dress?"

He suddenly seemed worried. "Do you want a big wedding? I'm up for that. You would be the most beautiful bride in the world." He set his glasses on the table, pulled her close, and they kissed for a while. "We'd better get married soon. I want you in my bed so I don't have to sneak out of here holding my coat in front of me."

When Beth stopped laughing, she said, "I'm not sure I ever really wanted to get married. Now I couldn't be more certain that I do. But I'm not the girl who dreamed of bouquets and wedding cakes. Far from it. No, I don't want a big wedding, but let's have two flower girls." She clasped her hands and brought them to her chest. "I can't stop the happy inside me. I want to run up and tell Grace the good news. But she already has a daddy. The most wonderful man she could ever hope to have."

They kissed for a while again, like two teenagers in the backseat of a car, with one ear listening for the patter of feet on the stairs.

Scott pulled back and gazed at her with a solemn expression. "Let's make plans. What kind of wedding reception would you like?" He locked eyes with her and held his breath a few seconds.

"Something small? Maybe a dinner with our family and a few close friends?"

"The Captain Linnell House Restaurant?" When she nodded, smiling, he said, "Shall I make a reservation?"

Beth felt as if she were melting, but her practical side spoke up first. "We should wait until Grace speaks again." Her eyes widened and her fingers slowly rose to her mouth. "No. That's not what's in my heart. I want to marry you as soon as possible, even if Grace never says another word." She laughed and kissed him. "Let's get married on Valentine's Day."

"That's what I wanted to hear. That's a perfect day. I'll make the reservations and we'll set the legalities in motion. Deal?"

"Deal. I'll arrange the wedding ceremony." She paused. "I might invite God. What do you think?"

"I think that's a great idea."

They held each other without speaking. Neither wanting to move away.

A few minutes later, she walked Scott and Kristi to their car. Beth couldn't stop smiling, even with the ache in her heart for the loss of Patrice.

Beth woke because Grace was shaking her shoulder, and Clara was barking. It was a bright morning. "What, Grace? Did I oversleep?"

"The door is locked," Grace signed with a perplexed expression.

"What door are you talking about?" Beth swung her legs out of bed and rose to her feet. She leaned over to pet Clara. Grace tugged on her sleeve.

"The lady's door," she signed.

"Oh," Beth said then signed, "It's probably just jammed. I closed it tightly last night because it was so cold out." She yawned as she went to the closet for her robe and slippers. "Wow." She turned and pointed to the window. "It snowed last night. It's beautiful. Come see." She held out her arm.

Grace shook her head. "Open the door," she signed, then headed for the stairs.

Beth frowned. She knew Grace often went into the sacred space to read if she was up early, but this felt different. She descended the stairs and saw Grace down the hall waiting at the door. Her lips were pressed tightly together in impatience.

Beth tried the door. She shoved it with her hip, kicked it with her foot. She bent down and checked the lock, it seemed to be engaged. "How could it be locked? I never lock it. I don't even know if there's a key." She scowled at Grace. Nothing would surprise her. "Do you have a key?"

A fast headshake was followed by a do-something look.

Beth went into the kitchen, flipping on the coffee on her way to the drawer with the odds and ends. She collected three loose keys and went back to the sacred space. Grace trailed her, and Clara trailed Grace.

The third key caused the telltale *thunk*. Beth turned the handle and opened the door. A wall of warm fragrant air washed over her. She froze, astonished, but Grace slipped by her into the room. Beth heard her intake of breath as she stood perfectly still in front of the table. Beth took a few steps in to gaze about her.

On the round white table—so fresh, dewdrops sparkled on them—were two perfect pink roses.

Beth's mouth dropped open. "Where—"

Grace spun around and ran down the hall. Beth could hear her pounding up the stairs. Was she frightened? Beth was a little. Who could have put the roses on the table? Who was inside the house while they slept? Scott didn't have a key—no one did.

She quick-stepped into the kitchen and opened the door. There were no footsteps in the snow on the porch. She went out, looked down the driveway and at the part of the front lawn she could view. No tire marks, no footprints. She went back inside, rubbing her arms against the cold. She heard Grace clattering downstairs as she ran past the kitchen door and back into the sacred space. Beth followed.

The first thing Beth saw was the purple print cochlear implants nested in her shiny black hair. Grace picked up the roses and hugged them gently to her chest. Beth stepped up beside her and put a hand on her shoulder. Grace handed her the florist card, bruised and creased, that came with the roses that were delivered after her implant surgery.

For my little angel. One pink rose for each cochlear implant. I love you, Mommy.

Beth stood as still as granite. It was like a miracle. Grace was hugging the roses, twisting back and forth as if she were rocking a baby. And then everything was clear. Beth didn't know how or why, but Grace didn't care. It was *her* message, and it was all she needed. Grace looked up at Beth and said in a strong voice, "Mommy."

"Yes," Beth said. And she knew in her heart it was true.

GERRI LeCLERC

Gerri LeClerc is a Pennsylvania native who received her nursing education in Vermont. An RN, her medical background is reflected in her stories. She lives on Cape Cod and insists it is magical. She shares her Cape cottage with her husband Ron, and Livia, her cat, who doubles as her muse.

She can be reached at www.gerrileclerc.com

Photograph by Kim Reilly
Studio K Photography. LLC PPA

Don't miss the third inspiring offering from
GERRI LeCLERC'S *Knoll Cottage Series*

Excerpt from DEAR ALICE

CHAPTER ONE

It was flu season and everyone was sharing. Julia stood in the hall of the clinic, reading a patient's chart. She could hear people coughing, babies crying, noses being blown. The sounds of February. The community clinic's waiting room was full, but Julia knew her task today would be handing out mostly comfort. That she would say a hundred times: Antibiotics won't cure a viral infection.

Hours later, she returned to her office. She was always glad to do some hands-on nursing. Since she'd moved into administration, she rarely saw a patient. *Beats paperwork any day.* And she *had* paperwork, a leaning stack of it in her inbox. It was going to be another late night.

A quick rap at her door was followed by the entrance of her boss, Makena. Julia smiled at her friend, but her smile faded as she saw the serious expression on Makena's face. She closed the door and sat down.

"We have big trouble, girlfriend. I've been in meetings all afternoon."

"What's up?" Julia asked, but somehow she knew it involved her and not in a good way.

Makena sucked in a deep breath. "I'm just going to spit it right out. Possible procurement fraud in the account you manage."

"*What?* What kind of fraud?"

"Remember when you mentioned the higher costs this year that were squeezing the budget?" When Julia nodded, Makena went on. "I ordered a special audit."

Julia felt herself stiffen. "And it showed fraud?"

"Let's keep it at *possible*. Special investigators are working on it now. Apparently, it's hard to detect *how* the fraud is being done, so they'll do a financial analysis."

"This is awful! Does James know?" Julia said, then raised a tight fist to her mouth.

"He will. As procurement officer, he's a suspect. Public Health's very tight internal controls make it difficult for anyone without login access to commit fraud. That narrows the field." Makena leaned forward in her chair.

"Unfortunately, you are also suspect as the approver."

"You're kidding." She held her breath. This couldn't be happening.

"I'm afraid not. I'm sorry, Julia, but both you and James are suspended without pay based on what they've found so far in the investigation." Makena handed her the legal notice of her suspension.

As soon as she passed the Honda sedan, cutting it too close and getting the horn for her trouble, Julia checked her watch. "I hope he's home. Please let him be there. He'll know what to do," she said aloud, as she wove her way through thick Boston rush hour traffic.

She hit the button to open the garage door and pulled right in. Ryan's Audi was already there. Grabbing her purse, she left her briefcase and the box of items she'd emptied from her desk on the passenger seat.

The garage opened into the kitchen. Julia dropped her purse on the counter. "Ryan?" She headed downstairs to the family room. "Ryan?" She descended quickly. He was standing still, a pained expression on his face.

The relief she felt when she saw him dissolved. "What's wrong? Is it my mother?" Her mother's advanced cancer was never far from her thoughts.

He raised a hand and ran fingers through his hair. "Not your mother. I'm sorry."

"For what? What's wrong, Ryan? You're scaring me." The gas fireplace was roaring. The too-warm room, mixing with her fear, made her lightheaded.

"Sit down." Ryan walked to the bar and poured a glass of white wine. "We need to talk."

She moved zombie-like to a leather bucket chair and eased herself into it, never taking her eyes from him. "Please. Tell me," she said, accepting the glass he handed her.

Ryan sat in the matching chair and swiveled to face her. "Julia. I don't even recognize you as the woman I fell in love with. Your life is your career now."

Her fingers dug into the soft arms of the chair. "What? You know my job is demanding. You were so proud of me when I was promoted."

"And since then you've been driven. You come home late most nights. We rarely do anything together." He lifted his eyebrows. "Not even sex."

Julia looked down at her feet on the floor. "Oh Ryan, I'm sorry. Just today—"

"Don't Julia. I get the message, but I can't do this anymore. When we were married, we planned a great life together. It included some beautiful kids." He lifted his glass of Scotch and took a swallow.

Julia raised a hand to her forehead. "Jeez, Ryan. Must we have the baby conversation again? Is that what this is about? Could we talk about it later? I'm in big trouble at work. You won't believe . . ." She trailed off, noticing that Ryan now held a manila envelope in his left hand.

"What is that?"

She heard every word he said. Watched his every movement as he paced the room.

Her throat was so tight she could barely speak. "Ryan. Wait. Let me explain—" Why hadn't she seen it coming? Talked to him. Told him the truth. Oh God. Now it was too late. Frozen in her chair, her right hand still grasped the glass of wine he'd handed her to soften the blow.

"Too late for talk, Julia. Too late for explanations."

"I—I'm sorry," she said, her voice barely above a whisper. "Please."

Ryan stared at her a minute, then blew out a long breath. "A marriage vow is a contract, Julia. You broke it," he said, always the consummate attorney. He dropped the manila envelope on the table. "This will make the contract null and void."

When she heard the door slam, she raised the wine glass to her lips and took a gulp. To soften the blow.

Made in the USA
Middletown, DE
13 February 2018